REQUIREMENTS OF GUILT

By

David Bazell

Copyright © David Bazell 2018
This book is sold subject to the condition that it shall not, by way of trade or otherwise, be lent, resold, hired out, or otherwise circulated without the publisher's prior consent in any form of binding or cover other than that in which it is published and without a similar condition including this condition being imposed on the subsequent publisher.
The moral right of David Bazell has been asserted.
ISBN: 9781976986277

While attention has been given to the established record relating to the Nazis' Auschwitz-Birkenau complex in Poland during the Second World War, the real-time action that takes place there in this work of fiction, and the personnel mentioned – apart from the camp commandant – are entirely the product of the author's imagination. All other names, characters, places and incidents throughout this novel, except in the case of historical fact, either are invented by the writer or are used fictitiously.

CONTENTS

1 1
2 8
3 13
4 18
5 21
6 26
7 30
8 38
9 43
10 50
11 55
12 59
13 66
14 70
15 73
16 76
17 81
18 85
19 91
20 98
21 105
22 112
23 116
24 121
25 126
26 131
27 136
28 141
29 147
30 153
31 161
32 168

33	175
34	177
35	182
36	188
37	196
38	201
39	208
40	214
41	218
42	222
43	228
44	236
45	244
46	253
47	259
48	261
49	270
50	273
51	277
52	284
53	288

ACKNOWLEDGEMENTS

I am indebted to the authors of such works as *Anatomy of the SS State*, *The Death Factory* and *The Theory and Practice of Hell* which so ably show the depth of hatred to which elements of the Third Reich could sink, and to my own experience of that most opposite of human traits – love.

AUTHOR'S NOTE

While attention has been given to the established record relating to the Nazis' Auschwitz-Birkenau complex in Poland during the Second World War, the real-time action that takes place there in this work of fiction, and the personnel mentioned – apart from the camp commandant – are entirely the product of the author's imagination. All other names, characters, places and incidents throughout this novel, except in the case of historical fact, either are invented by the writer or are used fictitiously.

Tarnów-born Polish prisoner Zbigniew Drecki, who lived in the UK, in Exmouth, Devon, was one of the first prisoners to enter Auschwitz on the 14th of June, 1940. He mentioned during the course of several visits I made to his home, the horrors he witnessed at the complex. But he also remembered small kindnesses – and this fact, for me, stood out on the broad canvas of gross inhumanity.

Mr Drecki would always rather talk about his first love, painting. Or – and this was recorded in his autobiography *Freedom and Justice spring from the ashes of Auschwitz* – hope for the creation of a world order that would help keep the planet's countries at peace. The world, he said shortly before his death, was a wonderful place; only people did not measure up.

So, enter the Nazi who did not really fit the mould, one who knew about love…

'All men make mistakes but a good man yields when he knows his course is wrong and repairs the evil…'
Sophocles *(Antigone)*

'So far, about morals, I know only that what is moral is what you feel good after, and what is immoral is what you feel bad after.'
Ernest Hemingway *(Death in the Afternoon)*

1

RASH imagination had joined him like a nuisance passenger on the night flight from London. And the intrusive voice was at its most bizarre as the Boeing sliced low cloud over Frankfurt International Airport. Reinhard shifted uneasily in the window seat. The energy from the mass of lights from the city below seemed to mock the exhaustion he felt. He tried to block intruding images but the aircraft still touched down on a runway of unset concrete, ravine-deep and boggy, and the passengers fought to free themselves from trick safety belts as the course mixture slowly drew up blinds over the windows, allowing a smudged glimpse of an orchestra of gaping mouths and bony hands stroking bows on barbs of wire.

When the telegram arrived at his Hammersmith apartment, he could think of nothing else but Dieter, lying badly injured in a Hannover hospital. That mood persisted until well after take-off. Then, as the aircraft left the Channel behind, two other names burst in. He didn't mind thinking about Stephanie - he even welcomed it - but Eichmann was something else. Adolf Eichmann, the Holocaust architect, the one with whom he had in 1943 so dramatically fallen out, so to speak, and who was again butting in just as the dawning Sixties could further distance him from his own far less infamous but nevertheless culpable war record. This first return to German soil had given Reinhard's mind the wild lurch of the half-crazed. No matter how unreasonable, he had become afraid of his old country, of stumbling into something bad, yet at the same time drawn on by the prospect, however tenuous, of reaching something good. Yet right now he wished to dwell on neither possibility. Dieter might be all tubes and bandages, arms straight out over stretched white sheets. He saw himself standing there, hating hospitals. Reinhard lagged behind as the plane emptied. Soon everyone was in front of him and he tried to think straight again. He checked his watch and wondered whether, if his years of borrowed time could be represented by the span of a single day, then the time right now might well be just a few minutes to midnight. He looked across the tarmac to the buildings. Absurdly, he imagined Stephanie at the airport. The truth was that she had come to mind not merely because he was travelling to his once beloved Fatherland, their land of love and promise pre-war, hers and his, but because he had never really forgotten her.

Twenty-five years of virtual silence had followed that fateful day in the restaurant when they stubbornly went their separate ways without, he was sure, either of them really wanting their standpoints to drive this kind of wedge between them. He had his reasons for later lying low but he could not remember a single week in which he had not thought about her. The burden of his administrative past with the camps sometimes tore at his mind and what he had felt to be right in his heart just after the war was submerged (though never drowned) by this inner guilt - and he became used to living out the unremarkable, tucked-away life of a municipal gardener in Hammersmith. Though that gave him self-destructive time to dwell on the old enemies: introspection, melancholy and regret. What he should have done, and what he now felt he would do, was to seek her out: find Stephanie. The sudden certainty of this future, late in the day notwithstanding, thrilled him. The decision had come to him almost as an impulse, as if it had been the first time he had had a real chance to act, and the fact that it had matured in the middle of a crisis, somehow made it all the more correct and natural. Of course, she would no longer look like his young Stephanie but it was the only image he had. And it was towards that image that he walked into the airport lounge, pretending she was actually waiting for him. He knew he should be thinking only about Dieter and cursed increasing bouts of self-absorption. He had asked the hospital to tell Dieter to hold on, that he would be with him soon. It was all he could think of to say. As for Eichmann, his name had cropped up over breakfast when his radio seemed to bellow the news that the former head of Jewish

REQUIREMENTS OF GUILT

Affairs and Evacuation at Reich Security had been captured and would probably face trial in Israel.

Over the years, he had been able, mostly, to put Eichmann to the back of his mind but this was different. It was stupid, he knew, but he felt that Eichmann's arrest had somehow put the spotlight on himself. He walked through the tunnel to the airport's main concourse and made for the onward flight departure lounge and checked on the details for Hannover. He had always wanted to hurry time along, to distance himself from what had happened. Now he wanted value for every second that ticked life by. Sixteen years had passed from the day, at war's end, when George welcomed him into his home. They had backed into each other on the platform at St Pancras, George train-spotting and Reinhard trying to occupy his little boy. After a few halting exchanges, the two men made their way to George's place and after Dieter had been settled with George's wife, Irma, she encouraged the pair to enjoy a few drinks at a nearby pub. He told George he'd come from a PoW camp in Yorkshire and George gestured with both hands saying that the war took too many prisoners. So this was the British, Reinhard thought; where did the two countries go wrong? They talked sparingly between lager halves, smiling often, and they needed each other to reach Hamming Way just after midnight. Mrs George was asleep and they bedded down in the lounge. Now his life had been turned upside down by the pending Eichmann trial and the telegram he took in with the milk at the peeling red door of his one-bedroom ground floor flat. Perhaps he could not expect much more settled time, though he had come to believe his council job would go on forever. He told George he felt heeled into the English soil and George said, 'Why, you're practically a Londoner.' But as he trudged to the flight desk, he could feel the full weight of himself.

He knew the trip would be more than being at Dieter's side. Nothing was ever going to prepare him for this moment, brought about more than likely by the single-mindedness of some emerging far right political party. There could eventually be so much. Back in the old country anything could blink into sharp focus without warning and he knew he would not be able to pick and choose the images. Smells, tastes, customs, phrases, the language itself. Instead of slowly mouthing the larger typefaces of the English press, he'd be able to swallow whole the newspapers and magazines, take in all that the radio had to offer and absorb street chatter. There would be places, things, signs. Already something - he could not be sure whether heard or seen - stirred in the back of his mind. He tapped his fingers on the arm of the bench he'd slumped into as anxiety overwhelmed him. The mastermind of the Holocaust was at work in his head. The barbarian had pushed in when all he wanted from his radio, once every year, was six English pips to take him to the anniversary of a very special day in the spring of 1943.

While he waited for Hannover to clatter into view he bought a coffee at a kiosk by the flights gantry and removed his brown tinted glasses which he wore whatever the light conditions. Eventually, he joined the boarding queue, running a hand over his once blonde, now burnt white hair. He wanted to tell the man in front of him who kept turning this way and that, to put his arms out and take off but he timed a smile at him and tried to relax on the second stage of the journey. After landing in Hannover, his mind sharpened and the form the hotel receptionist thrust towards him ahead of a proper welcome irritated him. He changed his glasses and filled it out in a deliberately slapdash fashion, replacing his tints against the starkness of neon strips, which bore down on him from above the half octagonal reception desk. He folded his arms high up on his chest, feet astride, and waited while the receptionist, a fat man with pebble glasses and a strange smile, gave each entry the importance of a silly nod of his head.

'Ah, there you are, Sir. There is a message for you.'

Reinhard remained as a statue.

'A Frau Irma Satchell, from London,' the receptionist added.

The message read: *Feel we need to help you through this. Travelling with George. Coach arrives Düsseldorf tomorrow 13.51. Catching 14.20 train to Hannover. Will telephone on arrival. Love Irma.*

Love Irma. Irma was coming. Into Stephanie country. He felt sinful. George's wife, he had to admit, was very attractive and on seemingly every available occasion attentive towards him. Naturally, the way things were, he liked her attention in those early days but George recognised a danger, and a possible solution - as on reflection he felt he should have done - when after dinner at his place one night George mentioned Senka from The Balkans. 'You should meet her,' he had announced quite matter-of-factly. Senka had married a German before the war but he had been killed during the lightening air raid over Belgrade just hours after the German-led Axis invasion of her beloved Kingdom of Yugoslavia when part of a city centre building was hit and half of the upper floor wall crushed the tram he was travelling on.

George said, 'Manfred had apparently been a very good husband. I met her the other day out shopping. I mentioned you and that was it - she wants to meet you!' He smiled, and then winked rather knowingly. Certainly Senka was a very pretty girl. She did not disguise her profession and Reinhard knew that his routine could not go on and that he would just have to cut down everything to manage matters. There was something about Senka that made him feel pleasant all the time and he began to resent it when others were with her and he was not. Eventually they married. In only a few months, however, she was stricken with some viral infection that could not be controlled and eventually became mentally ill and everything was ruined.

Reinhard hoped very much that Irma would not ruin everything now that she would be present and Stephanie would not. Before settling himself into his room, he phoned the hospital. Dieter was out of theatre. Restricted visiting would be fine from early afternoon.

Reinhard went for a short walk, taking his camera. He took a picture of the hotel and then crossed the street and relaxed on a bench in a small park. On the far side of the park, scaffolding struggled to follow the lines of a futuristic building and he could hear Dieter saying, 'Very arty picture there, dad.' He focussed his camera on the structure but an airline hoarding advertising Geneva, Karachi and Lagos caught his eye. G. K. L.

His hand moves over the desk blotter, an inch or so above the dried-up names. He cranes his neck to see around his slightly parted, slightly trembling fingers. He wonders about the names; who they are ... or were. He rests a hand on the alphabetic shambles but imagines movement beneath and snatches it away, transferring it to the safety of his other hand before taking both down between the black gabardine trousers stretched out beneath the heavy oak desk. He has driven across the city to arrive at Reich Security at lunchtime, to be alone before picking up his papers for leave and the onward journey to Auschwitz-Birkenau. In Prinz-Albrecht-Strasse he is at the heart of things, the place to test the resolve he has until so recently never doubted. He repeats the word heart with a censuring suffix. He reaches for a bound red record book on the desk, turns to the latest completed page, and compares entries with the blotter marks. Immediately Hauptsturmführer Reinhard Hansel, soon to be Sturmbannführer Hänsel, copperplate administrator of the Concentration Camps Inspectorate, visualizes a distant resting place. A female clerk interrupts his thoughts, striding heavily across the bare boards to sit at a typewriter where she transfers the noisy call of duty to her fingertips. He thinks of ordering her back out but he lets her be. It quietens the blotter. Even empty, the office appears full. Steel filing cabinets push out from dark green walls and the whiff of tobacco and immoderate mid-morning snacks make him gasp. Oddly mixed feelings engulf him, more powerfully than at any time since entering the place, more acute than at any time since starting at the huge, business enterprises arm of Nazi administration north of the city, at Oranienburg. Perhaps it had started earlier than Berlin and had nothing to do with the notion that it is natural anguish for anyone hoping to shape a future. He walks across the office to the grilled window. But it might as well be bricked up for all the light it provides from the grey city. From three storeys up, he can just make out the bent haste of rained-on figures. He looks back into the gloomy office. He knows the problem: the rail passages of the people in the bound red record book are scheduled eastwards but there is no allocation of return tickets. It is the blotters that should be forwarded to Eichmann.

Reinhard put the camera back in its case and hailed a taxi. As he rested back, he thought of how critical Dieter's condition might be. He could no longer think of hospitals as places where surgical chromium and starched linen, silences and mock cheerfulness dominated the wards and corridors with their constant tread of dread and layers of sickness on several levels of hope. There was only one bed in the whole building! He wished George and Irma were already by his side. He hung his coat over his arm and strode briskly towards the hospital. At the main entrance, he removed his fedora, releasing and capturing its brim in small, nervous movements with the thumb and forefinger and made for Jean-Paul Ward. The sister's voice attracted him as much as her face.

'May I help you?'

'My boy, Dieter.'

'Ah yes, your boy has been seriously injured. Head injuries mainly. He underwent an operation yesterday that went well but he has only just come out of intensive care. Only a short visit on this occasion. Oh, and please stop by my office when you leave, Herr Hänsel. Just a few details,' she smiled.

Reinhard fixed his eyes high up on the end wall as he strode down the ward, turning to his kind of prayer, offering up as he had so often done as a child, promises of butter and stuff for God to answer his beseeching. He looked down at Dieter, the top of him bound in bandages and something Reinhard had read about black being painted as white entered his head. He could imagine streaky red beneath the bandages and the canvas of his past thrust itself into view. He wanted to give the images labels of accurate but detached generality: ferocious humiliation, tortured anxiety, irrepressible sadism, degrading fun, the empty phrases of learned books, the bottle but not the poison. He looked away from the bed, trying to keep the phrases slumbering but they shook themselves free. Bandages unwound. History unwrapped itself. The blotter's limbed letters moved. Indifference, the protector, was impossible. Hateful load of bastards, the sergeant had said of them. Hate. Reinhard's father had always said that at least there was a chance with hate, so much more promising than indifference. Programmed punishment had seemed appropriate, a place to badge and restrain those who threatened to overthrow the legitimate government, or those who did not care about or actively hindered or purposely ignored the legitimate government …

Reinhard looked up. Monitors flickered above Dieter's head. Blue liquid advanced and drained. Occasionally it darted forward, forcing his heart into his throat. For a second, he turned to call the nurse. Forward, stop, stutter, back. Steady. One-eight-nine. The nurse stood by. One-nine-zero. One-eight-nine. One-eight-eight. One-eight-nine. She returned to her desk. He felt relieved to be by Dieter's side. Dieter had kept Reinhard going. The young man was huge consolation for everything. He recalled the early-on day when he bounced Dieter up and down with such vigour on the Z-bed bought at auction, that the little lad's ill-fitting shorts had fallen down around his socks and Reinhard had wrapped him in a big bath towel and Dieter had called him Dad.

2

HE wanted to contact Gottfried as soon as he returned to the hotel. The two of them had got on well in the old days. Basically they had been youngsters in an adult world and could easily see funny sides to what were undoubtedly quite serious matters. In fact, they developed their own absurd culture of fun during the early Thirties, almost certainly as an antidote to their often draining work as dedicated newspapermen. Reinhard supposed the work sapped him more than it did Gottfried because Gottfried seemed better able to dismiss morals like an errant child whereas he would agonise far too long over far too many of the stories that made up the daily routine in Berlin. They had their laughs, sometimes even laughing fits, but it was grown-up work and as the Führer gradually took over at the Reichstag they, like so many people, no longer saw him as a clown. They started to admire him. Reinhard certainly had. He shuddered as he remembered missing Stephanie, often hugely, yet allowing this parallel thing inside to dominate. Meeting Gottfried would be good. After so long, it would be relaxing to have a German to speak to. Reinhard had come across his old friend on the page of a faded newspaper that lined the top drawer of an Edwardian desk he'd viewed at auction during one of his days off from the council. There was a slight drag as he tested the slide of the long central drawer and he had straightened a curled edge of the page, folded it over and began settling it when the name jumped out at him beside his thumb. The by-line referred to a book review under the provocative heading *Revisionist claims Nazis not guilty of gas chamber Holocaust*. Reinhard had turned around and rested back, slowly closing the drawer with his backside. The lie shocked him, and initially he cursed Gottfried as the author rather than being merely the book reviewer. Reinhard re-examined the words, putting each of them on scrupulous trial as the auctioneer's strident voice and the soft babble of groups at either elbow, gradually drifted into the background. He saw it as charred remains being scraped like burnt toast, black being whitened. He would have none of it though he kept it all inside. Arrogance had been guttered long ago although he kept questioning how the change from black gabardine to rough boots and blue denim pants really changed anything very much. Reinhard challenged himself: exactly how big did he think was the fraction one six millionth? It was hardly anything and he knew it, though it satisfied him greatly. As Dieter had grown up, and eventually gone to university - and much to Reinhard's disquiet got himself interested in German affairs, and right-wing politics at that - he told him everything as objectively as he could, the way it had been. And still Dieter called him Dad. It worried him, though, that there might not always be such understanding. And now Eichmann, really his old boss, had re-surfaced. Bidding for the desk had started briskly but soon tailed off. He got the item for seventy pounds. He pulled the page out, folded it up and slipped it into his pocket. He would have to look up Revisionism later.

*

The voice at the newspaper office was short and dismissive: Gottfried rarely operated from the office, said an editorial assistant. Few colleagues ever knew where the man was, let alone when he might dignify the Springer empire with his presence. A bad day. Newspapers were sometimes like that. Reinhard wished he had been back in touch earlier. He had just missed Gottfried, the day before going on leave. He could have told him about his feelings. They could have gone for a beer and maybe sorted things out. The kind of Berlin they had known had probably never really been for either of them, though both of them had shared its considerable benefits.

Rest, after he'd slung himself on to his hotel bed, had been anything but. Dieter had been badly injured in a street fracas during a demonstration march by young right-wingers. The police were investigating. The hospital was cautious. Thoughts thrashed around his head so that he began to mix thoughts about Dieter from the beginning and about his mother who had perished and his Stephanie. He always called her *his* Stephanie and could easily justify his possessiveness, though it was he who had abandoned her for National Socialism. Already a mind friend, she had become a constant companion now that he was back on German soil. Even though Dieter was beckoning so strongly, Stephanie seemed to be trying to touch his hand as Irma had already done. Irma was a good friend with a kind heart and he was sure she would be a huge strength to him at Dieter's bedside, but he worried that she might be so available. Giving the radio a wide birth, he sat on the bed and began writing up his diary. His fountain pen had been the biggest survivor of them all, a present from father. It had hardly ever been out of his close reach since finishing high school. When he had asked for a reference from his headmaster for the *Telegraphen Union* news agency post, it was with this pen that Hans Grenscher had written carefully on crisp, yellowish semi-parchment paper words that Reinhard for so long cherished: 'a student of sound moral character who is well thought of in all ways, a young man with considerable potentiality'. Reinhard thought the testament was tailor-made for a noble cause. But confident years had become uncertain months, then guilt-ridden weeks, before his entire uniformed period with the Nazis condensed itself into one diabolical hour in Birkenau, an hour in which, mercifully, one second broke free from the clump of sweating mid-morning minutes at the building by the birch trees. Reinhard had told George, and he would tell Gottfried when they met, that it was as if old Grenscher had showed him how to use his hidden power and fulfil something of his natural, inborn capability and reject the transitory persuasion of a wicked messenger. But it could all go wrong now and he would be left with only the world overview of his kind, a consensus that, even five hundred, perhaps a thousand years or more from now, the breed, *his* breed as it would be perceived, would be associated with the worst inhumanity the world had ever witnessed. Within the space of fewer than twenty-four hours, everything seemed to have been turned on its head. Reinhard did, however, see one thing crystal clear: Dieter and Eichmann could be near to death. While Dieter had been cruelly struck down, Adolf Eichmann sneered across the front of the *London Evening News*, beneath the heading *This is plain revenge*. Yet despite the overwhelming feeling of apprehension for his own position that the name conjured, he could still marvel at what he saw as an attempt at editorial fair-mindedness. He took the cutting from his jacket pocket: *In a tension charged atmosphere at the Beit Haam courthouse ... Eichmann ... bullet-proof glass ... murder of millions ... stood for 70 minutes ... 5,000-word indictment ... story of mass murder ... country by country ... camp by camp ... Auschwitz, Belsen, Chelmno.*

Although it was only midday, Reinhard felt tired. He went back to his room for a nap but sleep would not come. He was restless. He forced his mind to settle, replaying the final moves of a remarkable game of chess he'd recently had with George, but it got out of hand when the knights ignored protocol and jumped all over the place, even to non-existent ninth and tenth ranks and the board got ever bigger to accommodate the extravagance of his imaginative play, to keep the game going, to keep his mind at bay. He went to reception and, still some way away from the desk, could see Funny Smile working up enthusiastic movements of his lips, eyes and hands on his approach. Reinhard responded, lolling over the counter as if engaged in some assignation, delivering quietly a question about the possibility of a hire car. Funny Smile, pulling himself together, said there was a small garage just a couple of streets away that did them.

Reinhard walked into Auto Merlin and made arrangements to take a Mercedes. Oil cans, rags and tyres were stacked up behind a desk with paper piled so high above the windowsill that much of the view of the yard was blocked. The garage brought back memories as permanently ingrained on his mind as the mechanical body fluids that had seeped into the thick planks of wood covering the inspection pit. As he walked away, a mechanic was talking to someone on an adjacent desk.

'*Ach, der Käfer, der tolle Käfer!* Your Beetle has stopped romping, eh? Only for a while, though. But while normally we'd be able to fix this in a couple of hours, one of our mechanics has gone down with a virus or something, another's on holiday and I've just had a call to go out to a crash car near Rastenkorb.'

Reinhard stiffened and had to steady himself against the desk. The place name had been yanked from some deep recess in his head, fleeting and blurred but powerful. He struggled to recall where or how it meant something. Already he was suffering with the twisted impertinence of Revisionism. Now there was this other word: Rastenkorb. And there was another word that had crept into his mind but would not properly form. He peered through a gap in the window. In one corner of the garage compound, there were scrap cars, a heap of tangled vehicles three and a bit high, doors hanging open, wheels sharply turned, floor pans on roofs, empty lamp sockets, bodies with almost every limb out of place, feet on heads, arms on legs, eyes staring.

3

NORMALLY he awoke refreshed with instant ability by a ready-for-action brain to recall or assess. Not this morning. Reinhard felt heavy, burdened by the weight of uncertainty. He managed to start a list.

Dieter ... brackets, little a, visits; little b, place for him

Meet George and Irma (Stephanie! Stephanie! Stephanie!)

Contact Gottfried.

Rastenkorb and???

Rastenkorb tore at his brain because he didn't know why. Gottfried would help. He might even turn it into a laugh. He was like that, Gottfried. Just seeing his old friend and colleague, before they uttered a word, would do him good. He saw them back at Habel's, down the Linden, not exactly drunk but nearly so. Laughing at things, silly things mostly, even themselves. Being youthful. Wanting to help the cause of course - who didn't? - but starting tomorrow. Reinhard knew he always had had his own ideas, naïve, even fanciful ideas at times, lurking in the background ever since those days when he would accompany his father to one or other of the ranting grounds of München where dad was regularly assigned by his newspaper to take pictures. Little Reinhard would scuff his feet while waiting for father to put down his camera and again take hold of his hand. Young though he was, he was somehow drawn to the sound of it all. There was something that thrilled him in the in and out of thundered then hushed words. He dared not tell father, who mocked the upstarts at every chance. But there was something that made him feel he wanted to be part of it, more than going to the pictures, playing hooky from school, being in a football team.

It was a long time ago, and yet for all the dedication he eventually applied to National Socialism, it was the likes of a snowball fight he had had with Gottfried that he remembered most vividly. Like when, on some special day, they both should have been polishing themselves to match the shiny shovels at Templehof, they totally lost themselves in winter fun behind the Reichstag. They'd whitened their uniforms and had to shake each other down, slap off the clinging crystals from each other's backs, every so often doubled up with throat-aching hysterical laughter.

In the dining room, Reinhard met the same group of breakfasters whose rowdiness had upset him worse than Funny Smile on arrival at the hotel. Their loud conversation again interrupted his thoughts about the day ahead. He studied them contemptuously. One of the group pointed vigorously at a rack of toast and the others fell about. Reinhard herded them into a huddle of civil servants from the clipboard division, with a competence simultaneously to deny and confirm the existence of any matter and to lean back importantly. They exaggerated everything. They used several serviettes to rub away at their greasy lips, brush off crumbs from fat thighs and settled on a newspaper as if they were shaking a mat, people who straightened out the world, dispensing justice over buttered toast as if they were civilisation's almighty judges. They bit off whole chunks of generalisation at breakfast time, crisp, three-cornered indictments. What would they say about Dieter? What political claptrap would they dwell on before, grudgingly addressing the issue of his life or death? And what, he thought, would they say about him? Oh, yes, SS. Naturally. The camps inspectorate. Dates, appointments, promotions, transports, the whole record. All of that. Bound to. But nothing about that special moment on Wednesday, April 4, 1943, that belonged to Reinhard and to Dieter. He finished his coffee, hoped Eichmann would hang and left the table. It had taken so many years since the end of the war for someone to nail him. He imagined that the motionless man in the Beit Haam courthouse - motionless, that is, apart from a lifelong twitch to the left side of his face - would surely renew the urge for justice worldwide. Suddenly Reinhard felt vulnerable. The anniversary that they felt so much about, Dieter and he, had been marked for the eighteenth time just days before Dieter's job-seeking trip to Hannover. Now, during this moment of extreme doubt and anxiety, he really did wonder whether there would be any more anniversaries to celebrate. He strolled out of the hotel. Dieter worried him. There was little strange or wrong in anyone being attracted to a language. It was also natural that the language Dieter should be attracted to was German, though Reinhard wished he had been drawn to his own attempts at French. Well before graduating from university, Dieter expressed a desire to live in the federal republic. The country was worth the while, was how it put it. No, what worried Reinhard was his siding with the nationalist-inclined parties that were springing up, that they should be given a chance, that it was better to have these committed politicians than a load of weary, armchair traditionalists. He even said that what was needed was for the country to get back to good old German ways. Well, here possibly was a taste of that! Reinhard tried to think of Stephanie but it was Eichmann who shared the bed as he tried to relax on it. Reinhard was generally able to let media revelations drift by. He took news in a hammock these days. On the other hand, this sudden focus on the Holocaust had made him take notice. He sprang off the bed, went to the window and then turned to face back into the room. Both hands took his weight as he leant over the bedroom table and looked at the judge. Out of his mouth came a cry that he coaxed into the open, stretching the lament until he tasted tears at the corners of his mouth. He sank to his knees until his voice was still.

*

The hospital reported that Dieter was stable but still not fully conscious. Reinhard walked the short distance to the hospital to clear his head. Everything was something else. Chess moves ... Feldherrnhalle manoeuvring; Hammersmith borough's carnival night ... Nürnberg's thundering Führer deification under the mesmerising lights and music of a breathless Zeppelinfeld; his own park gardens' masses of flowers back in Hammersmith ... weed-infested camps. He sat by Dieter's bed for half an hour. He saw the flicker the sister had spoken of and he prayed as he moved his gaze from the monitor of liquid despair. There was another flicker of Dieter's eyelids. And another. Then it stopped. Reinhard would have put up with the young man leading a right-wing party. He would have given anything at this moment to hear him repeat how he thought the party had the right to express its opinions and that some right wing parties' policies were not as extreme as reasons he had heard for decrying their existence, and Reinhard regretted saying that some of these parties were probably just trying to do after the second world war what had been attempted unsuccessfully immediately after the first. Just a hello would do, though. Hello dad.

Despite all the good times he had had with his own father early on, the dense layers of what too late he realised was party political nonsense had left them with little more to exchange than an occasional nod. Ten minutes before the end, however, with ideologies and indifferences sterilised by the crisp white sheets between them, the stiff folds of intolerance that had built up over the years to satisfy one trifling expedience after the other suddenly became as smooth as a bed pan. The thing was, time omega had revealed a fresh alpha at that bedside and Reinhard suddenly wanted more. Now, in the anxious present, he thought of those bloody red and black flags that had fluttered towards him to wipe away the tears as he left the hospital that day. And he wondered how much happier his life might have been had he tried harder to draw out the earlier bond the two had so much enjoyed. That set him thinking of Stephanie again and how much he wanted more of her.

He looked up. The liquid shot forward, almost three-quarters of its journey towards the end of the channel. Pictures snapped closed and he looked down at Dieter, whose lips parted slightly, momentarily, and his eyelids fluttered as a finger began a spasmodic muscular twitch. Then the barely audible words: '...arl einzlen. arl einzlen ... Heinz ... lengers.'

Reinhard called for the nurse. He waited, long and expectant minutes, but there was nothing more. The nurse put a hand on his shoulder. 'You should get some rest, Herr Hänsel. We will ring you immediately if there is any noticeable change.' After ten more minutes, Reinhard stood up at the bedside and slowly arched his back. He bent forward and touched Dieter's hand, turned and walked up the ward. He told the nurse he would be back in the morning, with friends. He walked out into a Hannover suburb that was far too chirpy for his mood. It had started to rain and by the time he reached the shops, there was a steady downpour. He bought an umbrella and took aloft its segments of grey, white and yellow. Then he suddenly realised he had not yet booked George and Irma into the hotel for the night. By the time he'd called the hotel, the rain had stopped and a weak sun was emerging between a long thin break in the clouds and he swung the umbrella rhythmically, immoderately, trying to bring the point down each time to stab the space between the paving slabs.

4

BILD screamed at him from the news stand and he responded, settling into a seat to scan its pages. The headlines were fatter, taller and redder and more insistent than he could ever recall. But he tried to make no judgement. He was grateful to be able to read a downright version of the fracas, even if the worst slant was being emphasised. The other, normally more watchful newspapers were too circumspect. There was this much to say for cheap journalism.

In addition to the front page, the centre spread was given over to the incident. A large picture showed an ugly scene, a close-up of two youngsters, one holding his head, his shirt heavily bloodstained, the other with a fiercely gaping mouth within inches of another's nose, the pair of them set against a battlefield background. Others were locked in combat. In newspaper terms, a good picture. Though Dieter might be in there, he realised. He looked closely. He turned to the report. Words matched the images. What a mess. He rested the conflict on his lap and looked out to just over his knees to shoes criss-crossing the heavy mosaic floor, scores of hurrying coat tails and swinging leather bags and umbrellas, brushing briefly, moving between the terminal entrance and the departure lounges, some legs turning one way to a large and busy restaurant, others opposite to equally packed in-house shops. Left and right selection.

'Your newspaper?'

Reinhard looked up at a hairy man with a weasel face who pawed his glasses as he excused his desire to share the seat.

'I've seen all I wish to,' Reinhard responded jerkily. 'Here, take it.'

The weasel said: 'Another bloody street fracas. Nazis still popping up all over the place. It's amazing, really, after all they did. We don't do enough about it. What a country! Thugs I call them, these nationalists. I lost my father in Buchenwald, you know. I don't want anyone to say that that did not matter.'

Reinhard did not know the means of drawing up the indictment of an entire nation, excused himself and left. If the Düsseldorf train was on time, he had another forty-five minutes to wait. He entered a bar where music and conversation fought for the upper hand, and bought a cognac. He downed this where he stood and asked for another, eventually making his way through the haze to a pillar seat. The strident politics of stretched newsprint seemed to encircle him as much as the cigar smoke. He looked over a reader's shoulder as he put the glass to his lips. Members from one of the parties that flooded the West German scene had split and formed a new party. 'Parties!' he exclaimed under his breath. Always so many parties. Dozens had risen up in the Thirties. Their crazy members had created fearsome scraps in Berlin. All but one had been *verboten* shortly after the multi-million cheer. It had been an exhausting time. But as he again put the glass to his lips he wondered how it had come about that he had not voted wholeheartedly for the outstanding figure of his time, his wonderful Stephanie? She had pleaded with him to ignore 'this false dawn'. She had been so right, and he so wrong. How had he not seen her point of view? 'Let's live our lives as two people in love,' she had said. 'Marry me, not National Socialism!' And immediately after the war, returning a move he had made to try to get back in touch with her, she had virtually repeated the offer but by then he knew he could not abandon Senka.

A young man drained a litre of ale in two gulps and set down the empty glass, froth running down his chin before being mopped by the back of a huge hand.

Reinhard is at the sink with his brother Siegfried.

'Another?'

Exhausted by a game of football, Siegfried and Reinhard pour the water down their throats. Reinhard is guzzling his second glass and eyeing his brother over the rim to see how far Siegfried has got, hoping he would not be pushed too far.

'Bet you can't drink a third!'

'Wanna bet!' swamps the front of Reinhard's shirt.

He wondered these years later whether during the sessions at the sink Siegfried had not detected the desperate need to win something that must have been etched on his face, and that brotherly love had not once or twice seemed more important than anything. Or was he kidding himself again; would Siegie have remembered nothing of the sort?

Reinhard hadn't noticed the Alsatian dog, which now suddenly appeared from beneath the table and came forward at him, lips curled, teeth bared. Collared by the young beer-swiller's chair leg, though, the dog could get no further.

'Here Jake!'

Reinhard stared.

The massive dog strains and growls, froth flicked about by an excited head, both its front feet pawing the air. Nearby stand a man and a woman and a small boy.

Something of the word that would not properly form came to him. It had been uttered in Auschwitz, he was sure, outside the political department. The man had called her this name. And she him. Fest... Fest-something. It would not come. But Rastenkorb. Of course! The dog-eared tram ticket. Reinhard now recalled it clearly. A greenish 30Pfennig ticket. It had fallen out of Dieter's pocket that first night as he fled from accursed Birkenau and out of Poland. Dieter had cried to keep it and Reinhard had placed it carefully into the back of an old wallet and given it to Dieter in the barn, two hours into their journey towards Switzerland. It had more than once been offered as fare as Reinhard drove an armchair around the front room of their Hammersmith flat. Incredibly, Reinhard realised that he was probably within relatively a few miles of the ticket's place of issue.

The dog moved forward again and then Reinhard got it: the man and a woman had been with a small boy. A fine looking pair, he remembered. They had spoken. He could not recall her Christian name but he remembered she had called him Rainer and near the end, before being separated, they had called each other Herr and Frau ... Fest ...Fest ... that was it! Festfortag! Herr Festfortag. And Frau Festfortag. They had been outside the political department building. Reinhard had been there, with the Commandant.

5

FAMILIES have slipped off Eichmann's mirror finish desk. They're here, heaped, more defined than at Prinz-Albrecht-Strasse. Leave is already a distant memory. He meets the commandant outside his villa by the camp. He is surprised at the bearing of the man: short, portly, a meticulous figure who seems he might not scratch his head without a plan. It is clear that Rudolf Höss has a passion for work, though even in the walk between the chief guardhouse and the political department buildings outside the wire ringed camp, the commandant seems to express both pleasure and sadness in what he is doing in this 'back of beyond' Polish swampland. He speaks of the coldness with which one of his officers herds people to their death and it seems that the commandant is referring to himself in this.

They approach the political department. There is bewilderment around the main doors. Höss leads the way. The now promoted Sturmbannführer feels important but the huddled mass of prisoners registers violently on his mind. Strands of reasonableness and hope try to envelope the rifled words that tear out of harsh mouths into the soft centre of perplexed, perhaps already unhinged souls. A dog menaces a young woman who holds the hand of a child. A huge guard is shoving them as the hysterical woman seeks to speak to both the guard and a young man on the other side of him.

'We're not together ... the three off us are ... stop ... I want to talk to someone ... please ... please ... it's a mistake.'

'Talk to me!' leers the guard. 'I will listen ... for two more seconds!'

'This -'

'Time's up!' cuts in the mountain, his thick, folded neck appearing to continue the physical line of the awful, parted lips. You can say one last thing to each other because you're going your separate ways. The man jumps towards the guard but the mountain's fist lands flush into his face. The man is down but he lifts his head and, mud and emotion on his lips, huskily says, 'God speed you darling ... Frau Festfortag-.'

'That's it!' says the guard, pushing the young woman away towards a group of people by a lorry.

'You too, my darling - Herr Festfortag -.'

Höss and his visitor stride on towards the main gate. Höss says, 'I will just show you around the camp - this place that I have made into what it is today only with some considerable effort, I don't mind telling you. Do you know that this was a quarantine camp at the beginning? So much reconstruction had to be carried out and all the time, even before the first couple of huts had been made ready, I was being pestered by those crazy people from the Security Service in Breslau to say when the first transports could be sent here!'

They cross the Apel square and walk left between Blocks 16 and 17, then again right and enter Block 10, the experimental block, and later Block 11.

'You'll be able to write a fuller report for your, let me see, ah yes, the Concentration Camps Inspectorate, yes? You'll be better placed to help fill up the files if you see it all,' encourages Höss, wrapping his sarcasm in the trace of a smile. 'We must concentrate on tomorrow. I warn you, though, Birkenau's not the same as the main camp here, but then Birkenau is, as you know, rather special in that regard. Still, we can talk about that later. First you will join me for dinner.'

*

The Birkenau camp is about two kilometres from Höss's playground and the SS-Sturmbannführer tries to stride contemptuously between the rough blocks. He walks, and alone, from the camp entrance between the men's and women's blocks in line with the course of the planned railway track that will later bring thousands of new arrivals right up to within yards of the first of the camp's crematoria. He prefers his solitude, spurning the company of both Höss and Höss's adjutant, not only because he wants to be as unprotected as possible, but because he feels a little sick from the whole fat haunch of hare, dumplings and red cabbage from the commandant's table.

The Arbeitskommando Krematorium, ready for the inspection of the most recently constructed crematorium, awaits the officer's arrival on the edge of Brzezinka Wood. As he walks, Reinhard's mind is battered by a cacophony of barked commands, stomping SS, shuffling skeletons, hideous screams and private sobs, desperation and clinging hope, and the vision of dazed, numbed prisoners surrounded by gulping dogs, en route to places for special treatment, for cleansing. There to see them pass are other remnants of once lively beings occasionally looking skywards towards great fat chimneys, perhaps to wonder about this warm peace at last ... Thoughts several shades darker than the most graphic words of hate assail Reinhard's mind as he fights to keep a straight path to the end of the blocks. He turns right to make for Brzezinka Wood and right again before reaching the steel-grey beeches. He passes the disinfection block, another of the crematoria and arrives at his destination, Crematorium V. He stretches out his arm for the work detail without removing his eyes from the open door leading to the entrance hall. From this entrance, straight ahead, is the changing room. To the right is the mortuary, and to the left, the first of three gaskammer. He stands alone inside the building. He sniffs the air, a long intake. He remains there a full minute, then turns to face the door. He looks back into the chamber, before turning his back on the building and walking to the officers' residential settlement area and straight to the mess and a drink.

In the morning, he acquaints himself with the rest of the camp. He is drawn to a disturbance but gives his body a tug to remove it from the scene. He marches quickly, thumping one foot down after the other, quicker yet, for he needs to stack up sandbags around his body, bloated with the chaff of Hitlertruth, to deflect a sharp cutting edge that dashes about him, threatening to spill the indexed order of Berlin. He stops. A cringing group he had seen earlier has disappeared. But there is another group, perhaps the same group moved on, half a dozen prisoners being urged towards a lorry. The group is misty, like before. Or is it the clarity of this couple? A woman and her child go from sight and the group sharpens. But her head reappears, now as a diamond set in papier-mâché. The group will be ready for a new death, he is sure of that, for even if all the crematoria are out of action - the ovens from Erfurt failing once again the cleansing programme - there are other means.

At command headquarters, he feels even more afraid of his thoughts. He looks out of his window, over to the left. He can see a large part of the camp. Preliminary construction work is going on to his right but to his left, as far as he can see, there are wooden huts, eight or nine ranks deep. And he knows that further still to his left, the original part of the camp, roughly where he entered the place, lies the mostly brick built barracks for the women.

The women.

The woman.

He rushes time. He wants it done and dresses himself with pace and style hardly born of care and precision. He is too quick; now he must wait. He does not want to think about it anymore. Just arrive, observe, know. He speaks to the man in charge.

'*Alles in Ordnung?*' he asks an orderly.

'*Jawohl, Herr Sturmbannführer!*'

The orderly carries on. The prisoners look weary but unafraid. Some even manage a smile. There is impatience that the doors have not yet been closed. But the mood changes. Prisoners' arms are raised, jerkily crossing faces. The doors close. The Sturmbannführer walks a little way into the wooded area, then deeper, picking his way around soggy areas, but the thumping boiler gets louder and he puts his hand over his ears. At the same time he looks at the perimeter fence and the watching guards. He walks back. A second group arrives. There is agitation by the changing room. A woman wants her small child looked after and when she says she does not want to expose it to any fierce flow or sudden burst of hot water, the orderly laughs: '*It's all new in there, perfectly controlled. No gushes of water, I promise you.*'

'*Mein Kind! Please take this child,*' the woman screams.

'*Nein. You must be responsible for your own possessions. This is purifying time.*'

'*Bitte! Nehmen Sie dieses Kind. Bitte!*' she pleads. But the SS man no longer looks her way. Reinhard does. The woman is holding the child across her shoulder, like a laundry bundle. Her searchlight eyes sweep the hallway and in a second lock into his gaze. It is she! This woman. He cannot pull away. There is a single beam that joins the two of them, making the edges all around indistinct. Like before, somehow like before this, like even that was not the first time. He sees in her searching eyes such earnestness and belief despite the uncompromising situation, eyes which seek just one small favour, one last wish so reasonable, an incredible trust in the most hopeless of situations, that suddenly it represents an understanding far beyond anything he can rationally explain. His broken voice calls out above the tumult.

'*Here!* Give the child to me!' He steps forward and reaches into the chamber, scolding the *Rapportführer*.

'*Infants are separated; they are treated specially,*' he says, improvising himself. '*We are not unreasonable,*' he adds, addressing the frightened prisoners. Then, almost inaudibly to the woman, he says, '*I shall look after him.*' The fleeting beam that has flickered between the jagged words of assurance seems to give her

REQUIREMENTS OF GUILT

silent contentment. And in its turn, this gratifies him to a degree that makes him reckless of the danger he now faces. He looks into her eyes for several seconds more. Then he whirls round on the stunned orderlies, realising that he must be even bolder.

'Some idiot has made a grave mistake, and for that person it's going to be a very costly mistake!' he barks. 'Have you nothing to do! You two, get out and help the Sonderkommando! And you, report to the Oberscharführer. Clear this entrance!'

Reinhard takes the child by the hand and leads him out of the crematorium, brushing by people without regard to any kind of pretence, except that as he passes a sergeant on the way to his car, he bawls: 'Some lunatic has fucked up. Get out of the way! You, move these people away from the entrance. Schnell! Schnell! Sergeant, make sure you get the names of those responsible!'

The bewildered sergeant comes stiffly to attention and is left half saluting as the officer sweeps on and gets into his car. He drives through gates between the central camp and the planned third camp and turns onto the main road to Command HQ. But he is not going to Command HQ. He slows down at the gate and furiously beckons the guard who is already approaching the car.

'Mention this to no one, but the Commandant's nephew has, God knows how, got into this bloody place,' he says. 'How long have you been on duty? Never mind! Telephone ahead that this vehicle has priority to Auschwitz Main Camp so this, er, little gentleman, can be returned swiftly and safely to the house. Understand?'

'Jawohl, Herr Sturmbannführer!'

Reinhard drives off, turns right outside the gate by Command HQ and the SS barracks along the heavily protected road, ignoring the guard posts. At the end of the road, opposite the large tower-topped main entrance archway, a clutch of SS personnel hold their hands up to vehicles to-ing and fro-ing, and one steps forward coming to attention as the officer's car slows. The SS man immediately raises his arm and points forward.

Reinhard hears a wailing alarm as he speeds out of Birkenau to begin the short journey to Auschwitz I but who, after a couple of minutes, swings off towards the town itself.

The commandant's nephew. The bigger the lie ...

6

IRMA looked lovely in a mint green suit and a straw hat with a dark green silk band. She sat in the station concourse, her hands, in off-white gloves, straight out in front of her, caught between her knees. Apart from sporting a rather wide and loud blue tie and what looked to be new black shoes, George didn't look as if he'd bothered too much. Her head went back, slightly to one side, a wide smile greeting Reinhard's approach. He embraced her lightly and shook George's hand.

'You are some friend, George. I do so thank you - both.'

'Steff, we had to come. Just take us to your lad.'

He never minded when George called him Steff; after they had bumped into each other at the station and settled little Dieter with George's wife, and gone out and quaffed a few ales, Reinhard had become a bit talkative and gone on about his Stephanie. George assumed it was his wife but Reinhard said he only wished she had been.

Irma stepped forward and raised a hand. 'I'd like to stay on,' she announced. 'To be with Dieter. You will need someone to help you, Reinhard, I am sure …'

Reinhard cut her short, catching hold of Irma's arm and picking up her suitcase. 'Are you hungry? Let's grab something to eat and we can talk there.'

All three settled down in high-backed, mock leather seats at a window table overlooking the concourse. George and Reinhard asked the waiter, a young man in a white jacket and black trousers, for Rémy Martins, and Irma chose a Jägermeister liqueur. When the waiter returned, George and Irma said they'd have what the stiffly folded menu called a Number 4 snack - slices of chicken, cheese and Salami with various breads, honey and jam and coffee - and Reinhard settled for a Wiener Würstchen mit Kartoffelsalat. George downed his Rémy Martin as if he'd suddenly realised he was on holiday and waved in another. When it came, he took one sip and said, 'After I've seen Dieter, I shall go on to my reunion. Irma, bless her, wants to stay and she will be a big help. I'll be in Enschede only a few days and then I'll return.'

Reinhard readily agreed. 'Of course it is George. It was good that you break your journey.' He stood up and pulled on his topcoat, and George and Irma followed suit. At the hotel, George and Irma freshened up while Reinhard sat in an armchair that practically enveloped him as he lay back, his head just touching the end of one of the long green limbs of an Areca Palm. Rastenkorb was beginning to spawn another word. He couldn't recall it fully but he knew he would and that it would probably draw him back to something bad. He wondered how much would be drawn out. He feared a deluge of suppressed matter.

Reinhard's attention was drawn to the girl at reception. He wanted to hear her voice and asked for a map of the area. As she bent down, her straight auburn hair fell over most of her face, giving her a secret appearance, sending him back to a place he and Stephanie frequented in Berlin's café quarter. Stephanie had waved her hands to describe the breadth of her love for him, accidentally flicking most of the ice cream from her spoon onto the carpet. Crouched over the stricken white and red blob like a paramedic, she looked back up to him with a scampish smile. It had been a forever moment.

Although at first they seemed to accept Reinhard and his journalistic aspirations, Stephanie's parents now openly opposed liaison with the Nazi he had become. And their influence had its effect on the couple's relationship. When a call came for Reinhard at the *Telegraphen* office, it was to announce that particular note had been made of some of his special newspaper articles. He was to be sent to London to report on the activities of Oswald Mosley. He had thought of Stephanie but concentrated on London. He wanted to contact her but every time he went to pick up the receiver, he drew back. It would be betrayal one way or another, whatever anyone said. That misguided thought heightened the remorse he now felt.

The appearance of Irma and George broke his reverie. Irma put a hand on Reinhard's shoulder. 'Here we are then. Ready for a drink?'

'Hello. Certainly! By the way, this family in Enschede, what are they like?'

'Oh, they are wonderful,' said George, adding, 'so kind, so pleasant, so eager to please.'

'Yes, particularly Renate!' Irma said, trying not to make it sound too much like fact.

'Well, yes, it was Renate, as you know Reinhard, who took me out of the battlefield, so to speak, before I went to hospital. I can never forget her kindness and the skill and application she applied on my account, so that it made it possible for me to live, really. It is as simple as that. And of course, to meet you, Irma!'

Irma smiled without moving her lips.

'Well, I just feel I need to repay her kindness. Visiting her and spending a little time with her every so often is the least I can do in the circumstances.'

In his room, the twisted impertinence of Revisionism was replaced by the fear he had of what lay behind the word Rastenkorb. He began to experience a sinking feeling he imagined worse than drowning as he splashed water on his face. He looked to see whether the foreboding was etched on his face.

He crosses to the large, gilt-edged mirror next to the office door. He does not know what he seeks but he has an anxiety that one day he will not see reflected what his training has imposed on him and runs a hand defensively over his mouth, touching the underside of his nose and up to high cheekbones, blue eyes thankfully betraying no hint that his career is not still set fair for the advancement he has sought for so long, and sought with passion, and which career has been improved at almost every step he has taken from his treasured moment of SS training at Bad Tölz. He slides the open hand down over his clean-shaven chin, bringing it to rest in the centre of his chest, before moving the palm slightly to the left where he lets it remain for some time. Orders, he whispers, are not everything.

Dieter was still unconscious but stable. Reinhard stayed an hour and then went to the station to see George off while Irma remained at the bedside. She had taken advantage of a room in the hospital's accommodation annexe.

George lowered the carriage window and said, 'Look after her, won't you Reinhard?'

'Hurry back,' Reinhard said to himself.

7

FESTFORTAG. The parents' name. The family Festfortag. Reinhard twice took the wrong turning and practically ended up on the bonnet of a taxi as he made his way back to the hotel deep in thought. Once in his room, he fully opened the widow and drew a deep breath before sitting down in the cane-backed chair, lips pursed, head back. It came out, clearly and proudly: April 4, 1943. He stared at the open window. In one of those swollen heaves of the chest that betray a disagreeable moment in life, the words Festfortag and Rastenkorb re-entered his mind. He felt ambushed and ensnared by them. His blood pumped wildly though he knew he could not and should not brush the words aside. He needed to pursue them and hope for the best. Festfortag. He needed to absorb all the torment that might await him so that he could suffer a permanent vision of the family home.

He would inch near the address hardly daring at first to look at the wall or hedge that led to the front gate, then stare and imagine how it might have been, one day before Auschwitz when he might have been able to look upon a happy family at play in the front garden so that in that moment it is realised that life is incredibly worthwhile. He would want to examine the gate, peer at the latch, and consider how many times it might have been pressed before the final depression, look at the gravel path that the postman would have walked up and down to deliver all the news of civilised life. Would the Gestapo have trodden the same path with express orders more shattering than all the worst news in all the letters that had fallen on every mat in every household in the street since its beginning? In the last few days before the Festfortags were taken, with their Dieter, were they resigned to whatever fate had in store for them, taking nothing for granted so that subconsciously their departures from their home might always be their last? Or did this couple, in their youth, never think of saying good-bye to anything in their home or look lovingly at anything that did not actually speak whenever they left home because life was ever present, automatic, always available, that it would never not be there? Had he curtailed some cherished occasion? And even if it was just an ordinary moment, it belonged to someone else and was not his to tamper with, not his to interrupt, however indirectly. Could he even now begin properly to understand how wretched and desperate the Festfortag family must have felt that day? Did he, SS-Sturmbannführer Reinhard Hänsel, never stop to think just what he might have been helping to set in train for people many miles away? Had he really not cared? Every action sent out its ripples. He knew that. A caring, thinking family had brought him up. He had learned to appreciate matters of the soul, things he had been taught that were important in life. He had gone to university. A thinking man. Yet in all this business he had been so clearly unthinking, until that special moment.

He had not smoked for ten years. The last time had been just after midday on September 3, 1949. He had tried to give up so many times before: smoking only five a day, smoking only in the open, only inside, on even days, on odd days, only at weekends, only during work time, only after meal times. He would smoke on rainy days and inhale only fresh, sunny air the rest of the time. By not smoking, he had once calculated having saved a willpower-boosting DM12,000. But today, he was going to smoke. He entered the tobacconist and the air of the practised smoker suddenly enveloped him again. He bought his favourite brand, lit one and inhaled, felt a little giddy, leant against the pavement railing and closed his eyes. He had done it now, too late to turn back. It did not matter any more, one or twenty this day or any other day. It was now an interval, nothing more. It felt nice, like it used to, when he had no need to care about anything, took life for granted. No longer would he have to divide his comfort with the other, less reliable accomplices of life. He could take long draws on the crackling cigarette and burn away distress that filtered through, the look of Frau Festfortag in the sealed chamber. He lit up another cigarette, inhaled deeply then drove out the smoke. He followed the wisp of bluish air out through the door, across one city, out the other side, pursuing it into the hotel room where he had lain there watching exhaled smoke encircle the cut glass lamp by his bedside, convinced of a bright and pleasant world that had been illuminated by the life-changing Nürnberg rally. Now his vision felt to be as elusive as the lingering smoke in the tobacconist's doorway as he tried to imagine again being able to put a loving arm around his brightest and most pleasant part of that world.

Irma joined Reinhard after breakfast at the hotel and suggested having a bite to eat and coffee somewhere swish after visiting Dieter.

'It would give me an excuse to sit in your lovely hire car,' she said.

He was nervous and felt himself lip-chewing as he lowered his eyes. She just stood there and he said, 'I am sorry, but I'm not going to be much company today, Frau G. Everything, it is over me.'

'On top of me,' she corrected with a smile.

He found an image of Stephanie, turning away a little. '*Ja*, on top.'

Now visibly squirming and without really knowing what he was about to say, Reinhard stood up, shook his head and began, 'Frau G …' She interrupted. 'Yes, Reinhard?'

'Things, they are hurting me, up here,' he choked, bumping the palm of his hand on his forehead.

'Things?'

He was hurting. Stephanie would probably not want him as things were. So he told Frau G, 'It is maybe nothing. I do not know yet. I say it is maybe nothing. I will try to explain but later, eh? I feel somehow confused. No more now; let's go and visit Dieter. OK?'

Irma's face suggested a smile. 'OK Reinhard. OK.'

There was no change in Dieter's condition but they stayed right up to midday, Irma every so often holding one of Dieter's hands and Reinhard the other. When their own hands touched, they looked up shyly and smiled. Sister Schlem assured them that the hospital would telephone any important news and they left for lunch. He opened the passenger door of the slate grey Mercedes and made an arm available before Irma sank into the age-lined leather seat. After the 300S had roared into life, Reinhard said, 'I think I shall be moving about quite a lot - might as well do it in comfort.'

'You know, Reinhard, you ought to get yourself a companion, perhaps even marry.'

'*Stimmt* ...' he said, adding in a whisper, 'Stephanie, I think!'

She practically snorted. 'It is lovely you still remember her. But that cannot be, eh? You must look elsewhere.'

'Then, her memory I will marry!'

She lowered her eyes.

Memory was stronger than presence now that he had suddenly spoken her name aloud. A housewarming party of a friend of George's came back to him vividly. He'd gone outside for a breather, away from the cocktail of noise, artifice, gulping and swaying and, if he were honest, the excitement of Frau G's hand that had found its way onto his when she sat next to him on a rather luxurious settee. He'd looked up into the night sky and talked to Stephanie, as sometimes he did. He re-wound the world to the first Plough they had seen together, the saucepan as they called it. It was to be their marker for the future when, no matter where they were, whatever trouble they were in or whatever needs they might have, they could look along the handle and round the bottom of the bowl and up to its rim then, springing four degrees upwards, a little to the right, they could be together, at the North Star. He smiled at the sheer extravagance of such an arrangement and in that instant remembered how he had hurriedly looked at his watch like someone who had remembered an appointment, wanting to turn and race away to catch a bus and a train and cross the water and ride and walk to where their Thirties' Plough had been.

'Where are you taking me, Reinhard?'

It took a moment or two for Irma's voice to reach him. He told her that he'd been to Max's and thought it was good. They drove off, and for a while she was silent, slowly winding down her window. Then, putting her head back and allowing the wind to rush through her hair, she said, 'I wish we had a car like this. Well, any car, really.'

'Companionship, as you say Frau G, it is the important thing. George, he is so much better than a Mercedes Benz. He is so much better than *any* car.'

Again, briefly, she fell silent. 'I like fast cars,' she said at length, looking out of the window she had now almost closed. Then, looking straight at Reinhard, she coaxed, 'Irma. Call me Irma. It is so much less formal. Let me hear you say it.'

'Irma.'

She sank further into her seat, like a cat settling down. 'You are OK Reinhard. Very OK. We … we get on well. Very well, *ja?*'

Reinhard ran a hand over the front of his head, a habit he had whenever he was the slightest self-conscious.

'It is only a little question, Reinhard,' she continued playfully.

He could not deny he was fond of Irma, though unsure of himself. He survived on Stephanie. Should he and Stephanie ever meet again, he wanted to be sure he'd been true to himself and to her memory. They found the restaurant but were held up by a delivery lorry and, as Reinhard drew the car up behind the vehicle, she turned to him with a resigned shake of the head, 'George is not very adventurous you know, Reinhard. He wants more and more to tinker with things around the house, things that do not really need the attention. It is either that, or he sits around fiddling with his radios. You know, I wish he would switch himself on sometimes. Then it is sleep. I often wonder what keeps him so contented.'

Reinhard adjusted the rear-view mirror, then his tie. Without looking at her, he said, *'Natürlich, Du, Frau G* … sorry, Irma,' resisting an urge to reach over to touch her hand but feeling as if he had already done so. She turned to look out on a crowded pavement, then straight ahead as the delivery man pulled down the lorry's roller back and went around to his cab.

'I do not think so,' she returned. 'He seems to change when these Dutch visits come round, the meetings with buyers at Enschede. As for the rest, well, he says stores work is easy but he comes home from the factory, flops into his chair and often just stays there. Perhaps he is less tired when there is chess. I don't begrudge him this reunion thing though normally I am left by myself. But this is different,' she said, shifting in her seat. 'I met the woman who tended him after he was injured at Arnhem, before he went to hospital. She is nice enough but a toucher, you know? I don't like touchers in that way,' she said, flashing Reinhard a glance. 'Also, the cousin, he kept looking at her. Odd it was.'

Reinhard glided the Merc into one of the few parking slots left in the park behind Max's. He walked round to help Irma out of the car, removing himself from her arm only slowly, running his hand down the sleeve to just touch her bare wrist. He had suddenly wanted to experience the feeling. He did not want to appear to distrust her friendship, but when they had settled at a table, he led in straight away with his concerns for Dieter and something of his new fear. He kept talking at a fair rate, pausing only to order mulligatawny soup and a crispy roll and butter, and some wine.

'I was worried before, but now, all this political nonsense,' he stressed, bringing an open hand down on the table top with such purpose that he almost upset the wine. It was an action of release, not exclusively linked to the subject matter. He mocked his own irritability, slapped his offending arm and, in seeing Irma's amused reaction, went as if to say something but drew back. They both laughed loudly when Irma accidentally sent a fork flying off the table in trying to administer a friendly rebuke. She picked it up and excused herself from the table.

Irma had come to regard Dieter as the child George and she had been denied by something George barely touched upon. George had been one of the survivors of the British 1st Airborne Division attempt to make a swift crossing of the Lower Rhine at Arnhem. He'd parachuted almost on top of a crack SS division and, though shot up badly in the middle region, made it into woods and later to the Hummel family. He'd been lucky Renate had nursing experience. She patched him up. Yet with all the bravery he could have alluded to, George was always the keener to dwell on Reinhard's situation nearly eighteen months earlier and the respect he had for what he had done. George would always sum up Reinhard by relating the occasion when, during a camping holiday in Spain they had enjoyed a couple of years into their friendship, Reinhard insisted on seeing a woman, Hagar, before they left. He'd befriended her at the bar. She was travelling alone following the death of her husband some years earlier. Hagar always seemed happy, singing to herself, despite her lonely situation. After knocking several times on her campervan door, a man appeared from around hedging to the rear of another van, caught Reinhard by the arm and led him back to it. Inside, Reinhard learned to his horror that Hagar had died during the night. Reinhard left the van gasping for air. He was so upset that George decided they should stay another night. During that evening, the man told them that Hagar was a Jew from Hungary who spent most of her time travelling and trying to learn how to sing. In particular, she wanted to perfect a rendering of Dvorak's *Song to he Moon* to a standard good enough to win a place at a music college and then pursue the singing career her daughter, Jael, had been denied by the Nazis. Jael had apparently perished during a three-day rail journey to Auschwitz-Birkenau following the German occupation of her country in the spring of 1944. She had been arrested while returning from private tuition at a house just four streets from her home in Györ. She had been perfecting the song for an important audition the following day. Reinhard bought a record of the song and had it played at Hagar's funeral. It became one of Reinhard's favourite pieces of music, George would say.

When Irma returned to the table, she said she always trusted someone who had the experience. Reinhard was concerned about Dieter, so therefore she was, too. The opinion of her sister in Salzburg, who could sometimes be quite boring on the subject, was far from re-assuring when it came to West Germany. Irma said she had recently given Dieter some of his favourite sweet cake when he called round and had tried to deflect him from pursuing a job in the country. 'And while he was there, my sister rang and referred to these young right wing politicians as "neo-fuckin'-Nazis".' They had both agreed, however, that Dieter was a very determined young man who had brains only for design engineering.

Reinhard was briefly taken by the way Irma had faithfully repeated her sister's description but let out a confirming and contemptuous, '*Stimmt.*'

Irma went on, 'Perhaps if he could take this girl of his, Hildegard, seriously. Dieter is such a dear.' Reinhard thought it was serious already and that they both loved the place. Sister Schlem understood that the girl was intending to visit the hospital. If so, Reinhard thought they might be lucky enough to meet her.

Irma was quiet on the journey to the hospital. Reinhard felt her presence again and glanced over to her. He wondered whether, if anything happened to George and he could not find Stephanie, he and Irma would get together. But the moment he thought it, he felt the pull of Stephanie and concentrated on the road. As they turned into the hospital grounds, Irma pulled her coat about her.

'Thank you for the little outing. I enjoyed today,' she said, resting her hand on Reinhard's as he took the car out of gear.

After they had stayed with Dieter for an hour and were having a cup of coffee in the hospital café, she repeated the action, urging him not to be late for Gottfried.

'I will look after Dieter, or Hildegard will if she comes today. I have my little book to read, anyway. You don't worry - just meet your friend. You know where we'll be,' she said. Then, lingering on the words, added, 'If I am not here, I will be up in my room.'

'Thank you, Fr ... Irma. Thank you,' he said as innocently as he could.

8

THE broad-brush memory Reinhard had of Gottfried was that he was always hungry, often patting his stomach either side of mealtimes, always ready and willing to down anything with cream on it. Which thought unashamedly presented the vision of a huge slice of Black Forest kirschtorte. Reinhard sort of licked his lips. The old friends had arranged to meet by the Schloss bridge at Bückeburg, south of Hannover, around mid-afternoon. Gottfried was currently working in the area. Reinhard found himself by the tall iron gates at midday and turned off into the town. *Zum Bahnhof.* He loved trains. The one on the single track to Michelstadt, years ago, when the tanker puffed its way through a peaceful land where spring had not yet entirely pulled back the blanket of snow from the fields. Such countryside invited travellers to open the windows and lean out and scream their delight of it, and he had opened a window and leant out as far as he could, bracing his head against the wind, shielding his eyes from the black bits that spat out from the full-ahead locomotive's chimney, took a long and contented sniff of the air and absorbed his country. He wished he had later just kept admiring countryside, extending a vague love of rooks to all the other 'wire-legged flutterers' and every other thing that moved so freely on the earth and who willingly shared their land with humans who called themselves nature lovers, ordinary folk who just loved picnics, riversides, mossy banks, tree roots, watching shadows being pushed across fields and up hills, cattle and sheep grazing, al fresco lunch and dosing off as the church clock struck three. He could have admired gliding wings instead of rigid arms. He had come to love rooks because so many people didn't, thinking of them only as rats of the air, whereas the real vermin, as always, walked around in smart suits and polished shoes, pressed uniforms and shiny boots.

He took a tram to the end of the street of arched poplars. It reminded Reinhard of another time, another place, when Stephanie had - old enough then to do so anyway - probably defied her parents and agreed to a secret rendezvous with him. He had stared past the entrance to a sloping path where Stephanie, some way off, was walking towards the railway station entrance, past a showy overhang of mature rhododendrons. He and Stephanie were to have spent the day in a nearby city. He'd gone on to the platform and waited but when he looked around she was nowhere to be seen. He rushed back out of the station but she had vanished. He returned to the platform and boarded the train and searched every carriage throughout the length of the journey but there was no sign of her. He even looked for her in the city, every young woman his Stephanie. It had not happened, after all. He wanted that time again, only this time he would keep her in view and, ignoring the protocol of secret lovers, go openly to her, hug her and tell her that the fact that they had both turned up, meant everything they needed to know.

Reinhard leant back against a high stone wall and realised again, and this time so powerfully, that although he had been able to grasp only a little of life's vast romantic offering, it had fed him for almost thirty years, even sometimes sustaining him during the short and tragic marriage to Senka.

Another tram returned him to the main street. He walked on past the Rathaus, standing by the Jägerweg to admire the brown-orange gateway to the Schloss. The first set of statues adorning the Schlossbrücke was visible and he still had plenty of time. Reinhard swept his gaze over the moat. Swans came to him as he made his way to the side of the still water. They would make a good photograph, he thought. He might return one day, with Dieter. But he guessed that when it came to it he would not return. And if he did, it was unlikely that there would be three pale, laughing old ladies dressed in black at rest upon a seat who had made him smile kindly. He returned to the bridge. Gottfried - it was easy to recognise him even at a distance and after such a long time - stood by the little parapet statues. The two men smiled widely as they approached and slung their arms about each other. They stood toe to toe like two lovers. It had been ages and their energies mixed joyfully.

Reinhard said, 'Why on earth have we not tried to get in touch before? You haven't tried, have you?'

'No, but I don' know why!'

They just looked at each other, suddenly astounded by the passage of time. They walked briskly back into the town.

'You managed to follow up ...'

'The story fell through,' Gottfried said. 'At least, the editor thought it was nothing. I have different ideas. But your boy - what happened, Reinhard?'

'Let's go for a meal, eh? I will tell you then. I've seen a good place. Fancy eating?' he said, looking Gottfried up and down and realising that food had continued to boss his life. He should talk! Lying in the bath the other day, he had had the water up to the overflow as usual, but the sponge no longer floated over him. It was now dry land and practically free of the flood tide that knees raised and rested had previously sent over his stomach. Though he still cringed at vested men, tattoos, beer bellies and bursting backsides. He felt he would never give in, even though the inner man was slowly winning.

'Yes, the same Gottfried! Lead the way. *Lieber Gott, Ich habe Hunger!*'

Gottfried mixed his Szegediner gulasch with a question: he was taking a few days off and wondered whether they could spend some time together. Reinhard said that would be great, adding that his neighbours and close friends George and Irma had come over from England, Irma particularly wanting to help him out but having Gottfried's support at this time would be wonderful.

'Good. Fact is, I would like to spend some time down this way, anyway. I have other enquiries to make that I am sure will interest you. Also, Reinhard, I've come into a spot of money, not a fortune but father and mother have both died recently and I feel the need for a rest from the routine of journalism, although, you know, I wouldn't turn down a biggie. Still have the stomach for that. How about you?'

'Well, I know what you mean, but no. Perhaps if we had started up that news agency we said we might after the war …'

Gottfried interrupted, 'You must tell me how it went after you left Oranienburg. Somehow I thought something was up. I wish we could have talked. But about Dieter, what has happened?'

Reinhard told him as much as he knew. At the end, silently, Gottfried thrust over a booklet and pointed to the name Forsthaus Heinemeyer on the edge of a forest a few miles south of Bückeburg. He said, 'Let's stay here. I'm told it's great …' and held up his hand towards Reinhard's protesting face. 'I said I had come into money. Actually, it's quite a lot, more than I ever imagined would come my way, and heaps more than I deserve, I'm sure. I'm not trying to be big about it. I'd just like to stay in this place and I would love you to be my guest.'

'I also. It is so good of you. But, Gottfried, I must be near Dieter at this time and I have a hotel nearby.'

Gottfried slapped an ample thigh. 'Idiot! Of course, what am I thinking of! All right then, I will stay at this hotel of yours, with you, and you shall be my guest there.'

'There is no … '

Gottfried again halted the protest. 'You know, Reinhard, I still remember the Max Schmeling fight night, our first meeting. You knew nothing about me then,' he said, leaning across the table and catching hold of Reinhard's arm.

'Yes, I recall it right enough, but it was only the entrance money, fuChrissake.'

'Not only. Spontaneous thoughtfulness to a stranger who said he'd forgotten his wallet! I so wanted to see the fight.'

'Well it was so unbelievable, it had to be true! My sort of forgetfulness, if you recall. I am still at it! Come on, at least let me pay for this, then.'

'Wouldn't hear of it. *Herr Ober!*'

As they walked out, Gottfried mentioned the other reason for being in the area: Holocaust Revisionism.

'That was how …'

'Yes. I've been going into this quite deeply. Maybe go out with a bang. Got rather a name for it now, with several by-lines in the big titles. I was thinking on the way over that there is nothing like first-hand experience. You were actually there, right?'

Reinhard looked away.

'Well, this has become a bit of a crusade for me. It's important that this thing, which is so outrageous, doesn't become a new suffering, if you know what I mean?'

Reinhard nodded. 'The fact, or rather fiction, that black is sort of white, eh?'

'Precisely. It did happen, didn't it, Reinhard? Tell you what, let's get to your hotel and we can talk there. In the meantime, tell me about your life in England.'

Reinhard started right away as he stepped with care into Gottfried's shining, split-screen VW Beetle with the hooded front lights, telling him enthusiastically about his own prized possession, that he was a municipal gardener, that he liked classical and folk music, chess and, yes, still thought about Stephanie. Gottfried straightened out his furrowed brow, hesitated, and went on with a lighter question.

'You play chess, then?'

'Yes, I do.'

Reinhard looked seriously at Gottfried. He said he felt threatened, as if in a weak end game, that he was suffering from an over aggressive opening.

9

'SO, tell me Reinhard; it did happen, didn't it?'

The bodies sway as the truck moves up. No group he has ever seen is so strangely out of focus as this one, a dense bewildered forest in which appears a clearing. A woman, holding the hand of a child who is dragging a soft toy. Strange. Reinhard is not drawn to her entirely because of the din she and the guard are making. Then they are loaded and the truck moves away. His eyes do not follow as his head begins to turn away.

Gottfried narrowed his eyes: 'Didn't it, Reinhard?'

Reinhard nodded, dreamlike.

Bitte nehmen Sie dieses Kind. Please, please take this child!

'Reinhard?'

The Berlin blotter names are here. All heaped up.

'Sorry, Gottfried. Oh yes, it happened all right,' Reinhard said, emphasising each word.

'Quite. This bloody Revisionism! When Dieter's on the mend, it's what I want to talk to you about and follow through. I told you I thought I might be on to something. Well, it's that. You'd hardly believe it.'

They left for the hotel. Gottfried said that the name Dieter had mumbled could be anything almost, but the police said one name, a Thomas something-or-another, had been mentioned in Dieter's diary.

'We could work together on this after Dieter pulls through. What do you say?'

Gottfried saw the look and changed course. 'Anyway, about yourself. Why didn't you ever return to Oranienburg. Where did you go? What happened in Auschwitz?'

The question was stifling. How could he sum it up? That this was the poison in an attractive bottle? That he had begun to inspect the bottle more closely in Berlin and that in Poland he tasted the vile contents? Well, it was a start.

'Let's have a drink. Cognac is for such a question.'

They sat down and Reinhard said, 'Helplessness, Gottfried, this was the worst. This woman, about to die, she held out her arms. Pathetic, it was, the look on her face. She was anxious for Dieter only, just Dieter. You could see. Even the night before, before No 5 crematorium was opened …'

'Dieter?' a puzzled Gottfried interrupted.

Reinhard drained his glass. *Ja,*' he said. *J-a.*'

Gottfried waited, reaching for his drink.

Reinhard could see it all but put his head back and covered his eyes as if to blacken the images that sprang forward. He remained in this position until Gottfried broke the silence.

'If you'd rather not, old friend.' And Gottfried switched his questioning. 'Your wife. Tell me about her. Did you get back with Stephanie after all? You said you might. Is Dieter…? Where is …? Oh, I'll get us another drink first, eh?'

Stephanie. Stephanie immediately pushed Auschwitz away.

They are lifted into the Nürnberg clouds. Greedily, they swallow the sixth Parteitag night atmosphere, walking with thousands of others from the Luitpoldarena. They gulp on thousands of riveting words and hold their ears as much against the cold air as to keep inside the ecstatic applause. They walk briskly through the crowded streets, as knight and maiden in slow motion through billowing mysticism and swirling Wagner. It is a city at the heart of a rejoicing Germany. They feel privileged, two privileged youngsters, a part of so much to admire. They're the young heartbeat of a new Reich. A speaker had said so and they believed it. They walk on. And on. They skip under the arch leading from the Rathaus to the Städtisches Amts-Gebäude and come out in Fünfer-platz. They turn to each other, hugging tightly. They draw back but keep hold of each other, just touching. But back they go to wrap their necks in arms. They skip as children up the steps that take them into the Rathaus-Keller. Reinhard lights a cigarette as the waiter arrives. Reinhard says, 'Let's drink.' They pick up their glasses and he looks slowly beyond the edge of his glass and thinks how beautiful she is. Her kind face is looking at him. He sits back, confident of the future, looking at and past the smouldering tip of his cigarette into the face with its talkative eyes. He moves forward across the table. She laughs lightly, shifting back a little further in her chair. He leans forward more as he notices a bending fingertip from a palm-up hand stretched lazily to the side of the table.

Gottfried noticed the look on Reinhard's face as he set down the fresh glasses. He went to re-join him and was about to say something when he looked at his watch and partially rose from his seat. 'Sorry old boy. This work is so demanding at times. I have to make a telephone call now. Almost forgot. Shan't be a tick.'

When they leave the Keller, their cuddled walk as public lovers loosens into fingertips that touch every so often as the crowds thin. They just keep walking, crossing the river without ever realising where they are going and they seem to have walked over half the city neither of them know, seeing the Hauptbahnhof ahead. Neither can remember how exactly they reached the hotel. He leads the way and laughingly presses his nose against the lop-sided number five on the door and, as she carelessly reaches for the low door handle in front of him, there is a buzz, like applause. It fills his head. It is something that he does not recognise from any other occasion ...

Gottfried returned with two doubles. They were not a couple of drunks, though it may have seemed that way to an onlooker that evening.

'Sorry about that, Reinhard. Young journalists these days, they think they know it all! Still, that's work. About Stephanie. Tell me more.'

Reinhard leant forward, trapping clasped hands between his knees. After a moment, he said, 'Neither she nor my brother Siegfried followed me, you know. "You and that bloody party!" they would say. Eventually they refused even a ride in my car let alone hopping aboard the National Socialist bandwagon. Whereas I had been fascinated by Nürnberg's clockwork arms and legs, they had not. Stephanie had been enthusiastic to begin with, very much so, but not later, when Hitler's rantings were as blood red as the flag. For me there was something beautiful in the jack-booted legions of the loyal as the Führer stopped along the street of fevered, outstretched hands, and how he leant over and ruffled the hair of a woman's delirious daughter. Here, I thought, was the mechanism of a huge precision timepiece, striking a mighty chord that would echo down so many Hitlermorrows. Here were arms that embraced, numbers that added up, glittering parts that needed no polishing, perfect works to drive Germany to lead the world …' Reinhard almost lunged at his new drink and downed it in a single gulp, his eyes closed and beads of perspiration evident on his forehead. He kept his eyes closed as he set down the empty glass and went on, 'She was lovely. I look back now, as I have for many years, and say to myself, "You fool, Reinhard!" To tell you once Gottfried and the honest truth, I am sustained by her memory. Yes, it has never diminished. We went our separate ways one night in the café we frequented but the bond was never broken, for me at least. It was not that I thought more of the portrait on the wall than of Stephanie. It was more that only through him could I hope to enjoy Stephanie. Crazy, I know, but that was what I felt. She walked out after an argument over the Nazis and I let her go, feeling like shit in front of that bloody portrait but somehow paralysed to do anything about it!'

The speed and intensity of Reinhard's voice rose with almost every word. He noticed Gottfried looking round.

'I lost everyone you know. Stephanie, dad, my brother Siegfried. Early on, before Ruhpolding, you know, when I was good for an unwelcome laugh, Siegfried would say, "Laugh back." My older brother would tell me, Laugh back - that's all you have to do. Older shoulders, wiser head. Easy now to see. All that foot shifting, head bowing, blushing even, and feelings of injustice. A laugh was all that would have been needed to get out of it and even come out on top. But oh no, Gottfried, there had to be bouts of reasoning, explaining, attempting to justify, all the time lowering myself into the hole out of which I could not eventually rise and from the rim of which all the people who had ever meant anything to me waved good-bye.'

Gottfried listened intently as Reinhard related the course of events at Ruhpolding.

He and Siegfried had gone there as usual. Just months before,

Reinhard had joined the Jungstahlhelm and he'd arranged to meet two or three of the members at the outing. They thought they would have some fun. Reinhard said, 'These people censured the Wandervogel movement, loudly. There was merciless ridicule of the one-day crusade of joyfulness to the cathedral in Erfurt. It went on most of the day. I hung about with them, almost ignoring Siegfried. They picked on a few, even Siegfried. I said nothing. Siegfried took me aside and told me how hard things were becoming. With a couple of my new friends nearby, the soft part of me had solidified by the time I responded.

'Imagine, Gottfried. I answered my brother with the Nazi salute. I stared straight into Siegfried's eyes, inwardly loving my brother in front of me but proudly aware of a new love welling up inside me, a greater love despite all that we as brothers had meant to each other over the years. Gottfried, the feeling of standing in front of my brother was like it was when I was very young, trundling behind my mother during an outing to the shops, me purposely lengthening the distance between us. It was like a fifth dimension, this unexplored territory of being alone, this danger, this excitement. It was an untested layer of life.'

Reinhard fell silent. Gottfried was just looking at him, still as a stone. Telling someone so many years later made Reinhard feel funny inside.

Tears fill Siegfried's eyes. The confrontation gives his face a lost, almost haunted, look that promotes in Reinhard power that takes over all but the miserably twitching fingers behind his back. Then comes a song. Reinhard is feeling frail but seeming tough.

'You know that bloody song: *In the German land we march for Adolf Hitler, we fight ... Et-effen-cetera,*' he said, practically shouting at Gottfried.

'I'm sorry, Gottfried.' Reinhard's eyes were fixed, tearful. Only his body remained facing his friend. 'If only I could go back to that afternoon in the woods around Ruhpolding. I remember it was three o'clock beside two bent pines. There was a moment of jollity, a few of us boys laughing our heads off. These other chaps came along. I recognised them from the Jungstahlhelm. They started and suddenly everything was more adult and worthwhile and my head went up. What I should have done was to laugh, like Siegie had said, carried on laughing. For years upon years I have wanted to go back and just laugh.' Now Reinhard was really crying and he covered his face with both hands.

Gottfried remained silent for a while and then said, 'I wish we had tried to get in touch again straight after the war.'

'Yes, I know,' Reinhard managed. He knew again why they had been such good friends.

'Tell me more, if you want,' he said.

Reinhard went on: 'Siegfried went to America. We lost touch. I wanted to speak to him. I felt unbelievably childish. Hello Siegfried, how about a kick around? Had his life been such that he would also wish for a second try? Wouldn't he like again the occasions of going to the newsagent to get their comic and be in charge of laughter while he read out pieces; finish that finely balanced football match in the lane between their house and the next that the war interrupted; pretending at the meal table that milk and beetroot was a desirable dish; encouraging the dog to hurry up and find the grounded brussels sprouts before mother re-entered the room? For whatever we did, it invariably ended in uncontrollable laughter, though if mum felt bad, perhaps in a few tears. Hitler should have had someone to play with, that's all I can say. It was a wonderful age, Gottfried. You will know that. It was our youth, our real happiness. Only joking, Siegie! If only I'd said, "Come on, let's continue playing," and led him away from those Jüngens. But I had joined the movement. I was impressed and had a desire to impress somehow. Then I liked what I did. Then I read and I wrote. I saw the, I thought I saw the way things were going and got my NSDAP number. Then the SS. *Führerprinzip*. Everything. Being hard. Being SS, Gottfried. Being bloody SS.'

Reinhard jumped up and strode away from the table. He faced the open window, looking out on to the hotel grounds. Then, as if in an about-turn manoeuvre on a parade ground, he turned to face Gottfried, angrily at first, with blazing eyes, but then he dropped his shoulders.

'Just for a moment there, Gottfried, I went through that *Ich schwöre Dir, Adolf Hitler* oath. I swear to you, AH as leader and chancellor of the German Reich loyalty and bravery. Like fuck! But you know, Gottfried, I even imagined in that moment, just then, looking out of the window as I was remembering the time of my own oath, actually going through the words, that somehow I had the opportunity to change my mind.'

'Just one more, old friend?' Gottfried said.

10

GOTTFRIED took a call at the bar. Reinhard was beginning to slump in the comfortable settee. He was feeling mellow. Increasingly, he had a hard time restricting thoughts about Stephanie. He could see her more clearly than ever. He closed his eyes and that fateful day returned.

'I have to go away, darling. I have this big chance. A real chance for advancement. The Goebbels Ministry …'

Stephanie looks away, her eyes glistening.

'Steph-an-ie, I want you to come with me. Really. I know you will have difficulty at …'

'The Nazis, yes?' she interrupts coldly.

Before he can rearrange his words, she says: 'Mum and dad made a fearful scene last night. They would never hear of anything like this. Help with my studies … well, this is conditional.' Her words trail into tears through hands tightly pressed against her face. Reinhard tries to take them into his own but she draws away. He says, 'I want you to come, Stephanie. I need you to come. There will be pressures. You will … help me.'

There is stillness in the restaurant, an unnerving silence, so severe that there is a noticeable tremor in his upper body.

Stephanie says, 'My parents, they do not want me to see you again, Reinhard, not the way things are. They do not like the politics. And I can't say I am wild about them, or the uniforms.'

Reinhard's body empties.

Stephanie leans forward. 'Dad says he has heard something from a friend of his in the Interior Ministry about the Gestapo being given national status and what this will mean for many people. There's also anti-Jewish restrictions ahead, to be made law in September.'

'They are the Nürnberg Laws,' he shoots back. But the words die in the barrel. 'They're designed to help, not hinder,' emerges as a whiff of pale smoke. 'Within the Nazi party, there are ... certain ...' enters the space between his face and Stephanie's disbelieving eyes as slightly disturbed air.

For a while, neither seeks to speak further. Then, when he can bear the silence no longer and he feels his whole body shake, Reinhard says: 'All right, I cannot pretend I know what everything means, but I don't feel in my heart the fears that others express. It looks good to me and you cannot say you had any doubts in Nürnberg.'

'That was Nürnberg, fu-Chrissake!' she explodes, sitting stiffly against the back of her chair, eyes wide and moist.

Reinhard lets himself be hurt and feels afraid. He would like to be able to hold out his arms to Stephanie and let things take their course. But something holds him back. They sip their beers in another strengthening silence. The searchlights of their eyes cross but the beams do not focus. Stephanie suddenly leans forward again and almost shouts: 'Do not go!'

He looks down.

'Do not go!' she repeats. 'I mean, just do not accept the job. Stay in Germany. Stay with me. Let's do all the things we said we would do. Let's do them all in the next twelve months you would have spent in England on this foo ... let's just enjoy ourselves, be ourselves.' She pauses. 'You remember dad once said he could probably help get you a position with the Stuttgarter Zeitungsverlag. Well, Robert Bosch is planning some changes ...'

Now he interrupts and matches the strength of her words. 'But I have a job. A good one. I am with the Telegraphen Union, remember?'

'Oh, you mean the Nachrichten-something-or-other!'

'It's the DNB as you very well know. Now come on, Stephanie, why are we discussing this? The Deutsche Nachrichten Büro is going well. It is probable that the Goebbels' ministry's say in the concern helped in my selection for this secondment.'

'Sure to have,' Stephanie says, looking away. 'After all, the ministry's say in this concern, as probably in all others, is absolute.'

Reinhard answers by ordering two more beers and says casually but with an urgency she recognises: 'Shall we go to Nürnberg? Shall we just ring up the hotel and go. To hell with the future just for the minute. Let's deal with the here and the now.'

Stephanie's mood is jolted. She looks down. Then, bringing her head up slowly, she says: 'We'll make that trip. I will go with you, tonight even. But you must tell me this Nazi idolisation is over. I will not share your love with the NSD...AP or whatever it is. I cannot share your love with the Nazi party.'

It is some time before the words that follow attack the magic of the first ones. The portrait over her shoulder looks sternly at him.

'Please do not make an issue over this. The Nazi party is a career I want to follow. But, Stephanie, you are the person I love.'

Stephanie replies, 'Oh, Reinhard. This nationalist movement is changing everyone. I have even felt myself changing on occasions. You have certainly changed. There have been times when I have reacted differently when I've met an old friend, different to how I used to. People and places, things I used to believe in so automatically, I have questioned. I know it is wrong and I am trying to put that right. Every time I have a thought like that, I think of what it used to be like and realise that how it used to be was just fine. I can mostly smile about those old times so I know there could never have been much wrong. Ideology is simply selfish obsession masquerading as importance and worthiness. I don't like it. Do not go on with this thing. Let us take what benefits come from the state naturally, as ordinary people and lead ordinary lives as much as we can. I don't want us to be clones of some design based on greed and domination. Reinhard, love me.'

Reinhard again bows his head. Those last three words came over so powerfully. His heart is bleeding. But he says: 'You speak as if a National Socialist can have neither heart nor mind. I have both. Remember what we had?'

'You see - the past. You are thinking of marriage but you would have me as a mistress.'

Stephanie gets up, touches his arm lightly, fleetingly and walks from the table towards the exit. He looks at the point on his sleeve. He feels sick, virtually unable to move. He wants to say he has only been teasing but there is this sensation in his stomach and he does not turn. He mimes the words to test his nerve. He wants her to return to the table and prays into the palms of his hands that his Stephanie will do so because of the inner mightiness with which he urges *it. He goes to speak but wipes his mouth. He looks back at his beer, then again towards the exit. She is pushing the door open. He turns suddenly to look at her empty seat. Tears come to his eyes but still he does not get up. His heart follows her out but his body remains obdurate in front of the portrait. She is gone.*

When Gottfried returned, Reinhard told him what he had been thinking, and continued: 'After the bust-up in that restaurant, we contacted each other a couple of times though nothing really changed. But it was not over. You could tell from letters we exchanged. I was with Senka but I let a meeting with Stephanie happen. I could not help myself, Gottfried. Really. My wife was very ill by then and I just could not leave her. Stephanie understood but her wound probably matched my pain.'

Gottfried could see Reinhard had been overcome by his tale and remained silent before he said, 'Stephanie did not wish to pursue the Nazi cause because she was convinced the Party would not just occupy the coat hooks in our home. I thought she was being too sensitive, that there were good reasons for most of the restrictions, that people ought to go and listen to *NSDAP* speakers, that as an industrialist, Stephanie's father should have appreciated the Laws. But I was wrong and she was right. So right.'

Gottfried kept his eyes fixed on his friend and Reinhard told him, 'But there it is. I lost Siegfried, mum went after a car accident and dad was to follow, a victim of a terrible 'flu epidemic. And Stephanie, the girl who had been in my heart from the moment I set eyes on her at the table tennis table, and who comes to me even now with the regularity of marriage, I let go. I would love to at least tell her how deep is my regret.'

He went on, softly, 'Then there was she of No 5. In Birkenau. Poor woman. No one, not anyone, went more certainly than she. I had been an onlooker of the previous batch. And onlooked death of that kind lasts forever, I can tell you.'

Reinhard seemed to be anaesthetised by his own words. Gottfried frowned deeply but said, 'You mentioned Dieter earlier, before I made that call. Who did you mean?'

Reinhard was silent for a while, recalling the momentous day. Then he suddenly shook himself and came out with how he came by Dieter. Gottfried hardly touched his drink as he listened to the story.

'The bigger the lie, eh?' Gottfried said.

But Reinhard was not finished. The bolt had been removed and reality had swung loose. He remembered little of the journey that eventually took him to within sight of the Swiss border. While watering forest plant life outside Lindau, he heard a man arguing furiously with Nazi officials, a party worker and an SS-Unnterscharführer on the roadway below a steep bank. The man said he was a doctor and had been visiting a cousin in Friedrichshafen. It was important he returned to St Gallen in time for a medical emergency the following day but the NCO said, 'No, the emergency is now' and shot him. He just shot him. No emotion, nothing. The officers rolled the doctor into the undergrowth and left on a motorcycle and sidecar without saying a further word.

Reinhard drew close to Gottfried. 'I told Dieter to be quiet, like a cat asleep at the foot of a tree and I went to the dead man. I checked his papers, took his suit and topcoat, covered him with my SS uniform and scrambled back up to Dieter. The papers were for a flight to England out of Zurich the following day. A St Gallen resident was booked for emergency surgery at a London hospital. That's how I got out. Just call me *Herr Doktor!*'

11

IRMA greeted them with a huge smile. With her arms straight out she said excitedly, 'The Sister says there are signs he's coming round. He's going to be all right, they think. He's been mumbling that stuff again. The police have been to the hospital. They want to interview this Thomas chap. Dieter has the name in his diary. The Sister will tell you all about it.'

Reinhard gave Irma a small hug and introduced Gottfried. They shook hands. The three of them strode side by side down the centre of the ward like school assembly teachers. They surrounded the bed and watched intently. There was nothing but steady breathing. Gottfried leant forward and touched Dieter's arm. 'So, this is your boy,' he said, looking round at Reinhard. 'Bloody politics!' Irma took Reinhard's arm as he nodded solemnly. Sister Schlem approached from behind curtains surrounding the bed opposite.

'Things are beginning to look up quite a bit, Herr Hänsel.'

Just as she spoke, Dieter's eyelids moved and the now familiar sound came from his lips. 'Karl ... Heinz ... lengers ...'

Sister Schlem twiddled with one of the monitors and made a mark on the board at the bed end. Reinhard suggested Irma took a rest while Gottfried and he remained for a while. Then they could meet back at the hotel and discuss the immediate future.

'I don't mind staying,' Irma said enthusiastically.

Gottfried said, 'Look, I'll tell you what. I've got some phoning to do and a story to file, as it happens. I'll go back to the hotel, it may take a little while. When I've finished, I'll have a bite to eat and come back in this evening for a spell. How does that sound? You'll want some time together anyway.'

Reinhard looked at Dieter before turning to face Irma. He said he'd certainly like to be present when Dieter regained consciousness. Gottfried put on his jacket, half turned up the collar in preparation for the deteriorating weather now clearly visible through the main window, and walked briskly out of the ward. They watched him until he disappeared through double doors. Only then did they slowly resume their positions on either side of Dieter, keeping their gaze on him and did not say anything for several moments. Even when the silence was broken - he said how white everything was - they both kept their eyes on Dieter. Reinhard eventually asked Irma, 'Where do you think Dieter would first like to go when he's out of here?'

'Back to England, probably!'

Reinhard disagreed. He said Dieter probably wanted to try to look for some job in West Germany. 'I imagine I will be looking for a house for him at some point. Now, though, I want to see Thomas whoever-it-is.'

She smiled as she sort of came to attention. 'Ah, I have his address,' and went to put her hand across the bed but Sister Schlem approached and said, 'We have some things to do in the ward. And shortly it will be mealtime, Herr Hänsel. You and your friend may of course return in a couple of hours, if you wish.' As they left, they found extended interest in the polished floor and pictures on the corridor walls until they reached the lifts when Irma said, 'This chap's address is in my room. Shall you take it now?'

'Might as well,' he said unguardedly.

Irma smiled again and pushed the button for Level 3. Reinhard did not like the silence and said, 'I hope everything is going to be all right. Dieter, he still looks a little weak.' He also wondered how George was getting on but said nothing. Irma stepped forward, then turned before stepping into the lift, inclining her head to rest lightly on his chest and taking a hand in both of hers.

'Everything is going to be just fine.'

Reinhard smoothed his hair. 'It is so hot.' He placed both hands over his face as he fought a delinquent awareness. Irma stepped back, blew playfully towards him and again smiled in a way that convinced him that he would have to hug Stephanie tightly. He put his hands behind his back and pressed against the lift manufacturer's cool brass plate. A ping announced arrival at Level 3 and provided temporary relief as Reinhard stepped out ahead of Irma, determined to lead rather than be led. She opened the room door, held it ajar and looked back at him, her eyes inviting him in. Reinhard remained awkwardly where he was.

'I wonder if it is very far from here,' Reinhard said, referring to the address.

She purposely misunderstood. 'Not at all!' she coaxed. 'In we go,' she said, trailing a hand behind her. Reinhard ignored it, putting out a hand for the address.

'Let's see, perhaps his place, it is within walking distance,' he said with pragmatic emphasis. She reached into a cabinet drawer and put a card on the table beside him, at the same time reaching up to kiss him. It had been a long, long time since he had experienced such a tender moment and it gave him a sensation that at once challenged the single-mindedness he had built up over the years into a crusading resolve not to let his Stephanie down again. He was suddenly aware of Irma's perfume and the fine texture of her hair, and for an instant she became Stephanie.

'There is Dieter,' he mumbled. 'There is this man. I should try to see him.' Then, in an effort to dispense practicality and gratefulness in equal measure, he said, 'It is not the right time,' knowing that in this falsely encouraging choice of words, he may have only temporarily taken her off the boil.

'I understand, Reinhard. You are right. Here is the card.' She picked it up from the table and slipped it into his trouser pocket, patting the pocket gently. 'Do you want me to come with you?'

Reinhard stepped back, 'Well, I was going to ask Gottfried if he would come. It might help him with a story he's doing.'

'Okay, then. You're back here again tonight?'

He raised a hand in her direction before pulling the door closed. He paused outside. He could neither deny the feelings he had had nor the temptation he had to re-open the door. Purposefully, he walked into the toilet and sought his guilt in the mirror. As he did so, he plunged his own hand into the same pocket she had entered and arched his back. Such moments had been rare. He continued to stare into the mirror above the washbasin at the same time levering water from the tap that he splashed over his flushed face. For a moment, he closed his eyes and took a deep breath, blinking as he stood back. He checked himself. Beneath the smile that emerged, there was shame. He felt manly but he judged his conduct, though moderate, had not been that of the man he thought he was. It had not been what he had done but the way he had felt. Reinhard gained a crumb of comfort from the fact that he had not initiated the physical contact but this was more than wiped out by the thought of what might happen next time.

12

REINHARD imagined himself standing on the last step of the old yellow post bus. One little jump and there he'd be. Siegie, too, and of course mum and dad. The gentle wooded slopes out from Iserlohn. Holiday time. All four of them jolly their way through the pines until they come to delightful grassland for a break - a mixture of refreshing food and ball games. Reinhard and Siegfried exhaust themselves. Dad joins in. Mum, too, eventually has a go for a while. Father, who fancies himself as an angler, has everything ready for the expected landing but his line breaks, most of the tackle is lost, but fair improbability of a huge specimen blue trout nevertheless turns to certainty with a smile. There is always a week of it, with gasthof accommodation at the end of each wonderful day.

The yellow post bus was in the distance; to the right in the top corner of the picture. Reinhard got up and had a closer look at the landscape oil on the wall. Thomas's mother entered the room with coffee and biscuits.

'Lovely old picture, that,' she said. 'I love old pictures.'

'It has reminded me of a holiday. Do you know the place?'

'Not a clue! Sorry. Black Forest somewhere, I've been told.'

As boys, neither Reinhard nor Siegfried ever thought about the expense involved but Reinhard reckoned it must have taken a lot of effort for mum and dad to raise the money for these annual outings. He once vowed that when he got married and had children, he would take the whole family to the Schwarzwald for an entire fortnight and, starting from the Enz Valley, make hay through all the lovely villages. They'd perhaps do even more. Spend a month there, even six months. Why, if the mood took them, they would all live in the Schwarzwald and get someone to bring out their provisions from time to time from Freiburg! Reinhard sat back.

'Thomas shouldn't be long now,' she said, setting up his drink on a small, ornate table of what looked like African ebony, and offering him a biscuit. He took two. She excused herself and left the room as he made slight mental changes to the picture on the wall.

The brothers each select six small stones that in turn they aim at the trunk of a tree. Siegfried strikes the trunk the most times in the first round and claims Nagold. He also takes another village in the second round. Reinhard manages Calw but as usual Siegfried ends up the best aimer. The villages can be recaptured but it requires even more of a knack and Reinhard sits down and dives into a slice of cream sponge.

The Wohlfahrt 'puffer' steamed from an envelope resting on a table shunting Reinhard to Michelstadt. He'd really been too young to travel unaccompanied. Mum thought he was with a friend but he had done it as a challenge to the daring side of his nature. Once he had decided to do it, he felt compelled to carry it through despite the force of fear within him. The train jerked forward and he knew there was no going back. He was on the train, young and alone. He had done his apprenticeship as a hand-held boy.

Thomas looked angry as he entered the room but his voice was soft and caring. 'You are Dieter's father, mother tells me. How is he?'

'Improving, happily. He's coming on. The police, they think it may have been an accident,' he lied. 'Did you see what happened?'

Kreit said he was near Dieter. They were waiting for the demonstration to start in earnest. There was a bit of activity, but it was more vocal than physical. 'Dieter moved a few yards away from me. He got talking to three chaps. I suppose they were party members. It got quite heated with a couple of them, one in particular. I don't know this chap but he and Dieter were shouting at each other near the end, about Jews. This chap said something to the effect that the Jewish state was financed on six million lies. Dieter said - and I remember clearly his words - 'My dad was there. He effen-well knows'. Dieter went as if to shoulder charge him but this chap turned and Dieter hit his head heavily against a lamppost and fell into the street in front of a motorcycle. Were you at this demonstration?'

Reinhard shook his head as he imagined the scene in slow motion and said, 'Do you know a Karl Heinzlinger or someone with a similar name?' Thomas did not know but recalled that this chap insisted that, far from being perpetrators, the Nazis were benefactors in putting people in concentration camps as an act of compassion to protect them from the wrath of others. Gas chambers, he said, were the product of Zionist propaganda. Kreit went on, 'I've known for some time that Dieter was at loggerheads with one or two of these people. They go too far. They don't represent the true nationalism in any part of the land, I can assure you.'

Reinhard doubted he could assure him of anything on this subject but he let it pass.

'Dieter's injuries were the result of an accident, then? Even though he had probably been provoked into action that led to it?'

'I suppose so,' said the young man, taking one of the biscuits.

'Why would anyone want to change history, say that what had happened, had not happened?' Reinhard asked.

Jutting out his chin, Kreit said, 'What is fact? I mean, how do we know anything, really know? As it happens, I believe you. Dieter has told me about you. Now Dieter is thinking about becoming a member, perhaps you would also like to join. We are not always so serious.'

Reinhard thought the Party could not be serious at all, but again he let it pass and thanked him.

*

Irma was at Dieter's bedside when Reinhard returned. Gottfried was still out. If it had not been for Dieter, he would not have entered. She sat with her back to the ward entrance, her hand resting on Dieter's. Her hair was up, apart from a few strands that had escaped a curved matt pink comb. As he walked up to within feet of her, he could see the fine hairs on her long neck. He wanted to reach out but instead went around her to the other side of the bed and put a hand on Dieter's shoulder.

'Hi, Dieter.'

Reinhard and Irma smiled at each other. He asked, 'How long have you been here?'

'Oh, I laid on my bed for a while, had a shower, changed and came down.'

Dieter's eyes were flickering more often and they called the nurse who alerted Sister Schlem. The Sister said, 'Earlier today the doctor thought your son would be out of this in a couple of days. He could well be right. But we shall have to keep Dieter sedated for a while after this. Strong though he obviously is, it will take time for him to recover completely.'

Irma stayed another fifteen minutes and then got up. 'I think I shall have an early night, Reinhard. First, though, I must phone George. Poor George, he will be missing me, I am sure. You know, I miss him too … in many ways. He has so many good points, does George. I do not know what I should do without him. Sometimes I also think I do not know what I should do *with* him, but there you are. Good night Reinhard. Call me in the morning, eh?'

'Wish George well from me.'

Reinhard waved her through the ward door. He looked back at Dieter and pressed his hand, like Irma had done. Reinhard wanted to hug him, like he had done after the graduation, and after he had dried out from the storm that had caught him as he made his way behind Dieter across the car park. Dieter had had his Masters gown to change into but Reinhard had to make for the cloakroom, the hair straddling his collar soaking several handfuls of toilet paper with more of the same screwed into a pad to try to restore the look of his new suede shoes. He then attempted to restore the creases in the smartest of his gabardines and gave his jacket a good shake before joining the good and the gowned. In the refreshment area he felt less than equal and damp cloth bonded to his limbs with the same persistence as the skin from a burning hot cup of coffee stuck to his lips. Efforts to tap into Dieter's work with its talk of energy changes in fluids made his head swim. He buried his head in his hands, elbows sinking into his damp thighs. Dieter's skills were something he might have been able to gain by study, text books and lots of eye-rubbing and sighing. It was nothing compared with the levelling that occurred in the moment they had clung to each other in that ghastly place. It was respectful, gratifying, accomplished in itself. In an instant, and there always. Like the photograph that father had taken of the bridge at Beuel, which he had seen him take, helped him compose. One click and it was captured. He had seen it with his own eyes and there it was, clicked into his mind, always available for viewing. Dad hadn't been half bad at photography and Reinhard had let him down, triumphant dad, who had had to savour his award alone. Erwin Hänsel had known his photograph was not an unquestionable masterpiece but he said he had captured the Rheinbrücke like he had always said he would, like he and Reinhard had always agreed it should be taken. But nothing that Reinhard later experienced in the family's favourite town had ever matched that first time when he and dad had chatted like two professors about the moment for a successful photograph of the new bridge while sitting on a low wall at the end of the Brückenstrasse looking across to Beuel. Well, dad suggesting and Reinhard agreeing. All the same, it was always a conciliatory presentation and his smile doubtless contributed to the discussion in a way that made everything else incidental. He would nod furiously when dad put the ultimate objective into words: the image had to capture the mood of the river and the beauty of the triple arch structure. Newspaper photography had been satisfying, sometimes pulsating, but dad's eyes showed that turning a shot of the bridge into a print of arguable magnificence held the greatest fulfilment. Reinhard had come to recognise that it had never necessarily been what dad had said but more the way he had enthused about it that had made him a special dad. Reinhard felt dad's picture would one day be magnificent but he had never seen it, except as glimpses in his mind. He had sought the framed finished article later but it had gone, like dad. It could have been his now, possessed like a testimonial to a wonderful shared experience, a kind of junior partnership diploma but, above all, a father and son thing.

'Now dad!'

'Not quite yet, Reinhard. You see that cloud - it obscures the sun just a little too much. When that knobbly bit goes...'

'Now then, dad,' shouts the little face behind the tiny Agfa.

'Wait, my boy. Just a bit more.'

'Aaah...'

The cloud moves but changes shape, keeping light from hitting the central arch of the bridge and the far bank.

'Verdammt!'

'Aaa-ah!'

Reinhard blows furiously at the sky, his lips eventually curving into tight disappointment.

'All right then, my boy, let's take it. This break will be just enough. Go on, you first, Reinhard.'

Reinhard's own, premature picture, dad's right hand cupping part of his beloved tripod-attached camera, edging in from the left, was all he had left of dad. When his dad's bridge picture had at last been created, and when it had slid out of the developing tray and come to pass undoubtedly in exciting fulfilment, he had not cared. The fixer had changed the scene for him. The impact of brooding clouds had turned to the cunning trap of clear skies. Not everyone had been fixed. Not dad. Not Stephanie. Not brother Siegfried. Not that poor woman of No 5. But he had been and it made him sick. When he had looked up in the big hall, waiting for Dieter's Masters to be awarded, he had imagined dad standing on the stage with his citation, smiling at the presenter, a smile that faded from the proud man's face as he turned to no one special.

'I'm here dad!' he croaked behind his hand as he cleared his throat into the Masters' programme.

What had helped him roar open-mouthed at the antics of the Circus Krone clowns in München - with perhaps just his delight causing dad to share the moment - and which had offered pathetic but willing photographic advice over so many good years, before politics intervened, hurt now with such intensity that tears forced their way through his tightly closed eyes. As the ceremony concluded, clouds seemed to tire of their spoiling tactics and allowed sunlight through the tall windows to ride the dust specs in the corridor of triumph. Cameramen set up their tripods to catch the brilliant light. Reinhard decided to go for the informal, the candid, reflecting some small but cherished occasion, an image probably lacking tonal distinction, perhaps even a touch out of focus, but it would be a moment he could treasure. And he reckoned he succeeded in the marquee when, against the social correctness of the occasion, stiffened by a trio's classical notes in one corner and the Dean to one side, Reinhard took a picture of Dieter trying to put a spoonful of strawberries and cream into his mouth while the remaining contents of the glass bowl slowly toppled into the mortar board he was desperately trying to hold on to with the same hand.

13

HEINZLENGER or something. Reinhard picked up the telephone book and took it back to the sleep-inducing seat in the hotel's lounge that he had managed to lay claim to on three occasions. For a moment, he let the book remain under his hand on the arm of the brown suede-leather armchair and looked out through the statue-adorned patio to the hotel's tiered gardens. Beyond, thick clumps of pond reeds and landlocked rhododendrons cast their bedtime shadows over the evenly lined lawn further out.

The telephone book offered up several Heinzlengers and one or two variations of the name. He couldn't go barging in on them in turn but he could select the estate agent he had noticed and combine his search for a house for Dieter with good old fashioned journalistic observation and questioning. As he sat in the agent's reception area, Reinhard gave the man of Dieter's murmurings an awful face and put obscenities into his mouth. The furniture became gnarled and the windows shrank as the walls grew taller and the young girls stopped flitting sweetly between desks and grew older, sitting stiffly behind inkwells that dispensed interminably and sharply the jagged four-lettered word. The clerks' features, too, were as abrupt as *Nein!* and as cheerless as the she-males who brought in the forms. And the male negotiators were uniform in their gait and garments, walking not on soft soles over deep red patterned carpet but strutting steel-tipped over worn pine boards. Fresh smooth lemon walls became heavy flaking brown partitions set against cubicles that were mean, like the business of confinement. Prinz-Albrecht-Strasse was beyond the window and there, in front of him, addressing an assistant with irritating correctness, was history's grotesque failed chicken farmer.

Reinhard checked himself. The man was just an unremarkable estate agent, while his assistant stood out as a very pretty woman. As soon as she was again free, he told her what he was looking for and followed her down a spiral iron stairway, keeping his eyes fixed firmly on her shoulder-length hair bouncing up and down as she lowered herself into a town-worth of housing. She flipped through an estate-worth of files and he marvelled at the crouched form. Here was practically the arrangement of the girl he still loved. How proud of Stephanie he had been, how fascinated he had been by her tomboyish behaviour. Sometimes he believed that the love had merely been interrupted by Hitler and that, with the maniac and his cronies out of the way, it was going on and that he could catch up with it again and carry on with the relationship. It was a love that was gratifying, even in separation, even after its natural (he could never bring myself to say final) break. Their love had never been tried by the rigours of everyday living, besmirched by the bores of propriety, the curse of sound stewardship, and the ever presence of everyday matters that he heard could sometimes taint a little here and a little there, leading sadly to corrosion. The love had been left to carry on through time and he felt he could catch up with it by waiting for a clear night and look skywards.

The assistant turned to him. She had found three possible homes but only one in the area of his choice. Yes, it did have a stream at the bottom of the garden. He looked at her as he slowly took the papers. The trouble was, every so often there was someone who reminded him of Stephanie, hair brushing against neck and cheeks in turn as she walked into the wind, strands sometimes catching in wide, slightly parted lips, eyes as if suddenly attacked by strong sunlight, narrowing so sensually at the slightest hint of fun, legs that were almost always hidden by slacks and body that in also being mostly covered was constantly an imagined beauty. He made for a café and ordered a coffee and cake. Stephanie swam into view. She'd taken over his retinas and the messages being sent to his brain were pictures that excited him. He realised he was wallowing in their distant love and soon he might be in a position to try to find her. The last address he had for her was well outside the present code area. Still, he could start there. His thoughts were bursting on German soil. He thought of the secret meeting that never was. How clearly he had seen her. Even when his train had reached its destination, he had walked for miles through the town, to nowhere in particular but treading on, yielding to the slim possibility that she had had to make her own way and that she was here now, trying to find him. The further he entered the place the thicker the crowds and the more hopeless the situation, the more he sought her out. He had leant against a shop doorway. Opposite *Triumph des Willens* was showing. He had thought of the litres of Party rally grounds magnetism, the hypnotic influence of crowds acting as one, and how much of a triumph of the will it had been, torches, floodlights, bonfires, silhouettes, flags, hatchments, crests, shields, music. Oh, the music! And the words, moulding thousands of people. Shiny shovels. Shiny boots. The path of obedience. Wilful acceptance. It had led on to awful things. The world knew. He knew. He wondered again whether international justice could yet step in between he and Dieter. They stood together every year on April 4, at 11.15 precisely. He would lift off the date from the calendar pad and paste the large red numbers into the book to join its neatly arranged predecessors, beginning 1946, and the three inked-in years before that. When this year's ceremony was over and he had firmed his hand over 1961, he had drawn back from the book and, as usual, Dieter and he had embraced, holding each other tightly for a moment, then hurry off together on some pre-arranged outing, the cinema, a picnic, a game of snooker, any place or thing that could act as some celebration of the bond between them.

'It's the 18th anniversary this year, Dieter. Why don't we have an 18th birthday party!' he had suggested.

'OK then. Stay in and drink ourselves silly!' Dieter responded. They did. And how they did! In the morning, they agreed they'd do the same every year, no matter what else they did to mark their special relationship. But plans had been overtaken by events.

Reinhard cursed Eichmann's effrontery to challenge the indictments that had taken him to Israel to face world justice, bringing everything to the front in all its ashen misery. He cursed the powers of retribution. He had Dieter, just, but he didn't have Stephanie. He opened his eyes as the waiter spoke. Reinhard ordered an Othello Becher, his favourite nut and chocolate ice cream dish. He realised what a fool he had been, what a fool he still was. He wanted to tell Stephanie everything, particularly the joy he had had in saving Dieter from the smoke. He wanted to bring her up to date on everything if, when he found her, she wanted to listen.

He unfolded the agent's sheet: Distinctive, with the advantages of isolation and proximity to amenities. Typical! It was always possible to be far away from something and yet be close. Hegeleninstrasse 5. He liked the number. He was crazy. Perhaps the number would be lop-sided. He *was* crazy.

14

THE brown leather armchair was again vacant when Reinhard returned to the hotel. First he phoned the hospital. There was no change. He asked to speak to Irma. She had bought a good book, she said, and was about to sit reading to Dieter.

'Thank you Irma. I'll be there shortly, within the hour. How was George?'

'Missing me, he says.'

'And you're missing him, *ja?*'

'Yes, Reinhard,' she said wearily.

Reinhard sank into the seat. He could feel himself wavering. He stretched himself out full-length, hands tight behind his head, toes thrusting forwards. He felt angst about everything. The exciting and the unthinkable churned around in his head. When everything had fallen into a heap, he nodded off before a hand descended on his shoulder. Gottfried was back.

'Listen, Reinhard. I've seen a policeman at headquarters. This cop was a good contact in the weeks I spent probing an alleged government scandal. The policeman was transferred shortly after this, a good policeman who knew most of the answers concerning the criminal element out there but who never got promotion because, within the station, he too often asked awkward questions. There is nothing known about any Karl Heinzlinger. Dieter's Holocaust protagonist is a rabid Revisionist and an explosives expert but it was a verbal blow-up and apparently nothing more. It has been concluded that there was no criminal intent. Nevertheless, I was counting on seeing the copper while I was down this way, you know, concerning the stories I've been filing over this Holocaust denial stuff. Well, the word is that an agent associated with a cell of the movement is masterminding some plot to target an important building somewhere in eastern Europe according to my usually very reliable source. I've been given a lead - an Anton something or another - and I'll see where that goes. The man is said to be in this area somewhere. The place is a bit run down by all accounts and he's rarely there. Anyway, I've booked a nearby hotel room for a week. After that, if needs be - either from your point of view, with Dieter I mean, or mine - we can use a friend's chalet a few miles outside Bad Eilsen. He'll be out of the country at that time and has given me a key. Nice to have friends who are often boarding planes, eh?'

Reinhard thanked Gottfried, surmising that George and Irma would by then have gone back to England. He told him he was off to the hospital and Gottfried, in a hurry to meet up with a contact just north of Hannover, said he would try to work it so that he could drive back and call into the hospital afterwards.

Irma was fed up with her book. She set it aside and looked at her watch, bringing up in front of her the hand she'd used to put the mystery man's address into Reinhard's pocket. She laid the slim fingers on her thigh and caressed them with her inexperienced other hand. She smoothed her denim skirt to the edge of the material, slowly moving over the edge. Reinhard, she knew, saw George as always ready to please, a kind and gentle man, with a good sense of humour, forever cheerful, constantly thoughtful, endlessly modest and profoundly genuine. And that was how she thought of him, too. He shied away from intimacy. He loved her, she was sure of that, and at times would fling his arms about her in breast-flattening enthusiasm, or with his strong hands hold her face in the gentlest of ways. He would suddenly get hold of her hand in the street and swing their linked limbs shoulder-high as if to show off his capture to the whole street. They had met and married within three weeks of George's recovery from his war-time injuries. Yet, she reflected for the umpteenth time, this was the trouble: he had not really recovered, not mentally. She convinced herself that the situation called for alternatives, and though he continued to express his love in many other ways, she felt sure he must feel the same. Irma sometimes likened herself to a doll, dressed up and ready to be shown off, but with no ability to express herself beyond meaninglessly flashing her eyes or crying.

Irma noticed Dieter stirring. She was calling the nurse as Reinhard walked down the corridor.

'He's coming round, I believe,' she said in a hushed, excited tone.

The nurse went for the Sister, who pushed a bell in her cubicle, and within a couple of minutes, curtains were being drawn around Dieter and a doctor appeared and slipped inside. Reinhard and Irma sat in an area outside the ward until the doctor re-appeared.

'It is good news. Dieter has regained consciousness. For now at least, however, I think it best that he should have complete rest. No visitors for the rest of the day. No distractions. It looks very much like he is going to be fine, but he must now be kept very quiet. Tomorrow, if all continues to be well, there are some tests I should like carried out. I think you may be able to again visit him the day after tomorrow.'

Reinhard accepted Irma's arm around his waist and she kept hold of him as he went to step back. The doctor interrupted them and they smiled. He smiled, too.

'Is good news, eh?'

Reinhard wanted to hug the doctor. He and Irma stood in the ward doorway and looked back towards the curtained bed space. They peeled away and Irma took Reinhard's hand. The sudden and uplifting news and Irma's skip-like steps towards the lift left Reinhard with the boyishness of a Christmas Eve. They were silent until she opened the door.

'Wait. I've left my coat on the ward chair. Must get that; it's got my wallet in it.'

Reinhard stepped out of the lift almost into the arms of Gottfried.

'Reinhard, there you are!'

'Gottfried!'

15

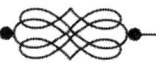

REINHARD left the main traffic stream to take a quieter road. He settled back into the seat and kept his foot just touching the pedal, reflecting the satisfaction he now felt over Dieter's condition, thankful for everything, glad of the enforced break and, thanks to Gottfried's timely arrival at the hospital, no additional guilt. Experts were now giving full attention to Dieter. He felt better out of the way and was being positive. House buying was for a future whereas hospital waiting, where the rhythmic movement of see-through tubes and fidgeting dials left too much time to feel that one breath was too heavy and another too light, or that breathing may become too rapid or suddenly stop. He briefly put his foot down, matching the well-being he felt. He would enjoy his visit, Dieter would pull through and be able to live in a house with a stream running by at the bottom of the garden. They could be close together. Irma would be back in England. He really would delve into the out-of-the-area telephone directories. He pulled over when he reached the centre of a smallish town, picturesque in the way so many visitors liked a town to be. He consulted his map. There were still a few more miles to travel. He rested for a while opposite a fountain in the cobbled square. The place was practically deserted, the sort of place he had loved as a youngster, even into late teens and early twenties. He wondered how long it would take before the two boys playing around the fountain would be lured away by something that glittered. They flicked water at each other. One tried to avoid a real handful and fell in. Such was life; avoid one thing and get hit by something else. The other one doubled up, laughing uncontrollably. Reinhard and his brother Siegfried had frequently fallen about laughing. Siegfried had borrowed a book from dad. They read from it as they walked one day to catch a bus somewhere. Siegfried had initially been attracted to *Three Men in a Boat* by the title, or more particularly the bit underneath *… to say nothing of the dog*. It had been a bit about the three men going into a maze by the Thames that had set the brothers off. When it was Reinhard's turn to read from the book, he broke down laughing and when he was able to open his eyes again, Siegfried had collapsed. They shrieked at each other, pointing at the book and at each other, neither of them able to say anything that the other could properly understand. Reinhard had hoped for this: the old good filtering through the old bad like rays of sunshine from heavy skies, weak but welcome, the smell of dampened hay and bracken, the comforting caw of rooks, cigar smoke, sausage and strong coffee and the lovely smell of *Bratkartoffeln* that always seemed to attend the café quarter. He thought of the many family outings that had included that delightful dish. In the family car of years ago, the windows of the old Mercedes were never wound down while the car was in motion. His father said that an open window gave him a stiff neck and mum did not like the noise. They had a private joke about this. Reinhard had once imagined the words tumbling out of their mouths, battering themselves at the closed driver's side window like trapped butterflies and falling exhausted at dad's feet, getting mixed up with the pedals and causing the car to veer off to one side and plough into a bus queue. He stiffened at the wheel and acknowledged with his hand a momentary driving lapse. He put his hand up again without need, this time more stiffly, remembering the scene. He had not saluted like that since 1943, on the edge of Brzezinka Wood when he came face to face with a group of senior officers during his assignment to Auschwitz-Birkenau to oversee the opening of Crematorium V. After all the years of dutiful compliance, he had thought he actually hated those officers as they stopped to question him.

'This is no place to be alone,' one of them says. An SS-Obersturmbannführer with an untidy collar, steps forward. 'You must be from the Inspectorate, ja? Your reputation precedes you, the supreme copperplate administrator. Out now, from behind your desk, I hope you will not find all this too much of a, shall we say, scribble. I say this because all is very efficient here. This you will see when you come to oversee No 1V.' Reinhard dislikes the tone of the man who does not

attempt to disguise a knowing wink in the direction of the towering Kreisleiter to his left. 'Jawohl, Herr Obersturmbannführer. I shall be officially overseeing the opening of Crematoria V,' putting as much emphasis on the number as he thinks prudent. 'Funf?' returns the other, sarcastically. And as a colleague leans forward towards the Obersturmbannführer, Reinhard says: 'It is the fourth to be built at Birkenau but official records put the one at the Main Camp (Auschwitz) as No 1, making the four at Birkenau II, III, IV and V.' 'See you at five tomorrow, then,' the senior officer replies coldly. Reinhard feels mischievous and wants to say that, with the official opening at 10am, this particular group of officers will be late if they turn up then! But he doesn't.

When he reached Rastenkorb, twenty miles or so away from where Dieter was slowly winning his fight for life, Reinhard practically drew a blank on locating a family called Festfortag. No tradesman he spoke to had even heard of the name. A milk roundsman thought the name rang a bell, but he could recall nothing specific. He said he would call Reinhard at his hotel if he did remember. And suddenly Reinhard felt too far away from Dieter and pulled over to telephone the hospital. Tests were still being carried out. He returned to his hotel, left a couple of messages at reception and went to his room. He lay on the bed, mentally tired. Thoughts were coming in as crossfire. There was an anxiety that he did not much like, made the more unpleasant by sensations at his back like creatures and knives, gnawing and slashing. What had underpinned his life seemed now to be less stable. He was tempted to say that there never had been a family of that name and try to carry on with his life. But he knew he could not just walk away. He picked up a magazine from the table, idly scanned a few of its pages, threw it back onto the table and laid flat out on the bed just as the phone on the wall rang sharply.

'Ja,' he said cautiously.

'Hello, you remember me? The milk roundsman. Well, I have recalled this name Festfortag. It's not a family; it's the name of a house - one that I used to deliver milk to before I was put on a new round. It's the name on a gate outside Hockbenderstrasse 4, which is just off the main square. Hope that helps.'

A house. It hardly made sense.

16

SMOOTH piano music. Smooth, like his drink. Just right for ragged days. Once more Gottfried startled him as he put a hand on Reinhard's shoulder. He spoke quietly: 'I'm not sure what I've got but I've a feeling I'm on the right track. Here's the thing: you remember Dieter's words: Karl Heinzlangers or something. Well, while I was sitting in a bar after visiting Anton's place, I played around with this name in my mind. A few beers later, I noticed a poster in the bar advertising some event in Ingersweg - and did the same with that street name. Eventually I came up with Karl and Heinz of Ingersweg!

'And there are...'

'*Stimmt!* They live there all right, and that's not all. I had to hang about quite a bit but I eventually got the chance to break in and they certainly have books about Auschwitz and the Holocaust. I shouldn't make judgements at this stage, I suppose, but it's surely more than a coincidence that they have one book that has quite detailed maps and diagrams of the place, the main camp and Birkenau. Also, my friendly policeman, after I told him about my enquiries, managed to fix up a tap on their phone and a recording at the exchange and I was able to pick up part of a conversation when this couple mentioned Aragua two or three times. There is an Aragua de Barcelona in Venezuela. So, Reinhard, I could be off to South America for a while. Not sure when or for how long. Thanks to my contact, I could have my story and maybe he'll get the promotion he deserves. And right now, I have to dash or I'll miss an appointment. Couldn't avoid this one, I'm afraid. It's all coming at the wrong time. I'd like to be around with Dieter but at least we can keep in touch. Anyway, I've got a totally free day tomorrow ... I'll see you then, OK?'

Reinhard thought how he could never return to that kind of life. He no longer got excited over stories, not in the way it used to be. Any stories, really. It was, he supposed, natural that his heart raced a little when he heard about the capture of Eichmann but these days he would classify those feelings more like apprehension than irresistible excitement. And again, when the trial reports started coming out of Israel, the effect on him swung in turn from unease to foreboding. Nothing about it had matched the raw excitement of some of the assignments during his newspaper days of old. As for promotion, this made him feel distinctly uncomfortable. Without the officer betterment he had pursued for so long and finally achieved through applying himself to his work, he might never have been assigned for the task at Auschwitz-Birkenau. He nearly had it out with himself, right there and then, aloud. But he argued that if he had not gone to Birkenau, he would have nothing honourable to cling on to. At least he had not ended up the office-bound pen and ink man, the dutiful, convenient, safe and comfortably compliant copperplate administrator.

When he met up with Gottfried at the hotel, he told him about his concerns. 'Even though I don't know where it will all lead, it is dominating me and I feel I have to go with it.' They freshened their glasses and Berlin and the good old days, which they agreed would never have been half as good or probably any good at all without each other's company, came back like Thirties' laughter. What they mostly remembered were the pleasant days, avoiding the other kind. They roared over their snowball fight in the city. They had looked forward to the Templehof show but this stuff was unscheduled, quite the opposite of shiny shovels, stiff backs and Do This! So instead they ended up round behind the Reichstag as wet as the Spree. Here was innocence, like well before. Soft and harmless. Drifting. Cold but warming. Like ... do-as-you-please time.

Gottfried looked a little like he was back at Habel's, down the Linden. He told Reinhard, 'Well, it could certainly be said that we toiled in the snow!'

'Pure then, as the driven,' Reinhard said. 'You nearly rolled me into the river, remember? I had to drain out one of my boots. It would never have done for the show at Tempelhof, with him there, boots all lustreless with a touch of weed about the heel!'

They eyed each other through the bottoms of their glasses, then brought them down together heavily. 'OK. Another each, eh?' Gottfried said, signalling to the bar.

'*Jawohl, Herr Hänsel,*' he said. 'Too much of the local Franconian stuff, that's what it was. Well, actually not too much, just bloody right. Potent, though. Don't suppose they've got any here!'

'And we found they had more bottles at The Tavern,' Gottfried recalled, turning round from the bar. 'You remember that Ristorante Italiano place where we pretended to be British and one of the waiters pretended he was German and threatened to arrest the both of us!'

'Very special day, you understand,' Gottfried told the grinning barman who gave the pair an approving nod. They were no drunks but they'd had enough to enable them to recall with picturesque glee some of the little sideshows to big occasions that one way or another occupied their time in Berlin. Like when the city's loudspeakers announced that England had declared herself at war with Germany and the pair of them, feeling relaxed after a few Sunday drinks, ran for the cover of another bar with such mock urgency and wailing as they went, coats held over their heads, that some folk along the Kaiserdamm and Wilhelmsplatz looked up to scan the skies while others, imagining instantaneous attack, eased themselves against the nearest building. Like when, as the Reichswehr's heavy artillery swept past birthday boy, powerfully at ease on a reviewing stand in front of the Technische Hochschule, a woman near the two of them stretched out her arm with such suddenness and force that there came a sound which no amount of mechanised armour could disguise and no amount of self-control could hold back their explosive laughter. Happy heads met in the middle of the settee and it was some time before either of them could speak. They had started shifting uneasily and both rose. By the time the barman had taken the opportunity to tell them about a conference being held in the main room in the morning and to be sure to take breakfast before 9am, Reinhard and Gottfried were a bit desperate. The stiff inner toilet door, which at first they thought was locked, and which thought provoked heavy curses, did not help. Inside, it appeared the conference was already under way and Gottfried fidgeted behind first one and then another stand-easy figure. Reinhard started laughing as he limped up and down the urinals, turning away every so often and squeezing himself. Then, as if all of the members were engaged in some unanimous low-level vote, they zipped up and left.

'You know, you looked like the *Herr Doktor* then!' Reinhard shrieked.

Gottfried had some difficulty in lining things up at first, and his concentration was worsened as, in pompous propaganda tone, Reinhard ordered him to pull himself together and take note of the fact that there was to be introduced a law for the re-creation of national defence forces with thirty-six divisions for the new army. Reinhard felt sure it sounded just like Goebbels. Gottfried said he could not pull himself together just yet. Reinhard selected a urinal for himself at last and gushed forth with, 'Do you know, Gottfried, that the *Herr Doktor* once asked me to sit in on a press conference he'd called when he tried to convince a hundred foreign Press representatives that conscription was being introduced because France wouldn't disarm, implying that it had nothing to do with tearing up the military section of the Versailles Treaty.'

'You should know,' Gottfried quipped in passable English, 'that we in Germany prefer to crush rather than to Press!' He rather liked the joke and walked away with a jaunt and burst into a bit of the *Egmont Overture*, against a continuing stream of applause from Reinhard. They met at the dangling towel and, for a moment, looked at each other, mouths firm, eyes still.

'*Egmont*,' Reinhard said, his mood suddenly serious. 'Remember that occasion?'

'Luitpold, *ja*?'

'*Stimmt*. Yet Nürnberg promised so much.'

Gottfried paid back the inner door with a meaningful back heel and Reinhard punched it for good measure. They supported each other back to the settee.

Reinhard said, 'I obviously didn't think so at the time but Goebbels' message that day, and its delivery, was so crass. Actually we must have had the thrill of the party rally still coursing our veins because that evening, if you remember, we were part of that huge crowd in the Wilhelmplatz cheering until A-f-H appeared at a Chancery window and saluted. Thank you for being strong, and giving Germany back its self-respect, *mein Führer*; that's what everyone was saying. We felt it, too, for God's sake!'

Gottfried muttered.

But they agreed they had loved a lot of it at the time. In recounting old Berlin, matters they now condemned in summary, were remembered in detail with a kind of banquet brightness. Like when the Sportpalast reverberated to Hitler's demands to have his Sudetenland and when the next day motorised divisions paraded down the Linden, thundering columns of righteous men and metal. Like when Tannhäuser enraptured the audience, the both of them present at the Opera, just a week after war had been declared. Like when the Orient Express stopped in Berlin. Like when the Hindenburg flew over Berlin and when the Lindberghs were in the city. They agreed that everything then had seemed so important, every vehicle on every road, every person's pavement destiny. The city hosting those Olympics; the emotion inside the stadium! Things were happening. Well, Hitler was in power! The Saar. The Rhineland. The purge on the SA. Protective custody. He could do no wrong.

They put down their glasses and clasped hands behind their heads, leaning back against the settee. Reinhard stiffened. 'Burning books was criminal!' he said, adding after a sudden silence between the two men, 'But compared with ...'

Gottfried stiffened, too.

17

REINHARD couldn't forget about newspaper journalism altogether. As he sat in a café, en route to the Hochbenderstrasse address, he considered the oft-used ploy of the newshound to enter Festfortag. He'd pretend he was doing an article on unusual house names (it would more likely be a life story on just the one name). And if he were told to push off, he'd put his foot in the door. Newsmen were supposed to be notorious for that sort of thing. Yet this was somehow more difficult. He paid the bill, steadied himself by lighting a cigarette, again felt dizzy, slipped in behind the wheel of the Merc and slowly moved off.

Hochbenderstrasse was classy and tree-lined. He parked up and assumed as detached an attitude as he could muster. He inched his way along the roadway until No 4 came into view. There, on an old thick gatepost, its original paint long since undermined by the elements and dark green ivy beginning to give it a new coat, was the word: FESTFORTAG. He stared at the name. He read every letter individually, then the whole word slowly. He drew a deep breath and moved towards the gatepost, holding back the gathering gloom he associated with the name. He tried to concentrate his gaze only on the name on the warped piece of wood. Eventually he placed a hand on its top edge, holding it gently for several seconds, as if ready to offer condolences, before letting it slide gently over the letters. Parts of each letter stood proud on the aged wood, refusing to give up. He let his hand drop. For just those few moments, the power of the ten letters had been total matter, with no place for any morbid analysis or awkward attack of contrition. Up- and downstair windows were either partially or totally closed over with old shuttering, giving the house a look of despair. To one side of the front door, a thick rope led up to a verdigris-encrusted bell that came from the mouth of a hideous gargoyle. There was no reply to the two quick tugs Reinhard gave the shoddy hemp. He wanted to break in and compared levels of criminality. Exercising another journalist's ploy, he enquired next door, where, even in the clamped single-mindedness of his mission, the beauty of its garden could not be ignored. A middle-aged man leaned forward and answered Reinhard.

'There's no couple there ... just one.'

Unprompted, he went on: 'You never know with this man. He's often away for weeks or more at time. He has very, very few visitors. You'd be only about the third I know of and I have lived here nearly five years. Is there anything I can help you with?'

Reinhard said: 'I'm a freelance journalist doing a series of features on unusual names. Such people usually have interesting backgrounds.

'He could be Martin Bormann in disguise for all I know,' the neighbour said. And labouring the point, 'He could be anything from a saint to a murderer. But you don't need to wait for him. The brother of Father Dohl, the priest of St Nicholas Church, is very much the local historian around here. I'd say he'd be your best bet. Quite a friendly man.'

A two-handed assault was needed on the iron ring handle of the church door, and the heavy panelled portal gave way only reluctantly. Reinhard immediately felt a foreboding about almost everything he could see inside the church. He shook himself and walked resolutely forward and sat at the back by the south aisle. He picked up a hymn book and flicked through its songs of praise, recalling his youth. He sought out hymn number eighty-four. The last time he had sung the words of that hymn was as a member of the Frauen-Kirche choir in München's inner town. And he hadn't managed to sing all the words on the occasion. He had fainted, sprawling all over the stalls in an embarrassing heap, mechanically blasting forth on a fading verse. He looked towards the choir stalls. Wooden figures were here, too, just like those that had been ascribed to Erasmus Grasser. In the Frauen-Kirche, the figure fourth from the left had been so grotesque. He had

had to sit level and within a sideways glance of its bulging eyes, rude tongue and right-angled ears. It was in such ghastly proximity as to regularly tempt him as a youngster to pervert the heavenly silence between one verse of this or that and another by a sometimes violent, one fingered backwards jab. That is until, clearly able to conceal mirth better than his fellow choristers, Reinhard had been made head boy. In this new position, he need only face the remains of King Ludwig II and his consort Marie Therese beneath the high altar at a respectable distance and soon enough became bored with the whole idea of the divine life.

Father Dohl introduced himself and Reinhard explained his presence. 'I hear that your brother is a local historian, who might be able to help me. There's a -'

The priest's brother, Georg, had died recently, in a car crash near the French border. 'He was a good man, was Georg. All his papers came to me only yesterday.'

Reinhard told Father Dohl about the name.

'That will be HJB. I only know him by this; he prefers it that way. I'm sorry. He's very... well quiet, shall we say. You can view some of my brother's papers if you wish.'

*

At the vicarage, a mass of envelopes, files, books and tapes were laid out on a table ready for Reinhard who went straight to the task. With Father Dohl's problems relating to falling congregation attendances, the choir and money needed to repair the church organ and roof gradually becoming a drone, Reinhard thought about the possibilities and the improbabilities of finding anything during the visit, his mind never allowing the thoughts to run to natural conclusions. He flipped through the pages of a fat indexed book and another, similar book contained cuttings, writings and photographs loosely filed between half-finished pages and two sizeable envelopes at the back stuffed with similar material. He sat back after two hours, and was about to ask if he could continue his research in the morning when he saw a picture of a man lying on the ground - on a road or courtyard, with the unmistakable boots of a braided Nazi officer just captured in the bottom right hand corner of the frame. It was not the boots that had caught his attention, however, or straight away, but rather a contraption that protruded from the underside of the man's right arm towards the boots. The print bent as his free hand slammed into the arm of the leather chair. He looked away, into a blackness that eyes shut had never previously achieved, before he again looked at the print. The more he stared, the more possible it became: the contraption looked like a version of his own crude design, circa March, 1943. His idea, idly turned into a rough drawing while on leave, had fallen from his pocket in front of the braided officer who had questioned Reinhard about it during a café interlude en route to Poland. Enthusiastically at first, he had said it could be put to use to reprimand anyone who did not show proper allegiance to Hitler by saluting. The patchy, light brown walls of the café's interior became the surrounds of the vicarage lounge as the hot memory of that time brought sweat to his brow. The senior officer had entered the café and taken charge of an awkward situation, his small, round rimless glasses so tight against a waxen, colourless face, that the lenses had almost seemed to be his eyes, magnified, piercing. The braided officer had stood there, silently yet totally commanding.

Reinhard peered at the photograph. The device, he felt sure, was from his rough design. The officer had probably arranged for the drawing to have a life of its own. Guilt swept over Reinhard as he realised he may have been responsible for the death of an almost certainly innocent person even before reaching Auschwitz. On the back of the print was lightly pencilled HJB. Reinhard trawled on through the prints before coming to a photograph that gave him a second shock. He thought the figure in the middle of a group of five was this café führer. His general stature looked remarkably like the one Reinhard recalled. If so, then these pictures probably recorded the result of the try-out of his *heil-holz*, the saluting wood as he had so pompously called it. If true, the place was probably the former Gestapo 7 headquarters at nearby Planz. The officer had uttered the word during the dressing down he had received that day, a name that sounded like it was being ground out through a mincer, oozing out over his fat chin as dribble.

18

THE municipal gardener and the old SS Sturmbannführer were falling out with each other. It was of a different kind but command and compliance was in the air. Reinhard could not dispose of unwanted things like dead-heading flowers and in the morning he wanted to get on with his Festfortag enquiries. Dieter was continuing to improve and visiting could be resumed, possibly as early as the following day. Reinhard contacted the hospital, then Gottfried. His old friend was so understanding. 'It's fine, Reinhard. Really. You go right ahead and try to sort things out.' They agreed there was nothing much either of them could do at the hospital for the time being so they'd both keep checking at reception for any messages.

An hour later, Reinhard pulled up outside HJB's house in a hurry. There was a car in the driveway. His knock was answered almost immediately.

'Mm!' grunted a tall, slightly stooped man, who appeared put out by the visit. His face must often have been turned towards the sun and this had given it a bloom that the sunken neck surrounded by a dirty shirt, did not possess. Oval life stuck on a rotting stick, given added gloom by indifferent light. Reinhard's introduction sounded artificial.

'Unusual house names, you say? I'm afraid your series is not going to benefit much from the addition of this name because I know precious little about it. Festfortag - it's just a name. It's nothing to me. I inherited it with the house. I cannot really see how anyone could be interested in that. You journalists are all the same. Are you sure you have the right house? Really, I am at a loss. It's just an ordinary name.'

He was hiding something. Reinhard recognised deception within the embellished sentence and stared at the man, hardly moving a muscle. Reinhard was a reporter again, prizing information out of people who did not wish to talk. His stance gave him an almost lawful force that had often been so effective. Throughout an unnatural hiatus, Reinhard kept his gaze on the other's face, right between his eyes.

'Really, I know hardly anything worthwhile about the name.' And he moved as if to end the discussion, looking strangely into the middle distance. Reinhard kept perfectly still.

'Well, you had better come in. I'll tell you all I *do* know,' he said uncomfortably.

Inside was evidence of neglect and a stuffiness that shortened Reinhard's breath as he followed HJB into a large room. Broad framed pictures fought for space on walls and the dark, heavily patterned flock paper took up more of the air. Reinhard accepted a cold drink and sank into an armchair. On top of a radiogram was a picture of a young man, to which HJB now referred.

'That's my son,' he said. 'He's the one who could have told you as much as anyone about the name. But he's dead.' HJB hesitated and then added in a strong, high-pitched voice, 'He was murdered.'

The adjudication accused Reinhard, renewed guilt enveloping him as he got up and walked towards the radiogram just as the grandfather clock in the hallway boomed out the fifteenth hour of the day. It jolted his mind and he asked HJB if he could pay for a call to the hospital. 'My own son is there and I promised I would check in at about this time. Do you mind?'

'I want an assurance that the address here will not be published. The name - that is all right, but not the address.'

'Certainly.'

HJB inclined his head towards the door. 'It's in the hall by the grand old man.'

HJB paced the floor as the call was made and when Reinhard re-entered the room, the man said, 'I've made it a habit of keeping what little I know much to myself. But it won't matter soon. Not because I'm not proud or anything like that. It was worthwhile but the pain is still there. It will be even after it's all finished.'

The sad, yet powerful-looking man sighed deeply. 'You wouldn't understand. You cannot. Few people could. However, I do know more than I have said. I've lived with it for so many years, ever since 1943. Things are changing now, anyway, finishing really. I cannot be many years from the end now and I've really always wanted people to know of Rainer's bravery.'

Reinhard tried to keep his balance as Rainer lurched forward. HJB's further explanation consisted mostly of unlinked words. Reinhard tried to concentrate. HJB's son and his fiancée, Ingrid, were engaged in a resistance plot. Complicated and extremely dangerous. HJB could hardly understand how it was possible. It was secret anyway. He trusted Rainer.

Rainer ...

He had been a level-headed young man, HJB said. His fiancée, too, was a realistic young woman. He loved his son. He hated the way the Nazis were plunging the country into the mire. Above all, he loathed the target of their resistance plan as much as Rainer did. They planned to do away with Heinrich Himmler.'

Rainer ... Reinhard straightened. Now the words came more clearly. 'You longed for the day...' Reinhard encouraged.

HJB nodded. 'There was something to do with a mineshaft. The area was full of SS and the Gestapo. Himmler had apparently been examining the possibility of a site for a new, special concentration camp, not too far away from here. And his route - the couple somehow got hold of the information through a clerk - took him close to the Gestapo 7 headquarters.'

HJB's voice trailed off. Reinhard hardly heard that fire jets had been involved, that the couple thought it was appropriate to incinerate the Reichführer-SS.

'They never made it. A few days before Himmler's visit to the site in the early spring of 1943, the Gestapo arrived in numbers to clear the line.'

The spring of 1943.

'Rainer and his fiancée, and Fritz were arrested, separately. My boy and Ingrid were taken in because they were said to have been acting suspiciously. They weren't anywhere near the mineshaft area or anything. The Gestapo just wanted to put the wind up everyone and my two just happened to be around. They would have been right about their intentions but there was no way they could have known. Fritz - he was a very good friend of mine - was taken in a mile or so away for failing to give the Nazi salute, would you believe.'

Reinhard's mind reeled. He wanted to consider the date but asked where the name Festfortag came into the story.

'Yes, Festfortag. It was the operation code name for the proposed assassination of this monster. It was coined by Rainer when, in the early days of talking about doing something positive against the Nazis, Ingrid's understandably cautious reaction made Rainer think again about carrying on. In fact, the couple had about given up any idea of assassination, however justified, when Ingrid's parents were killed after being dragged from their home on a charge devoid of any truth or justification. Their deaths refocused Rainer and Ingrid on the mission. I'll never forget their reaction: almost together, in unison, they said 'Right, we'll carry on with the plan, then, in their memory.'

Reinhard's memory flashes slopped about inside his head. Thoughts darkened and he said, almost as if he wished his words to be missed, 'Did they ever use the name Festfortag, to call each other I mean?'

Steel shuttered confirmation.

Speaking softly to himself as if he were alone, his eyes viewing something far beyond the lounge wall, HJB said they had started calling each other by that name. Frau Festfortag, Rainer would call out to her. Herr Festfortag, she would answer.

Reinhard shivered, an ice-pick at his back. And the silence that froze the next few moments promoted around him an even greater chill. So, her name had been Ingrid. Rainer and Ingrid. Reinhard sat down and, again, did not catch everything as HJB spoke of forged papers and the use of that name and how he wished he knew everything because they were no longer around to ask. However, Reinhard did clearly hear him say, 'There is no one now who would know.'

REQUIREMENTS OF GUILT

Reinhard was bathed in sweat. He looked at HJB. Above his shoulder, taking up the whole of the picture over the fireplace, then filling the space on the bookshelf, now fitting into the carpet pattern, was a plastic white face. He pictured the scene outside the camp's political department, the couple and the giant of a guard. He had heard their choking goodbyes. Herr Festfortag ... Frau Festfortag.

Places, dates. Now names.

HJB, now with the manner of a man who had unburdened himself, offered Reinhard something stronger to drink. Reinhard asked for another cold drink. And when they had settled back, he reached into his pocket and took out the two photographs from Father Dohl's collection. HJB was not finished, however, and went on as rigidly aggressive as Reinhard was feeling despondently limp. HJB was eager to relate the circumstances, even though confined to just an intention as it turned out. Reinhard thought that if more people had had thoughts like this young couple, there would have been less chance of people like Himmler ever ruling in the way they did. HJB leant forward militantly, 'And who knows what would have happened with the Number 2 out of the way, the man who would vomit if he saw a speck of blood. He, the SS and the Gestapo.' HJB sighed but continued, even more aggressively, 'They were all so evil that an Hiroshima or Nagasaki, or both together, on this country at the right time would have seen off good people, yes, but it would have swilled away the stench that will still be potent when the last chapter on this country is written.'

HJB said Rainer and Ingrid were taken to Gestapo 7 and Fritz was murdered right enough in the butchers' quadrangle. He said someone who actually saw it happen had told him the sequence of events. Fritz was punished for his insolence by having to stand with his arm outstretched for half an hour or so. What none of them knew or cared about was that Fritz had a serious heart condition and some contraption, some bell warning, went off long before even they expected it when Fritz collapsed - and that sentenced Rainer and Ingrid and some child to death. The justification was as flimsy as that.

Reinhard nervously rubbed the two photographs together. The device was his. The bent man who failed to salute Reinhard in the Café Wien was Fritz. He knew at that moment that he had sent him to his death and Rainer and Ingrid, too. And was the boy Dieter?

'Was this Fritz?' he said, thrusting one of the photographs forward.

HJB looked at the print.

'Where did you get this from,' he demanded angrily.

'Father Dohl. His brother's-'

'Yes, I know. I gave his brother this photograph some years ago, but it was only for his personal records. Enough of this subject anyway. The war is a bitter memory.'

Reinhard's request for the negative, to make it easier from which to reproduce a good print, was met with a curt decline. He felt no longer welcome but knew he would have to return to Festfortag.

19

IGNORING a spiteful wind, Reinhard unfolded the map, forced it down onto the roof of the car and looked at his watch. He still had plenty of time before ringing Irma. He couldn't just sit around and wait. He was being consumed by the mystery. Eagerly he sought out the place HJB had described. He feared the findings but buried truth would prey on him. Reinhard tucked the map's extremities under the target area in an untidy fold, looked up for a moment, and then bore down in a frantic search for Planz. He found it, across the deep centre crease of the map, under which the freshening wind was whistling it into a kind of topographer's three-dimensional model of the area. Nearby would be where Gestapo 7 had been. A café had not been too far from this place, its name forgotten but its form intact in his mind. He leaned back behind the wheel and stretched out as straight as possible. That particular day in the cafe had epitomised it all. He had had nothing against the man. He just wanted to exercise the power the uniform, his new uniform, gave him. Otherwise he would have taken the man aside, and told him the virtues of obedience and allegiance and duty and all of that. He could have been more human and, with nothing lost, Fritz's death wouldn't now burden him and make him bang his fists on the steering wheel. He turned the key, slammed his foot on the clutch, threw the stick forward and drove off with protesting tyres. A sign showed eighteen kilometres. He drove slowly through the town and, as he was completing a second circuit through its streets, Reinhard stopped and asked someone about the café. It was the Café Wien. The pedestrian had just had breakfast there. Reinhard eased the car around the corner and there it was. He pulled up outside the door which was not in the same place as before but when he entered the cafe, he saw that the bar, though modernised, was in the same position and for a second he saw Fritz's bent body. Reinhard had not even known the man's name. Somebody who asked for a beer and was sent to his death. Reinhard sat down, turned towards the door he had just entered and went through the torment of that day's incident.

The door bell's dull chimes are just losing their persistence as a slightly stooped, middle aged man with a serious but somehow contented face brushes past him into the café.

Reinhard ordered a strong coffee with cream. He would certainly go to Planz but not just yet. Wooden blocks had replaced the old red carpet. Reinhard looked across to the right-hand side of the cafe where everyone apart from he had sat. Bent by the weight of what he had seen as insolence, he let the man walk to the counter and begin to place his order before shattering the mood of the café by his raised voice.

'You! Insolent swine!'

The man turns, but slowly.

'Yes, you! Tell me, do you consider this establishment, this café here, as part and parcel of the Third Reich?'

'Natürlich, ja,' the man returns.

'Here, then, is another simple question: why did you not acknowledge the same by recognising me?'

The man lowers his head. Then, looking up and straight ahead, he replies: 'But I do not know you.'

Reinhard looks down. With silence in the café complete, he says: 'It is all probably well beyond you, but what I am asking for is the courtesy of a salute.'

The man stands motionless with the bearing of a plough.

Reinhard commands, 'Salute!'

There man remains unmoved.

'I am arresting you for insulting the Führer!'

Reinhard goes to pull his gun when the little bell again becomes agitated. A braided officer enters.

'Having trouble Herr Sturmbannführer?' the senior officer says with a swift movement of his hand, sending the man shuffling to the far corner of the café. Reinhard is struck by a large green stone ring on the index finger of the officer's left hand. The senior officer icily indicates that everyone should continue dining as normal before motioning Reinhard to sit down, as he does himself, the two officers facing each other across a small table on the quiet side of the café.

'An officer should never lose his temper,' he says straight away. 'Right must deal with wrong. You learned that during training, surely. What is wrong? Together we will put it right, eh?'

Reinhard tells him, switching his gaze between the piercing look of the officer and the glittering ring on his finger. The Standartenführer's eyes darken. Such insolence he himself would not tolerate, he says. But the voice has to retain its cutting edge. The stronger the tone, the weaker the effect, he says with frozen soundness. 'Coffee, Sturmbannführer?'

'Thank you, Sir,' Reinhard says, reaching for his wallet which he then fiddles with, unsure whether to offer to pay.

'Relax, Herr Sturmbannführer!'

Reinhard fumbles to replace the wallet when a folded sheet of paper falls from it to the ground by the Standartenführer's feet. He bends to retrieve it but not before the officer, with surprising agility for a man his size, picks up the now partly unfolded sheet from the floor and examines it.

'Looks interesting. An amateur architect, are you?'

'It is nothing, really. Just idling one day at home.'

The officer inclines his head towards Reinhard in a manner that leaves no doubt that prevarication at any level annoys.

'Well, it is, Herr Standartenführer ... when I was in my home town, a soldier passed me without saluting. I checked him but it got me thinking about punishment for this kind of effrontery. It may seem petty -'

'Get to the point, Herr Sturmbannführer!'

'I devised a kind of saluting wood, a heil-holz I call it, that can be attached to an outstretched arm as punishment; if the arm falters, a mechanism will be triggered which will result in a sharp electrical reminder of the importance of recognising allegiance and superiority in the first place. It's not much of a ... I wanted only ...'

'Leave judgement to me,' Herr Sturmbannführer. Firm opinion can come later. Others will decide. I shall keep this.'

Reinhard, formerly the confident Café Führer, becomes the lowly Café Unterführer. He is made to wait through ten more minutes of the virtues of SS discipline before the senior officer returns to the subject of his heil-holz. Then the senior officer presses Reinhard's uniform and puts shine back on his leathers when he says the idea has grown on him; he will take the design as a model that might be perfected. The stooping man leaves. The SS-Standartenführer follows. Reinhard slowly brings his arm down and resumes his seat. He looks around the café, defensively, his gaze stopping in the right-hand corner. There are still five other customers present, who carry on chatting.

Reinhard had wanted rest, some ordinary place, some nondescript eating house in an unimportant German town, where he could wile away several hours in two or three sessions, privately, because of the meeting ahead, in Poland, when for the first time he would see the Berlin file papers come alive. He had been ordered east by his office of the Concentration Camp Inspectorate and his particular duty - to oversee the opening of Crematorium V in Birkenau - would start with a meeting in the lavish office of SS-General Eric von dem Boch Zelewski in Breslau before joining the Camp Commandant, Rudolf Höss, at Auschwitz.

He now ordered a meal and, as he waited, his eyes drifted to the corner where the group of young people had sat all those years ago. He saw the group again, clearly, the five of them chatting, laughing, throwing heads back or bringing them forward, hands occasionally pounding the wooden table, cigarette smoke darting and swirling as hands circled and bodies rocked. They were all so youthfully carefree.

His focus tries to cast shoulders aside so he can concentrate on the girl to the right of the group. He can see most of the youngsters but the essential parts of this particular girl in a long, cream coloured floppy jumper, her face, her hands, her ears even, remain hidden to him. His attention is gradually drawn almost entirely to this girl. Yet although she moves this way and that, nothing of her is revealed to Reinhard. He will call to her. He will remain silent. His imagination drapes over her table, to peep at her properly. She has slightly curving hair that hangs just below her neck. There are a few strands caught carelessly on the jumper with the apricot cable stitch around the lower half-inch of the garment which loosely envelops the top of her black jeans. A pair of cream coloured socks covers the gap between these and the brown, ankle length boots that are drawn close together beneath the table. Her imagined beauty fascinates him. It is simple to fashion her into Stephanie and readily gives her the contours of kindness and sweetness, with impishness, class and poise. He keeps on building up a picture of her. She returns a sweet odour on which he draws fresh breath and later he imagines their talking of little things that seem to matter.

An unexciting waitress slid the Kartoffelsalat in front of him. Reinhard noted the blue of her blouse, and its pattern, nearly matching that of the plate. He went to speak but drew back.

As he knew it would, loneliness would always befriend such as this finely fashioned woollen shape. He should buy second hand somewhere, change out of his uniform and greet them. He should smile when they roar, nod when they speak, be asked to join them, possibly. He is always so full of serious talk, with a face of thoughtful creases instead of laughter lines. He thinks he wants to spit out all the scholarly philosophy he has absorbed from the writings of Alfred the Ungreat, he of the Nazi thinkers, and the rest of the psycho political clap-trap. She gets up and he lifts his face towards hers. She does not turn his way and he sinks back but keeps looking. He is not disappointed, nor is there any kind of frustration. It is simply the culmination of a fascinating encounter, untested but by no means sterile. She walks away, intermittently cloaked by her friends and with others near the bar, and he lets her go as he turns to look around the restaurant. But his eyes return to the door. There she is, moving out, her face still invisible to his gaze. Suddenly she swings round to answer one of her friends. She is beautiful. He has been in the company of an angel.

If only nothing could always have been like that, Reinhard thought, taking a lump of Kartoffel into his mouth and holding it there, staring again into the empty corner and then towards the exit. He could still see her. He walked to the window.

He watches the girl walk on down the pavement and sees a young man cross the road. She walks out of Reinhard's view but a minute later, he sees her cross over further down and she joins the young man though they walk slightly one behind the other and quickly. Military vehicles arrive and there is a clatter of soldiers running down the street, iron tip noise and soldierly shouts. Before the couple reach the corner, a child runs from open ground carrying a bright yellow, star-like object, and stumbles into them, the girl having to readjust her stride to avoid colliding with him. The child ends up in her arms just as a group of Gestapo personnel draw level. A lorry draws up.

Reinhard stepped back and resumed his seat. The blue-bloused waitress approached and he ordered another coffee. The street scene had been almost clear enough to be contemporary. Back then, he had been able - just - to see the three of them swept up by a group of officials and put into the back of a truck that was following the Gestapo. Reinhard closed his eyes.

He sees a clearing in a dense forest of bewildered branches outside the political department in Auschwitz ... a woman, holding the hand of a child who is gripping the tattered arm of a soft toy.

Of course, it was why she had appeared as diamonds set in papier mâché! It had been her, the girl from the café! He flushed and gripped the table in front of him, knocking his plate.

'Have you finished?' blue blouse asked.

Reinhard nodded and crossed to the window again. The girl was as clear now in his mind as she had been before. It had been the same person. He had been close to her even before No 5. Almost certainly he had been close to Frau Festfortag and probably been only scores of feet from Herr Festfortag.

'Do you want anything else?' the waitress asked.

He shook his head. Had he also seen Dieter? He looked at his watch. Still time. Reinhard rang Irma.

'Yes, everything, it is OK. The doctor says there has been a slight interruption to his progress but all is again well. However, a further full day of complete rest will be necessary.'

Reinhard wanted to go straight away but Irma said, 'See this bit through, Reinhard, for your own good. I'll see you this evening. Gottfried may be here, too.'

Reinhard certainly wanted to see Fritz's death through. Right now though, he wildly imagined, so close to the place where there was pain in Fritz's arm, agony, gloating men, Fritz was still alive. Reinhard momentarily put his foot down hard on the pedal, as if life and death might still be in the balance. He went around a bend on the wrong side of the road. He cried out. He slowed down. The old station had been off Seckterstrasse, a semi-derelict building now, partly used as a discount carpet store. To the side was a high wall in which was a large wooden door that fitted badly against rotting posts and a crumbling arch. He looked through one of the slits and saw a small covered courtyard with vans tight against the far wall blocking a gap beyond which he could make out what appeared to be a larger quadrangle. The death-bed. For a moment, he could see the shiny boots still banging about, the smirks, the taunts, the hatred, visions that were gradually replaced by tufts of grass and weed which had grown up after it had all gone quiet. Reinhard pulled himself away from the door and returned to his car. He knew he would have to return to Festfortag. Whatever it was he was following - and it was part of the trouble that he didn't really know - he felt gloomily that it would turn out to be something bad and he did not know if he could cope with any of it, even if Dieter was happily married, settled in Germany with a good job.

Here was the thing: whenever there was something important to do, that something would have to be done more or less instantly. It had always been the same. It was the way Reinhard was. What at this time was there more important than Dieter? Reinhard made for the hospital.

20

REINHARD arranged to meet Irma at the hospital entrance and even from a distance he could tell she was somewhat animated. She rushed forward to embrace him, took his hand and pulled him through the doorway before breaking loose and spurting ahead, urging him to hurry up.

'Come on,' she yelled, offering no explanation for her demeanour though he dared conjure one. She merely put a finger to her lips every time Reinhard tried to question her. When they reached the ward, Irma stepped back and let Reinhard enter first. As he neared the bed, Dieter turned his head towards him and smiled. Reinhard ran the last few steps, practically skidding to a halt by the bed and fell upon its fragile occupant. With both arms around Dieter's shoulders, the sight of the bandaged head moving, the sound of his breathing and hearing him say Dad, Reinhard felt the world was again spinning in the right direction. Despite the distraction of Irma (on cue she gave him a big smile) Reinhard had been suffering inside. He still had Festfortag to sort out and Stephanie was looming larger by the day, but for now he could relax. Neither of them said anything for quite a while before Reinhard withdrew himself to arms length but still gripping Dieter's shoulders. They spoke only of what was to come, a future home with a garden stream, books, celebration, a game of snooker, nothing of the incident that had almost claimed his life. Dieter was given just ten minutes before a nurse appeared, indicating that visiting time for the moment was at an end.

'You are tired, Dieter. Of course. It's just that I am so happy.'

'Me, too, Dad. Thank you for coming out, and you Irma. I'm OK, just a little groggy. I will see you both again later, eh?'

Dieter covered Reinhard's hand with his own. Irma gave Dieter a cuddle and turned around to beam at Reinhard. He felt strong and tried to smile as a polite stranger.

'I didn't want to spoil the surprise for you,' Irma said.

Accepting the challenge of a hand thrust towards him, Reinhard managed 'And what a surprise it was!' But Irma's closeness made him suddenly nervous as they walked along the corridor. His mind raced on the subject of which way he should turn at the end of it. He spun round on her, said how wonderful it was about Dieter but that he would have to dash because he was expecting a call from Gottfried. When he reached the hotel, Gottfried had left a message at reception. He had had a very successful trip and would be back in Hannover the following day. Reinhard tried not to analyse the hand-in-hand walk down the hospital corridor and was at the hospital first thing in the morning after a good night's rest. He went immediately to see Dieter but he was asleep. He stayed for a while but the nurse said it would be best to let Dieter rest. Reinhard could return mid-afternoon when Dieter would have probably woken naturally and been seen by the doctor.

Before Irma went shopping, she emphasised that she would not be long and asked Reinhard to wait. He had a coffee, several coffees in fact, and thought about their meeting up again. He tried to think of Stephanie but Irma kept hanging about. He read almost every newspaper lying around and he fidgeted and he sighed. The hotel receptionist with pebble glasses appeared in the corridor just as Reinhard decided to stretch his legs.

'Care for a lift back to the hotel? I've been visiting a relative. I'll be glad to get back.'

'Thanks, but I'm waiting for someone.'

Reinhard continued his little walk but after a few moments he turned and galloped down three flights of stairs, across the entrance hall and out onto the car park, scanning the areas between the cars. He slapped his side in frustration. Suddenly, he had wanted to go with Funny Smile. Reinhard was practically planning this thing. It was not the way. There really shouldn't be any way at all, but certainly not in this place, laying in wait for Irma and making it easy for her to ply her magic within yards of Dieter. Nothing had so far happened, no situation had arisen that was irreversible and he wanted fantasy, if it struck him, to end at that. He returned to the Hotel Bahnhof. In his room, he looked into the full-length mirror. He had seen the look in other people on occasions and now thought he detected suspicion etched all over his face, the sort of look that he was told crossed his face when he went through the green channel at airport customs. Without even the most paltry of items to declare, he become quite unable to walk casually or appear at ease and as a result probably always ended up having as guilty a look about him as it was possible to have! Gottfried had left a message saying he had been delayed and was not sure whether he could make it even by the evening, though he would try. Irma rang. She was back from shopping and wanted an update. Reinhard told her he had only just left the hospital and that they must have missed each other by only a few minutes.

'They were letting him sleep on ahead of a visit from the doctor. I would not be able to see him until later in the afternoon. But they all appear very optimistic.'

'That's wonderful; we'll go together, eh? I've got something for you, from my little outing this morning. I'll come over straight away,' she said, putting the phone down and preventing him from delaying the visit. Reinhard almost phoned back but shrugged and changed into a pair of light gabardines and dark green zip-up. He still felt strong. After pausing in the foyer, where he had intended to wait for Irma, he asked about good eating houses. The Kreutzkamm, just around the corner, was recommended. It was perfect, anywhere but the hotel and her hospital room. When Irma arrived, she looked radiant, like she had just come from a wedding, wearing a pink outfit with a straw hat that she delighted in telling him she had bought for a song during the shopping spree but without hinting at the cost of the rest of the outfit.

'You look smart,' she said, smoothing the end of his sleeve, and going up on her toes to kiss his cheek. 'Green suits you.'

Reinhard caught her perfume and forgot the name of the restaurant. 'Shall we have a drink?' he said inclining towards the bar. She took hold of his hand and gently tugged him in the direction of the lift. 'We can have something sent up, why don't we? Anyway, I want you to try this on,' she said, thrusting a carrier bag towards him. He let himself be gently tugged and momentarily toyed with the idea of surrender. It was the look on her face and the flick of the head as she took off her hat, holding it by her side. By the time they emerged from the lift, composure was difficult as they walked down the corridor to Room 34. Inside, she opened the bag and brought out a shirt and jumper.

'I think you'll like this,' she began. 'Here, change into this,' she said, holding out with one hand a pastel green shirt with barely discernible silvery horizontal stripes and pulling at his jumper with the other. He complied, with the feeling that this would be the removal of the first layer of decency that had thus far kept them respectable. And when it came to removing his shirt, he was bothered. As he restrained her hand on the buckle of his belt, he stared down at the shirt he had discarded, caught on the back of the armchair, its sleeves stretching down into the seat, their cuffs pleadingly wrung one into the other. He raised his head towards Irma in pitiful explanation, rendered wordless by the ring of the telephone. It was Gottfried, back from his travels and downstairs. Irma, already with more to gather up at her feet, ran her head down past Reinhard's hands, smiling into his face as she disappeared into the toilet, calling behind her, 'Tell me more about Dieter in a minute.'

'Coming right down,' Reinhard told Gottfried who said he had lots of news. 'But to tell you first,' Reinhard said excitedly, when he reached reception and took Gottfried by the arm, 'Dieter, he has sat up in bed and has sat in a chair! He's going to be all right.'

'*Gott sei Dank!* Reinhard, that's wonderful! Really wonderful.'

'He is sitting up, and talking. That is all I want, well for now.'

'When can I see him?'

'Probably tomorrow. I'll let you know. Doctors and nurses have been all over him for most of the day.'

'That's fine, only for a short time, though. I've got a story to crack and a favour to ask you. I've got some good news for you, too.' Gottfried went on: 'My aunt Amelia, a painter, who lives near Goslar, I've had a word with her and she would be truly delighted to have Dieter stay with her for a week while he fully recovers. She was herself in a serious accident - skiing in Italy, I believe. She cannot make it longer than a week because she starts a painting course the following week in Augsburg.'

'I ...' Reinhard hesitated, his mind suddenly on Rastenkorb, Stephanie and Irma and all the things connected with his past.

'It's only a week.'

'*Only*, Gottfried. Why, I -'

'Well, it's only a week in the Harz. Actually Dieter can look forward to three further weeks of convalescence, if it takes that long. After Goslar, it's the Ojcow Valley in Poland for your lad. I've talked with my cousin Marek and his wife Jo and they say they'd be delighted to help him through this. Well, it would be mostly Jo, because Marek's a schedules manager with the railway at Kattowice, though he's trying to take some of his leave. They've both said they'd be delighted to help out and it only requires you to say yes.'

Inwardly, Reinhard felt pleased that this would probably give him the time to track himself down properly, beginning with another visit to Festfortag. HJB had said he was off to Peru shortly; perhaps things would work out. How much time he actually had alone, however, would depend on other things.

'Gottfried, this is so special.'

'Actually, you can help me. The favour I spoke of. Can you come with me tomorrow, to Enschede? Nothing sinister. I just need company ... and a driver,' he smiled. 'I'll have some copy to get in by the time we're on the road and need time to write the bloody stuff for a grumpy news editor.'

Reinhard said, 'Sure. Sure, we could leave straight after seeing Dieter,' relieved that the test of his willpower would again be delayed. He decided to be bold. 'Irma will be on hand. Actually, Irma's in the hotel at the moment. I was just about to tell her the latest on Dieter when you called. Do you know, just to see him move, just a little, and to hear a few words ... come up and I'll tell you both together.' As they walked up the stairs, Gottfried said, 'It's on the outskirts of Enschede.'

'That's where George is, Enschede, isn't he?'

'Well, we'd be a few kilometres apart but I guess it's not too far.

Why, do you want to call in and see him?'

Reinhard said, 'He's due back the day after tomorrow, but I could surprise him. Maybe, if you don't mind and he's ready to come, we could bring him back here.'

'I'd be delighted.'

When they reached Reinhard's room, Irma smiled her welcome to Gottfried and immediately ordered coffees and, thinking of Gottfried and Reinhard, asked for a tray of fancies to be brought up. Minutes later, as the waiter laid the tray on the low glass-topped table, Reinhard thought about one of Hitler's maids, who in a book she had written, alluded to the fact that the Führer had been partial to the sticky carbohydrates with their cholesterol-filled slits. He also thought of his own first experiences with fancies at grandfather Otto's. He had missed out on some of his favourites because of a defiant excursion to see hammers and nails asleep in grandfather's old shed at the back of the house, sniff at rust and oil, crunch wood shavings underfoot, invite the bite of chisel points and then comfort a finger in little pyramids of sawdust close to a vice on the workbench. Grandfather had kept looking, and grunting, over his broadsheet to see how much Reinhard was missing the cakes. But when a log rolled from the fire, father took advantage of the old man's agitation and thrust what remained on his own plate into Reinhard's mouth, the disappearing cream grinning back at him. The burning log had caught the edge of the newspaper and, for a moment, there was quite a fire. Grandfather cursed and went off to paint. Of those visits to Berlin, Reinhard remembered red the most and had thought of it as blood, wondering how much paint was left in grandfather's body, how much longer he could keep grunting before he was drained.

The talk of the entire coffee break was of Dieter and all of them rejoiced in the young man's recovery. Gottfried repeated the tentative convalescence arrangements that had been made and Irma, now feeling relaxed enough to flash several looks at Reinhard as she spoke, said she would be happy to take Dieter to Goslar before he went off to Poland, if Reinhard wanted time with Gottfried. Reinhard said defensively, 'Well, yes, there's Gottfried. But also, I've stumbled on something that's worrying me a bit, something to do with years ago. It's maybe nothing, but I feel it's primary, you know. A life can be enormously rewarding even though nothing special happens, yet at another time, life can be full to overflowing but depressed. Just now, Dieter provides a thrilling diversion from heavy thoughts. I want not to say more. I hope you understand.'

Gottfried said, 'If you need space, OK? Do you need any help?'

'I wish I knew. Maybe later. Or, hopefully, not at all.'

Irma suggested Reinhard had a few days to himself and when he felt relaxed he could join Dieter and her in Goslar.

Gottfried agreed.

21

WITH Gottfried quietly scribbling away for the best part of the journey to Enschede - apart from an occasional expletive that he later explained related to an inability to decipher his shorthand - Reinhard tried to relax at the wheel and reassess his position. He liked using driving time to think. Back home, he often did his best thinking behind the wheel of a car, particularly at night because he could see very little to distract him left or right and headlights acted as a focus. Irma and George were out there in the twin shafts of light. Reinhard wished they were as entwined as the beams and that he could make them disappear by switching them off. A problem Reinhard had was that the stronger his feelings for Stephanie (and how brightly she was sometimes glowing now that he was back in the old country) the weaker he seemed to become in the presence of Irma. He was afraid that in some random and totally unsolicited moment, Irma's match could ignite Stephanie's flame. Stephanie filled his head like a wonderful occasion while at every opportunity Irma slipped her arm into his. Stephanie was easy to imagine wherever he was or whatever he was doing. What worried Reinhard was the prospect that in quiet moments Irma might gradually provide telling features of her own.

If only Dieter was out of hospital, the Festfortag mystery sorted and the possible personal ramifications of the Eichmann hue and cry proving to be a fear without foundation, he could concentrate on his love for Stephanie. He did the lefts, rights and straight aheads to Gottfried's bidding as they went through the centre of Enschede, and reached the address two or three miles further on, up a narrow lane. Reinhard switched on the radio and lent back for a long stay, but Gottfried walked back to the car after twenty minutes, with a bounce in his step that indicated he'd already got at least something of what he'd gone for.

'Right, George it is. I've got to go in that direction myself now; the trail gets longer.'

Gottfried took over the wheel and told Reinhard: 'It's the money side of this Revisionism crap, I'm sure. Ironic, isn't it, cutting corners in greed-inspired property development to fund the destruction of memorials in Germany and Poland, places where people were starved of everything that a good life had to offer, as part of a perverted and criminal attempt to change history. Do you know, Reinhard, the chap I've just seen even spoke of working against the Revisionists!'

Gottfried picked up on Reinhard's response to this - 'a fat fucker pretending he's trying to take a couple of bricks out of the wall, whereas in reality he's one of the load bearing joists for this whole sickening movement'. Gottfried said, 'Are you sure you don't want to return to journalism; that would have looked good in print - what you just said. But honestly, that's about it, Reinhard.'

They lapsed into silence, both squinting through the rain-lashed windscreen out on to a roadway of flickering reflections that trembled then disappeared beneath the bonnet of the car. As he entered an underpass, Gottfried said he had a name and address to follow up. He had got it off the desk when the man went into the hall to take a call.

'I think I recognised the surname from a report in my office,' Gottfried said and, thumping the wheel added, 'I'll nail these bastards somehow!'

The rain eased for a while as they chatted about old times and entered a second underpass, leaden skies now giving way to central rows of orange lamps. When they re-emerged at street level, there was again two of everything.

Gottfried said, 'Wonder what this chap will have to say for himself. I'll drop you off at George's place and go on to my contact. I believe it's quite close by.' By the time Gottfried pulled up in the railinged mews of George's wartime benefactor, the rain had eased off.

Reinhard waved him off around the corner, pulled up his collar and tugged simultaneously at both sides of his hat. George was not in.

'Neither, of course, is Renate,' said the man who answered the door. He spoke with hardly disguised indifference, adding, 'I suppose they'll be back some time, though I cannot say when. Do you want to wait? You can if you want.'

The off-hand delivery gave the man's tone a sadly bitter quality. But it would not be long before an exclamation mark would be flung in after almost every sentence. As he turned to retreat into a rather dreary and dark building, Reinhard said, half apologetically, 'I've only popped in on the off chance of seeing George. We've actually arranged a meeting in Hannover the day after tomorrow but I am with a friend who has business here and ... well, here I am.'

'Come on then, if you're coming in,' said the hunched keeper of the house, his baggy wool waistcoat slung low over the front of his slightly bent frame by hands plunged into ragged, shallow pockets. Several strands of grey hair fought for prominence on top of a mottled scalp. Neither did the several finger plasters that had been pinched around the bridge area of his spectacles help his appearance.

'It's cold standing on the step,' he said.

There was hardly any light to help guide Reinhard as he followed the man down the hallway. It was the other's footsteps over creaking boards that mainly kept Reinhard on track. Reinhard practically bumped into him as the man stopped suddenly to depress a clanky latch and enter a room illuminated by a small lamp with a tasselled purple shade in the corner of a room heavy with books. The man immediately sank into an armchair, crossing his legs and indicating with both hands what Reinhard imagined was an invitation to sit in the only other chair in the room but which might just as easily have meant that he could please himself what he did, sit down or turn around and leave.

'I am Reinhard, a friend of George ...'

'George!' the man repeated loudly, leaning forward.

'Yes. He's ...'

'I know,' he interrupted, getting up and putting his hands behind his back and walking backwards and forwards. 'I know.'

Despite the years he had been out of practice, and his increasing disrespect for what some newspapers had to say these days, Reinhard felt an instinct slot home like first gear. It was the way the man spoke. The practised procedure had Reinhard nodding slowly with tightened lips.

'Quite,' he said hopefully.

'He and Renate, well … do you want a drink?'

Reinhard nodded. 'Thanks. May I have a brandy?'

The man poured from a decanter. Reinhard said, 'George has always said how lucky he was that Renate was around at the time.'

'Lucky for Renate, more like,' scoffed the man, passing Reinhard his brandy and downing a gin in two gulps before pouring another.

Reinhard needed to take a chance. 'Well that, yes, but …'

It worked. The man quietened him with a slow wave of a hand, clearly wanting to lead the discussion. Renate was his cousin and they had been proud to give George shelter where they previously lived. There was no argument about that. And he was particularly proud of Renate, who had always been such a shy woman at heart. He sometimes went out but it suited them both to stay in most times because they liked each other's company, playing cards or listening to the radio - and then there was their mutual interest in reading which often more than filled a day's leisure. The man recounted it all, affectionately. Then his mood shifted and he went on, gruffly: 'This all changed when George's visits started. Naturally, George would have been grateful for the way Renate had dealt with his initial, medical situation. You obviously know about that.'

'A little,' Reinhard lied, declining a refill.

'Oh, well, it was a hell of a time for George. Apparently he was struggling over a high bank on the edge of some field when part of a shell passed right between his legs skimming the inside of his left knee and entering the upper thigh of his right leg. In one way, he was lucky. As it was, it …' The man hesitated, sliding his tongue over his top teeth, as if uncertain of how to proceed.

Reinhard encouraged, 'It must have been a testing time for you and Renate in the circumstances.'

'We just had to take him in. People did what they could during those dreadful times. We were no different. Eventually, of course, he had to go to hospital. But Renate was marvellous. They say first aid is so important. It really is ... He was all bloodied and in so much pain. I felt so sorry for him.'

'Renate nursed him for a while?'

'Of course! She was a nurse!'

Reinhard fell silent, considering George's injuries and the possible aftermath. He said, 'Oh, I see,' his thoughts turning to Irma.

'Yes, well, that was then,' said the man, reintroducing the edge to his voice. He added, 'That was the war; it was a time for extraordinary things. Hostilities, for all its sadness, bloodshed and misery, foster kindnesses and this, naturally, promoted gratefulness. But the war ended and lives, our lives, I hoped would resume.'

He got up and paced the room again before sitting back and putting a hand on his forehead. 'George's increasingly frequent visits over the years would have been welcome and I would have been glad to spend a couple of days with him whenever he came over, but he spent more and more time with Renate. And now he comes to see only her, I'm sure. He must have told you how much he likes her. Did he ever tell you about the man he replaced in Renate's heart?'

This was getting too deep for Reinhard and he stalled. 'He loves the reunion. You can always tell.'

'Which one?'

Reinhard covered his interest with a slow, matter-of-fact statement, 'September 1944. Arnhem. Operation Market Garden, I believe.'

'Huhh!' the man puffed, getting up and shuffling to the window. He shook his head and took a deep breath.

'Look, Reinhard ... Emiel, by the way,' he said extending his hand. 'Look, she ... he... well ... you sure you won't have another?' he said, returning to the decanter and refilling his glass.

Reinhard was overwhelmed with an unstoppable fondness; a light kiss for Irma and a massive hug for Stephanie

'You know George's situation,' the man said. 'I feel for him, really.

If it were just for that, I could possibly accept it. I even studied psychology, once. So I know some things may not be straightforward. But it's not that; they're together now and it is always the same whenever he comes, which, as I say, is now quite often. Not just September but once every couple of months and the stays seem to get longer each time, two, three, four days. He says it is for his factory, but I struggle to see what it is he does during his time here apart from take up Renate's time. Renate and I were great before. Now she's practically told me she feels a kind of calling to nurse him for life.'

Reinhard felt compelled to repeat the word: psychology.

'Why, yes. She dealt with the situation in the raw, so to speak. So he feels comfortable with her, only with her, apparently. And yet, the whole thing revolves around a couple of …

'A couple of what? I didn't realise it went this far,' Reinhard said.

The man poured himself another drink and sank back into his chair, the expiry of the leather seat's air pocket coinciding with the first thrust of the final gush of information. 'It's not so much Renate - at least that's what I hope because I still want her - but rather the circumstances that necessarily surrounded his early care that ties him to her. I don't know … the dressing rather than the dress, perhaps. Well, I just wish he'd find another nurse.'

Shortly afterwards, Gottfried drove up outside the house. Reinhard told Emiel, 'If George has a date, I won't hang around. That will be my friend Gottfried now. We're all meeting up the day after tomorrow anyway, as I told you, so I'll see him then. Thanks.'

'If you are sure.'

Gottfried's visit had left him very talkative and by the time he reached the point where he said he would have to fly to South America again next day, Reinhard felt a slight but indecent weightlessness, punctured by a sudden recall of his old love. He drove again while Gottfried started transcribing his notes. They travelled in silence. When the car pulled up outside the hotel, it was quite late but Gottfried immediately went for the telephone. While Gottfried cupped the mouthpiece, Reinhard said he'd visit Dieter, and again in the morning. 'It could be the last time before he comes out.'

'I'll definitely come with you tomorrow, Reinhard,' Gottfried said enthusiastically before starting to read over his story to the news desk.

Reinhard went to his room and crossed to the window with its rooftops view. He flicked at the blind, then turned away and walked into the bathroom where he expected to find a stranger. But there was no smile on his face and the front of his head was cool to the touch. It was the head of Reinhard Hänsel and as he turned back into the room and looked at the telephone, he was lifting the handset near the Hofbräuhaus Festhalle during his first Oktoberfest. Father and mother were still inside the huge marquee, cheering along with the *musikmeister* as the band on the centre stage blew, thumped and sang to raised steins, slopped beer, lolling heads and hands that waved the imaginary batons of a thousand conductors. His head was singing, too, with its own drum beat from his chest. He had been banned from contacting Stephanie so he could concentrate on exams but mum had lost her glasses - round by the bratwurst stand she thought - and dad was tired and just wanted to sit down and agreed that Reinhard had younger legs and could buy an ice-cream for his trouble. Reinhard's hand had trembled when he mouthed the letters of her name as he dialled her number. But it was just a signal. Three rings and down. He so wanted to know her number now.

22

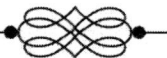

DIETER was fine. He had practically been told to go to sleep. Sister Schlem said his lad would be ready to leave hospital soon. Reinhard thought he would sit by Dieter's bed and read a few pages of Irma's book. As his hand hovered over the replaced phone, it began to tremble like it had outside the beer tent and his stomach contracted, like it had as he left that huge canvas marquee of merriment on the Theresienwiese site all those years ago. Reinhard snatched at the handset and phoned the hospital again. He thought of letting her phone ring just three times and imagine it was Stephanie but Irma spoke on two, throwing him somewhat. She said how pleasantly late it was. Reinhard told her about Dieter and she said that was wonderful.

'He's asleep now,' Reinhard added and was about to say it was time he was, too, but she cut in.

'The timing would be perfect, then,' she said.

The word 'then' entered his body and spread itself thickly: the timing would be perfect, then. On the way over, other words of hers about a dark green velvet pencil skirt and light green top she had bought pressed down on his spinning mind until they deepened and distorted through seductive soprano to husky tenor and depraved base. Reinhard went straight up to her room at the hospital and, by the time he stood outside her door, he wanted her to open it and for the both of them to turn and go straight back out. He didn't want to knock. He pressed on the door and peeped around. She was sitting on the bed brushing her hair, only a brief covering above the green pencil skirt she had talked of.

'Come and sit down,' she said, patting the counterpane.

Reinhard slowly pushed the door to its full extent, walked past the end of the bed, reached the window and turned around to face her.

'Irma!' he whispered hoarsely, aware that he was twiddling with his hands.

'Yes, Reinhard?'

He paced around the room, talking more or less to himself. Every time she went to say something, he held up a hand and said, 'I know.' Every Yes or No was the full stop he intended should destroy the web she was weaving. Reinhard did not want to hear anything, however subtle or reasonable. He also wanted to strangle his own thoughts before they re-emerged and gave his weakness strength. Bringing both hands up level with his chest and rubbing them vigorously while looking towards the door, he said abruptly, 'I promised I'd pop in and see Dieter when I came back from Enschede.'

'Plenty of time then ... he's asleep right now.'

'And I have this thing on my mind ...'

'I, too, Reinhard!'

He sighed quietly, turning towards the window. 'This thing from the past I must find out something tomorrow. Don't ask me about it now. Trust me, it's important to me.'

Irma got up and walked towards him, running a hand behind her hair and over the side of her neck. She then lowered her arms, bent her head forwards and walked slowly up to Reinhard before taking both his hands in hers. 'Then you need to be at peace with yourself,' she said. He did not move away. 'It's only fair,' he stumbled. 'You've been great during this trip, standing in at the bedside and all that. We must not -' They stood toe to toe. 'Come on!' he pleaded urgently, turning her away from the bedroom door. The grip on her shoulder lingered beyond the intention of spontaneous touch and he spun her into his arms, trying to believe it was Stephanie. She had Stephanie's eyes and the arrangement of her head, widish mouth, narrowing, sparkling eyes ... everything in that moment seemed to match. The perfume, which had slowed his advance around the room, smoothed things out and now cast its net more widely. Reinhard kissed her tenderly. It was some moments before he released his hands from a soft embrace that seemed to last an hour for every year he had known her. He wanted to explore his thoughts at that moment but pocketed his hands and stood back.

'You're lovely,' he managed.

Stephanie smiled more widely, leaving her lips parted. She stood by the doorway as Reinhard again moved towards it. He imagined it was Stephanie. 'You've been lovely all the time, every moment, every year.' She took her arms up, slowly, like a ballet dancer, and rested them around his neck. He allowed his hands to glide over her ears, using his thumbs to edge back strands of hair that had fallen over her eyes. 'You have always been lovely … but George,' he said agitatedly, jerking his hand away and replacing her arms by her side before moving towards the door again. Irma's face sagged. 'Don't say it, Reinhard,' she said, following him. Reinhard turned the door handle. Stephanie seemed to smile at him, a kind of consensual smile, he thought. The tension of his youthful uncertainty released its grip on his body as he turned away from the door and saw the look on her face. He was tempted to allow his arms and mouth freedom from imprisoned years but the sudden and quite loud knock at the door pleased one and irritated the other.

'Room service, Frau Satchell.'

She had forgotten. He threw her a jumper and disappeared into the toilet.

'Thank you. Put it down there please,' he heard her say, imagining she referred to the glass topped coffee table in the centre of the room.

'Enjoy your meal, Frau Satchell. Oh, I hope you don't mind my mentioning it but I was coming on duty when your boy came in that night. I am happy he is recovering so well. Good luck.'

'That is kind of you,' Irma said softly.

Reinhard came out of the toilet, hands miming applause. 'Such timing, Irma. How you can at this time think of food, it is amazing!' Irma laughed, dropping her head coyly. Reinhard held out his hand and said with a wink, 'Let's eat. This kind of food, it will not mature with time.'

They ate in virtual silence. All he knew was that what he had felt before the knock on the door had satisfied him and he wanted to go no further. It would be Stephanie or no one.

And Dieter needed him. Reinhard would go to him, accompanied by Irma or not.

'I understand,' she said sympathetically, after they had finished eating. She was obviously a little irritated but she completed dressing as she had intended. The green ensemble looked even more stunning to Reinhard now she had it on and they took the lift down to Dieter's ward. He lightly squeezed her arm on the way down, thanking her for being so understanding. His sponge rubber soles monitored his progress over the highly-polished linoleum squares of the corridor but he was listening to his heart, a heart that in the sensations he had experienced in the last half hour, made him recall yet again what a fool he had been over Stephanie. The energy of those times flowed through his body. And it was always at the same level as then. It was always the same, year after year, as if the small Thirties' interlude upon the globe that had ignited so much love and happiness between two young people had been condensed into something eternal, and there was no one or anything that could diminish it in the slightest. From the first time George had introduced his wife to him, Reinhard liked Irma. Always kind to him, and occasionally flirting with him, she had become someone he would look forward to see and when, on the few occasions they met unexpectedly, in a store or in the street, he would always acknowledge her pleasantly, momentarily remove his tinted glasses and smooth the front of his hair. George's Enschede trips had changed matters. The door was open and it required a giving-up-cigarettes strategy. Having an unopened cigarette packet in a pocket seemed to strengthen the resolve to keep it untouched. Some of the cables of decency had been loosened by what had happened recently but Reinhard was now more than ever certain that he could continue to consider Irma as a safe substitute for the absent Stephanie. He should keep smiling and saying hello. Just be happy in her presence. But nothing more.

23

THE concrete coal-bunker helped Reinhard lift himself back to his childhood bedroom, with a pocket full of apples. It appeared to be further down from this cold top, further up and further down. He could taste the fruit. He looked up at the quarter light on the side of the building. It was small but it looked open. Reinhard was going back; a tight squeeze then home early without a key. A staggered down pipe. Same as before. He'd shinned this just for devilment, to show off, to equal brother Siegfried. He got a good foothold and tested its ability to hold downward pressure. It held. The quarter light opened easily, in went his hand and the the main window became his front door. Taking a deep breath, he made his way downstairs, entered the lounge and drew the curtains before making for the small bookcase that contained the album. The slim beam from his torch lit its brownish red covers. He skipped through the pages of war images and text and examined the book properly, reading about Rainer's childhood. What he wanted was photographs. Two pages near the centre had pictures, though two appeared to be missing. He snatched the photographs from his pocket. They fitted. There was another photograph on the page showing virtually the same scene in the picture Reinhard had. The photographs would probably have formed a trio beneath which was a single legend: Gestapo Seven - Death to them all. Reinhard counted the men. Eight with the man on the ground, probably Fritz. He looked closely at the third picture, but the left hand of the pig was almost hidden.

REQUIREMENTS OF GUILT

Reinhard turned the page, where the prose thickened: '*Fritz died at the hands of Nazis. He was murdered. Werner took the pictures. He told me about it following a shooting incident in the town. They came out gradually to join two who had dragged Fritz out on to the quadrangle. It was treated as a new toy - this wood contraption. It amused them. One click on the camera recorded it. Fritz had to stand to attention, right arm raised in the Nazi salute. If his arm fell half an inch, a bell would ring - and in would go the shiny boots. Another officer interrupted. He shouted up to two or three other people being held at Gestapo 7 and they had better hope the bell did not sound and confirm their own destination. If it went off, so too would they - off east with all the others captured that night, which included Rainer and Ingrid. Fritz lasted just ten minutes. He died of a heart attack.*'

Reinhard studied the photographs again. A ring like the one he'd seem on the finger of the Standartenführer was there on the officer standing third from the left, who could well be the same café führer. But he could see no detail on the ring. He needed the negatives to enlarge the image. On the ground, near the edge of the frame, was what seemed to be a crude construction of his *heil-holz*. Reinhard thumbed on through the book. On the inside of the padded cover he found an old style key with its ring end in a roughly hewn recess. He swung the torch around looking for anything that might take such a key. It did not have to be a door, he realised and he was soon looking everywhere at everything. He went into the home's large kitchen with its adjoining scullery, then into the hall. He thought about leaving just as his beam caught what looked like a cloakroom under the stairs next to the big clock. Inside was a trench coat. It was hanging in front of an inner door and with some excitement he saw the door had a large keyhole. He dropped the coat and rammed the iron into the recess. It fitted and he clicked it open. Almost at his feet when he pulled the door open was a set of stairs leading downwards to a platform about fifteen feet below. He entered the shaft and reached the platform that gave access to another door. Beyond this was a few more steps down to a long narrow basement room with roughly whitewashed ceiling and walls, brick and stonework mixed on both sides. At one end, to the left of a double door, was a complex of steel cabinets and a desk. He had not noticed it at first but as he moved slowly down the room he saw an enormous wall-mounted board that looked like some kind of historiography. It was a picture strip of heads and shoulders, linked by a thick black line - portraits that only rarely showed a full face and in a couple of instances only the back of the head was visible. He recognised one face in the gallery, and quickly surmised that they might be the heads of the offending officers and possibly taken at the same time as the picture he had in his pocket. From each of the rogues in the gallery sprang two further thick black lines, central to each of the portraits - lines that went upwards to a box enclosing the name, and downwards to another box, exactly the same size as the photograph and etched in grey, white or black. Beneath this, yet another box, identical in size to the name box and containing a date. Five of the boxes beneath the photographs were black, the first one was white and the penultimate in the row was grey. Only the white and grey boxes were undated. Beneath the row were two maps, one, a part of an area north east of Madrid and the other, Asuncion in Paraguay. The whole board, he now saw, was headed *Operation New Festfortag*. He labelled his discovery Death Row. The black boxes - probably death on the noted date; the grey one - marked out for death; and the white one - this could mean that the name and whereabouts were unknown. If his theory was correct, coloured pins on a large map related to the last known location of the two officers still alive. The named grey officer had been spotted in Paraguay at one time, but there was no name under the white officer, although Asuncion was linked to his box. The cabinets were not locked and he feverishly searched for negatives. There were hundreds of letters, documents and photographs, detailing what looked like a search network. HJB was methodical, a touch of the WVHA business enterprises efficiency, Reinhard thought, and the elaborate index gave him what he wanted. Everything in the file of photographs before him was also simply and effectively arranged - such a formation as to briefly return his searching fingers to Oranienburg. HJB probably believed these officers caused Fritz's death and indirectly Rainer's and Ingrid's. HJB would probably record their deaths when he came to know them and take appropriate action. He looked at the negatives and pocketed them.

    Reinhard had once been told that he had one of the most efficient filing systems in the Third Reich and that his application to the tasks he was called upon to perform, the records it was his duty to organise, and the initiative he in general brought to the job, had been at least partly responsible for the SS taking over camp administration as the industries became such big business. When Reinhard thought about this kind of thing, in his early days in London, he even sweated over the possibility that in some oblique way his very dedication had contributed to a decision on the so-called final solution of the Jewish question. It's the way he had been, overloaded with guilt and condemnation, what a psychologist might have concluded was a prima facie case of moral anxiety. The trip back onto German soil had taken him out of himself in so many ways. The fact was that Stephanie was a few hundred miles closer and this had really lightened him up and given him an unstoppable resolve to try to meet up with her. Of course, there was this other thing to sort out, and it looked like he might struggle with the outcome, but Stephanie was now a powerful personal objective that had belatedly leapt out of a long slumber.

He opened double doors. At first, he could make nothing of the sight before him and very little of the trace smell. He swept the torch around a room twice as big as the one he had just left. Down the centre ran a narrow gauge rail at the far end of which was a platform with a set of bogie wheels. Suspended above the rail, at about the half-way point, was a number of metal objects. To the left was a cupboard and further into the gloom Reinhard could make out a table and chair. Fear hugged him like a bout of angina. He had a loathsome tingling at his back and there were sensations that distorted his body. He seemed to have difficulty closing his mouth and the torch's erratic movement served to make his fear the more acute. He found himself gulping uncontrollably as the beam danced its way over nothing whole … oven hinges … platform straps … metal plates … chain links. But there was a huge and heavily pixelated face with eyes that looked at Reinhard, despondent, wretched, wasted eyes. Quietness screamed. Strangely, he felt he wanted to join in. He stepped forward without wanting to move. He turned to face someone who wasn't there. The smell grew ever stronger and he saw the smiling face of the Kapo, standing by the blackened door, reaching down with the air of someone lifting potatoes.

'This is nothing. They are nothing. It is just work, and it is work that has to be done, and more speedily. Orders are orders. But who needs encouragement with this lot,' the Kapo sneers. 'The decisions have already been made; we are just following orders,' repeats the Kapo, as if he had noted something. Reinhard looks away, the bolts tighten. Reinhard shouts, 'Orders are …'

He turned to the Kapo but he wasn't there. '… not everything,' he whispered towards the oven-like apparatus. He imagined he saw a man topple backwards and a hand move against a foot. He heard a smell. Falling against the door, he dropped his torch. He wanted the darkness. He felt insane, yet a sudden calmness took him to the point of laughing. He was back on the pavement, crouching down as mother strode on to the shops believing him to be behind her. Exciting fear. He hurried from the room and up the iron ladder into the hall cupboard area, up the stairs, out of the window and into the front garden.

The Kapo had had it all wrong. Reinhard wished he had told him so.

24

THE tape yielded cryptic stuff, easier to understand because Reinhard had been keen on the game, and still played when he got the chance. Reading from a police transcript, Gottfried said: 'Bonaventure is on after ven-ven. Difficulties for the O's pairing overcome by 21-9, 10-21, 21-10.' There had also been some small talk, Anton saying he would have to get an early night for the flight.

'Well, it's tighter than we ever played out in Oranienburg but those numbers sound like a table tennis score,' Reinhard suggested. They mixed memory with detective work, the old days to begin with being far more productive. They would have talked after the bar had closed but Gottfried had to fly to Caracas. 'I'm following this one to the end,' he said.

Reinhard studied his friend's powerful frame as they mounted the stairs. Although he could no longer share Gottfried's enthusiasm for the old craft, Reinhard was able to admire his single-mindedness, his ability to keep advancing his daily routine with apparent confidence, because of his fresh resolve. Too easily in the past Reinhard could feel compromised. Now he had a mission that he could not wait to get to just as soon as he had tracked himself down and fathomed the mystery. His thoughts blotted out much of Gottfried had to say but as he reached the top of the stairs, Reinhard did hear that the police had established from the tape that Anton, Heinz and Karl were probably the three people who were said to have taunted Dieter. Maybe they didn't actually push Dieter but their twisting of the truth had led to the accident.

*

It was a simple printing job that could be undertaken by any photographer in Germany but Reinhard needed privacy. He could not face anyone with this negative; he could hardly face himself. His nervousness intensified as he approached the outer limits of Hannover where Gottfried had offered the use of a darkroom he sometimes used, and Reinhard was at near fever pitch as he pulled up outside the building. He entered a general store and bought a bottle of coke, placing the side of its metal top against the edge of a low brick wall and brought the palm of his hand sharply down upon it, sending the cap flying across the pavement. He took a swig and carried the bottle into the building. Inside the darkroom, he took out the negative. He wished he were sitting with Gottfried in the plane en route to South America, concerned only with the possible wrongdoing of these misguided Revisionists. He set up the enlarger, pulled down a yellow box and switched over to the red lamp that set a tone for the work ahead that gave him as many doubts as the shadows around him. He took out a sheet of paper from the black plastic wrapping inside the box, dropping it clumsily before finally trapping it under the steel frame. Almost simultaneously he switched on the enlarger while fiddling the *heil-holz* into focus. He waited half a minute, shading an area with a hand that needed little persuasion to feather. He stared at the image that discharged its truth as pus. Very probably it was the product of his accursed drawing, the primitive but lethally descriptive lines that, had he not been so anxious to impress, so boot-lickingly obsequious, would have remained as indifferent pencil marks on a scruffy piece of paper idly to be rolled into a little hard ball of rubbish and flicked into oblivion or accidentally machine-washed into fluffy insignificance.

Reinhard fixed the second negative to enlarge the extended right hand of the man he reckoned was the Standartenführer. Displaying scant regard to good darkroom practice, he raced ahead to the point where he was lifting the edge of the developing tray up and down to send waves of the solution backwards and forwards across the increasingly detailed print. A second hot flush made his face and neck prickle as the image emerged. The dragon was there! It was the ring. Very little doubt indeed; it was the café Standartenführer. The clammy feeling would not recede and soon he was covered in sweat. Reinhard blinked a path to the window on the print, to the left of the officer's extended hand. Ignoring the tongs, he plunged his fingers into the developing tray and snatched at the print. He rushed it close to his face. Though not fully in view, he was sure he could see her, leaning against the half-shuttered window on the upper floor, she of Crematoria V and, of course ... the cafe girl, which was why ... Stephanie ... attracted to her ... Frau Festfortag ... Rainer's girl, the woman in Birkenau on that day that changed everything. The beautiful café face, here grey and soon to turn plastic white, the face that was engraved on his mind, was looking at him again. Alive. Perplexed, frightened and cursed, yet without any doubt that Reinhard's mind could concede, alive. He sagged against the table, knocking off the tray and paper. His mind filled with the probable truth, becoming clear with the speed of book pages being thumb released, a horror book he had helped to write. Just to think: once there had been journalistic pride in creating respect with words, then, following a visit to the darkrooms of Berlin's *Telegraphen Union* and a subsequent Nürnberg rally assignment, foul utterances became natural and fulfilling accomplices to the seeming four-dimensional pageant of spellbinding passion. Here she was looking at him now. As it was, with her there and he, Reinhard, standing in front of her, she could be saved; for she died later. Reinhard sank to his knees, holding the dripping photograph out in front of him, the poor wretched girl weeping out her anguish. He brought the print to his face and kissed the dots around the window. For a moment, he felt elation. While this poor woman's life had been so tragically ended at No 5, her memory had been preserved. She had been found and embraced. Reinhard snatched at the print again, but it was darkened beyond recognition. He repeated the process, this time fixing the image. There she was. Frau Festfortag was permanent. Reinhard would keep her. Frame her face. Talk to her sometimes. Respect her. For he knew now he had influenced her 'selection'.

He left the darkroom still clutching the print and leant against the corridor wall. So, this was it. He had acted as judge as well as executioner. She had gone to the concentration camp and he had sort of pursued her, or so it might be said, and helped kill her there. HJB had said a couple would have been sent there if the *heil-holz* - *his heil-holz* - sounded off. It must have done so. There was the dead man.

Retribution had had to be exacted. All his years of effort had been wasted. The intervening years had been impostors, swallowing up time he should have spent in death. A corridor anaesthetised by midweek silence gave his presence the prominence of rampant bacteria. He re-entered the darkroom. He released the negative from the enlarger, slid it next to the others and picked up his stuff from the bench. The mother. The son. Who? Where? Shadows crossed his mind as he stared at the fixer and a pair of scissors. He walked to the end of the corridor, entering an anti-room and sat on the edge of a low window recess.

The arrangement of this part of the room reminded him of the side of Dieter's bedroom and of the *Dictionary of Modern Prose Usage* he'd idly glanced at before setting off for Hannover, and the author's attempts to determine which of two alternatives was correct - 'I have read many deutsche (or deutschen) novels' - and how crass such a question could be.

*

One of his suitcases had remained unopened in the corner of the hotel room. Now Reinhard opened it and almost immediately discovered he had mistakenly thrown Dieter's desk diary in with other items. He flicked over several pages of the diary, skimming entries he imagined might be very private. He turned to the front, read Dieter's details and flipped to the inside back. Two scribbled words rushed up from the page of telephone numbers: Karl and Heinz. Beneath their names was an address. He shot out of bed. He looked at his watch and reached for the telephone. Gottfried was travelling via Heathrow. There still might be time. The call from Le Bouget was pounced on. 'Gottfried, thank goodness I caught you.'

'You almost didn't. Some hitch with a red light has delayed take-off. Still...'

'This Karl and Heinz. I know where they might be heading. Their names are in one of Dieter's diaries. Remember Bonneventure? Take a note of this address in Gasparillo, Trinidad. After ven-ven, perhaps? Just a chance, eh? And, Gottfried, it came to me: the O's pairing. Auschwitz is the German word for that place, Oswięçim. The score could be a code for date and time. Perhaps the first set of numbers, 21-9, meant September 21 (Sept being the ninth month) and the second set of numbers 21 minutes after ten on that morning.

Or perhaps target blocks, 21 and 10. Block 10 had been notorious and Block 21, well, I think I remember that that was about opposite. Well, it's something to go on.'

When Reinhard returned the handset, he was shaking.

25

IRMA, Gottfried and Reinhard followed Sister Schlem to Hardterwald Ward. Reinhard peered around her white overall to scan the ward but the bed was empty.

'It's all right, Herr Hänsel, Dieter's in the day room, over there,' the Sister pointed beyond the final pair of beds. 'He is out only for a little while today. Longer tomorrow, hopefully, and then in a couple of days he should be about ready to leave.'

They found Dieter in a surprisingly alert state, listening to the radio. Reinhard was surprised at the strength of Dieter's clasp as they shook hands. Irma bent down and kissed Dieter, whose face, while still some way from showing its normal bloom, looked healthy compared with how it had been. Reinhard introduced Gottfried but Gottfried said he could stay only a short while.

'Newspaper duty's always calling,' he said, shaking Dieter's hand. 'I'll be glad when I've had enough! Good to see you on the mend.' Irma stood back, giving the men their space. After a while, Dieter said, 'Actually, I do feel a bit tired. I'm sorry. I was just thinking of going back to lie on the bed. Perhaps you'll escort me, Dad?' Dieter said, looking round for his crutches.

'Certainly, Sir,' Reinhard said, bowing majestically, projecting a crooked arm for him to hold on to. Gottfried took up a similar position on the other side of Dieter.

'You must be tired, too, Dad.'

Reinhard indicated with his forefinger and thumb. 'So much has happened. But first we must get you out. In a few days, the Sister says - and then, it is off to the Harz. That will be with Irma's aunt, in Goslar. It's all arranged.'

'It's so good of Amelia.'

'She is really looking forward to caring for you,' said Irma, stepping up level with the trio. 'Me, too. I'm planning to stay on for a while, if Reinhard agrees. We've got on well together, haven't we Dieter?' she said.

Dieter thanked her. 'Where is George?'

They explained and Reinhard added, 'Gottfried says you can also go for a spell with his cousin in eastern Poland. It's a wonderful place, I'm told. So ther-ra-putic by all accounts. That, too, is all arranged.'

'Blimey, it's not so bad being injured, after all!' He said it sleepily, though, and as soon as he had levered himself on to the bed, his eyes began to droop. Gottfried left for his appointment. Reinhard and Irma stayed only a few minutes longer. It was all the time they had before George had to be picked up. At the station, Reinhard thought George looked a little flushed as he said, 'Sorry I was out when you called, Reinhard. That would have been a nice surprise. Renate didn't tell me about your visit until just before I left for the train this morning but it wouldn't really have been possible to come back with you; I was out for the whole evening and was a bit tired when I returned.'

Reinhard left it at that, quickly filling George in on Dieter's condition and the plans for his convalescence. This prompted Irma to repeat her plan to stay on to be able to help out in the Harz. Still thinking of George, Reinhard said, 'This is very good of you Irma, but you've done enough already.'

'George won't miss me for a week more, will you George? George is so good at occupying himself. Besides, you're trying to sort out another problem, Reinhard.'

'Yes, but Dieter comes first.'

'Precisely. And I am a woman. I can help mother him!'

Reinhard said, 'It is true that this problem is certainly something I should like to sort out. And Gottfried can help perhaps.'

Irma spoke with the charitable air of someone willing to put herself out. 'Besides, I have been reading to Dieter in hospital - a hell of a good book, I must say.' Then, glancing in Reinhard's direction, she said, 'We've reached a very exciting part.' Reinhard ignored the symbolism.

George ventured, 'Well there! That appears to be settled. It seems right. I want things to be right, the way they should be. Never mind my having to return. Things have a way of righting themselves if they take the course that seems proper. And this does.' Both Irma and Reinhard came forth with resigned affirmations. George stressed, 'I want to see Dieter. When can we go?'

'You can see him later today; in the meanwhile, I'll show you Hannover,' Irma said, adding that it would give her a chance to look at the fashion houses. They would bus to the shops.

George, Irma and Reinhard contented themselves with their own thoughts as they walked towards the Mercedes for the short journey to the Bahnhof Hotel where they had a coffee and talked about Dieter. Reinhard excused himself and on the way to and from the toilet, he thought of the bugged line message and the paradise island that could be the nerve centre of a hideous attempt to wipe out an international truth. Then there were the actual disciples of the new and dishonest creed who had sprung out at him from the newspaper cutting back in England, malcontents who probably included Anton and this Karl and Heinz. Then there was the right-wingers involved in the street fracas he'd read about that had put Dieter in hospital. As he regained his seat, Irma's poised body on the barstool formed an image that again took him back to Thirties' Berlin. It was getting to the point where Stephanie was practically taking up residence in his optic nerve.

*

George told Reinhard he had enjoyed the city excursion when they met up again in the hotel. When Irma appeared, she had hold of two bulging carrier bags. She sat in the back on the journey to the hospital, peering ahead between George and Reinhard. Anticipating a change in the flow of traffic on approaching lights, she leaned forward on one hand close to the gear lever. Reinhard straightened up and saw her in the interior mirror. Irma, now lying back with her head on one side, hands folded together on her lap, had the look of an innocent who knew magic had been applied. They both knew magic had been applied and he had to admit he was tempted to trail his hand back between the seats. He still felt insulated though. It was only flirting. George was taking in the view. With what Reinhard knew, and Irma almost certainly didn't, and considering his own mostly lonely existence, physically he could justify much but his heart had let him down once before and if his head were to do any deciding for him now, that should tell him not to let down either Stephanie or George. As they neared the hospital car park, George re-focussed on the immediate future. He said, 'The Harz idea is fine with me, really, Irma. It depends on Reinhard.'

Reinhard hesitated, calling himself into question. What was he doing? Where was he going? It was true that Irma's offer would provide him with time to try to sort out his problems. Yet Irma's presence, especially without George, would be dangerous. Perhaps he would take George at his word; things had a way of righting themselves if they took the course that seemed proper. It seemed right to follow through what he had discovered and Irma's presence would certainly enable him more time comfortably to do this. He would just have to deal with the fact that this argument could apply to both his problems.

'That's settled then,' Irma said, as if reading his mind.

They collected Dieter from hospital and, thanks to generous prior arrangement by Gottfried, a room with an annex was available at the hotel for George, Irma and Dieter for the three days before Irma's aunt in Goslar returned from a business trip to Brussels when Dieter could start some real convalescence. They had a meal in a nearby restaurant Reinhard had sought out for himself and Irma. Even though Dieter looked remarkably refreshed, they didn't linger afterwards, Irma insisting that they all had an early night. George seemed content to leave them all to it and travel back to England alone. However, Reinhard took him to the station for the train to Düsseldorf, wondering whether George might be tempted to divert to Enschede.

Reinhard was anxious to resume his enquiries but stayed with Dieter the rest of the day and, while they were having their evening meal, Irma thoughtfully suggested that Reinhard could in the morning get on to some of his personal business while she and Dieter spent time listening to music, playing cards and just talking. Reinhard smiled his thanks.

26

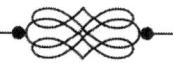

THE day got up in a mood. The sky grizzled before breakfast and as soon as Reinhard set out, ready to be a reporter again, rain had begun a slow descent which left him pretty well soaked before he gained the protection of a shelter on the edge of what looked like open common land. It was inquiry time. Questions about a shoot-out following the arrival of special detachments to cleanse the area before Himmler arrived in the spring of 1943. Who in this area had lost a child in bizarre circumstances, a child there one moment and not the next? Who was the mother? Where was she now? Towards a group of houses to the side of an open space was a hedge-ringed grass area with several discoloured, rectangular shapes that might recently have been used for a visiting fair or some community event. As he walked towards the homes he murmured softly, 'Sun-powered life, sodden emptiness.'

A severe looking woman answered his knock at the central house of a group of five. She stared back over his shoulder before saying she had seen nothing although she had heard the noise, a mighty din one night just as she was preparing a meal. Someone had let off a flare in the path of an armoured truck. There was apparently a vicious and frightening response. 'Frau Dilsen will know more,' she said, pointing back over the green to a detached house between trees. 'That's her place, right of the church.' She had known the people in a nearby house that had been virtually blown apart in a massive explosion. Her finger picked out a gap in another line of homes.

Reinhard returned his gaze to Frau Dilsen's home. When he reached it, a woman emerged as he opened the garden gate. She was carrying a teacloth that she put over her shoulder as she walked briskly down the path to meet him. She readily responded to his enquiry.

'It was a terrible night. Frau Wimmer's pain was the greater because this was just a silly sideshow in the crazy circus that was the war. Frau Wimmer lost her husband and three children that night and her sister went mad all because of a stray bullet. It's not easy to forget things like that.'

Reinhard leant on the fence. He did not want to appear personally involved but his posture seemed to offend her and he pulled himself back up and sank his hands deep into his trouser pockets. She seemed just as upset by this bearing and self-consciously he pulled out his hands and put them by his side. She smiled and told Reinhard that the bullet, or whatever it was, had hit a huge gasoline tank Kurt Wimmer kept at the side of the house for his pre-war sport of flying. The tank went up in a fireball and, eventually, the house with it. She said: 'We thought at first that a bomb had dropped on the property, so fierce was the explosion and fire. At the end of it all, his wife Gertrud Wimmer - Gertrud and a babbling sister, Traudi - were all that was left of a very happy night over there. I'd been there earlier in the evening. Ilse, their eldest girl, had just passed her piano examinations and Wilhelm was enjoying the attention on his sixth birthday. The Wimmers had four children: Dietrich, who was three or four, was upstairs and he didn't stand a chance. Well, actually, they found only three bodies, but I'm surprised anything, let alone anyone, was found. You could feel the heat from over here.'

Reinhard spoke hurriedly: 'I'm doing a series of articles for my magazine about some of the agonies of the war that have persisted to this day. Our information is that a boy went missing from this town when soldiers checked out the area before the visit of a high-ranking officer. Do you know who this boy might have been? Only you mentioned just three of Frau Wimmer's four children were found. She brought the tea cloth down from her shoulder like a race marshal and moved to end the conversation.

'Though matters like this are impossible to forget, I think it is best not to speak of them, much less put the matter in print. Writing articles about this boy is not going to bring him back now, any more than an article about my husband would bring poor Manfred back to me from stinking Stalingrad, frozen or otherwise.'

Reinhard withdrew from the tears. This was not going to be more cream for a bloated stomach, like it had sometimes been with the agency. This story was personal to him and the parents, whoever and wherever they were, and to the largish woman who was also caught up in the family of people whose lives had been twisted by the incident. HJB. Rainer. Plastic white. Because he did not come as family, or was at this time unwilling to admit his involvement, he felt bulky and surplus, the interfering journalist he was pretending to be, someone on the outside trying to look in even though the truth of the matter was that he was on the inside all right and would so love to be out of it altogether. He tried other houses but drew blanks. He almost felt glad. He was going through the motions. Yet if he didn't ask, he might cheat himself. He sat down on a seat around the green. A few left-over balloons were acting up around a tree in one corner, jostling irritably in a gathering breeze on their tight reigns. He wandered away towards a large house covered on one side with glistening ivy, green and reddish. The house looked worse than HJB's. An odd-looking woman opened the door after peering out from one of two cluttered windows. She did not seem normal and he wanted to turn around and go. Rain dripped noisily from every leaf, splashing into a muddy puddle outside the front door. Reinhard was left to stand, straddling the puddle, as she replied to his question: 'I remember a boy. He came here and we played. We played on the floor over there with some yellow wallpaper,' she said, pointing a bony hand towards a corner of a room into which she now disappeared. Reinhard followed. 'We played while they fought out there. We cut out planets and stars and had a fine game, until he won my Saturn. He could have Pluto or Mercury or even Big Jupe but not my rings. He ran out with all he had left, one of the stars and even that was captured.'

'Captured? How do you mean?'

The funny woman drew closer and breathed a rancid gust towards his face. 'I peeped through the window and saw two people, a man and a woman, grab the boy and question him. He must have said he wanted Saturn and everyone knew the rings were mine whatever happened. So they took him away for punishment. All three went with the soldiers who also probably asked about Saturn.'

Reinhard nodded, thinking wildly about the star, the yellow star.

'I see,' he said.

'Children must understand,' she counselled.

'Where did the soldiers take the boy? And this couple?'

'Away!'

Reinhard endorsed the indignation she expressed. 'Well, they would, I can see that. Did you see where they took them?'

'Serves them all right. My rings. They were my rings, don't you see. Look, I still have them - here,' she said excitedly, shuffling over to a sideboard and bringing out a small, seemingly much-used presentation box, its lid held in place with an elastic band. She opened the box and took out two rings - an engagement ring and a wedding ring.

Reinhard continued his mock anguish: the boy should have known, you did right to insist, and the couple outside did right to punish him. 'What, was he cuffed around the ear or something?'

'No, no, no, no. Oh dear, no,' she said, her head bobbing. 'He and this couple - his mother and father more than likely, on the streets and not looking after him much, I'd say - they were all bundled into the back of this dark truck,' she said gleefully, laughing widely, mocking the scene she seemed still to witness as she gazed towards drapes of dirty linen behind which, at one time long ago, had probably afforded her clear sight of the scene she had just described but which now gave only the slightest resemblance of being a window at all.

'The truck left and went up the Rinterstrasse. The star was big and bright but I had the real gems here. The police knew that, the day they came to see me about him.'

'Him?'

She twisted her face and reached for a cardboard tube and pulled out a newspaper cutting onto her table and flattened it as she smoothed both hands across a story and picture of a man.

'Your husband?'

She sat down. 'We had been married a week when he died,' she said, smiling in folds as she scanned the cutting. She went back to the table and shook the cardboard tube until another, smaller newspaper cutting emerged, an advertisement showing a number of rings. Two were circled.

*

Reinhard returned to Father Dohl and re-engaged the leather seat. Reinhard asked outright about the razed house. The minister said he remembered the incident. The property had belonged to the Wimmer family. Four of them died in the resultant fire, Kurt Wimmer, two daughters and a son. Another son was never found.

Reinhard went to interrupt but settled back as Father Dohl continued, 'I knew the Wimmers, not directly through the church, although they did sometimes attend services, but mainly through their work at the social club. For years, many of us at St Nicholas marvelled at their energy. Frau Wimmer, Gertrude Wimmer, helped in so many ways, and Herr Wimmer was chairman of the committee and our handyman. Gertrude used to help organise and take part in the entertainments. So happy, you know. Even today, I can easily see the smiling Wimmers and visualise the despair of that night, the contrast, the misery. There is a sister, Fräulein Traudi Kursten, but I did not know her at the time - and I suppose I still really do not know her. She was also there the night of the fire; there were some birthday celebrations going on. I fear she was unable to hold on to God at this time, unlike her sister whose eyes showed the hurt, but whose hands were clasped in the Lord Jesus rather than in anguish. Fräulein Kursten, in some strange way, regarded the whole tragedy as hers. I have listened but have never fully understood. You see, I'm afraid she has since then had to be given an extra helping hand through life. Some of us need this, you know. Anyway, Frau Wimmer lives somewhere in Niedersachsen. I'll give you her address. It is not far from a military base run by the British. I remember that, because she told me she felt she would always be protected in the future if her own countrymen tried to finish off what was left of a once tremendously happy family.'

The reply to Reinhard's blurted question caught helplessly on Father Dohl's lips.

'I remember one of the girls was called Ilse. The other was ... yes, Erda. And there were two boys, Wilhelm and ... I think Dieter.'

27

REINHARD kicked out at a stone. If it struck the poplar's trunk, Bayern would be ahead. It just missed, like so often. He smiled. Even years ago, on the rare occasions when he did score the first goal in their frequent pretend football matches, Siegfried would soon equalise, and invariably go into the lead. Never mind. He bent down and selected another two stones and looked about. With the coast clear, Reinhard threw them one after the other at the same tree. They both hit its base, smack in the middle. There, beat that, bruv!

Reinhard stayed with Dieter for a couple of days before leaving Irma to continue little trips with his lad out into the Harz countryside. Now he wanted to get back to Hannover and hopefully to be able to tell Dieter some good news. The sooner he sorted things out, the sooner he could return. He had explained a little of what was bothering him but nothing about Frau Wimmer. They hugged and Reinhard gave Irma a light kiss and a quick squeeze of the hand. He took the Mercedes slowly down the gravel drive passed Amelia's log-sided home, running a hand over his head from front to back, and exhaling a long, slow funnel of air through tight lips. He suddenly feared that he was starting to interchange Irma and Stephanie in his mind and the thought that one might become the other filled him with guilt. As he gained the main road north, his pedal foot sought instantaneous travel but was eased back to a steady determination to make sure he reached Dieter's mother. Yet as he drove he wished his headlong flight to Bad Tölz and SS training had not gone so well and that Stephanie had been the good inner reason why he should have felt immediately repulsed by what he pursued. Should he not put that experience to good use now and steer clear of something he felt urged to do but which would in all probability not turn out well? True, he had gone to Bad Tölz to build a future whereas this mission was to try to repair a past. He'd joined the new order against the wishes of his father, who often spat at the regime while mother stirred the gravy. Reinhard had ignored their advice, and that of brother Siegfried and his beloved Stephanie. How, he kept asking himself, was a regimented future more attractive than a relaxed present, how were disturbing dictums better than letters from friends, belligerent Him preferable to peaceable Her?

In Hannover, Reinhard made straight for the psychiatric unit. He paused by large, iron gates. Black clouds were darkening the scene and the wind was getting up. He hated the wind. It tore at a group of trees off to the right where, for a moment, restless branches formed a mournful human feature, some birds forming the toothy centre of a face. Reinhard hated order now as much as the wind. Even sign posting annoyed him. He saw the sign, Kirsthofklinic, and thought of turning about and taking an earlier side street, to find his own way. But sometimes, like now as a storm threatened, principles could chill to the marrow and he continued.

'I'm looking for Peter Fortsheim,' Reinhard announced at reception in a voice that mirrored his disquiet. 'Will you tell him I'm a friend of Father Dohl. I am Reinhard Hänsel.'

The receptionist got through to the registrar on a white phone, marshalled to the left foreground of a square formed by three other coloured phones and guarded on one side by a wire basket, empty apart from a single pink sheet, and on the other by a box file with the letters A-L on the spine. Ah, there was a crack in the efficiency of the place right here at reception: where was the file that carried on from L? M for Missing! He looked around the hanger-like reception area. Perhaps all the patients with surnames from Herr and Frau Mad onwards had escaped. Or perhaps letters had had to be sent off to relatives detailing the sorrow the clinic felt in such unfortunate circumstances that had resulted in their death through pneumonia, say, a heart attack or tuberculosis or some pulmonary failure or mystery virus, even suicide while expressing the assurance that all had been done for the patient that could humanly have been done and offering to help the family in disposal of the, er, body.

Peter Fortsheim led the way along a corridor and opened a door that bore the simplest of legends - a blue circle. The office was simple, too, its furniture dominantly pine wood with tubular limbs. There were stacks of plastic trays, and boring brown carpet and magnolia walls.

'Please sit down,' he said, exactly right. 'What can I do for you?' completing the perfection.

Reinhard wanted to push over a large filing cabinet and daub the walls with a dotty pattern but said gently, 'I would like to have a word with Fräulein Traudi Kursten. I am a freelance journalist writing the first of what I hope will be a series of articles on how ordinary people tried to oppose the war-time regime and record how some suffered as a result. Incidents way below the magnitude of July 20 but nevertheless big enough for the individual and certainly something that needs to be told since it is becoming increasingly clear that there was a lot more small-time opposition to Hitler than has ever been officially recorded. Not the titled leader of organised resistance but a forgotten Frau Defiance, so to speak. My understanding is that Fräulein Kursten could feature.'

The registrar stared straight ahead to a clock on the wall. It looked like a no but he said, 'Of course I will have to observe but she will not know I am there. The moment she shows any sign of distress, however, you must leave by the red door. *Verstehen Sie?*'

Reinhard nodded and again trod a corridor path behind the klinic official.

'Wait, please, I will get her for you.'

Her face would be pale. She would stare at him, and beyond, without blinking. She would be dressed loosely, in off white. Her hair would be damp and her hands cold. She would wear slippers, shuffle across the room, unafraid, aggressively even. Any greeting would be met with silence. Later, babbling might be accompanied by twitching, but it would return to reference room silence. Her mind would have sealed everything in. But the woman who came through the door resembled his vision of her not at all. Her greeting put the finishing touches to what appeared to be a complete misjudgement.

REQUIREMENTS OF GUILT

'Hello, I don't get many visitors. How nice of you to come. You are...?'

'I am Reinhard.'

She extended her right arm from behind her back, transferring a soft toy, a small bear, to her free hand. She asked him to sit down.

'Thank you,' Reinhard said matter-of-factly, reflecting on his misjudgement. He explained his position and added: 'I am doing a story on the war, and think you can help me. I'm trying to find out about the explosion at ...'

'You,' she shouted. And then, with diminishing volume, went on: '... are trying to find out about the explosion,' the final word trailing off to almost nothing. Her eyes indicated a startled abstraction, almost nothingness. For a while, she continued to moon ahead, her mouth slightly open, everything motionless except for her right hand, which jerked a smoothing palm over the head of the bear. Reinhard was about to reassure her when the woman, who now looked rather old and unattractive, began muttering, incoherently at first, but gradually making some sort of sense as the frequency of joined up words increased.

'No one blames me ... they cannot. They see no guilt. In the house, but not be in my mind. Those who find me blameless were not there ... it is so important ... how I thought of it at the time ... just before ... I did not act ... let the moment go to attend to a button on a dress I did not like nor ever wore again ... a piece of cloth, not a living soul ... no reason to go that anyone will know ... I know ... I felt something but hesitated like you'd drink that last mouthful of tea and miss the bus ... had I gone then, he would have been safe ... to cuddle teddy.' As she murmured the final words, she turned to the somewhat grubby yellow soft toy and said, much more clearly, now with tears in her eyes and with her nose burying into what remained of one of its ears, 'Blackface won't be long.'

The name turned into an ice pick that attacked Reinhard. He shuffled his feet before asking her, 'Blackface, did you say? Who is Blackface?'

'His brother!' She gushed out the words irritably, stroking the bear's head alternately with her own hair, which now he noticed did look damp.

'Yes, of course,' he said, bending down to look closely into the small buttons on either side of a well-worn nose. Reinhard swallowed hard as he gathered the strength to ask: 'Who has Blackface, then?'

Fräulein Kursten sighed, looking up to the ceiling, and announced with weary annoyance, 'Dieter, of course.'

'Such people can be upsetting,' said the registrar sympathetically in his office. He confirmed that Fräulein Kursten had a sister, Frau Wimmer, and wrote down the address for Reinhard. Outside, as he walked back through the avenue of trees that he had admired on the way in, his brain seemed not to function. Nor did he want it to.

28

TIME seemed to be as short as ever Reinhard had known it as he left the hotel the next morning. He'd hardly had time to dress properly. Cleaning his teeth and combing his hair were huge impositions on precious minutes. He kept up a frantic pace, and skipped breakfast. He stayed with Dieter only an hour before leaving him with Irma. Only when he climbed in behind the wheel of the Merc for the trip did he relax. He wanted to get there without any reasoning of the mind, doubts or preparedness. He longed to reach Berlinerstrasse and, when he did, he felt no nervousness. The house was very attractive with Spanish-style walling linking the home with a garage that had attracted the attention of a large petal clematis. Reinhard looked for signs of life but nothing stirred. He was halfway down the path and still refused to work out the first thing he should say. As he waited for the door to be opened, his mind went a blank.

'Frau Wimmer is asleep,' announced a man appearing from over the garden fence. His tone was definitive, promoting an aggression Reinhard did not much care for.

'Oh, I see.'

'Yes, she always sleeps in the afternoon,' the man persisted, pursuing Reinhard along his side of the fence. 'She would not like to be disturbed,' said the thickset man with less edge to his voice as Reinhard spun round to face him. Not only did the man know when she would be available but what she would do afterwards, what time she would go to bed, and, lo and behold, what time she would rise.

He probably also knew whether she preferred strawberries or raspberries and whether brown or white bread was her favourite. Reinhard encouraged the fisherwoman, now gripping the top of the fence as if he meant to jump over it.

'Well,' Reinhard said, 'I am an old friend of Frau Wimmer. I knew her from her days down south, quite a few years ago now, and I thought I would look the family up as I was on my way to Hamburg. Business, you know. Are they all still together?'

The fisherwoman confirmed what he already knew. 'She's only one, I'm afraid.' And shaking his head, he added, almost silently 'She is very, very ill. She's being taken to the Marien-Krankenhaus any day now, I believe.'

Reinhard recalled how only the other day he had clipped his elbow on a wall and rampaged menacingly. And how, years ago now, he had moaned because he badly cut a knee just hours before a rally where Hitler was due to speak. What kind of armour was it that protected this woman so that she could take a nap or be bothered one way or the other about the merits of soft fruit or bread flour?

Reinhard had seen the Führer for the first time in the flesh while tagging on behind dad who was covering the event for his newspaper.

Reinhard peers between the uniformed officers in Kurt Ludecke's party, just two lengths of his bed away from the man with the pale face and defiant forelock. Everyone around him is staring attentively into the man's face like his classmates do when Herr Dormer turns back to the class from his blackboard scribbling. To begin with, they do nothing but look. No clapping. Reinhard's hands come together but only quietly. He wants to clap just once, a loud clap like he managed in the playground, bringing his hands together suddenly and having the other kids come round. Howjerdothat? Words shoot out of the man's mouth and his hands follow them out of view. Reinhard expects rabbits and playing cards but when the man's mouth closes and tightens and his thickly coated arms bring back his hands, they are stiff or curled, but empty. Reinhard stares open mouthed and nearly misses his father rest his camera and turn around, and when he does, Reinhard scuffs the ground with his shoe, pretending to be bored or something.

What he did not then understand, he came later to interpret as sarcasm-laced sense, force mixed with finesse, mesmerising, energised oratory that, later still, he began to think of as a special

REQUIREMENTS OF GUILT

collection of shell words, designed to explode the mind. And in suffering narrow office corridors to glimpse wide ceremonial avenues, he had helped in a country's devastation. Reinhard could be particular: he had pulled bitter rank on an unassuming man with a weak heart so that he would have to stand saluting on a bleak quadrangle to teach him a lesson about authority and obedience and that there had been a mortifying by-product of that, twice as nasty; that he had bowed his head outside a full-ahead gas chamber. That particular day had led to compassion taking over for the first time in all his SS time, yet even this was going wrong.

Reinhard tried to concentrate on Frau Wimmer's garden as he leant over the steering wheel. But he had to keep pruning his thoughts. The towering forsythia, rhododendron and wisteria and particularly the honeysuckle and clematis which bent over to form archways met by moss-covered stepping stones cuddled by the greenest grass he thought he had ever seen, kept his mind at peace before autumn came and people fell as leaves in front of his tired eyes.

There is a frame on a sideboard. It is Dieter. Reinhard has snatched someone else's son. His calendars of satisfaction, starting in 1943, now swell into heavy chunks of wooden type, every date hugely accusing. The very day; it rears up inside his belly, contorting his body. A one and a two squeeze in and they hurt. Then the next day and it hurts more. In turn they all present themselves, each day settling into Reinhard's body, hurting more and more as the first month progresses. But they come again. He tries to count the months but the days pain him and he keeps losing count. The big ones hurt the most. The first of the month is best but it is scant relief and the heavy wooden dates are affecting all the functions of his body. He is losing blood as they make their entrances and exits and he is thinning. What has been his life's plus, his action carried out without command, compliance or blind following, something he has done spontaneously without any plan to cover up, no last greedy grab, now becomes a shrivelling minus. When he is tired and wants to die, a bony hand, attached to a length of cardigan, rises slowly out from its stricken trunk as if to comfort him around the face, but it snaps on contact.

Reinhard jerked his head from the steering wheel, looked down at himself and wiped his mouth. There was relief but it was only momentary; there might be no framed photograph but he feared the rest. His head buzzed as he began to think of this woman's longing for her youngster over the years. Her son. A longing denied. He drove around the area, returning after an hour, boldly walked up to the front door and knocked. He still didn't know what to say and he didn't care. The door would open and he would say something. The door opened and he said nothing. Frau Wimmer stood there, sago pale. Reinhard thought of it as the end for both of them.

'Ja?'

'I ... I am sorry to bother you. I am looking for a Frau Stein. Frau Gertrud Stein,' he pretended.

Her voice was laboured and Reinhard felt bad that his senseless question had further burdened her.

Dieter might miss the hearse: Reinhard couldn't stop the words forming. Frau Wimmer's skin was as washed-out linen. Supposing she got so bad that he might have to tell her himself before Dieter had convalesced and was strong enough to face her. He knew he would if he had to but he would be an inadequate, perhaps ridiculous, and certainly a cruel substitute. Yet he would want to give her the slim chance that she might welcome at least part of the news. Reinhard prayed that Frau Wimmer would hold on. He did not wonder how her treatment was going at the Marien-Krankenhaus or whether she would survive. She was going; circumstances had sucked her practically dry. Her luck was out. Yet perhaps there was one last top-up, a full gulp at the last that would enable her to enjoy at least a little of what nature - without any interference from hands that sought to rectify an injustice only to create another - had very likely intended. The hospital authorities could be told some of the tale and if the doctors agreed, she could be told. And if she agreed, Dieter could visit her and, miracle of miracles, they could smile at one another. Reinhard so much wanted to see them smile at one another. If there was anything in the belief that a will to live was all-important in many cases of illness, her life might be given a better chance. It might be just the kind of tonic a doctor would support. As soon as he reached the Marien-Krankenhaus, he explained.

'Remarkable,' said the doctor. 'Have a drink or a bite to eat; I'll come to the restaurant and we'll talk further. It's on the next level down.'

Reinhard scolded his mouth on the coffee he took with shaking hands to a white plastic-topped table. He pushed the mug aside and stared at the doorway. The doctor strode through and sat down.

REQUIREMENTS OF GUILT

'I don't believe in miracles, mind you, but the hospital administrators both here and at Dieter's hospital think a meeting might be a good idea. Of course, we will have to have the permissions though I don't foresee a problem. I also think such a meeting should take place. It would be very cruel to deny it but please understand that the decay in Frau Wimmer's body is very far advanced. Also Dieter's recuperation must be complete.'

As Reinhard returned to the car, he thought of his father's death in hospital and about the cruel force that had come between them. Tales from Teutonic myth and legend that father read to him as a child had enthralled Reinhard. It was not, as he was to learn from his own reading, father's vast knowledge of the subject but the passion with which he told what little he did know that had left its mark. Father had always tried so hard in whatever he did that it was difficult for anyone to criticise him. Reinhard had never been able, despite what happened later, to bring himself to ridicule any of those nights when father would leave Reinhard's bedroom with that special smile of his face when his own head would slowly slide beneath the sheets where he would be safe from any stray monster that had not been gathered up and put back to sleep within the pages of the red clothbound book with goldish lettering. Neither would he now. He would not hint that Teutonic myth and legend stories such as *The Land of the Not-dead and Many Marvels*, *Siegfried and the Nibelungs* or *The Coming of Beowulf* had at all influenced his destiny though he had to admit that National Socialism's blazing theatricals at Nürnberg - he could still easily visualise centre stage the hypnotic, almost pagan atmosphere of the Zeppelinfeld - had seemed equally captivating. He had willingly followed father around the ranting grounds of München. Father's interest in political meetings was based solely on the fact that they were often an explosive cocktail which could provide good pictures for his beloved *Münchener Post* and that interest almost always stopped the moment his assignment of the day had ended. Father had been neither for nor against Hitler at this time, though he did invariably tell mum of 'the rabble' that surrounded the man. And he had been impressed by a couple of the Circus Krone gatherings. All this began rapidly to change when the *Post*'s presses were smashed in a Nazi raid. When Reinhard did not come out wholeheartedly against the action, relative child though he was, he and father increasingly kept to their own sides of the road. Yet, standing by father's hospital bed in the middle of many party glory days, when red, white and black handkerchiefs were always at the ready to take care of leaking emotions, he suddenly felt he had missed out on so much else. All he could see in those few anaesthetised moments was that against the gravity of father succumbing to complications following a nasty bout of flu, how petty had been his excuse of a heavy cold to forgive attendance at father's modest newspaper awards ceremony for a brilliant bridge photograph in the landscape section and a street fight in München in a hard news category. Reinhard now reckoned that there would have been in those glittering and polished years of National Socialism nothing to compare with father's two shiny prints and that some recognition of them by his son would have outshone everything.

The time between the beginning, when Hitler butted into their conversations, and the end, when the long illness really took a hold, and aided walks around the bed ended, had generated between father and son little more than a few sentences of indifferent chatter. Yet this final day had been so beautifully different. In the few moments they were together in hospital, father held rigid by fearsomely crisp white sheets, their exchanges were constant, though they said nothing. Reinhard liked to believe that their hearts romped in the carefree dust of reunion and that feint but unmistakable reconciliation obliterated the corrupting passages from the nationalist bible. So that when father sighed his last, Reinhard let grief have its way ignoring the clamouring Nazi flags, stretching fawningly towards him.

29

REINHARD waved excitedly as he reached Amelia's place and practically brushed past Irma. He gave her a kiss that almost missed its mark as he ran on down the drive to greet Dieter. Irma, who had obviously anticipated his arrival and stationed herself at the gate, walked slowly back towards Dieter and Reinhard. After hugging Dieter, Reinhard felt obliged to return to Irma.

'Sorry Irma. Here!' he said, pulling her into a light embrace. She let her head loll sideways as she rested a hand on his back.

Reinhard became defensive. 'Irma, I am at a very important stage in, you know, trying to clear up a mystery, what I spoke of before.' But Irma looked off to one side.

Apart from a small plaster on the side of his head, where his hair had begun to grow back, Dieter looked almost like his old self. 'The hospital here says I'm fine again. And I feel it,' he said brightly.

'And you look fine,' Reinhard confirmed, hugging him all the way to the covered doorway. He wanted to tell him about his mother but knew he had other things to tell him first and that would have to wait for a quieter time.

Dieter said, 'We're going out tonight, dad - all of us. It's Amelia's treat. She's taking us to a special restaurant that comes highly recommended.'

Reinhard whispered to Dieter, 'And you and I are going out tomorrow. A secret. OK?'

The evening restaurant turned out to be a quite exclusive place set in woods several miles from Goslar by a lake that shimmered in the glorious evening light. They all ate at a table under a large poplar whose canopy cast a dappled net of rays as they drank Hock. They moved on to a flower-festooned veranda to finish off a very successful evening with coffee and schnapps.

*

The week was fast coming to an end, and Irma, her duty done, started preparations for her trip back to London. Amelia had said she would drive Irma for her early evening night flight from Düsseldorf before attending a lecture in nearby Rheydt ahead of the painting week she was looking forward to. Dieter thanked Irma for being so kind and considerate. Reinhard just looked at her, nodded and put a hand around her shoulder, pressing his face against the side of hers. He said something to the effect that he did not know how the week would have gone without Irma's presence but at the same time trying not to give her any sort of encouragement.

'I have loved it,' she said, excusing herself and walking back into the house. 'Support is strength. I have really loved it,' she called back over her shoulder.

The conversation Reinhard had with Dieter about the Polish part of the convalescence was interrupted when Amelia's car turned into the drive. Dieter spun round on Reinhard. 'Oh, dad, Amelia's taking me into town just for a while. Well, in an hour's time,' he said, looking at his watch. 'We'll only be an hour at the most? There's a public unveiling of some plans for an interesting new stadium in the area and a journalist friend of hers is going to pick us up and drop us back. She's heard the design is quite futuristic and obviously I'd like to see it. My kind of construction, you know. You two'll be all right here for a while, won't you? We're all off to a concert tonight, anyway. Your kind of music, dad.'

Amelia reversed her Opel Kapitan into a carport and stepped out smiling. She suddenly looked serious, putting a hand to her mouth. 'I've just remembered ...'

Reinhard interrupted. 'Dieter, he has just told me. You two go right along. I need a bath, anyway. I believe we have a concert later. Thank you. What's the music?'

REQUIREMENTS OF GUILT

'Monteverdi and Mahler. The *Vespers* and I think it's Mahler's *Kindertotenlieder*.'

Not wishing to be late for the concert, Reinhard splashed around in the bath for fewer than ten minutes. Yet the firm intention he had of trying to seek out Stephanie again after so many years made him feel like a boy before his first date, fussing and fixing nothing, thinking wishfully, fantasising, assuming wildly. Yet it was Irma he would next be meeting, and very soon. Though he no longer had any presumption or desire in regard to Irma, he knew her presence would weave its particular spell which he would accept and enjoy as long as the flirt was just that. Yet he was totally unprepared when Irma appeared at the top of the stairs and bent forward to tug at the towel around him as he left the bathroom ...

The interval between Monteverdi and Mahler left Irma and Reinhard paying particular attention to the coffee cups on the varnished table in front of them. Irma declared, 'You know, I'm sure I saw this very design in one of the Staffordshire pottery outlets George and I visited one day. Burslem I fancy it was.' And when that subject was pretty well exhausted, Reinhard tried to make something of the chocolates and their silvery wrappings that lay on a plate by the milk and sugar. Irma and Reinhard never looked at each other. He turned to architectural innovation and let Dieter expand on the more tangible and fathomable characteristics of the recently viewed stadium plans but occasionally Irma and Reinhard yielded to the soft leather settee provided in the hall's luxury lounge, allowing the outer parts of their opposing hands, resting innocently against their thighs, to generate surges of excitement by the gentlest of movements towards each other. Consequently, they both found it difficult to take in architecture and all its works - no matter how interesting it might have been to a fellow professional - especially when the talking got down to concrete type, structure and stress. They nodded ambitiously and left the questioning to Dieter and Amelia, though Reinhard did at one point unwisely ask Amelia's *Spiegel* newspaper acquaintance, Hans, whether he thought there were any particular pressures existing these days to conform with any agreed standards in German architecture.

Hans replied, somewhat tardily, 'What, fears of decadence and all that? No, I don't think so. I mean, what did you think of Goebbels' talk in the Thirties when he spoke of degeneration in modern art?' And the journalist wasted no time at all and answered the question himself, leading on from that to changing times. In little more than a couple of minutes, he seemingly covered the whole spectrum of West German life (plus a rather turgid view of the DDR) including denazification and the bearing of guilt for the sins of the fathers. And he went on: 'You know, numerous trials of Nazi murderers are still being held all over the country.' Reinhard gauged *Ja'* was sufficient since what the man had said constituted a statement rather than a question and he bent down and re-tied a shoelace. Hans was still looking Reinhard's way when he straightened up. There were questions bursting in the man's eyes and his lips moved excitedly. He wound himself up to say: 'What do you think about a statute of limitation for Nazi murders being extended?' Reinhard felt certain: if Dieter had not recovered and anyone had then asked him the same question, he thought he would have said it could be a permanent arrangement so far as he was concerned but his being alive generated real purpose again and he felt like saying he wished the statute's term could be shortened to right now, this afternoon. Instead, he went on a wide-front attack - again somewhat unwisely - with a cannon blast on the questioner's own doorstep.

'Nazi crimes cannot be rationalised and, while I would not go with the notion of collective guilt, there has to be collective responsibility and that means having the legal framework to bring Nazi murderers to justice - no matter how long it takes.' Reinhard heard himself as a professor in contemporary German studies but he continued, striking out boldly. 'What sort of mandatory training is there for journalists these days?'

From the twitching in the *Spiegel* man's face as Reinhard spoke, it was almost possible to predict what response was being assembled. Judging it would not be complimentary, he waited for the man's mouth to open before he continued, 'The Press - and the radio, of course - were thoroughly purged institutions after the war, politically that is. You'd think the press would be united in wanting to cleanse the soul, so to speak. On the other hand, the courts, the civil service and the police were practically left to carry on.' And he wanted to add that in public opinion polls aimed at rating professions, journalists fared pretty badly, but he thought that would be too provocative. In the end he settled for, 'Of course I hear this only second hand, living in England.'

The newshound had relaxed his face and surprised Reinhard with silence. It was of an unnerving duration, too, typical of a probing, investigative journalist.

'*Der Spiegel's* my main outlet and this publication is a credit to the country. The title shrinks from nothing. It has the low-down on anyone who's anyone and will go after anyone who's no one but believed to be dodgy.' Then, after lapsing into another longer silence, he added, 'Tell me, are you following the Eichmann trial?'

'Defence council Servatius has a job on there,' Reinhard suggested.

Noticeably irritated, the man said, *Ja, ja*. The bastard's guilty. But who else should be there? Two of Eichmann's henchmen look like they're having to stand trial. Bloody good, I say. As far down the line as possible, I'd go. Right to the bottom, to the bloody clerks whose pens packed them off east; they must have known what they were doing, they are just as guilty.' Then, drawing breath, he said in increasing volume and pointedness, 'Guilty, the lot of them, wouldn't you say, Herr Hänsel?' his head raised and tilted in the most inflammatory of attitudes.

Reinhard responded boldly as he stood in a sturdy dock flanked by two guards in a packed courtroom of dark oak panelling, where the judge's words arrowed away from the black gown and fell where they were levelled.

'Guilty,' Reinhard said.

Irma allowed her little finger to climb over Reinhard's, pressing down on it gently.

Widening the argument, Amelia said, 'I read somewhere that there's some Zeitgeschichte institute in München that provides expert opinions at trials of former Nazis …' before suddenly looking at her watch and cutting herself short. 'We'll not get a drink before the bell if we go on about that, though. What shall we have then?' As they moved to the bar, Hans quick-stepped up to Reinhard's side. 'How do you like England?' he enquired in a sort of whisper.

Reinhard felt he could easily deal with this question and relaxed. 'Right now, I love the Harz. I was saying only yesterday I find it difficult to believe how a place like this could have escaped my attention for so long.'

'Well, I suppose that depends on how pre-occupied one can be elsewhere,' Hans said obliquely.

Reinhard fell silent, tightening again. He thought how much a *Spiegel* man he looked, sparse but somehow dominant, and while he smiled a lot, his eyes seemed to question everything around him so that Reinhard found himself editing his own words as he spoke. The journalist had an irritating habit of smoothing one set of fingers against the other, alternately, when he spoke. What with his beaky nose, and thin lips, he looked to Reinhard as if he had somehow devolved from Rattus norvegicus, Amelia's friend or not. Reinhard decided he would think of him as the Herr Rat.

Amelia, sipping her sherry, said, 'You certainly get around, Hans. The strange thing is, you never seem to get tired, do you?' But just as he began preparing some fingers for another severe stroking, the final bell rang and they relaxed and rose. Reinhard held his hand out to help Irma from the settee saying, 'Right, give it to me, Mahler.'

30

OVER breakfast, Amelia took out Gottfried's written instructions and the largess that went with the Polish trip and also read from notes she had made after ringing his cousin Jósef. Flight 203 would be out of Frankfurt Terminal One at 13.35hrs on Sunday. She announced: 'Gottfried is coming here on Saturday, driving you to Frankfurt, Dieter, where you'll spend the night before he takes you to the airport in the morning. Jósef's wife, Janina, will meet you at Warsaw's Okecie Airport.'

Amelia said she would be back from Rheydt late on the Sunday. In the meantime rest here; the house is yours.' Then she hesitated, consideration of what she was to say reflected in the way she slowly spread and re-spread marmalade over her slice of dark rye bread. 'You are much better, Dieter, but please, you take it easy, eh? You, too, Herr Hänsel.'

Reinhard was pleased that Irma was going home. He said goodbye with a swift embrace, smoothed the front of his head and thanked Amelia for all her kindness. Amelia smiled, swung her legs into the car and, with Irma turning around to wave, the car moved off over the crunching gravel, disappearing behind the weeping willow at the end of the drive. Two hours later, Reinhard drove Dieter down the same drive, Dieter's hands behind his head, elbows protectively tight into the sides of his face. Reinhard kept referring to the political demonstration incident, what it was probably connected with, how he felt in the hours that followed the telegram, Irma's kindness during Dieter's recovery and how wonderful it was now to have him next to him and on the mend. But he kept the real reasons for the journey to himself and Dieter did not press him. After a little under an hour, the Mercedes reached Hannover and in an outer suburb of the city was inched into a parking bay on one of the main shopping streets. Reinhard pointed through the screen. 'First we have something to eat, eh?' Reinhard had the contented look of someone emerging triumphantly from a lost property office, putting an arm around Dieter and tugging his parcel towards his side. They both smiled. Reinhard wondered whether this might be the last time he would see Dieter cast anything like a benevolent gaze his way. They were shown to the table Reinhard had booked, the reddish light from the ornate table lamp giving the corner nook something of the appearance of a photographer's dark room. Diffused lighting was what was needed in the circumstances. Reinhard wanted to put everything this trip had uncovered to Dieter coldly and straight, facts without comment or trimmings, the most unbiased report he had ever filed. Dieter had the right to hear it all as a stranger would. Only then could the full impact be fairly judged. And the reaction had to be instant: bad, if that was the way it had to be, rather than 'Well OK', then gradually festering to become terrible. Only from the lowest point could matters stand any chance of getting better.

'I am not sure ...' Reinhard began. 'I cannot be sure how my story will sound to you, how you will think of me ...'

Dieter protested, 'You really do not have to apologise for anything.'

'Dieter, I do. You say to me Dad, you always do because I bring you up. But you do not know everything about me. I now have more I must tell you, more that I have just discovered here in West Germany.'

Dieter looked puzzled. Reinhard felt graceless. He had brought up episodes of his past in many private moments. Sitting openly in a restaurant, however, away from the confines of home, where the cushions and the curtains absorbed the force of disclosure, was much more like a public autopsy. And flanked by strangers that Reinhard could imagine were judge and jury, the process of telling the new truth to the boy he loved could be more than equal to the rigours of an international tribunal. He began his story with Rastenkorb, the word that had started him off. He left nothing out as he retreated into the umbra of his Third Reich time. Reinhard spoke of the plans devised for misbehaving folk, the names, the journeys, the ends that might have been, the ends that were, right up to the end that would have been but for that one move in his life that he felt comfortable with but countered now by what he had found out. They were utterances of no half measure, self-condemnation as rough as he sometimes felt the occasions really were. He would know soon enough ...

Dieter's eyes remained on Reinhard for only a split second before passing on to somewhere between the edges of a heavy velvet curtain and a gilt-edged picture on the wall by the exit. Dieter held his head and saw Reinhard's anxious look.

'It's nothing, dad. Just a bit of a headache.'

Dad.

It had been said. One fabulous word, from Dieter's mouth, directed at Reinhard Hänsel. Fact. Mighty fact. Fact that had already passed into history. Something that could never ever be taken back. Sorry, I didn't mean that, you disgustingly deceptive, snivelling man. Reinhard waited. No. It was simply Dad. Nothing more, nothing less. And it had been said without emphasis, without any particular tone, just normally, like he would have said it in asking whether Reinhard would be much longer in the bathroom. Dad.

Reinhard kept his eyes on Dieter. He waited for the verbal response on the huge matter of culpable weakness.

Dieter simply said, 'I love you.'

Reinhard pressed his hands hard against his face to provide maturity for the child-like response he felt surging up through him. Not *still* loved. Just loved. As always. He cried his love of life. His eyes burst in front of Dieter. Dieter leaned forward across the table and took hold of him. 'My dear, lovely dad.'

'*Lieber Gott, Dieter ...*'

'Do not speak. Never say anything more about all that. Just be as you have always been, as I have always known you. No son would ever be able to ask for more. Not any son. Not anybody.'

Reinhard stood back, smiling just a little and said that there was more, another big moment for them. 'I have traced your mother. She is very ill but she lives.'

Dieter jerked himself from his chair to stand rigidly, half bent, his mouth widely open, his eyes shut, before he exploded with 'Where! I want to see her! When can we see her?'

We. Another word of love.

'It is arranged. We go now. But she is very, very ill, Dieter. I must tell you she is very ill.'

*

Brisk footsteps, then slow, reverent paces. They spoke only in glances as they neared the ward. After initial exchanges, the doctor was silent, too, until he said, 'Don't please expect anything much at all. Frau Wimmer is very ill and any improvement as a result of this kind of therapy might in the first instant be more visual than real. She is deteriorating rapidly, even within the last forty-eight hours. Medicine and surgery are only ... well, they sometimes help in such cases but at this stage you must expect the worst while hoping slimly for more.' Dr Weiss swung round yet another corridor before turning into Zweig Ward. He spoke briefly to a Sister and left the two men alone with their thoughts, both scanning the ward for a woman who might experience a momentary life more brilliant that the sunniest of her seventy-odd years.

Reinhard had always believed that someone, somewhere, might speak up for him but he never would seek out that person. He knew at this latest moment of truth that his face was ready to crease into ever-joy or crust over in ever-woe. He said to Dieter, slowly and deliberately, 'For all this, I am sorry. So very sorry.' There was no embarrassment. Dieter held his arm. The Sister called them over.

'Your mother has been told nothing. I will leave that entirely to you.'

The crisp white figure of mercy turned and they followed. Reinhard tried not to look at any of the faces in the ward, keeping his eyes on the bed ends and soon it was quite impossible for him to distinguish very much at all as his mind wandered.

The extended arm of the Sonderkommando directs Reinhard's hesitant gaze to the side of Crematoria V, where bodies are being draped one upon the other.

'Dad?'

The sergeant says, 'You are in luck, Herr Sturmbannführer; there are about six hundred or so bodies for the pits this time.'

Dieter touched Reinhard's arm and smiled encouragement. The Sister also smiled.

He sees a young woman, in such a position that had she been upright she would have been standing to attention, her right arm close to saluting. He recalls Stephanie had once mocked his Nazi tendencies in a similar sort of way, a half-homage-half-jeer. He had looked away but now he turns back to the victim and says he is sorry. He steps back in horror, his mouth opening for a yell that enters upon the diabolical scene as a whimper. He turns away, feeling the contrast between the naked dead and the freshly laundered living. He strikes out for SS Command headquarters, passing the new Crematorium V. He thinks of Stephanie and how one number can represent both bliss and despair.

'Dad, come on.'

The Sister smiled again at both men. 'Good luck,' she said before carrying on down the ward. Dieter and Reinhard stood at the end of the bed. Both men looked shocked.

Bumpy letters ... there are postures and bearing of warmth and compassion. Arms drape. Stephanie's arm draped off the bed by the cut-glass lamp. Reinhard knows that in a world of pleasure, there is nothing quite as exciting as a late summer night of 1936. He also knows now that in a world capable of unremitting hatred and sorrow, there is nothing so horrible as the spring day of 1943.

'Shall I take your coat, dad? It is rather hot in here.'

Reinhard slowly removed his coat. They looked at each other, seriously. Reinhard felt very uneasy. Dieter, too. They stared at the waxen figure and Reinhard could only imagine what Dieter was feeling inside and in that moment he was glad he didn't have to find the strength to be the first to speak or initiate anything because he felt lifeless. At length Dieter moved round to her side and uttered a hardly audible 'Mum.' Suddenly, Dieter's mother opened her eyes and slowly parted her lips. At first there was nothing. Then, after what seemed an eternity, she found the strength to utter: 'Is that ... ?' But the voice trailed off. Dieter spoke out clearly, almost shockingly. 'It's me, mum, Dieter. I am here. I know it is incredible, but it is true. I know you have thought me dead all these years, but I am not. I have come just as soon as I knew where you were. I will explain later. It's me, Dieter.' There was something in her face, beyond the decaying skin and dull eyes, that suggested she had made some sense of what he had said and Dieter continued, 'It is a wonderful story, mum. It's me, Dieter.'

Reinhard could not remain. He took a few silent steps backwards and felt as if he were floating away from the bed, his eyes fixed on the two tragic souls. Dieter would tell him how it went. Reinhard just wanted to experience, alone, a few moments of fulfilment now that mother and son were together, the link made. There might be more, for mercy's sake he hoped there would be, but there definitely had been this much. He was sure that for now it would be best for him to remain in the background. In the likelihood of her surviving for no more than a few weeks, or just a few days, all her time should be spent with Dieter and certainly not have to sustain any kind of obligation to a third party.

In the waiting room Reinhard straightened Dieter's jacket that he had thrown onto a chair when earlier he'd paced the room. As he folded it neatly, a letter fell from the inner pocket with a flashy *Partei* heading at the top. He read from the letter an invitation to a rally and convention ... important policy matters to be announced ... nothing of the contents to be disclosed to non-party members. Reinhard looked towards the corridor. Dieter's face would announce the verdict and he tried to imagine him smiling broadly and both of them walking briskly from the hospital. He had just about returned the letter and placed the jacket back on the seat when Dieter entered the room. Reinhard knew it was bad.

'She has just died,' Dieter announced as he crossed the room to sit down next to Reinhard. 'She said hello son, I think, but she slipped away. I don't properly know how I feel, Dad.'

They both looked down, deep in thought, before both men stood up to face each other before seeking comfort in a long embrace. The silence was grievous. For Dieter it had been instant hope dashed. Reinhard felt his unrealised expectation would affect his remaining days.

'How long had you known, Dad?'

'Just a couple of days. It was a chance only. I am so sorry.'

'You tried, Dad. You tried.'

REQUIREMENTS OF GUILT

*

They walked into the Bahnhof Hotel, the one constant comfort that was now little more than cold housing for numbed minds. Reinhard felt nervous. Dieter managed a smile and said he would rest for a while. Reinhard read a message from Gottfried; his friend would telephone again at six. Reinhard checked the time, sank a brandy and took a second to the phone to hear Gottfried say the table tennis configuration was correct.

'But we have to be fairly quick to win this particular game.'

'Understood.'

'That address you gave me was spot on, though I had to spend a lot of time at the Coral Reef on Tobago and was forced to do some snorkelling from a glass bottom boat!'

Reinhard cut in: 'I am sorry, Gottfried. Bad news, I'm afraid. Not Dieter. He's fine. No, this is something else; I will tell you later. Must thank you again for the Harz; Amelia's a super woman. And for seeing Dieter safely aboard the flight to Poland.'

'Think nothing of it, old friend. I'm glad I can do it. You are all right, aren't you?'

'Yeah, yeah, I'll tell you later.'

'OK then. Now listen. I've booked a flight for you to Warsaw from Frankfurt the day after tomorrow, flight W504, for us to be able to choose the right table for this very important sporting engagement, *ja*? Take a taxi to the Checkers Hotel, not far from the airport. Speak to Piotr, the manager; he'll give you all the necessary directions to get down to Krakow and then Auschwitz and the place where we're staying. It has all been arranged. Got to go now. See you in Auschwitz town, Oswiecim.'

Auschwitz. Probably the State Museum, the Monument to the Martyrdom of Nations, according to the Polish Seym parliament. This was to be a terrorist act to eliminate ghastly evidence of Nazi atrocities, one of the most ghastly in history, where a lot of the worst had happened. They wanted to muddy its existence and boost the crap claim: Nazis not guilty of gas chamber holocaust! Reinhard again heard each word brawl its lie. He had read them. Dieter had read them. Thousands of people had read them and the words had been spread, but Gottfried was on to this particular wrong and Reinhard felt like joining in. He went up to Dieter's room. They spoke almost in whispers.

'It's all right,' Dieter said, sitting on the edge of the bed.

No 'Dad' this time.

'Really, Dad.'

Reinhard smiled.

'You know, I actually saw her and spoke to her. It was not in vain. She died knowing I am alive. It is obviously so massively more ... it is difficult to take this in, that I could ever see my mother again but I did.'

Reinhard remained silent, looking out of the window. He stood there for a full minute. Then he turned and sat down on the bed next to Dieter, putting an arm around the young man's shoulders.

'She died knowing I am alive, Dad. That must have given her some peace. Thank you for that.'

Still Reinhard did not speak. He hugged Dieter tighter and resumed his position at the window, staring into space. Dieter rose and joined him.

'It's the Ojcow Valley this weekend then.'

Reinhard nodded slowly and told him about the Revisionists' threat at Auschwitz.

Dieter stressed that he'd like to join him to go to Birkenau afterwards.

'That's fine. We'll keep in touch anyway.'

31

DIETER wandered around the old and proud city before taking the train to join Reinhard and Gottfried at Auschwitz.

Apart from an illuminated red box sign advertising its three-lettered ware above a door in a seedy side street off Kracòw's central area, the greyness he witnessed through a ninety degrees sweep of his eyes seemed total. The reason he was in Kraków was because he wanted to travel the 70 kilometres to Oswieçim by train as Reinhard had done, to the Auschwitz-Birkenau complex, those many years ago. He was too close to Birkenau and the man he was longing to re-join to benefit from any extended relaxation in the Ojcow Valley, though he hugged his host as they parted in the city centre like she was his mother.

Dieter strolled around several markets and religious edifices. He took a tram east across the Wista, peering out onto the river's black waters. There was a drab, colourless feel about the place with city architecture gradually giving way to stacked concrete blocks. He got off at the Ul.Konopnickiej flats tower, and strolled around aimlessly in its hideous shadow before crossing the road for the return journey to the city centre. He took a deep breath as he stepped aboard the Oswieçim train. He was thinking of Reinhard's journey. It may have been as it was, yet, equally he may have sat with his back to the engine. So he moved to the opposite seat. Again, he looked right and left and returned to the first seat. Sitting this way was positive; he was sure Reinhard would have tried to be positive despite misgivings he would almost certainly have harboured at this time. Dieter sought old, mature scenery outside, left and right. Which first? What scene had Reinhard gazed upon? Right, that clump of trees? Left, that isolated, winding and crumbling stone wall? He tried to imagine Reinhard not being as certain of the future as he had once been and how he may have reacted to everything including his fellow officers. He kept moving from one side of the train to the other as the fields and the small communities came and went. He wanted to think about any small part of what Reinhard's eyes may have taken in or what thoughts he may have had as the train carried him through the Polish countryside that springtime nearly two decades earlier to a mission that in the end was to mean so much to them both. Reinhard would have been on the last lap of a life-changing journey and now only a few miles and almost certainly only a relatively few hours from that moment when he would enter that place and slowly move up to that crematorium, stand in that doorway and be confronted after a few moments by that one person out of so many scores times scores, so many hundreds times hundreds, so many thousands times thousands and who had become such a major part of his life.

At the station, Dieter rested a hand on Reinhard's arm as he said, 'I want to back myself into that doorway and face you as I had once done so trustingly as an infant.' Reinhard's throat hurt as he swallowed. They left the station and Dieter asked, 'How much of the business has been done?' Reinhard paused. 'We will talk after lunch. I think maybe we are here for two days. Gottfried has it arranged. We have a little guest house not far from Osmus.' Oswieçim Museum. Dieter thought he would hear a fair sprinkling of coded talk over the course of the next few days.

They took a taxi to the guest house. where light meals were eagerly consumed and all three then joined the rest of the small team in a private room. Gottfried immediately got down to business, introducing the others. 'Zbigniew and Tadeusz, are under cover police officers who will be with us in the Main Camp, that is Auschwitz I. Birkenau is Auschwitz II. These policemen are also expert bomb disposal officers. And we have an explosives expert, Max, a friend of mine from Berlin. All the information about our plan is on paper and with another colleague. He will inform Kraków police headquarters if there is a major stumble. We think Karl X and Heinz Y will strike inside the main camp tomorrow, probably in the afternoon. Four blocks, at both ends of the camp, may be targets. By examining a map of Auschwitz I, and using the later hut numbering, explosives could be set at 10 and 21 at the eastern end of the camp and 22 and 24 on the western side, nearest the main gate. That's what we read into the latest *Neues Deutschland* personal column entry.

The self-appointed anti-terrorist group was there to foil this attack. It was believed that the bombers would go in as an amateur ciné group, carrying their equipment. It was assumed that the intention would be to destroy the camp virtually in its entirety and that meant there had to be a fair amount of explosives planted, although the huts were wooden and there were only twenty eight of them, fairly close together. With an unknown number of members of the public being present in the camp at the time, they would have to act extremely responsibly in trying to nail the would-be bombers. Reinhard outlined the lesson they would be taught after they had been 'arrested' and before they were handed over to police to face justice. He said, 'Thanks to Gottfried's brother and his police contacts we can go right back to school and give these so-called Revisionists – criminal liars I would call them - an unforgettable detention!'

Gottfried stopped the laughter with a raised hand. 'Police headquarters are going to co-operate with this, but only if everything goes according to plan. Our little game is up if there is any kind of trouble. We must be very careful, as professional as we know how.'

Dieter would stay at the guest house until the operation had been completed.

Outside Oswieçim railway station, the members of the group allowed the other half dozen or so people waiting at the stop to filter between them as they waited for the bus. The dark green single-decker ended its journey at the edge of a small housing estate, pulling into a service road, and the five of them stood up slowly so they could be the last passengers off. Across the road was a rough track that Reinhard knew eventually led to an arch under which the first batch of prisoners - more than 700 political prisoners - had entered Auschwitz on June 14, 1940 - and which Reinhard had entered a little under three years later. There was no longer direct access to the camp. Now a new building fronted the notorious place housing a cinema and other aids to acquaint, acclimatise, and forewarn visitors about what they would face once past the iron announcement *Arbeit*

Macht Frei. Separated by a dozen or so paces, and leaning against the left-hand wall of the museum entrance, Gottfried and Zbigniew studied leaflets they had picked up on entering the reception area. They ignored Tadeusz and Reinhard as they moved further into the hallway. By rubbing his chin on a shoulder or occasionally massaging the back of his neck, Reinhard was able to keep a fairly wide-angle observation over much of this part of the camp, including windows overlooking the grassed area leading to the entrance. Gottfried looked at his watch and back towards the point where the group had entered. He spoke to Zbigniew and the two moved over close to the reception counter, Gottfried reaching down to the back of his lower leg, a sign that the film-makers were in the building. Tadeusz and Reinhard, with their backs to the entrance and talking lightly about nothing, looked across in the direction of the other two and Gottfried sneezed - a further sign that the two men carrying film-making paraphernalia were Karl X and Heinz Y.

The would-be bombers acknowledged a greeting from the woman behind the counter and made straight for the door leading to the grounds surrounding the camp. Tadeusz and Reinhard were already on the semi-circular path to the notorious gates. The so-called film-makers were almost upon Reinhard who made way for them. Inside, Reinhard stopped against the kitchen wall and suddenly the pointing of the old brickwork presented itself as music staves and he could hear the little orchestra that had met anxious and exhausted prisoners that April day eighteen years before. Tadeusz took hold of Reinhard's arm and led him towards Block 10. Gottfried and Zbigniew went off to the left. Karl X and Heinz Y trailed wires and set up tripods in the road outside the blocks and, after a few moments, Karl started taking still pictures, on one occasion clicking from ground level close to the base of Block 22. The rest of the equipment was then carted off to the other end of the camp where Tadeusz and Reinhard had just emerged from Block 11 - 10's infamous partner in crime. Reinhard met up with Gottfried between Blocks 17 and 18 - roughly in the middle of the camp.

'Just what you might expect of film-makers, eh?' Gottfried said.

Karl, the taller of the two, had been taking pictures, or pretending to, with a still camera and got very close to the base of 22. Reinhard reckoned that might be where they intended to set a bomb. He added, 'It could even be in the camera itself because these large format jobs are pretty bulky. Check with Tadeusz when you go back. If Heinz Y does the same there, we may not have long to wait. See you in ten minutes at Point B if there's any need.'

A small crowd had gathered in the roadway between Blocks 10 and 21. No one turned away or hid their faces as Karl X panned his cine camera around the area. He stopped filming, looked at his watch and walked to his MPP where he appeared to change the plate, pointed the camera a couple of times at the black wall between Blocks 10 and 11 - where so many prisoners had been shot - and then put it down against the wall. When Karl X started walking towards Block 21, Tadeusz stiffened and moved through the crowd towards the block just as the man picked up another camera and started going through the same routine. It was time to act. The operation was co-ordinated when Tadeusz signalled Zbigniew before stepping forward, pulling his gun.

'Halt! You are under arrest. Put your hands in the air!'

The public was cleared from the camp. Karl X was marched back to join his accomplice and lined up outside the kitchen by the gallows while Max went to work on defusing incendiary devices. Tadeusz said: 'There are two people still in this camp who would like both of you to be strung up right here and now and I wonder whether I should let natural law take its course. With the public now gone, it would be very possible,' he said, lingering on the words. 'However, there are certain procedures. Move!'

Tadeusz and Reinhard followed the handcuffed bombers out of Auschwitz I to an unmarked police car. It had travelled only a few miles out on the road to Kraków when it was forced to pull over on to some common land when a car overtook them and cut in, bringing both vehicles to a halt. Gottfried got out of this car and pointed an imitation gun at the men. The police officers were lightly bundled out and had their arms loosely bound and left on the ground behind Gottfried's car. Gottfried piled in with Reinhard and the would-be bombers and made a show of speeding away.

*

The blind-folded Karl X and Heinz Y looked down, though they could not see the cringing weeds leaning against each other as if wearied by the stiff, cold breeze. Life, stunted so cruelly long ago, exposed to the poisonous liquids, burning lubricant, the thrust of youth or the dribble of old age, had slowly risen again, close to the oily patches that had left their indelible mark on the aged sleepers. Sudden, clanking halts had always meant a spillage of one kind or another. Gottfried's railwayman friend, Marek, who had agreed to take some leave to help out with this part of the plan, walked behind the uncertain pair and, pointing his imitation revolver at the pair, said. 'You are going to be resettled. Your changes of clothing are just inside the sliding door.' He removed the elastic bandages and tape from around their eyes and mouths, and announced, 'Get in … no, no, not out here! Do not soil this ground. These weeds do not appreciate it. Inside is your home; that is where you can be private. It is maybe a little difficult. I will help you. Give me your arm.' Marek was enjoying his part in all this and the label he got for his trouble offended him. 'You bastard!' exploded Karl X, jerking himself away. 'What the fuck are you playing at?'

Heinz Y accepted some help in mounting the two-foot gap between ground and the floor of the truck. Inside the wagon, Karl X was the first to speak, and only then to curse. Heinz Y remained silent, leaning against the door. Unlike Karl X, Heinz Y was trying to keep calm. Karl X continued to curse, and Heinz Y was becoming too depressed and appeared not to hear what his friend was saying.

'*Verdammt!*' cursed Karl X. But suddenly there was something. 'What's that smell?' he spat, kicking his clothes bundle fiercely into the dark interior of the wagon. But the bundle struck something mid-flight and it fell between two lumps that shifted uneasily.

'What the shit are we doing with stinking cattle!' exclaimed Karl X. Before the calculating Heinz Y could answer, a damp mass pressed against him as an excited lover but then left, as if rejected, to be quickly followed by another, and another. They pressed against him hard now, and then backed off slightly, only to return. Both men sought each other across the dangerous centre of their prison. Terror gradually gripped Karl X. Heinz Y, still within himself, hardly knew whether it was his friend, or the cattle, or these things that kept hitting his lower limbs. 'What's going on?' attempted the angry Karl. 'I mean, this is crazy. Who is that bloody guy?'

The stench was unrelenting but neither man could get relief from

REQUIREMENTS OF GUILT

it and they were slapped by slippery lumps on some sort of rotating gantry. Putrefying carcasses. Karl tried to force his way forward but became lodged between clamminess and sweating hide. There came a thud and a yell. Karl X, pinned against the back wall, screamed, 'For Christ's sake get over here. Get this thing away! There's a herd of them!' Then the wagon started moving. Karl yelled. He was pinned against the back wall by a rear end. Gradually, the stimulated beast got off which allowed Karl X to slump to the floor. He laughed, a laugh tinged with fear but still the lightest relief either had had in the hour they had been in the wagon. Heinz Y looked across to his companion. In the gloom, he appeared like the high-up father of a friend he had known. And suddenly, he knew where they were and why there were here. He knew what this was supposed to represent. The resigned Heinz slumped against the side of the truck and slowly slid to the floor. Then, as his bottom pressed into the rough wooden slats of the floor, he was convinced this was part of the Auschwitz complex. A cattle truck, a box car service was being revived. Marek thought Heinz did not have the will or the wit to think out how, but he looked resigned to their being herded to their deaths. He told Karl X but his fellow prisoner had no more to say. The next time either would speak would be in the police station in Krakow.

32

REINHARD did the sums: two into two hundred thousand, walk where you want time, Birkenau space. He could just see to the other side of a vast, lifeless area, dotted with chimney stacks. At first, Dieter started walking as if trespassing and after a few hesitant steps they stopped, turned to each other and smiled nervously. They strode on, passed what remained of the women's camp to their left and, to their right, the town-loads of space for the men, just a single rank of huts still intact. They created an immensity of isolation but yet a feeling of suffocation. Wrapped by the chill Upper Silesian air, the occasion promoted in neither men the desire to speak but to extract what seemed intended from the crunching ground beneath their feet. They moved straight ahead, stopping every so often along the length of Section BII. Stretching deep into the greyness were the crumbling chimney-stacks, the only purpose-built humanity in the camp of two square kilometres. They pointed here and there and they murmured to themselves but neither man let words strung together become irreverent intrusions on minds that thought mainly of journey's end on the other side of camp and of their own beginnings. They followed the line of the old railway. The silence between them was broken by Dieter just before they reached the remains of the first pair of crematoria, his words finding a strange echo among the silvery trees, their arms bared, frozen and still, near the perimeter fence.

'What do you feel, dad?'

There it was again. Dad. He needed that.

Reinhard looked slowly around, turning almost a complete circle and returned to face the second of the closest chambers, then towards the disinfection buildings away to the north of the site and in the area where the second pair of chambers had been. He went to speak, but stopped. Gradually, it seemed as if in slow motion, the land in front of him regained its platform on which meatless bones were crushed by men and she-men. Visions and voices stacked for years in the envelopes of his mind rushed out to settle where they had originated. Barked commands, stomping SS, skeletons shuffling to and fro, hideous screams and suffocating, private sobs, desperation mixing crazily with clinging hope, dogs gulping at once beautiful frames and remnant ranks of dazed and numbed victims of racial insanity packed into lorries bound for special buildings to foul the air from great fat chimneys, leaving others to fix their gaze on the night's blood blotched sky and perhaps even yearn for this warm peace at last.

'Dad?'

Reinhard looked at Dieter. 'I really do not know. Most of all, I feel depressed. For everyone, you know? You, Dieter. Everybody. This whole thing, it was so terrible. It still is. I want so much for everyone to have back everything. I do not know how returning to the old *gaskammer* will be but we are almost there.'

They passed the first of the stricken crematoria and reached the remains of the second, larger one. Dieter stopped by the steps that led down to the basement and gazed over the ground of rubble and weed, once the undressing room and gas chamber under the fifteen three-stage furnaces. Reinhard walked on a little, slow, scuffing steps, head bent, hearing again the sounds that occasionally came to him.

'No!' he yelled.

'Dad?'

Reinhard crouched, tracing lines in the dry earth with a twig.

'N-o ... n-o ...' he started, finally letting the word go in a long, low and pained bellow, the word smashing into the trees and skimming off into the mist. Dieter walked back and helped him up.

'Christ!' Reinhard said quietly. Then, looking straight at Dieter, he said, 'This is Terrorplatz! I had heard things. But nothing to what it was. I walked over this ground, this ground here! ... There!' Reinhard yelled, pointing out in front. He walked quickly forward a few paces and, waving his hand over the area, continued, 'Here, just here it would have been, the officers came by me, those who say how I am a copperplate admin man. I think how good I am to tell them they have the crematorium numbering wrong when they speak of IV instead of V, they forgetting the No I gas chamber at the main camp. I should have killed them and died *wie ein Mann!*' He walked up to Dieter and looked into his eyes. 'When I came to you, I was to that point more needing you, perhaps even more than you me. Do you understand?'

Dieter looked intently at Reinhard.

'Up there, Dieter, through the wood. A kind of playground ...'

'Dad, do not upset yourself -'

'I *am* upset.'

'Please, Dad -'

Reinhard said, 'Dieter, I am *very* upset. I save you, trying to clean my hands. Here, I know for sure something that bothered me in Berlin. I had always wanted victory for Germany, definitely victory, but the contest, it had to be fair. And Birkenau was not fair.'

Dieter said, 'Dad, you actually saved someone from this place. You saved me! How many others who were here could say that they had saved anyone from such a place? Maybe there were a few, I don't know. All I know is that there was one.'

Reinhard interrupted, 'Look how many in Berlin I helped travel. Some lousy trip. *Konzentrationslager:* I believed in them to begin with, Dieter, I really did. Places to change thinking. I should have raged against it all.'

Dieter looked serious. 'First of all, if you had done that, you and I would almost certainly not be here today. Such outspokenness may have led to some change that might have been for the good, though more likely things would have become worse, for you almost certainly. But in Birkenau, in the spring of 1943, with things as they were, there was salvation for one at least. And that person stands in front of the man I am proud to call my father because of that single act that single day. We are not talking about someone you saved and how good a thing that was and you wonder now and again if that person still thinks of the occasion or whether he or she is even still alive or whether that person at all cares or understands. This is about me, the person you saved and have watched grow up and who has been with you ever since that day. It would have been great to have been responsible for saving the lives of hundreds of anonymous people but I can tell you for sure how it ranks among wonders without words that you saved just one.'

Both men became one big coat on the rough path that led to death. They walked in silence for a while before Dieter halted. 'And Dad, you have made me want to go to this place of salvation to do something that I was unable to do at the time.'

They passed what remained of the huge disinfection buildings and, leaving Brzezinka Wood to their left, they turned between the ground-level remains of the third and fourth crematoria at Birkenau - Reinhard leading the way to the furthest one away. For a full minute, still as a stake, Reinhard stared into the ground. Then, lifting his head to view the broken walls, weeds, crumbled concrete and bits of crooked iron poking out of the ground, he said, 'Here was Crematorium V.' They stared silently into the space before them. Reinhard had stopped by a break in the broken wall, four or five brick courses high. He took a few paces forward, into the rectangle and turned to Dieter. 'My attention, it was drawn from this point, the entrance hall, to what I thought was your mother. She was screaming for attention.' Reinhard beckoned Dieter forward. Dieter joined him and followed Reinhard's gaze left into an area he explained was the first of three gas chambers. Still in a halting voice, he said, 'On the occasion, she would have been among the last into here. An orderly, he was holding them all back with a stick so he could close the doors. The stick, it was against her arms as she held you out towards the entrance door and her eyes searched for anyone who would listen.' Reinhard said he had seen her. *'Bitte nehmen Sie dieses Kind!'* the woman had pleaded. 'It was the look on her face. She was asking me to take you. I see it always so clearly, then as now. I reached forward like this and took you. I said there'd been a terrible mistake. I made out later you were the Commandant's nephew. Well, the bigger the lie ...'

Dieter stepped forward but went two paces past Reinhard to stand in the old gas chamber entrance. He stood looking out over the area, turning to stand just inside the doorway, facing Reinhard. Dieter said,

'Thank you.' He paused, then added, 'That's what I wanted to say. Thank you, Dad.'

They wrapped their arms around each other and remained in the doorway, silent and grateful. When their arms slackened, Reinhard immediately put his back around Dieter's middle and lifted him clean off the ground with a huge and audible effort and said: 'And I swung you out of this damned, rotten, unforgiving place and -' But he was losing his balance and tripped over one of the crooked iron bars protruding just above the ground and staggered backwards, falling towards the low entrance wall. Still holding on to Dieter, he connected violently with the uneven brickwork and Dieter was released as they both fell to the ground. The momentum took Dieter over the wall and he caught his head on it as his body twisted on the other side. There was a heavy thud and Dieter remained where he had fallen. Reinhard picked himself up and lunged forward.

'So sorry, Dieter. Not so young any more, *nicht wahr*? Are you OK Dieter? I'm sorry. I am so happy.'

Dieter's head was close to one of the protruding iron bars and Reinhard suddenly drew back. Blood was pouring from a wound just behind his ear. He got a handkerchief and held it tightly to Dieter's head. Dieter's eyes were open but he was quite still. Reinhard's persecuted cry dropped back at his feet. He stood up and yelled again across the lifeless acres in a long, half strangled voice - diagonally, over the BII avenue of extinguished hope to where he and Dieter had left Gottfried.

'Gott-fried! ... Gott-*fried!*' Reinhard's voice ricocheted off the staggered ranks of chimney-stacks. The reply was a muffled echo and gripped in panic he swung round to Dieter, blood now visible as a pool beside a bleached and silent face.

'Dieter!' Reinhard screamed. He stretched forward to take hold of him under the arms and lift him off the low wall and onto his back in the dusty track. He smoothed his hair as again he yelled for Gottfried, turning almost a full circle before facing an approaching couple.

'*Was ist los?*'

'*Mein Sohn. Es ist mein Sohn.* Look, he has an accident. I take him out, you see, to swing him out of this place. I tripped. *Hilfe, sofort,*

REQUIREMENTS OF GUILT

bitte. Bitte, ein Krankenwagen. Schnell! Bitte, schnell! Oh, schnell, schnell -'

'I am a nurse; I will stay, said the young woman, already bending over Dieter, pulling her scarf from around her neck. 'Hans, go to the main gate,' she shouted.

Reinhard cradled Dieter against the doorway where the bewildered orderlies had once stood. Now he was back. He and Dieter were back and it was as if they had never left. It was just as if he had never intervened. Dieter had lived a while longer but he was probably dead. Reinhard was sure his son was dead. He had not been gassed but he was dead. He had not subsequently been burned but he was dead. He was dead.

'I am sorry,' said the nurse as she stood up, slowly shaking her head. Reinhard stared at Dieter. The young woman spoke again but Reinhard neither heard what she said nor did he move. Soon Gottfried was at his side and an ambulance came along the rough road Reinhard and Dieter had specially trodden to reach this chosen place in their lives.

Special treatment.

Gottfried turned Reinhard towards the ambulance. 'We shall both go,' he announced.

Reinhard was doubled up, yelling into his coat collar, flinging himself by Dieter's side and putting his arms around him. Reinhard kept repeating, softly and as if expectantly, 'Dieter.' Then he said, 'You left here, you never stayed. I could not let you stay. Don't now, not now that I took you away. *Kommst Du mit? Jetzt.* Now, please. Let us go from this place.'

Gottfried reached down to touch Reinhard's arm. 'Come on old friend. Come on Reinhard.'

'Yes Gottfried,' he whispered, repeating the phrase *Sonderbehandlung* as the ambulance drove away. Some special treatment! Dieter was another body being taken away from the *gaskammer*. And he was travelling over the same road out of the camp as he had done in 1943. Be ever so quiet, Dieter, he had said. So that he should not be noticed. Now there was no need. Yet he said, 'Be still, my boy. Be still.'

The ambulance went out through the gateway to the right, leaving the old SS quarters on the left, no black cloth moving in and out through the double doors, no vehicles drawing up or leaving to transport or deposit black cloth. Gottfried sat opposite Reinhard as the ambulance left Birkenau camp behind, and he leant forward until their heads touched. Reinhard's tears were the silent expression of a terrible lament that ended when he broke free suddenly to kneel at the side of Dieter. He several times smoothed Dieter's hair and brought Dieter's right hand up to take into both of his. 'Forgive me,' he cried.

Reinhard turned to Gottfried. 'I ... I ... saved him. Now ...' Gottfried put both arms around Reinhard but said nothing. Reinhard stood up and yelled, 'It is not true. Tell me it is not. Dieter! Answer me, please!' And then, in a gradually fading voice, he added, 'Son, answer me ... what shall I do with Black Face? Dieter?'

Reinhard looked up abruptly, as if he had been called to answer for something.

33

TIGHTLY holding the plastic bag he had carried from the boarding house, Reinhard lowered himself to sit on the newly dug, cold Harz soil, and, for a moment, he let it rest on his middle while awkwardly supporting himself. At this moment, he felt no emotion. The hitherto almost unattainable nothingness that had for so long done little more than knock at his mind before running away whenever he tried to confront it, was practically ready to swamp him. Consequently, he felt very little of anything. But there was one thing to do before he would be able to let the previously illusive state of nothingness take its course and leave him wherever it would. Reinhard opened the plastic bag Irma had handed over in Goslar where, according to Amelia, he had been pacing for several hours before Irma was able to respond to his disturbed telephone call. He took out the box, lifting its lid slowly. He stared at Black Face and the strong strands of nothingness reverently retreated as the mostly threadbare animal repeated some of its more memorable past performances before his eyes. Reinhard buried his face into the still fluffy centre of the little bear's left ear.

'Goodbye old friend. You were never mine but I loved you, too. Everything you have seen, the good and the bad. Shortly I will leave you but Dieter, he will be with you soon.'

For a while longer, Reinhard looked intently at Black Face before taking the trowel from his inside pocket to begin picking at the side of the grave. He wondered whether Dieter would wish to face with his head towards the church or the lychgate; whether he, too, preferred facing the engine as it were. He should have asked him. The space that had been allotted within his state of nothingness did not allow much room for anger but he had been unable to avoid feeling annoyed that in this small thing he had also failed Dieter. Neither was it such a small thing: if it were not right, it would forever be wrong. Here it could happen, after the darkest of nights, that four strangers would lower Dieter into this black hole, then make it blacker still in which to spend a death-time the wrong way around. It was important, not just because of the long journey ahead but because as a youngster, Dieter had always had his Black Face to his left hand as he would lie in bed at home. Reinhard decided to follow his own preference and offered up the cardboard coffin to the little hole, but before placing it in, he made sure the tram ticket was in the pocket of the colourful cardigan Irma had made just two weeks after they had known each other.

For the first time, Reinhard noticed how cold it was. He looked upwards to a huge oak tree whose branches seemed to clutch at the mist, keeping out what little sunlight had begun to break through. It would be cold for Dieter. And the mist strengthened as he stood up and leaned against the earth. He thought he would try to warm the earth himself and sank back down, spreading his legs out and laying stretched hands flat on the soil. In this position, he realised that he was close to his own end.

As he shuffled back along a gravel path through the community of bones, as heavily hung in his crumpled suit as the lead on the church roof, a foot occasionally caught the top of one of the stones, unsettling his measured gait but jolting nothing else. Nothing now came into his hollow head that allowed any appreciation or interest in the kind of afternoon it was, nothing that provided any recognition of light, shade or temperature, nothing that could automatically tell what else surrounded him, certainly no mind or spirit that would spur him to curse his stumble, let alone entertain any thought or consideration for any other course than the one he had set for himself. Nothingness was everywhere. He was on a journey through a void that after the funeral would exclude everyone but HJB.

34

REINHARD was gripped by isolation as stark as tundra. Land, but slipping away into a slow-motion heave of bluish green, going under but not sinking, somehow weightless. No more thinking, no more problems to weigh the mind, no conscience to wrestle with. Only The Forsthaus had to be found, the restaurant Father Dohl said HJB frequented. Table Six gave him a fair view of the area he wished to watch.

The arrangement of tables reminded him of confession time with Dieter. It might be days before HJB ate out in this restaurant again but Reinhard nevertheless looked about expectantly. And only about half an later, the man approached. Reinhard stiffened. Before HJB sat down, Reinhard walked out through the swing glass doors and entered the reception area. Partially masked by one of a number of large pillars in this exclusive eating-place were two adjacent telephone kiosks. He entered the toilets, gave himself his new identity and walked out to one of the booths. He made a note and entered the other booth, picked up the receiver and dialled. He let it ring briefly, put down the receiver and re-entered the toilet, leaned on the inner door and drew breath on his plan. Reinhard returned to the booth, dialled and after a few rings someone from reception approached.

'Guten Abend, Forsthaus. How may I help you?'

Reinhard said HJB often ate at the restaurant and he wondered whether the man was in this night.

'I believe so. I will check. Who shall I say is calling?'

'He doesn't know my name: it is Ernst Mouer. I have important information he will want.'

'*Moment, bitte.*'

Reinhard watched the receptionist walk into the restaurant, entered the booth and pressed down the cradle, leaving the handset to the side. He then moved into the adjoining booth, left the door open, held the receiver to his ear but did not dial. As HJB neared the other kiosk, Reinhard started talking.

'Give me Hermann ... Hermann? I have a good story for you. An important old SS officer has turned up locally. If we're quick, we'll have a great scoop and this Nazi will get his comeuppance.'

HJB entered the booth and Reinhard heard him curse into the dead phone. Reinhard sprang the name and went on: 'Yes, of course I am sure it's him. I would not otherwise ask for the picture desk. He's there now, at the Stern Hotel, according to my reliable source but for how much longer, I do not know.' HJB was fiddling in his pockets and Reinhard drove home his trap. 'I want Georg for this. This is a great story and no other paper knows. Tell him to meet me in Sturmstrasse by the milk depot. We need someone at the back also. *Volkszeitung* has a reputation to keep up in this town. This man was a big Nazi fish hereabouts. Tell the police but not before we move in. Do not forget, the only cover we have here is silver bromide.'

Out of the corner of his eye, Reinhard could see HJB react. He was pretending to look at the telephone directory. As soon as Reinhard put down the receiver, HJB cast the directory aside and hurried back into the restaurant. Reinhard knew he would have to be quick to complete the deception. The thought of capturing the final filth in his list of scum and giving the former officer his just rewards undoubtedly stimulated HJB. Reinhard was pretty sure he would feel they all deserved their fate and that probably Germany, if not humanity itself, would recognise his actions, his devotion to making sure that good in the end triumphed over evil. More than likely HJB thought that tracking down such vermin and ensuring that they paid for their sins, had to be public-spirited. Reinhard wondered what HJB would do when all the old officers on his list had been accounted for? How would he occupy his time when there were no questions left to ask, no leads to follow up, no plans to devise, no deaths? He would not been keen on resting. The thought would give him a cold, empty feeling ... Reinhard realised at the same time, though, that HJB had not come as far as he had by planning and acting carelessly and he almost certainly knew that to capture the final officer, even with the lucky break that would give him the advantage of surprise, he would need to exercise care and cunning.

Reinhard reached the hotel within ten minutes, booked in and went to his room. HJB arrived not long afterwards and also booked in. He glanced down the visitors' list and entered the lift. He had spotted the name, and if this was really the man he was after, he was not far from his own room. He sat down, breathing heavily as he fumbled through papers from his jacket pocket. He opened a small notebook and extracted the picture he had had with him for seven years. This was the only photograph he had ever had of the man. It was only just a side view. He had the who and the where. The when would be this night. The former SS man was due to have a rude awakening - press photographs and all, if he knew *Volkszeitung* - but he had to be first. Speed was everything. He would need some luck because he knew so little about the man's features - except that he would look like a rat, and would almost certainly squirm. HJB would not just to barge in, however. At reception, he fabled a yarn and was told his friend had not long ago gone up to his room.

HJB told the receptionist, 'I wonder if I could go up unannounced; I'd love to give him a surprise, you know.'

'I see, Sir.'

'It's unbelievable,' HJB went on. 'We haven't seen each other since the war, and last week, quite by the most outrageous chance, I heard he was not only still alive but living in the same town as I. Can you imagine, living in the same town as someone you've not seen for so long, and yet not know about it until now? So here I am. I believe the press - *Volkszeitung* no less - are coming for the occasion.'

The receptionist adjusted her hair and took her hand away with a sweep saying, 'Might do trade some good for a while, then!'

'Certain to,' said HJB. 'Anyway, here I am. Just cannot contain myself any longer. I just want to see him face to face, suddenly, to see the look on his face. *Verstehen Sie?*' he said, again picking up the truth.

The receptionist tried to enthuse. 'Well, he is in No 25. Give him a while, though because he looks a little exhausted.'

'I will.'

Reinhard reckoned that a man of HJB's fanaticism would mean that he would be sure to make the first move. Reinhard would have only to wait in his own room, where he now stared out of the window. On the street below people were walking this way and that, everyone seemingly with a purpose. No one looked remotely like HJB. Perhaps he was in disguise. Everyone was HJB! Theatrical make-up could turn anyone into anyone else. The man was coming from all angles. Would HJB find him? Of course he would. Reinhard would leave everything else to the thorough German, settling down to whatever length of peace and contemplation was left to him. He returned to lie on the bed, done with everything. He had the time to run but would not. Though had he really finished with life and Stephanie? For a second, nothingness receded. He did not want to die; he needed to. He could walk away with hardly any questions asked, except self-interrogation and that was the trouble. He knew he would be deceiving himself. Nothingness nestled up close to him again. Reinhard returned to the window. There was a small child and a woman walking along the road. Reinhard breathed deeply. What a beautiful picture. Nothingness did not stand a chance. What freshness, innocence, expectation. Not nothing. Suddenly, briefly, he wanted to be that child, someone who had not yet been accountable. He should have been concerned that he had never seen Bruno Walter perform at the *Deutsches Opernhaus* or the fact that people like Fritz Lang, Kurt Weil, Thomas Mann and Berthold Brecht had left the Fatherland and the horrors that would likely lie ahead in the Third Reich and taken more note of the sad face of Eric Kästner as he watched the works of 'undesirable and pernicious' authors burn in Franz-Josef-Platz rather than be delighted that Hitler's share of the poll had gone up more than six points to 36.8 per cent. Schoolchildren should not major on maths and geography but be introduced to those things that kept the spirit free and the soul clean, to have textbooks on kindness and thoughtfulness, on love and how to apply it. He went back to lie on his bed.

The knock came as an explosion. His heart sprang. *'Moment, bitte.'*

Reinhard rose from the bed and stumbled across to open the

window as noisily as he could as HJB burst through the door and spat out, *'Halt! Bundeskriminalamt!* We have reason to believe you are wanted for crimes against peace, war crimes and crimes against humanity. You are under arrest.'

'Never!' Reinhard bellowed, launching himself towards the open window. HJB was as alert as he had imagined he would be and threw himself in a dive towards Reinhard's legs, bringing both men to the floor. Reinhard tried to make his resistance adequate. HJB was like an animal that had tasted blood and his claws were into his long sought prey. Reinhard said, 'Right. OK, I'll come. Nothing heavy, please. The hotel chief, he is an old friend and I don't want any questions. Can we walk, normally?'

HJB lied, 'I am not alone on this operation. If you try anything you may not be alive even to get your little Nürnberg trial.'

As they were leaving the hotel, Reinhard felt a sharp jab against his thigh. After he was pushed into HJB's car, blackness swallowed everything up. When he awoke, he knew exactly where he was.

35

A CLAP of thunder prefaced HJB's voice like a behemoth clearing its throat: 'As you will by now have guessed, I am not from the police. I am your executioner. This is Festfortag dispensing its own justice. I do not care how many people you have murdered. Nor does it matter that you may not actually have done the killing with your own hands. You have been responsible for removing, indiscriminately, people from this earth for some unfathomable reason. Now you, too, will be removed. I know how long you were in the SS, where you were and what you did and, if I had the time, your death would last those 84 months and 13 days - each day becoming progressively more unbearable in the type of punishment I have dedicated years of my life in getting rid of scum like you.'

Nothingness was becoming a real friend.

'And with me,' added HJB, eyes blazing, 'you get no last request. Also, it all starts now.'

The Nazi-hater stood up and signalled for Reinhard to enter the room he had already seen, where there were all sorts of machinery, benches and pits and what looked like a short conveyor belt with a rail of spikes over. HJB reached over to press a red button. The spikes jerked into life and Reinhard was roughly directed to a wooden bench beneath them. HJB started to immobilise one of Reinhard's wrists with a strap attached to the side of the bench. The storm now raged and provided an increasingly dramatic backdrop to what Reinhard saw as a theatrical performance. His state of mind, with an unswerving resolve to die, acted as pain relief.

HJB went on, 'You are one of God's deformed sons. Whom God seems unwilling to punish for his wickedness, I intend to put to death. May God be with you.'

Reinhard did not hate him. He was doing a duty and a kindness. As Reinhard's ending became clear, there swept over him the most comforting and purest level of nothingness that he had ever imagined. Previously he had been able to hold on to this image - absolutely nothing anywhere - for only a split second. Suddenly, however, this feeling was almost upon him totally. He was alone. HJB was not there. He could not see Dieter. Dad. His mother. Stephanie. Irma. George. Gottfried. Everyone had gone. Every*thing* was going. The spikes moved forward, high, lower, faster ... they passed from tip to toe ... then back again ... closer, ever closer. Eventually the spikes would slice nothing for the last time. Reinhard closed his eyes to take nothingness to its final level of peace. His head swam with an unfamiliar dizziness as he looked up at the greedily waiting blades ...

HJB suddenly clutches his chest and collapses as rain enters the basement, rises quickly through weakened brickwork and sweeps him out of sight. Then the log-like Nazi-hater returns briefly before again being swept away. The top end carries eyes that take an extra look back, dead eyes alive with glee. The body is rushed away. Reinhard hates water that masks its depth but shows how deeply you can drown. The spikes are upon him, slashing close to his scalp. He seems to look back at his own face, scarlet dye from inkwell eyes ... crying blood ... his clothes stretch across his threshing limbs. Diabolical words hang in the air. He clutches at them, gathering in handfuls of letters. He sorts out nine and tosses the rest aside, holding the precious letters close to his heart. The water continues to rise and suddenly the machine falters and the spikes are halted. But at the same time burning hot tallow drips from huge candles above him. One blob begins to look like Stephanie. His body is rigid, his neck straining to raise his head to see her properly. She seems to be beckoning tenderly. Blood vessels pound. Wait, he tells her. Where is that book? Damn you book, where are you? He wants to bring back the people in the bound red record book but the pages are stuck together. More, much more water, rushes into the basement, weir-like. Water comes for him, with its stinking coat of decay, forcing him to the final, futile act of jutting up his chin momentarily to stop the foul liquid entering his mouth and nostrils. Minute particles of leather, the gathered-up shame from so many jackboots, collect around him and go ashore and enter the double fronted cave. HJB comes round the headland and rubs up against his face when the bubbles cease. He comes up to the jetty on a new wave. Their arms brush and he tries to grab a sleeve just as the accursed man veers away. Footwear reappears and this time the capture is made. His fingers strain to get HJB's key. His legs nearly jack-knife but his mouth is too far away from his right hand for his tongue to help. HJB moves again and Reinhard can reach the key. Tallow falls and there is a sharp pain on his right wrist and the key springs loose from his weak grasp and sinks to the basement floor like an angler's lead. He curses the candles, but smiles at Stephanie. Stephanie's face. More tallow falls and her head joins a body on his thigh. The mass snuggles up to him but bites a displeasure and the pain is bad. He jerks his leg to let her slip to the other side of him but succeeds in making her role between his legs. He repeatedly smashes his thighs together to put out the searching flame. The tongues will not be stilled, however. He is burning in several places. She passes between his thighs and rests on the couch beneath him, sheltered now to feed in peace. He threshes uncontrollably but this only helps her in her search for food. He screams his agony. His movements become a frenzied spasm. Tallow and flame stagger but stay together. Thunderous screaming fans the flames and the smell of his raging hair and flesh irritates his eyes and nostrils. With all his energy, he blows at the flames. They reel, bent as sprinters. But they regroup to return with even greater vigour. He directs another hurricane towards the orange mass but the wind is only just strong enough to carry his screams to the ceiling as his head jerks back in anguish. Stephanie seems to consume him, her face is so beautiful. She is the only pain and suddenly the hurting stops. He rests back and opens his mouth in hideous joy. She is looking at him, open-mouthed, as if about to speak. He wants to pick her up. She is saying something. But he cannot. He wants to tell her something but he cannot move. The heat around him makes him boil. He starts to suck away the flames from her beautiful body but his throat catches fire. He wants to squeeze her hand but he will never be able to squeeze her hand because ...

Reinhard's mind crashed through to consciousness.

Had he really been kidding himself about dying all along? He *would* squeeze her hand!

Every sinew strained to jerk his body upwards as he resisted HJB putting the final buckle around his other wrist. Just as assuredly as he had wanted to go, he now wanted to carry on. He had wanted to go because, no matter his intent those years ago, no matter what he did finally, no matter how Dieter had repaid him by calling him Dad, it had all cost others. He had built up his layers of contentment on top of burdens of distress. And now he didn't have Dieter. To those who could put it all together, add up the good points and take away the bad, it would still come down to failure - and to the most cynical among them, Dieter's death could be seen as his finishing off personally a job he had pursued in Berlin.

But Stephanie, how could he leave her just like that?

She would always be beautiful, so wonderful. It would be a nightmare in hell to be totally unable to remember her, see her in his mind's eye. And now he knew that in committing suicide he would be thinking only of himself, releasing himself from the agony of living while abandoning Stephanie and, yet again, failing properly to consider the consequences of an action. It would be an extension of wrongdoing. Plain, simple and tragic.

He ripped his hand away from HJB's hold, the momentum taking his knuckles flush into the other's nose. The man clutched at his face and Reinhard slung his free arm around HJB's neck and brought the startled face back down towards his own, braced forehead. The dazed man's nose burst, shattered blood vessels discharging in several directions. He grabbed the key from HJB's hand, giving his own fist greater steel for the punch that landed directly on the man's chin, sending him cold to the stone floor. He released his other hand and in the same instant jumped clear of the bench. A clap of thunder reverberated around the basement just as a brick gave way near a corner of the room and water started entering. Huge and prolonged claps of thunder completed the diabolical scene in the basement room - dank, dark, evil looking, smelly, somewhere beneath the stained soil of Germany. He stumbled across the airless basement towards the exit. Freed now from dark imagination, reality was nevertheless course grained and he picked out only strips and stripes in front of him. He cannoned into the iron railings and suddenly felt sick and clasped a hand to his mouth against the heave. He was terror-stricken. The space behind him appeared packed with heads, rising above a swamp, each a hollowed face and gaping mouth. Sticks stretched towards him, seemingly coming to him neither hatefully nor hopefully. It was not until he had dragged himself up one rung of the ladder that his head cleared. He looked back. Below him everyone had now laid back and there was only a dampish, crumbling brickwork floor. He was violently sick, a full and lasting rush of it, emptying him of everything. He felt cold, thin, weightless, destined. He saw Dieter's crumpled body, then the brilliance of Stephanie's face. He ran, legs suddenly lightened and he ran and he ran.

He was out of breath and practically doubled up and had no reason to wonder about the man with horn-rimmed glasses and a panama hat on the other side of the road talking earnestly in a telephone kiosk. He had no breath left as he clasped at the pebble-dashed wall of a house. People looked at him from over their shoulders as they walked on. One person, middle-aged and concerned, stopped and checked on him. A laugh mopped up the spilled explanation, 'Too - old - for- runnin' - s'ppose.'

She laughed, too, as Reinhard straightened up.

'You must be in a hurry,' she said.

'Yes, I really want a taxi. To the nearest station for a train to Goslar.'

'I'll take you to the railhead in my car,' she said. 'I live here - over there,' she pointed.

He began to thank her but she said, 'It's nothing, really. You are in a hurry and I don't really have anything much to do. Your appointment must be important,' she said, beginning to turn out on to the main road and continuing as another vehicle flashed her on.

'I am going to surprise a lady,' he said after recovering his breath.

'Ah! I love surprises, especially surprises of love. Tell me about this lady.'

'OK,' he said, turning to her and feeling much younger. He told her everything. The honest truth came rushing out, though he said he'd torn his jacket on a hedge. Putting it all into actual words, he seemed to hear things almost for the first time and knew for certain how much he still loved Stephanie. It took up the whole journey and she thanked him enthusiastically for the story as she pulled up outside the station.

'I am a writer,' she explained. 'Romantic novels. This will make a good book. Why, it's practically written itself. Just the ending to do, virtually. Very good luck. Promise to let me know how close I get with the ending,' she said, passing over a card.

'I will,' he said eagerly, like a young man, again not being concerned when he again saw the man in the panama hat at the station standing close to him at the ticket office before bringing up his arm across his face and holding the rim of his hat as he peeled off back to the station telephones by the taxi rank.

Reinhard phoned Irma. She answered somewhat shakily.

'It's Reinhard. I have had a terrible time. I will tell you about it when I see you again in two or three hours probably.'

'I'll pick you up; where are you?'

'No, Irma, thank you. I know the way ... ahead.'

'Excuse me?'

'See you, Irma.'

36

IRMA had obviously been waiting at the window. Reinhard was hardly out of the cab when she came out of the house and ran forward to wrap her arms around his neck. He already felt uncomfortable and tried to end the greeting without appearing too eager to do so. He was further embarrassed when, still locked into Irma, the waiting cabbie was seemingly enjoying the embrace. Amelia also emerged and paid the cabbie who briefly raised his eyebrows before pulling away. Reinhard uneasily gripped the top of his open neck shirt collar, buttoned his jacket and sank his hands into his trouser pockets.

Amelia said, 'Shall we go in. Let's have a drink. We can all do with one. You two can talk about everything when the police have gone.'

Reinhard tried to appear casual but *'Die Polizei!'* had shot out like a cannon.

Amelia said: *'Natürlich, Reinhard.* We had to call them. We were concerned for you and had no idea where you were. Detective Sergeant Rudolf Knabel is here now. Apparently a top wanted Nazi has surfaced and he is in the area. Some journalist set the ball rolling when he rang up Central Office in Ludwigsburg seeking an official comment for a story his paper is running. Not everyone has faith in that office but there it is. We understand officers are on their way over here. They could be here quite soon.' She explained that the sergeant had requested being updated if anything new occurred and she telephoned straight away after Reinhard had called to say he was safe. The sergeant said he'd call in on his way home anyway. Apparently he finished early. He's been so good, Reinhard. It's just to finalise matters.'

'Detective Sergeant ... finalise ...'

'Come on,' Irma said slipping her hand into his. 'Let's meet him; he's such a nice chap. Gottfried will be back in a minute. And you've met Hans already - you remember, the journalist, the night of the sports centre plans?'

Reinhard took his hand from Irma's and plunged it deeper into his pocket. He felt wrong and out of place. It was as if he was entering a head-high diameter pipe that would eventually become ankle-high. He felt trapped by Irma, even though in his mind he had released her. Her concern for him had blinded her to the possible difficulties of involving the police. She had gone to the one source that he would have preferred knew nothing about his disappearance. And the rat-like *Spiegel* stringer would doubtless try to lay some slimy trail before his retching public, whether the case was all over or not.

Amelia told Reinhard that Gottfried had felt he had perhaps not looked after his friend as surely as he should have. Because he'd suddenly lost touch with him after Birkenau and he'd left it to his cousin to ask the police to make the checks. Now he wished he had given work a miss and done the whole thing himself because police in Hamburg and the local force were on to it. While that need not necessarily be any problem, it was something he and Reinhard would not have wished for. Still, Reinhard had been missing. He could have been in some danger. Gottfried, who just then re-entered the house, immediately repeated this to Reinhard as 'I only wanted discreet enquiries. Not all this. Still, you're safe. You are here.'

'I am here,' Reinhard replied, trying to smile.

Gottfried put an arm around his friend as Reinhard explained that he had had a rough time although, for now, he did not wish to say more.

Gottfried changed the subject. He said, 'Look, I'm going to Scotland soon to do a piece on Dali's Christ of St John of The Cross painting that's been vandalised in Glasgow on exhibition. I want to speak to the guard who discovered it. We could return to England together. What do you say?'

Reinhard felt uncomfortable and frustrated. He wanted to concentrate on finding Stephanie and yet here he would now be bogged down for God knew how long with police enquiries that could take him straight into the one imagined area, this feared consequence of his poor past judgement, that every so often pounded away at the back of his mind. He slowly shook his head and was about to say something general about re-kindled fascination with the old country when Gottfried, glancing in Irma's direction, said he quite understood. Reinhard looked at Irma and her demeanour assured Reinhard that she had got the wrong idea. He clapped his hands together louder than he intended and said, 'My, Ludwigsburg officers, eh?'

Behind Irma, Amelia, Hans, Amelia's doctor friend and the Goslar policeman stood near the entrance to the dining room and, for a moment, there was complete silence in the hallway, with everyone as still as a collection of museum long case clocks. Reinhard felt his heart was ticking loud enough for all the timepieces for miles around. Within the constraints of the emerging situation, Reinhard's homecoming was a time for relief, even of jubilation. Irma particularly but also Amelia and Gottfried were overjoyed to see Reinhard again, though naturally everyone felt obliged to hold back on anything approaching relaxed jollification. The doctor friend of Amelia also popped in but, clearly aware of the situation, tried to take a sober medical view of him as he extended a hand. Reinhard did his best to be gracious but he did not wish to hear any of it and kept shifting his feet, adjusting his glasses and smoothing his hair. The policeman worried Reinhard. A statement to close the file on a missing person meant an explanation, going back over things. 'Reinhard Hänsel, who was missing for a few days, has turned up safe and well' would satisfy no one. He looked at the detective sergeant, who had the kind of face that displayed a fixed smile. To all those present, Reinhard said: 'You will have to excuse me; I would like to be alone for a while.' They all mumbled understanding, shifting backwards, forwards and sideways and, as he passed the smiling policeman, said, 'Give me a few minutes, please' without wishing to be given any time at all, minutes or years. The policeman nodded, saying he would return in the morning when it was more appropriate, and Irma left the room with Reinhard, Amelia calling out, 'Show Reinhard into the conservatory, Irma.'

REQUIREMENTS OF GUILT

Out among the rubber and Swiss cheese plants, Irma said, 'I am so sorry about everything Reinhard, everything except for you and me. So very sorry.' Reinhard's smiled reply was forced and brief and he turned away and sank into a cane lounger. 'I could do with a drink,' he said, as the telephone rang.

Amelia knocked on the glass door of the conservatory, with a folded hand to her ear and pointed with the other.

'It's for you, Reinhard. It's George. Take it in the dining room.'

George could hardly speak at first and for a while mention of Dieter made them both choke. Reinhard had the strong impression that George felt the loss almost as much as he did and loved him for his call. But at the same time he was aware of a remoteness in his friend's voice and once they had spoken at length about Dieter, George particularly spoke as if short of air. They both knew that Dieter's death was not the only thing that was massively different now and eventually George supposed that Irma had told Reinhard about the change, about what had been going on for some time. He probably wished it wasn't so but it had happened and he implored him to look after Irma. The way he said it left Reinhard with the view that George meant for longer than the journey home so he told George that his return to England was going to be delayed because of the Ludwigsburg nonsense and that he intended to look for Stephanie.

'OK, then,' George said. 'Anyway, look after Irma, won't you, until she travels back, with Gottfried now, I understand. I know you've always had a special place in your heart for her,' George added with what Reinhard interpreted as words of hope. When he put the receiver down, Reinhard did not experience the boyish thrill that those words some time ago might have given him. He no longer wanted licence and it was Stephanie he thought of first as he stared at the curtains on waking next morning. He tormented himself and got out of bed as if she were actually there. He put his hands around the material and allowed the sun to caress his body. He must have been at the back end of a dream because the particularly powerful images suddenly faded and were replaced by a numbness in full consciousness. The chasm left by Dieter's absence made him drop his head into his hands as he sat on the side of the bed. His lad's tragic passing was so incomprehensible to him, worse now than when it happened, that once again, in waves of misery, he imagined that nothing mattered. Once again he felt desperate. Once more he cried.

When he had pulled himself together and re-joined the others, he realised that there was only one person who could provide the depth of solace he needed and was the reason he did not reach out for Irma's hand as she moved towards him with hers extended. But he did take her aside and told her briefly what he'd been through. There was no discussion because just then the morning newspaper had made its noisy entrance through the letterbox and he made straight for it. He took it out of the door and threw it on to the table, where the background of a plain off-white tablecloth helped promote the headline's pushy and vulgar message: *Spa town sighting of Nazi murderer.* His chest tightened at the sight of the name he had assumed. His hands jerked instinctively to hide the paper but he took possession of the ranting tabloid and sat down in a corner of the room and read the story. Waves of apprehension enveloped him. As members of the household made their way to the breakfast table, yawning their Good Mornings, he wished he were still asleep. Apart from Irma, no one looked at him especially but he knew they soon would. And though he had thoroughly made up his mind about Irma, he still wanted George to storm back over the Channel and demand his wife back.

Irma smiled at Reinhard and pressed her knee against his leg. He left the paper folded on the seat and moved away, irritated, as she looked up at him. He filled a glass with fruit juice and fiddled with rye bread and Jarlesburg as he noticed the Herr Rat circling before making for the discarded newspaper. The *Spiegel* man straightened it out and showed it to Gottfried and Amelia as they were about to sit down. Irma joined them and all four were soon pouring over the front page.

'The bastard ... in our midst ... Bloody hell ... Right here ... What's he doing here ... How? ... Why?'

Reinhard narrowed his eyes from outside the room, taking in only as much as keyhole sight of the group. He was about to break into the peering cluster when there was a knock at the door and the policeman entered.

'Just in time to protect us!' Amelia said. 'And have a little breakfast with us, of course, officer! Please take a seat and join us. What's the latest, then?'

REQUIREMENTS OF GUILT

'I won't, if you don't mind,' he said formally, leaving the door open and signalling to a police car on the drive. Two other officers appeared. Realising what was happening, Reinhard brushed forward and stood facing all three. The senior policeman formally addressed him by the assumed name and Reinhard faced the problem outright. He struck out boldly, 'Someone will have told you that I am he and that person will have done so because for a short while I pretended that I was. That person has reason to harm him. I wanted to be hurt, killed if necessary, after what I have been through recently. But I am in fact Reinhard Hänsel.'

The senior officer, a middle-aged man with calm eyes and lively crop of reddish hair, listened with head bowed while a young second officer, stout and sweating in a dark blue suit, thrust his head forward and stared at Reinhard. They asked the local sergeant to stay with the others in another room and when the door had closed, the senior officer said: 'You assumed someone else's identity so you could die? Now why should anyone want to do that?'

Reinhard went to speak but words piled up and jammed in his mouth, beginnings and endings in turn trying to impose themselves, fixing his jaws open and giving him the look of a half wit. He wanted to ask for George's presence. Mostly he wanted Stephanie by his side.

'I think you had better come with us,' the senior officer said, slowly lifting his head, the words restraining him more securely than any official caution would have done.

'We have reason to believe -'

'Look, I tell you I am Reinhard Hänsel. I lost my son in an accident. My fault and I will tell you everything but at the end of it all I'll still be Reinhard Hänsel.'

'You do that, Sir,' the other officer said, leading him out to the car while the senior policeman fetched the Goslar sergeant. As Reinhard was led away, an agitated Irma called out. 'What are you doing to him? Where are you taking him? He's just come. It's a mistake. For God's sake!' Tears poured down her face as hysterically she yelled out, 'The poor man's been through hell already! He's just returned from burying his son. Is there no decen -' But the words trailed off into the gravel on to which Irma had collapsed in the driveway. Gottfried skirted her coiled body as he hurried up to the police car.

'I am sure there has been a mistake, officer. Reinhard -'

'Please remove your hand from the car, Sir. We will be back in touch.'

Although the situation looked serious for him, Reinhard placed a lot of trust in an outcome that would prove the truth of what he was saying. He even relaxed between the two officers and actually thought of Irma lying in a heap on the gravel driveway back at the house and what she might now be thinking and doing. He imagined her passing through phases of anger (at police stupidity), to disappointment, even disgust with him (for his thought of suicide). For a moment, she would probably harbour a conclusion of his guilt and the fact that in any full relationship with him she would be spending time with a killer.

He was taken to Ludwigsburg, spending the night under guard in accommodation close by, being confined to a room that had only a quarter light high up. In the morning, in a windowless room half the size, he told the whole story to officers without pausing. He emphasised his own actions, from the time he first joined the SS. He kept returning to the Berlin days and the *heil-holz* and Auschwitz-Birkenau, to the woman and to the boy. He repeated himself, as if the telling and re-telling could act as witnesses' testimony, the chance - away from the private condemnation and reprieve he had tried to offer himself - to test official reaction in an office specifically seeking justice for anything up to and including mass murder. They kept asking him to confirm that he was a former district court councillor and telling him he was wanted for the murder of six prisoners being taken to the concentration camp in the moor of Esterwegen where he allegedly ordered their hanging on butcher's hooks. Reinhard had, according to the interrogator, treated anyone who had been the slightest antifascist with a cruelty that turned the stomach of even diehard Nazis and was once involved, at a timber plant, in tying together one set of opposing feet and arms of two forestry employees working near Mulheim and pulling them apart with winches.

'Their crime,' said a square-featured man whose rounded nose spoiled the symmetry of his face, 'had been to be overheard questioning the accuracy of a radio report on German successes in the autumn of 1943.'

Reinhard listened impassively. Relating his personal and military history had left his accusers completely cold. Another officer, weedy and with bad breath detectable from near the back wall of the room, stepped forward and added, 'With others, you were also responsible for the death of two Jewish families, including grandparents and children, during a visit to Krakow in 1940 who were forced at gunpoint to walk naked into a blazing pit of old tractor tyres. Other indictments are being prepared.'

They both leaned forward, like examining doctors.

'Well?' they said together.

37

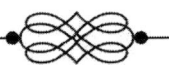

A REMARKABLE freedom enveloped Reinhard in the few moments after a Ludwigsburg officer delivered him back to the house. What he had said checked out and he was no longer suspected of being the wanted officer. They had turned over what details they now had on the other man to the federal police. Reinhard had been purposely vague as to where the place was and said that in the Forsthaus restaurant he had overheard the man talking about what he called his anti-Nazi retribution ring, and had set up his telephone call hoax because he had been overwhelmed by Dieter's tragic death and had been drugged as he left the establishment.

'His activities ought to be stopped. A bloody madman,' the officer had said.

It crossed Reinhard's mind that this actually was another way of saying that old Nazis should be left alone. Then, typical of Reinhard, he imagined that there had therefore been a bit of a whitewash of his case, that the activities he had laboriously chronicled for the Ludwigsburg office had been condoned rather than examined and found reasonable in the circumstances. As a result, he had suddenly felt less free than a minute or two earlier but he felt a bit better again when the officer had pressed him further about the location he was taken to. Reinhard had spoken only of rain, thunder and crumbling brickwork during the first part of the capture and that when he was eventually taken from the basement he said he was gagged and blindfolded and remembered only that the car went up a long hill almost immediately after leaving the place. He said he'd travelled for something like half an hour to forty-five minutes before having the gag and blindfold removed.

'And you overpowered him when he drew into the track by this copse.' The officer had suddenly stood up and snapped 'OK then. Well, we have your description of this man so we'll see. No name, though. A pity.'

Reinhard felt unshackled. He thought to himself: What a waste it had been over such a long time, dwelling on the unreasonable. And it was at that point, when he hoarsely whispered, 'I'm free!' into his hand, that he realised he was completely free to do what he liked about anything. Fresh and heightened desire to be with Stephanie again flooded his mind and body as if he would be a more worthy partner. Of course, Reinhard reminded himself, at this stage he was pure day-dreaming.

He called out to Irma from the hallway and she ran downstairs to him just as Amelia entered from the kitchen, releasing the fine smell of a goulash and the news that there would be a celebration dinner in two hours in the garden since it looked like being such a nice evening. What Amelia then said gave Reinhard a decided guilty feeling, 'My, you do make a great couple!' Irma laughed but Reinhard was unimpressed. As he made for the staircase, Amelia called after him. 'I'll leave the celebration wine to you. Take my car and get whatever you like. The more expensive the better, they tell me! And put it on my account. It's Gustav's, by the railway station. Get Hans to serve you, OK?'

Reinhard went upstairs to the toilet deep in thought about Stephanie, whether she could be found, what he might discover if he found her and what he would feel if he did not, or worse, if he found her but she wanted nothing to do with him. The things that George had said on the phone he now put out of his mind, about the special place Irma had always had in his heart. It was only mildly true. Had George spoken of 'a special place' with a hint of resignation or of hope? Was George making do with small doses of Renate to make life tolerable with Irma when really he would like to enjoy a full relationship with Irma, if only Irma would help him along the way? He should waste no more time on such questions.

Spiegel man Hans interrupted Reinhard's thoughts, banging shut the front door and calling out that he was back. He was uncommonly pleasant when Reinhard rejoined the family downstairs and discovered that Hans had taken over the role of transport provider to the late-night wine shop because he had to go to Gustav's part of town to check a couple of facts to do with some story he was working on and invited Reinhard into his Mercedes. Reinhard tried hard to put up with its unpleasant occupant by listening to the purr of the engine and admiring the bodily curves of what was undoubtedly a very beautiful piece of automobile engineering. He looked out on the pleasant evening Amelia had forecast and hardly heard the Herr Rat suggest his story would make interesting reading. Distant buildings and some tall trees had begun to make silhouettes against the fading skyline that Reinhard made into romantic profiles.

'I mean I could almost certainly get you a four-figure sum,' the *Spiegel* man enthused, massaging fingers on the steering wheel as he pulled up at traffic lights.

Reinhard briefly met the rodent's eyes but again looked out through the car's open window, up into the night sky. And when for a second he compared his freedom to that of the heavens, he felt his magnitude to be greater than that of Sirius. He located Ursa Major as the car moved left. But without looking at the *Spiegel* man said, a touch sarcastically, 'Can you now?'

As the car turned favourably again, Reinhard traced the seven stars of the Plough. He halted his journey along the bottom of the saucepan, like he knew the way from there, like he wanted to make the final stretch of the journey ceremonial and diverted his gaze back into the car, to the driver.

'Yes, but it must be exclusive,' the Herr Rat said.

'Oh, it is very exclusive,' Reinhard said.

Hans brought the Mercedes to a smooth stop by a parking island. Reinhard got out and said, 'I'll choose some wine then,' looking around for the entrance to the railway station. Hans said, 'OK. I've got this call to make. Won't be long; see you back here in, what, fifteen minutes or so?' Reinhard did not reply and set off. But as he pulled out, Hans called through the car window, 'There! The wine shop is just over there! Goodness knows what you'll be like when we've had a few!'

Reinhard forced a smile and changed direction but when the car re-engaged the traffic, he turned and made for the railway station. He looked up. He knew the way. He should have gone a long time ago. And now with his mind made up and the way clear, he practically long-jumped on to the platform with a surge of joy from that special place somewhere in the centre of his body, that rush of adrenaline, that told him he was glowing with Stephanie anticipation. The platform was empty but a train waited with doors open on Platform 2 and he ran down the stairs, clanking on the perforated metal treads two steps at a time. He walked briskly towards one of the open doors and no sooner had he seated himself in the quietest part of the carriage then a whistle blew, the doors slammed shut and the train started, inching so slowly at first that he felt it necessary to slump a little into his seat and keep an eye on the platform just in case the *Spiegel* man had suspected something and had made his way on to the station.

He was free. Free from Irma, dear Irma, who in recent years had made it possible for him to be able to breathe in the girl he had always loved, sometimes casually brush by her, touch her hand lightly, while smiling warm-heartedly as a good friend and neighbour, then, so recently, to embrace her and imagine it was Stephanie with the full force of that night – an occasion which, however, he wondered whether he had made up during nights of tortured imagination. He got out at the first stop, a small station with candle-strength lighting and no one around. Reinhard went to pay for his journey but was waved through as the ticket man turned another page of a paperback novel. The station, with the bustle and profile of an empty hay barn, was all he wanted, to be unnoticed. Just a few yards away, the light under a rusty lamp shade dangling from a wall suffered the anaemic thrust of a funnel of cigarette smoke blown towards it by the driver of a lone taxi positioned on the station's cobbled forecourt. Reinhard moved towards the vehicle but stopped in the middle of the road and looked up. They were still visible, his markers for the future. Though he held back, resisting a peep at a future he could have called on many times over, sometimes pretended he would, a future that he now faced with sudden, impatient urgency, as if everything before this moment had been a fill-in, surrogate activity in a make-do life, kept tolerable only by Dieter and his other private thoughts. Now he had no one and yet he had his eight bright friends and a ceremonial intent that was one brief look away. He counted the stars along the line of the saucepan. One, two, three, four, five, six ... seven. For a full minute, as he stood on the cobbled road, the taxi driver looking intently at his suspected fare, Reinhard held his gaze on star number seven, the lip of the saucepan. But it was not a test; he was ready as never before. He just wanted to enjoy the anticipation, the excitement, to make it very special, allow the moment to mature, to fix her, to let her know he was coming.

'Wait, I'll be with you in a minute,' he told the taxi driver.

He spoke to Amelia, then Gottfried and Irma from an ill-lit kiosk. He explained and thanked them for everything. He said he was sorry but the thought of Stephanie was directing everything and he felt as if every hour counted. When Reinhard stepped away, he breathed deeply and once more looked skywards. Clouds had begun to obscure the night sky.

Reinhard walked towards the taxi driver, who was also looking upwards as he sent out a final stream of smoke between pursed lips, and opened the rear door.

'You see that star ...' Reinhard said, pointing.

38

HE thought he was hurrying between the tall firs on the forest track to the wooden lodge café near the staggering fence posts held upright by rusting wire where he was sure they had seen glow worms - and that soon he would be with Stephanie. Then earlier when he first met her in the club and gave her a bottle of Coca-Cola and asked her for a game of table tennis. He wanted to hurry on down the street and get into a telephone kiosk and look up the number and go now, with a bottle in his hand. He started to hurry away, looking at his watch as if to make sure he was on time for the bus that he'd always intended to catch.

Reinhard had thought of her a lot but never acted on the urge to do something about it because there was this shame, his past, the way he had treated her and the way his Nazi work had turned out. Sometimes, when he was really low, he would think of her for quite some time, perhaps ten minutes or so at a time, and there had been times when she would put him to bed and smooth his head until he fell asleep. Sometimes his thoughts would trail away into tears. Always he would end up saying what a fool he had been, what an unadulterated simpleton, what a regular half witted, feeble-minded, unadventurous, self-centred, profligate idiot he had been, especially recognising the way he felt. For if there were flash thoughts of her, these were surely sharp reminders that she still really meant something to him. Thoughts, even at one a week, amounted to a fair amount of imaging about someone supposedly discarded. She had been someone he had really loved, someone he still loved.

Somehow he and Stephanie imagined, all those years ago, that they would know, whichever one of them it was, that the other was in need. They had said they could always do that, that they need never suffer alone. Reinhard was convinced that something would tell her how he felt at this moment. She would, he said to himself, have looked skywards as his desire grew and his resolve strengthened. Whenever it was possible he would at this point in his thinking always look up into the night sky, find the seven stars, then look those small degrees to the right where the North star would be, their star, their waiting saviour. As he moved on down the street, he felt passionately that they could one day soon be together and there would be comfort. Whatever the outcome, it could never be a waste of time. Nothing of this kind could ever be a waste of time, giving in to something like this, real and important to the soul, the one thing save breathing that kept things going, even though they were in the background, not forming part of everyday working and living life yet somehow being the whole of it. Because, even if he went no further with this, if he stopped now, and turned back to Irma, or a car should hit him as he crossed to the café, or he was shot by a stray bullet by some maniac hell bent on some political machination, then even what he had thought during the last few minutes would have been worthwhile, rich in honesty and gratifying and exciting, the honouring of some extravagant youthful accord that might be as far-fetched as the distant stars he so relied on for his comforts in times of stress, yet so what! It had always made him cry, and he knew he was again crying, because his cheeks were wet. After a while, he was hardly able to see in front of him as he picked his way along the pavement. Neither did he turn away or cover his face with a hand, or rub his forehead with the newspaper he carried. He just cried, head up and happy. When eventually he blew his nose, as he waited to cross the road, he saw the skin of his hand and it shocked him. How could he be so old? He looked at his feet. Tired but urged on by the messages his brain was still putting out. Stationary by the lights, he shifted impatiently like a young boy wanting the toilet, until the road cleared when he forced his stride to the limits of that pace he had always taken for granted.

Reinhard was not on his romantic forest track, among the pine trees of those carefree days before the Nazis interrupted. It was the tedium of a shopping street. Yet he did not want to return the pine trees to

REQUIREMENTS OF GUILT

telegraph poles, those trees that had leant in on them from both sides as they walked towards the timber beer house along the spongy path of pine needles, holding hands, chattering like birds. His love for her had seemed to increase every time the Kellner ticked off another drink on his beer mat - marks, he noted, that gradually formed a kind of chain around the colourful cardboard coaster. He had mentioned this and they expansively agreed that the chain should be completed, right around the beer mat until the marks linked up. And when it was, they said it would form a ring and that they should marry!

Most people had regrets in their lives. And if he were asked to say what he felt his biggest one was, it would be this failure to act on the question he had put to her that night when they had slopped the last drop of beer at the tavern in the woods. He could see the forest, the beer house, the Biro marks around the beer mat, Stephanie. He had later handed her a ring. He remembered the jewellers, the walk to the bus stop, her look at that moment. But he had never took it to its natural conclusion. He had taken a picture of Stephanie at the picnic in the forest that he still had on a small piece of glossy paper. And there was that time when they were together on the hill overlooking the Francorchamps Spa track for the Belgium Grand Prix during that wonderful June day of that wonderfully romantic year. Yet he could not recall her birthday, just one special day in so many lonely others that he could have slowly savoured once a year, with perhaps a Coca Cola. Because she meant so much to him still, he always signed himself Rheinhardt as an extra thrilling reminder of her and places that they knew.

Reinhard spent the night in a moderately poor hotel but was glad to be resting. Again he thought of Stephanie. Yet despite trying to recall where it had been she had said this or when she had laughed at that, he could not. Yet Stephanie's voice and her looks were in every street and beer garden, on every tram, and in every room he occupied. Her ways and expressions came to him in turn, like all those little things that made up masses of sweet memory and were called love. He could not analyse this love for Stephanie. It just was.

He smiled his way through the dull corridors of the hotel, up and around the red floral carpet with its blotchy, once polished stair rods holding the well-worn twill more or less in place, letting his hand slide along the top of the banister rail in the idle action of a far-off mind. He stopped at the door to his room and looked it up and down. He shook his head. He turned out the light on his brown-burdened room as soon as he had undressed and, sitting on the edge of the bed, head in hands, allowed himself to flop into it, slowly pulling the bedclothes tight around his shoulders.

*

If at one time there had been a boyish face that showed up in the mirror when he cleaned his teeth and brushed his hair, it had long since ceased to exist in the years he had spent in his Hammersmith flat. Yet this morning, as he quick marched his towel and washing kit along the short corridor to the third-floor bathroom, he felt as young as tent life, the feel of youthful expectancy replacing casual adult hope. Reinhard ached with vigour and playfulness, so much energy inside of him that when he addressed the huge, white washbasin, it was his father who looked out of the stain-edged mirror. Reinhard stood back, running his hands over his face, closing his eyes, as much to remember those times when he faced his father like this as to keep the image going. Reinhard wondered what particular time he was remembering when he saw his father exactly as then, what either of them next said.

'Tell me dad,' he said looking deep into the mirror. Perhaps it was a row over politics, the final parting-of-the-ways row. Or not a row at all. Perhaps just a kind of vacuum in which there was no air either could breath. The attraction of Hitler or the hatred of an Upstart. Reinhard leaned further towards the mirror, as if he wanted to go through it. Their noses almost touched.

'Sorry dad. You're right. Enough of this. Let's forget the whole crazy bandwagon and photograph the bridge again, you and I. I'll get my bag ... come on!' For a moment, Reinhard stood still against the mirror, relishing the image and going through the process down at the Rheinbrücke by Beuel, taking out his little camera, waiting for the cloud to release the sun a little and click. He had never pointed it at his dad. Dad was always around. He could see him whenever he liked. If only he had clicked at him, just once.

Back in his room Reinhard sat on the bed, his young heart regaining its beat as the thought of his mission took over his mind. If he had been himself, he might by now have lain back on the bed and cried out the loss of Stephanie but he was no longer himself and could not see how he would ever again be himself. He felt his cheeks again and looked into the mirror in his room. He narrowed his eyes to the point where he could imagine the age to match his mood. He knew he had to do the rounds where Stephanie and he had been all those years ago, to feel her as she had been, to enjoy her again, before he picked up the telephone to ring her. Only then would he go and see her, if she wanted to see him. Because if he were to go and see her straight away, if she were there to see, everything might go wrong and he would then not wish to recapture anything. Powerful though his thoughts of her had always been, if she did not want him now, even to see him, for a moment, then there might be nothing for his mind to recapture. He had always said nothing could ever take away the wonderful memory he had of Stephanie but suddenly he realised ... well he would no longer have the desire to wander round the past, yet, of course, the memory could never be expunged. Not picking up the telephone could mean he could go on enjoying what they had experienced - because it truly had happened - believing he could rediscover, almost to the point of experiencing it again, the love that had fortified his life. Whereas she could kill everything by an adverse reaction to his call, take away the huge plank in his life. In going back over his old stamping grounds, he would go from one memory to the other stripped of all the bombast and pretence that he would with the Nazis employ with such devastating failure and regret. He would take lungs full of what had been during those earlier times. He would for now settle for her memory and the scenes that recalled her so vividly - stinging nettles and the buzz of the summer fly, the aircraft's passage overhead that they could control by slowly bending their heads towards the ground and back up again, the breathtaking smells of mown grass and resurfaced roads and the hush and contentment of a riverbank or a clearing beneath autumn's forest canopy. Stephanie had really always been the most important thing for him, deep down, in the sub-conscious. She was the sub-text of his reasoning. And it would be the most important thing because it was the one thing left that had expectancy. The rest was death. All those hugely significant other people in his life - his brother, his dad and his mum, that poor woman of number five (that representation of all the poor souls who perished in the camps) and lovely, loving Dieter. They were available now only in memory. And though they spun round in his head, providing wonderful moments, yet they were not alive. It could have been that within days, perhaps even hours, or minutes after the letters stopped, Stephanie might have been run over by a bus or succumbed to some disease of which neither she nor he had ever been aware. Or that the final break in their relationship had been so powerful that at that moment, and increasingly as the days went by, she had lost that normal ability to assess risk, deal with disappointment, vanquish disaster and had put up shutters that blocked out everything including the hurt. Worse than his own loneliness. Who knows? Reinhard thought it could be any one of those things. But equally it could be that Stephanie was well in the sense of physical and mental condition, well enough either to have carried on a life with occasional smiled glimpses into the past or made do with life with recurrent regret that Reinhard had simply not come up to scratch.

He'd go to Nürnberg, then München. That would keep him busy. Berlin he would tackle later if necessary. In Nürnberg, in what Hitler had called the most German of all German cities, the city of the Party Rallies he recalled so easily, he would try to recapture just one or two instances that had so much helped to influence his life. It was a bitter-sweet recall in respect that the wretched place led on to so much that was bad but it was still the place that, for a while at least, had fortified true love. So he decided to try to retread the steps they had taken in September, 1936. He would relive as much of their time together as a loving couple - all those places they had visited during time off from those cataclysmic seven days. It might take a whole week, of smiles and tears no doubt. Then she could tell him to clear off. And he would, unwilling any more to as much as look at a building, a tram, a café or a beer hall, or face any of the city's folk. If she said no ... he refused to accept the thought. He would be empty. Cleaned out of everything. Everything he had ever been able to call on in the shallow days and deep pits of the night would drain out of him and he did not dare to think of what might remain on which he could try to draw strength. But she would say yes! When he met her, she would put out her hands. They would both put out their hands. They would acknowledge each other and he would be so happy. He hoped their hands would touch, then wrap around each other, for a moment, at least, expressing in that natural action a simple, physical anthology of all the thoughts they might both have had over the years. He stopped and stared at the telephone kiosk. Then walked on.

He would walk around Nürnberg. But as he approached the next kiosk, he tested himself without money, picking up the receiver and putting it to his ear.

Stephanie? Stephanie, it's Reinhard. You know.

Reinhard? Reinhard Fürth?

No, Stephanie, Reinhard Hänsel.

Reinhard! Wie Gehts? Wie schön!

Imagining tears, he said, *'Do not cry, Stephanie. It is so wonderful I hear you but laugh, with your eyes, like you always did. Would you show me again if I come to see you?'*

Natürlich.

Reinhard wandered on foot, hopped on and off trams and eventually caught an R-Bahn out to the Dutzendteich. He would walk from Zeppelinwiese to the site of the old Congress Hall set in the wonderful grounds of the old recreation area around the lake and, though much would almost certainly have changed, from there he would look for pointers along the long walk they had made. He visited beer gardens, cafés and restaurants, hoping he could remember one of the venues in which he could wallow in the past, but there was nothing really, though he did think there was something about one he passed and excitedly swung his arm up in the air and hit a man in the back.

'Hey, watch what you're doing!'

39

IF he never telephoned her, Stephanie would remain young.

Her old house was there still but not the family. The owner knew little about their movements beyond the fact that they had moved to live near the Austrian border. Neighbours confirmed that the family had moved to Hausham. They had met up on a couple of occasions but things had become increasingly difficult and then the war started. The parents died within months of each other and daughter Stephanie had married a doctor, Theodore, who was in general practice with a brother in Nürnberg. Next morning, Reinhard returned there but it was Thomas who answered the door and nodded pleasantly when Reinhard said he had been an old friend of Stephanie before the war. Thomas said his brother had been killed in one of the last Allied air raids over the city while out on call just weeks before the war ended.

The two men immediately got on well together and they talked freely. Had he come far? Hamburg, Reinhard lied.

'Been meaning to do it for years and with a few days off, I decided to come on the chance of being able to see her.'

It was not long before they were enjoying coffee and cakes, and Thomas enquired whether Reinhard wished to stay the night. 'I've plenty of space here. I'd be happy for you to be my guest.'

Reinhard accepted the offer. The doctor said he'd looked after Theodore's wife for quite a few years now and they had until recently spent a fair amount of time together. A brilliant card player who also loved almost every board game, she was also interested in politics and was a great humourist and conversationalist.

Thomas said: 'You know, she does the *Die Zeit* crossword in about the same time it takes me to drive to my practice of a morning. She also loves dinner parties and has helped with the administration of the practice. She reads a lot and listens to a fair amount of classical music. We've had some great evenings here, I can tell you. Great fun is Stephanie most of the time: her wicked analysis of our politicians' attempts to govern this country is a speciality. And she's got another kind of back-hander; table tennis. She still plays. On that table over there sometimes,' he said, pointing to an extendable dining room table. Very recently, however, he'd had to put up with increasing occasions when she rather isolated herself.

'Silly, really, but I suppose I actually felt a bit jealous when it became clear, well to me, that she'd probably met someone. She went out more but, strangely, she began to withdraw into herself. On the decreasing number of occasions when we talked for any length of time, she began linking her dead husband to places and occasions that I am fairly certain he had never known or ever visited. Strangely, I've even heard her refer to Theodore by a different name. She sometimes seemed confused. Perhaps she felt some guilt about becoming attached to another man, if that was it. I don't know. I tried to reassure her but she didn't always seem to be listening. It got to the point that any time she had to herself, when she was not painting - oh yes, she is an artist, in oils, and a good one - she spent either in town or in her room.' Thomas added, 'Look, that's one of hers, the moody clouds painting over the fireplace.'

Reinhard walked over to the painting. The canvas gave him a thrill. He imagined her hand guiding a brush to achieve the softer area of the central cloud. 'Is Stephanie ...' he began.

Thomas interrupted. 'She no longer lives here. One morning a couple of weeks ago, she came down to breakfast and announced she was moving to München. Just like that. Never mentioned this bloke of my imagination or anything. She spoke of the move over toast as if it had been a moment that we've both known about for a long time. She said we should keep in touch but she needed space to work things out. I can tell you, if she had been my wife, I would gladly have put up with periods of apparent melancholy for the overall delight of having her under the same roof. The next day she said she intended going into the phone book under her maiden name. "I'm who I once was," she announced quite matter-of-factly. She's not listed yet but if you wish I'll give you her number. Have you ever been to Nürnberg before?'

'Once. That was in ... 1936.'

'Ah, the rally? I was there then. What a week. Probably a bit out of order to say so – well, certainly out of order! - but I feel we need some direction like that in Bonn at the moment. Without the consequences, of course!'

Reinhard again thanked Thomas for putting him up for the night and took a note of Stephanie's telephone number. After discussing over a couple of brandies the merits of Thomas Mann and Stefan Zweig, dealing briefly with the Eichmann trial and drifting off to lighter matters and eventually back to Stephanie, he retired to his room. It was a smart room in a smart house, with minimal but well positioned, quality furniture, paintings and ornaments. Reinhard contrasted the splendour of ease with the clamouring items of necessity or convenience that cluttered his Hammersmith flat. Above the bedroom, so he understood, was Stephanie's old room. He would peep in before he left if the door was open. For tonight, however, he was happy to allow whatever vibes might drift from there to rest upon the sheet he now pulled up around his face.

*

He'd packed away his heart so securely that when in the morning he eventually telephoned Stephanie he started speaking of the weather. The beating practically stopped when she answered. He managed an echoed 'Hello' before his mouth dried up and, covering his now thumping heart, he said nervously, 'It's Reinhard. Reinhard Hänsel.'

'Reinhard!' she exploded. It did not sound like anger though he dared not guess. There were sounds from both ends of the line but not exactly words. Eventually, they started - and talked about everything and nothing, giving each other no time to dwell on anything. Their timing was all over the place and they kept pardoning and apologising, laughing a little. Reinhard felt he was floating. Both of them kept to the past mainly. Neither seemed to know where to start or when to stop, without ever saying very much. They did not refer to what they were doing now. Reinhard wanted to say, 'May I see you?' but he thought she might think he was making promises again.

'Come on round, please; I'd like to see you,' she said.

His heart leapt and, for a moment, he felt he was going into some sort of spasm. He pressed a hand firmly against the kiosk and as calmly as he could, he said, 'Yes, I hoped we could meet. When then?'

'Any time, really. I've just moved in here, still got a few boxes to unpack, so I don't yet have a routine. Where are you? How did you find me?'

As he told her he felt he was defying gravity, aloft with joy. He wished he could throw himself at her feet and smother her with thanks. Again, however, he did not want to assume.

'I'll ring you when you're settled in -'

'No, no, Reinhard,' she cut in. 'You could *help* me settle in!'

His laugh was too loud, he thought. It was darkening outside. He looked up but could not see what he sought but came right out with the Plough thing.

'Ah, you remember! It's odd but I had a funny feeling about that the other week ... just before I decided to move.'

Reinhard was about to say he had never forgotten and that on such nights as this he thought about it powerfully and talked to her and sometimes cried for the love he had thrown away but, with a voice that only just formed the words audibly, he said, 'Yes, I have thought of that from time to time.'

'You talked about it only yesterday!' she said.

'Eh? What do you mean?'

She continued, 'Well, yesterday; you said it then.'

He could feel the fun in her voice.

'Not, of course, for the first time yesterday; years ago now, right at the beginning. Do you recall, Reinhard?'

'I -'

'I still have the recording you made to ask me out!'

Reinhard's heart felt as if would burst through his chest. He was all those years younger. Making the tape, in his office, secretly, before wrapping it up and slipping it into her raincoat pocket in the cloakroom after he'd left the dance floor to use the toilet. He had been like a kid, too shy to face her with such a powerful proposition! The memory of it came rushing back. He was a kid now and could hardly speak and nearly lost her when he miss-fed the phone and only just managed to catch the coin between his knees. He kept fumbling with coins and words.

'Oh that!' It came out like he'd dismissed what she had said with an unwanted emphasis on the second word and so he said it again, swapping the words around and putting distance between them. But now it was overdone. She laughed and Reinhard visualised her eyes shining and full of life.

'You also promised something. Nothing particularly big, but something in the way you said it excited me all the same. For years I thought about it. Every time it came around. Bet you can't tell me what it was.'

Reinhard knew. Because he had never really been practiced at what his friends commonly referred to as an art, he remembered feeling grown-up and adventurous when proposing all those years ago a date at the München Oktoberfest. And here they were in München, some meters' worth of well-worn telegraphic cable length apart and no doubt within a mile or two, perhaps even walking distance of the Theresienwiese, where he had already seen on several street lamp frothing notices that the event would open in just a couple of days' time.

'May we go this Friday?' Reinhard ventured, suddenly reckless. He tried to hold his breath but the air made a jerky, foolish din and he began to prepare a fresh statement.

'That would be marvellous, Reinhard. Thank you. I shall look forward to that very much.'

'Great,' he said, trying to sound casual, and adding unnecessarily, 'I've heard the Augustiner-Festhalle is one of the best on the site. But we could also go to the Schottenhamel where it all starts. Shall we make for that?'

'*Stimmt*. To start with!'

A noon start. Stephanie invited him to meet her at her apartment on the Friday and added that she had to catch the shops. He rounded onto the street and bumped into an elderly woman who was unfurling her umbrella and obviously put out by the wait to use the phone. It was pouring with rain now and Reinhard felt like stretching out his arms high into the sky and singing. He felt so good he would have given a solo performance to the elderly woman if he thought it would have done any good.

40

STEPHANIE replaced the receiver and aeroplaned around the kitchen with a smile as wide as her wings. As she halted at the sink she began humming a refrain from Nicolai's engaging overture to the *The Merry Wives of Windsor*, ending it with a full-blooded yell of joy and a few pirouettes. But suddenly she stopped her jig and stood perfectly still in the centre of the lounge. Reinhard had telephoned her. He was to visit her. That's all. She poured herself a brandy and held the glass to her lips, sipping thoughtfully, a deep frown evident beneath a casually layered fringe of dark auburn hair that now slipped between the fingers of her free hand as she ran it over her forehead. Stephanie glanced at the *Die Zeit* crossword she had been doing. If only she had clues to work out what questions the telephone conversation had generated. She knew what he had looked like, back before the war and Stephanie could match the voice with her vision of him. But what did he actually look like now? Had he perhaps let himself go? Perhaps his camps work had changed the person she had so fallen in love with? Why had he tried to reconnect with her after so long an interval and not before? In all the rehearsals for such a moment she had imagined over the years, there had been no such misgivings. Surely last-minute nerves - even if such silliness was to last the entire three days before he came - would be no match for the day-dreamed hope of thirty years? No. She slumped into her lounge corner seat. As the golden liquid took its effect she announced to herself that no matter what probabilities could be listed as to his intentions, she preferred to dwell on the very much shorter list of possibilities. Anyway, what of herself, she wondered. She walked to the mirror and pulled at the skin beneath her eyes, seeking signs of the tomboyish look Reinhard had so loved in her. But it achieved nothing beyond a distortion of her face that made her burst into laughter. No matter what, he had telephoned her. Nothing could ever be the same again.

She made her way through to the bedroom where she bent to the bottom of the wardrobe and took out a cardboard box. She put it on her still unmade bed and lifted its lid with delighted ceremony, tears again making their way around the lines that her smiles created. She wrapped both hands around a reel of tape and pressed it next to her cheek. She breathed heavily at the ceiling. She had played its message scores of times over the years. He had recorded it before their courtship had really begun. She reckoned he had been too shy to say very much to her face. The spoken words had held her together through some difficult times. It was the only thing, apart from a photograph, that she had of him. Now, she thought extravagantly, she might have him. Hark at me! she said out loud. Stephanie returned the box to the wardrobe and stood facing the back of one of the doors. There was a life-size photograph of Reinhard, one she had taken when they'd picnicked in their favourite forest clearing when they'd tested each other's command of English. She went up on her toes and gently pressed her face into his, remaining there for several seconds before walking to a full-length mirror in the hall. She stood this way and that, holding her hair up and smoothing the front of her dress, leaning backwards just a little. Should she buy as a lady or an urchin? she asked the mirror. She was torn between a completely new and stylish outfit or choosing a lazy-day combination of white blouse with rolled up sleeves and pale blue chequered turn-up jeans. She ranged over whether the former ensemble should be pink, green, mauve or black. 'Or any other colour!' she conceded with a wide grin. Then there was the question of the food she should have in. She thought of much but came up with bread and raspberry jam; it had been his favourite. He'd want a slice at one point, if he stayed. Hark at me! Stephanie said, rubbing the words into the back of her hand. One day, possibly a couple of hours at most! Not that food would make him stay. It would be that something else, she said to herself as she poured out a little more brandy. 'Really, just hark at me!' she chastised.

She hardly slept but though she rushed next morning to the mirror, the flush of happiness that had toned her skin better than any foundation and had already lasted longer, and the sparkle in her eye that she'd caught after glancing at her hair in the mirror on putting down the phone was still there, if anything diamond-like now, and she wondered whether it would show. It was not far off her birthday, just a couple of days. Perhaps he had remembered, planned it this way. Should she help peel off his coat when he arrived? Oh, hark this question: should she tell him she still loved him!

Stephanie decided not to stop for breakfast. It was no use sloppily occupying an impressive property, not even if he still loved her. What was she saying, love! He was arriving to see her. Hello, good-bye, more like it. Well, it mightn't be quite like that but it might have the same meaning. It could be just a courtesy call: I'm in the area, so nice to see you again, shall we go for a meal together, that would be nice, well that was great, good luck in the future. Maybe he was here with an exciting purpose. She threatened herself, putting two fingers to her temple. He wouldn't even know I'm alone now, Stephanie reminded herself. Perhaps he was married anyway! Still, she almost skipped from her usual car park, anxious not to waste a moment of this special day.

She had four material hours, holding up cloth and slipping in and out of garments, breaking the routine but once for a coffee where she looked at everyone, people on adjoining tables and out on the street where passers-by were suddenly bathed in bright sunshine she reckoned had broken through for her personally. She felt a wider interest in life that had been absent for so long and in which she cared for everyone, smiled at the slightest happiness and positively beamed when she saw a young couple put their heads together across their café table. She thought how wonderful the world was and of how, suddenly, she felt herself to have been lifted onto its stage. She finally made for an exclusive shop near to the popular Hofhaus where she normally but seldom shopped. But the window nearby that had sometimes challenged her to go in, she now dared to keep her out, defiantly staring into its interior, then pressing down the door handle so fiercely that she stumbled in but kept her head up. She settled on a light fawn pencil suit which had natural wood buttons, toning with a delightful silk neckerchief which the assistant had described as an imaginatively creative brown and lemon yellow, shot with beige and which, she noted, complemented madam's suit perfectly. Also, if madam didn't mind her saying, it even extended its matching influence to her hair and her shoes. Stephanie was so pleased she almost giggled, putting a hand up to her mouth, correcting it into a small cough.

'I hope madam enjoys her rendezvous,' the assistant said.

As Stephanie crossed over the road, her intention was to slip down the alley opposite the dull Hofhaus to the car park. She thought she saw a car out of the corner of her eye. It seemed to be bearing down on her faster than the rest of the traffic. But it was all right. It was only the sky, although a little crowded by fussy clouds bending out of the blueness, going from the sulking Hofhaus towards her shop of understanding creativity but slowing as they passed over and tending towards her, just above her head, just above her nose. She felt weightless and fluffy like a piece of lightly chloroformed cotton wool, really like the wispy, bending clouds that quite suddenly darkened blackly.

41

DOWN this street, across the road by the memorial, along a bit, then … No, still too early. Reinhard was young then, distance was nothing. Now, off to the left? Yes.

Part of Reinhard wanted to go back and make it a simple appointment at the first photographer's studio he found. In the city centre, it would be easy. But another part, the strongest part, implored him to go on. The proprietor, Gustav, might not still be alive but the shop could be virtually as Reinhard had known it. Where was the place! Had he been mistaken? Perhaps it really was the case that walking as a youngster was always half the length of any adult distance, striding out with dad, arms around his shoulder.

Good pictures, Dad?

Great, I think.

Why was that man telling everyone off?

Well, he wags a finger at the world.

What do you mean?

Oh, he's always like that

What do they call him?

Depends, son. Today, he's wonderful! Stirred up the crowd just right! Should make the front page.

But …

That's Hitler. Adolf Hitler.

I think he's wonderful, too.

The son had taken over the business although the old man still put in appearances. One day a week mostly and Reinhard had struck lucky.

'It keeps me active,' Gustav said brightly. 'I still take the odd photograph, you know, mostly unconventional - whacky, some might call them. Experimental, I call it. Not that Erich seems interested in any of my ideas. That's my son. I would really like for him to move away from safe retail and be bold, open a gallery or something, create rather than just utilise the produce of others, be able to leave something behind, something worthwhile. 'That's my aim, you know, to leave something behind in this life,' Gustav said, gathering his hands together and taking a pace forward as if prepared right away to start on something. 'Erich seems more interested in politics, I am loathe to admit. Still, how wonderful it is to see you again, Reinhard. They were good old days. Honest days, eh?'

They went into a back room, the orange of a dim central light getting no help from windows partially obscured by heavy brown curtains. The room smelled of liquor and cigar smoke, slightly airless but chummy. Gustav opened a glass-fronted cabinet and projected a bottle of brandy at arm's length towards Reinhard, his raised eyebrows anticipating acceptance. Reinhard thanked him. Gustav lit a large cigar, sucking eagerly on it before sinking into a leather armchair, lifting his head, a long, slow exhale ending with, 'Honest days indeed.' An aromatic haze from the expensive Havana eventually formed a lazy ring that matched the shape of an oval gate-legged table under the window. Accepting the comfort of a matching armchair, Reinhard felt at ease. He told Gustav about his part in all the dishonesty that followed those early days when he would often fetch and carry for dad. And he kept going through all the other years. He kept to the salient points but covered them all, right up to the night of the strange dream he had which still bothered him and which he described to Gustav in detail. As Reinhard spoke, he edited his life like a news story emerging from his old typewriter. Just the facts, as objectively as any personal memory could be. Powerful, corroborative quotes that he normally would have injected high up into his stories, he let express themselves with facial movements of obvious misgivings or well-remembered joy.

The telephone rang and when it was not answered in the shop, Gustav called out urgently, raising his eyes to the ceiling with a look of annoyance that Reinhard had seen earlier while hearing about his son. 'Take that will you Erich!' he yelled, sending up another ring of cigar smoke. There was sudden movement outside the room. Erich's reply came as a raised hand into the gap left by the partially open door. Gustav sighed. 'Erich's a man of few words - and fewer ideas, I'm afraid.'

Or manners, Reinhard thought as he listened to the young man's receding steps. Reinhard said outright, 'Well, he's interested in something.'

Gustav apologised. 'I'll speak to him. I'd like to think he was checking that you were not here for any bad purpose but that would mean he'd turned over a new leaf and, to be frank, I have long since given up any hope that he will change in any meaningful way. Now politics - he'd have you up half the night, listening to his right-wing views. You can guess what I call them! Anyway, perhaps we could talk again, Reinhard. Another visit, now that we've found each other. I'd like that.'

Reinhard said he would ring him and left it at that. Momentarily the room dimmed as if covered by some opaque film. Bewildering shadows shifted in front of him. He felt vulnerable. Erich worried him.

'I'll have a head-and-shoulders-only, normal size, and a full-length of her, same size, so I can have them in a frame side by side with this one,' he said, reaching into his pocket. He produced a rather battered picture of Stephanie, taken on a picnic close to the Neurer See lake in Berlin's Tiergarten before any of the upsets. Gustav smiled, leaning back in his armchair.

Reinhard heard someone in the doorway and noticed Erich again. 'You're the next best thing to invisibility I've ever seen!' Reinhard said.

Without taking his eyes off Reinhard, Erich monotoned, 'The phone call was nothing, Dad, just a reprint order. No hurry.' Then he said, looking away, still with a flat, uninterested tenor to his voice, 'How soon do you want your work, Herr Hänsel?'

Reinhard shot a glance at Gustav but the old man was snoring lightly.

'As soon as possible. Tomorrow?'

Erich nodded, took the pictures and turned. 'I'll leave you to finish your drink, then.'

42

IT dawned on Reinhard that regret had suffocated his life. He had abandoned Stephanie in pursuit of political idealism that he came to realise was nothing more than acquired madness. And although he had finally acted something like a real man, he had more or less accepted a punishment of endless repentance. Now things would be different. He had jettisoned the bad but not replaced any of it with the good, except in his mind, as if memory was all that he was entitled to or able to acquire. How had he managed for so long to keep virtually dormant thoughts that now so violently hammered away beneath his skull? He tapped his head as if expecting an answer. What he did know was that he was again taking in teenage gulps of fresh air with the ability to think clearly and logically, with little interest in anything but the present. Right now - and this is what took him forward - he had everything before him and as a result actually felt like a teenager. But instead of contenting himself with the knowledge that he had successfully arranged a polite social engagement - and little else - he allowed his brain to promote such extravagant expectation surrounding the date (as he liked to think of it) that his demeanour might have been classified by a psychiatrist as certifiably optimistic. Even so, he lapped up every imagination. He congratulated himself on the courage he had summoned and the risk he had taken, virtually ignoring the obvious, that most men would have acted a very long time ago or completely put it from their minds. Stephanie had been as pleasant and correct as he could have dared to hope for over the telephone. And as he locked the door to his rooms in the Hotterstrasse, and descended the well-worn stone steps to the street below, the city's dawn sounding a bit rough and in patches smelling even rougher, Reinhard was rearing to go and he wanted to be part of today's largely unrehearsed world. What he faced would be unpredictable in detail yet set in outline. He had a project and was bursting with energy and kindly thoughts, the exciting presumption that all would be well, to the extent that by the time he reached the tram stop he was already imagining a life together with Stephanie.

It was not long before the conductor announced Merkenweg and Reinhard alighted. He consulted his street map and began walking in the direction of her home. It was not far now. He tried to imagine the Stephanie who would open the door. During those far-off days when they had been so good for each other, she had a tomboyish look - invariably combined with a cheeky smile - and often dressed casually. A flimsy jumper and lightweight slacks seemed to him to be her favourite combination though it was probably nothing of the kind. Reinhard knew from other occasions that she could match the class around her just in the way she stood, answered someone or queried something. He particularly loved to be by her side when she was dressed elegantly, perhaps with the choice of a simple but stunning two-piece outfit with a plain silk or art print chiffon neck scarf.

Reinhard recalled the night when, during an interval of a first night performance of *La Boheme* in Hamburg, as they began inching their way to a crowded bar, she was jostled from behind by a heavily sweating, thick-necked, jacketless middle-aged man, his rolled-up sleeves revealing a rather course love-related tattoo. As he attempted to get round her, the man said, 'Thirst of this magnitude needs quenching, and quickly. Sorry, darling. Needs must.' She answered quietly but firmly. 'Manners that lacking need correction,' she retorted, turning to bar his further progress. 'Don't we all agree?' she said, raising her head towards the queue behind. She took a 10DM note from her purse and offered it up. 'Take it,' she said, with the slightest smile while indicating for those people immediately behind her to budge up. 'It will help pay for the extra drink you'll need by the time you reach the bar,' she announced to the queuing concert goers, suddenly emboldened by the exchange. The man puffed and fidgeted but remained in a secondary place.

Stephanie's hair often appeared in playful attitudes of unceremonious layers, the result of no more than two- or three-fingered combing this way and that across the top of her head but that night at the opera house, her neck-length hair was straight and to the point. It met up with a silky orange neckerchief that contrasted attractively with her lightweight cream jacket beneath which emerged seductively around her wrists and neckline the gentle frills of a paler blouse. Classy it was, made the more so by her dark brown and cream pencil skirt and matching calf-length boots. So easily did this vision of Stephanie come to mind that it was easy for him to imagine the beauty of really falling in love with her again. Had anyone been watching as he reached her home, they could easily have seen the joy he felt. Boring realism had been put to flight and the situation on the telephone that had so delighted him attended him again with renewed excitement. He counted the numbers on the doors of the homes he passed. She would fling her arms in the air on opening the door to him. Or she might offer a limpish hand to shake! She might have a beaming face; then again, she might frown and be subdued. Stephanie might open her house unreservedly to him. Just as easily, however, she might offer him an hour at most because something important had come up. There might be an open top car ride into the countryside, radio music mixing with laughter and outrageous suggestions, with so much left undone that there would have to be another trip next day and the day after. Equally, however, pushed for time at the end of a rather strained hour, she would point to the bus stop and announce as brightly as she thought prudent, that the green line service ran fairly often so that he should not have long to wait. What nonsense; her telephone response had been delightful, everything would be all right. The time he had often thought about had arrived and he knew he should not shrink from it.

Her home was in a new development of attractively terraced properties varied in both footprint and facade, with assorted garden areas wrapped around the staggered buildings, giving the overall design of the complex, with its medley of tree species, a very engaging appearance. Stephanie's place was brick-faced and set between rendered homes, to the left in very pale pink and to the right in light cream. The number seven, in ceramics, was adjacent to a post-horn letterbox. And to its right, he noted, was the name of the house: *Die Sterne*. The stars. Reinhard whispered to himself, 'Of course, it was the Seven Stars, *Grosser Wagen*, Ursa Major, the Plough or Saucepan.' He had not after all been foolish. It had never been for nothing, just like he had always wanted to believe. Here was brass-plated proof. He looked up, even though it was not yet noon. As he stepped forward, his mind nevertheless recalled that time when she took him to her home to meet her parents for the first time. He had been nervous, just like he was now. He had entered the impressive house, where the mother invited him to take a seat in the lounge, full of drapes and small statues, deep red flock wallpaper and, Reinhard surmised, a Hereke floor covering, no doubt in the traditional combination of wool, cotton and silk and threads of gold. He had felt as heavy as the massive, thick-legged table, covered with green baize, at which he was invited to sit as Stephanie's father walked in slowly through double doors, a cigar in one hand and a drink in the other. When he was seated, the top of Stephanie's father's head was partly hidden by the large green glass shade that presented itself on the end of a loose link chain within a couple of feet of the table top, illuminating the space between them but leaving his face in less light than was enjoyed by the huge bowl of fruit off to one side.

As he responded to a question about what he planned to do in life, Reinhard - almost certainly wrongly - suddenly felt his plan to pursue journalism was unworthy; that it could never hope to match the stratum of the north German industrial scene. Perhaps it was the way Stephanie's father had slid his hands inwards across the cloth where they gathered each other up, fingers interlocked, and then leaned back. Yet perhaps it had been the way he himself had delivered his plans for the future, a performance he had later interpreted as uncertain, timid and possibly apologetic. Reinhard longed to say he wanted to marry Stephanie but though the forefingers of the man opposite broke free and formed a sort of church steeple against his chin, he did not think this sort of proposition would gain approval. Reinhard had just felt overwhelmed in his surroundings and was likely making a poor impression and certainly some wrong assumptions.

Reinhard knocked. Stephanie did not answer. He tried again, and again. But there was no reply. He looked at his watch and the door. He took a couple of steps back to survey the entire frontage of the building. He again checked the time and knocked again, much louder this time. As he did so, a young man appeared from a passageway to the left of her home.

'Can I help you?' And without waiting for a reply, he went on, 'Only I happen to know that the lady of the house is not at home at the moment.'

The man, wearing a bomber jacket and jeans, with a cheerful looking face beaming out from beneath one of those Mao worker caps, took a couple more paces forward. 'Are you Reinhard?' he asked, stepping close to him.

'Yes, I am,' Reinhard said, standing his ground and staring back at the man, whose face did now look a little Chinese.

'I was listening out for you but nature called when you first knocked. I am her neighbour and she wanted me to tell you when you arrived that she had been called away suddenly but that she would meet you at the Theresienwiese, at the Schwaben Bräu marquee. At 15.00 hours, she said. And that's all. Does that make sense?'

Reinhard thought she had more than likely managed to turn a business inconvenience or some boring but necessary duty into an exciting initiative. They could drink to their being together again, however brief the reunion might turn out to be.

'Do you know if one of the buses goes close to the Oktoberfest site?' Reinhard asked, pointing.

'I don't know, I'm afraid. Never use them. But I expect one or two of them do, especially at this time of the year.' He turned as if to go back indoors but stopped, put both hands in the surrender position, wheeled round and said: 'Well, why not come with me? I was going a little later, but, hey, it's where I'm headed today anyway. I have to pick up someone else on the way but he'll not mind spending more time there than he thought. Nor me, come to that. In fact, five of us have planned to go. We'll all go early. I can arrange it. Going early won't displease any of us at all. I'll phone them and we'll jump into my old Kapitän around the corner and head for the U-bahn. No good trying to park around the Theresienwiese. It's Hans, by the way,' he said, offering a fleeting hand that skimmed the vigorous overhang of rhododendrons as he skipped off down the passageway between his and Stephanie's home.

Reinhard walked to the corner and studied the bright blue Opel.

Its abundance of chrome and American-style grill of the third generation Kapitän model did its best but Reinhard felt it did not match his stately Mercedes-Benz back home.

43

HIS new-found acquaintances engaged Sendglr Tor's underground network of echoing stone staircases with such speed and agility that by the time they reached the platform for the trip to their change stop at Goetheplatz, Reinhard was some way behind and feeling quite wretched. They seemed not to notice him and he only just made it, panting up to the open carriage doors. As he paused to get his breath, the doors started to close and he stumbled in. Hans and his friend, Ernst, briefly turned towards him but he thought their looks mocked rather than expressed concern. Before he had time to say anything, they had turned and engaged each other in whispered conversation. Reinhard studied them for a while. Every so often they laughed but never looked his way. Reinhard inched his way sideways to hang on to one of two slim chromium pillars that extended to the ceiling from the framework of a seat into which two hysterical young women had fallen helplessly in a heap. They created a convenient diversion. The females could hardly speak for laughing, apart from shrieking the word Oktoberfest at each other, and gave every indication that alcohol would be no new experience for them this day. As he looked away for a second, he noticed Hans and Ernst, now holding on to straps in the middle of the carriage as the train gathered speed, were still deep in conversation. Still they did not look his way. Reinhard returned his gaze on the amusing antics of the two women. Simultaneously a young man bumped into Reinhard's back. He was carrying a head-high object wrapped in brown paper. He apologised and cursed the package, muttering something about how the festival authorities imagined advertising of this kind could be transported without fear of damage or possible injury to passengers through a crowded underground was all quite beyond him. He added that he would nevertheless enjoy himself at the festival - as he always did - asking whether Reinhard was going and introducing himself as Heinrich. The information all came out in a single, breathless moment, a burst of bonhomie that rather jarred Reinhard's reflective mood. 'Reinhard,' he responded with a quick smile.

At the next station, two more young men boarded through doors a set away from Reinhard's. They attracted his attention by their animated conversation, one of them struggling with his words over the top of what could have been a cased musical instrument. They inched their way towards Reinhard and both stopped to greet the other three. It was then that Hans and Siggi turned towards Reinhard and, speaking to him for the first time since they had parked the car, said: 'This is Gandolf, and this fat bastard whom we call Siggi, is one of the bandsmen you'll hear in the Paulaner marquee where we're headed.' Reinhard greeted them.

'Yes, Reinhard here is making his debut, so to speak,' said Hans. 'He has a date but it's not for a few hours. In the meantime, we all aim to have some real fun, eh?' All of them nodded.

Gandolf said, 'Yes, our kind of fun. Serious fun, really.' All of them looked at Reinhard with the precision of robotic pre-programming. 'Oh yes,' they said in unison.

Reinhard hesitated, rubbing his hand over his breast pocket.

'Oh, come on!' Siggi said, trumpeting some kind of marching melody between tight lips. 'It's no good being alone at the Oktoberfest. Not that there's much chance of that!'

The man had no idea just how alone Reinhard wished to be. He wouldn't mind a drink with them, get it over as quickly as possible but he wanted the solitude of detachment before the meeting, to be alone in the jostling crowd where he could absorb the atmosphere and talk openly to Stephanie as if she were next to him without being heard or bothered. These strangers were usurping his private time, yet he felt he could not reasonably deny them without appearing to spurn the hand of friendship.

'Yes OK. For a while, then. Thank you. But I mustn't be too long.

As Hans knows, I'm meeting someone.' Reinhard went on, 'I suppose you're all practiced hands at this event.'

'Not really,' Hans said dismissively.

Heinrich added quickly, 'Well, Siggi is ... it's the only place where his many bum notes go more or less unnoticed. I have been once or twice before but for Hans it's a first.' Hans, said Heinrich, was also meeting a lady friend. 'Hans mustn't have too many drinks. He would not wish to stand her up,' he said, shooting a mischievous look towards the others. 'He's quite excited about it, aren't you Hans? I've said, though, this kind of rendezvous has a habit of not always turning out quite as one would like. Tread carefully, I've warned him. The years, they do have a nasty way of ganging up on what might otherwise be a pleasant and fruitful reunion.' The other two nodded their heads in unison, smiling mechanically. Reinhard felt they could have been speaking for him and gained the impression that they were nodding at him rather than answering their friend.

When the train reached Goetheplatz station, practically the whole train emptied and Reinhard was swept forward trying to keep his acquaintances in view as they sought the platform for the Theresienwiese site. It reminded him of a football stadium emptying after a big match. It was the same at the other end and they were all glad when they settled into the marquee. Hans looked at his watch and said they had half an hour before Siggi had to start spreading his notes as thinly as possible among the trombones and tubas and ordered eight steins from one of the serving wenches.

'Give us some pretzels, too,' Heinrich added with bumptious authority.

'Eight!' Reinhard exclaimed.

'Yes, I like a drink,' Hans said, keeping a straight face. 'You others must order your own!' He looked at Reinhard, kept up an unnerving stare and then suddenly smiled. 'That's only two each in sixty minutes, Reinhard. Were you thinking of more?'

Reinhard laughed, relieved by the utterance of his name, the return to normality. 'No, no. No, that's fine,' he said, already wondering at what point he could safely detach himself from their company. He watched as the five of them practically halved the contents of their first steins in single guzzles. Then he found them looking at him again, their glasses resting on their lower lips waiting for breath.

'Is your friend also a lady, like Hans' date?' Heinrich asked.

Reinhard confirmed with a mixture of pride and uneasiness.

'Well now,' Heinrich said.

'That'd be something ...' Hans added, now lifting the second stein to his lips.

'What?' Reinhard asked, trying to match Hans' drinking.

'Well, if it was the same woman! I mean, conceivably, it could be. I like dealing with improbable but undeniably possible situations. If they were one and the same woman, why, we'd have a fight on our hands, wouldn't we Reinhard? Just think - a ready ringside of thousands ...'

The use of his name this time seemed distinctly unfriendly. Reinhard decided to back off and leave. He'd say he'd listen out for Siggi's musical endeavours. Reinhard took a couple of mouthfuls and set his stein back on to the beer-spotted wooden table, rather heavily, slopping some out on to the table. He smiled and stretched his arms. 'Damn good,' he said, feeling the strength of the beer on an empty stomach. Avoiding their faces, he studied the emptiness of his first stein and the couple of mouthfuls at the bottom of his second stein - plus the rivulet of alcohol making its way to the edge of the slightly bowed wooden table - and reckoned he had finished most of his commitment to the drinking session. He again looked at his watch and without planning his words, he said, 'I think I should be getting along now. I'll listen out for you, Siggi,' he said, leaning over to pat the man's shoulder. 'I'll get some in for you chaps,' Reinhard said, raising by mistake a full stein of beer to his lips which he quickly realised belonged to Hans.

There was no response. They just looked at him, impassively. The noisy animation that had surrounded him since his arrival in the marquee had, for a moment, been replaced by a buzzing in his ears, the five of them still out in front of him but now behind fuzzy plate glass, their talk muffled. Reinhard waited for his head to clear, slowly replacing the stein in front of Hans, who remained, like the others, expressionless. Unnerved, Reinhard found himself trying to reverse the situation as in childhood where he would always be the one to break any silences or offer an answer whenever there was uncertainty. He wished he were on the other side of the bandstand, even the world, among people he did not know, milling with them instead.

'Now who does that remind us of?' said Ernst, who had so far contributed little to the conversation. They closed ranks, put their heads together as if grouping for a family photograph, opened their mouths and held the line of juicy apertures for several seconds before announcing in unison, 'Konrad!'

Ernst spat out the words. 'Indeed, Konrad! I unfortunately bumped into him in town the other day. Somehow he knew we had this, eh, project on but not when and where, fortunately. He said he'd got some of the real stuff and would be happy to apply it.'

'A bad lot, Reinhard,' said Heinrich. 'Konrad goes overboard with everything. Always has. He's always trying to go further than the far right. Right-right, you might say - except he is mostly wrong-wrong. He was a member of the old Socialist Reich Party, Reinhard, you know the one that was banned a few years back by this high and mighty Constitutional Court of ours. His cohorts slunk back into the Empire Party from which, as you will also be aware, it sprang openly to espouse *Führer* worship. Now he wages a one-man battle to find listeners for his twisted vision of the kingdom he aims to create. We may be extremist on occasions but he is obsessed all the time. He stands squarely behind old Nazi legal thought that whatever is useful to the State is lawful: *Recht ist was dem Staate nutzt* and all that. And most of what he considers useful would turn most people's stomachs. We're different, Reinhard. Different and much cleverer than the likes of Konrad.'

Heinrich, face down over his beer throughout the discourse about Konrad, suddenly looked up and addressed Reinhard. 'You don't play?' he asked with grave inquiry, at the same time inviting him, with a proffered gentle open hand and a pleasant smile, to resume his seat. Reinhard flushed. He could feel his face and neck burning.

'No, though I like listening.'

'That surprises me. I thought you would have played. I can see you with some reflective instrument, like the double-reeded oboe deployed at its most plaintive or the cello or perhaps the clarinet. Yes, an introverted player, you would be. Good but rather mournful, at times perhaps even depressive going far beyond the capabilities of even the most versatile instrument. I deduce this from your physical demeanour, the way you sit, particularly, perhaps, the way you stand, hold your head and, notably, the way these actions match what words you use and the times when you say nothing more revealing than anything. At best, you look regretful. Do I come near the mark, Reinhard?'

Reinhard tried to ignore the tormenting tone of Heinrich's voice. 'No, it's just the way I look,' he said as lightly as he could muster the words, feeling inside that he was being mocked and that even this dismissively casual retort had been delivered in a manner that had given his true feelings away.

'Inside, I'm bursting with quite ordinary thoughts about how much of a good time I'm going to have here against the background of the uplifting sound from all those lusty notes emanating from the likes of Siggi and similar companies of musicians.'

Heinrich persisted. He leant forward, his face closer to Reinhard than Reinhard much cared for.

'No regrets, then?' he said. 'There's nothing that's ever happened in your life that you'd like to rectify? People of your years usually have some deep regret and it's usually about a woman, pretty or otherwise.'

The swirling effects of the strong lager inside him suddenly put Reinhard in the role of a casting director and the corpulent Heinrich sat naked at an audition, shifting uneasily to conceal excesses of flesh around his middle, sweating in the effort to justify himself as a sleek male model. Reinhard maintained a steadily penetrating and meaningful gaze into the rather bloodshot eyes of Heinrich, generating a silent but powerful counter to the oral imbalance thus far. The jutting jaw sank back, resuming an unimportant role, the head bowed slightly and the eyes narrowed. Reinhard inched closer towards Heinrich who sat back, pulling his light jacket together in front of his stomach, with nothing more to say and, not wishing to provoke anything or anyone, Reinhard also sat back, at once troubled and emboldened by what he had achieved.

Hans took over. 'Well, it's like this: Siggi, here, doesn't regret anything. His woman is his musical instrument, and she's with him most of the time.'

Standing behind Reinhard, Siggi beamed. He loved banter that concerned him and brought out what looked like a penny whistle that he put to his lips and raspberried a few notes of some marching tune. Then he leaned over Reinhard and brought the reed down hard on the left side of Reinhard's chest. Reinhard winced and clutched the spot.

'It gets you there, doesn't it Reinhard?' Siggi said.

Heinrich still looked as if he really had missed out on a modelling career but the others said in turn, 'Right there!' repeating the action with their fingers on the table.

Reinhard stood up, less sure of himself again and just wanting to get away.

'All very interesting,' he said, somewhat stiffly. 'I'll have to go now. Thanks for the company.'

Heinrich said, 'No, please, Reinhard, sit down. We like your company. We get a bit carried away sometimes. It's the way we are. We're passionate about things; I'm sure you will have noticed. You doubtless were in your time, perhaps still are. We'll buy you another stein to show there's no hard feelings about your indiscretions, to cement our friendship,' and he left to locate one of the serving wenches.

Indiscretions? What was this? Reinhard thought.

Hans took over again. 'Take politics and our most unimaginative government for instance. This annual piss-up we call the Oktoberfest gets more international acclaim than anything that emanates from the Foreign Office in Bonn. We need some positive action. About lands outside our borders, for one thing, and people need unburdening, if you follow me. Anyway, the Oktoberfest is not really for us. It may for most people be an excuse - almost a licence - to get very drunk in public, but it is a special occasion that has driven us to this place this year. Intoxication for us is induced by something far less basic than collaborative drinking. Not that we don't like beer. It helps lubricate our minds, Reinhard, as you would soon enough discover should you ever think of joining us for one of our meetings. But it's only a small joy on the way to a big hurrah. We never, ever pursue wasteful, delinquent drunkenness. Eh, chaps? What I am talking about, and

REQUIREMENTS OF GUILT

what all of us at this table are talking about, you included may we hope, is the creation of a new regime dedicated to the betterment of our country, and more particularly, the building of a nation populated only by folk who, if they are not naturally redoubtable, can after a while demonstrate courage and a steadfast willingness to defer to command and compliance. It goes without saying, therefore - and here I and my colleagues hope that we are not boring you in any way, Reinhard - that we shall not tolerate weak, spineless, diffident specimens, especially men who allow sentiment to cloud a noble vision forged and shaped for the good of the majority. A new regime for our Fatherland, Reinhard. Just think of it. One with tried and tested policies from a previous era, if you follow my drift.'

44

HEINRICH returned with fresh beers and he and his friends could hardly have set about them with greater gusto than if they had been parched from a fruitless trek into the desert. Reinhard mopped his brow, now somewhat alarmed at the way things were going. The thrust of the conversation disturbed him and the invitation felt like he was being pushed out into quicksand. Reinhard started on his fresh stein feeling decidedly apprehensive and not a little unsteady.

'But all that is for later,' continued Heinrich. 'To this special occasion I mentioned. Would you like to know what it is?'

Reinhard went to speak but Hans, smiling widely, cut in.

'Actually, it affects you. Something very close to your heart. Down that and come with us; we'll meet my lady friend.'

Reinhard shifted uneasily. His discomfort was not just upstairs.

'It's over in the corner,' Hans pointed perceptively. 'Don't be long, though. It's getting late now and we don't want to keep her waiting any longer than we have to, do we?'

Reinhard hurried to the toilet, his mind and legs at the point of breakdown. He stopped suddenly, at first to regain some composure, and then because he could see it looked like the toilet of his dream, with ill-fitting double doors and a decorative palm just off to the left. In the hideous nightmare, he had propped up a stiffened life-size photograph of Stephanie behind the palm before entering the toilet. Inside now, his forearms held him unpredictably off the wall as he recalled the rantings of the group of self-styled political trailblazers who sounded more like reactionaries trying to repackage old evils, and how much he wanted to avoid anything that might spoil an occasion, now only an hour away. Reinhard's head swam as he turned and stepped onto one of the springy planks that formed the toilet's loosely suspended wooden flooring. He reeled like a deck stroller in rough waters. Daylight had so far brought him no joy whatsoever and it got worse. When he stepped outside the toilet, he saw Stephanie, she of his dream! Here she was. His body crumpled, and only the palm saved him from collapsing. He heaved and spat, repeatedly, but the need seemed endless. He sank to his knees, holding on to the large pot in which the palm sprouted so proudly. Reinhard looked up, out towards Stephanie. She was gone! He got up. Blood coursed feverishly through his body. Then he saw her again, standing off to the right with four strangers. As he stared, Reinhard gradually realised what was happening, what this was all about. His photographer friend's son Erich had obviously kept himself in the wings of this pantomime, having laid the elaborate groundwork while his friends invented a finale to his dream. The figures out in front had formed themselves into a circle and had begun passing a life-size cardboard cut-out of Stephanie from one to the other. The dream was continuing. They were laying him back in his bed and closing his eyes. He found himself bathed in sweat.

The group divided itself, its members holding her horizontally, two at the shoulders and two at the feet, shaking her like straightening a blanket. Lunging forward, Reinhard managed to get hold of his Stephanie. There was a struggle and he ended up being clubbed to the floor. They started chanting, shoving her from one to the other. He tried to get to his feet but in turn they abused his cardboard Stephanie while threatening him.

'You have her!'

'No, you have her!'

'OK, you then!'

'There's nothing there. Look, it's all flat around her lovely jumper.'

'Poor maid!'

Reinhard opened his mouth to shout but nothing emerged. He tried again: 'Hey, whad'you doing; who do you think you are? Give her to me. She's mine.'

They answered: 'Ooooohhhhh.'

Ernst said: 'Who do we think we are?'

'We're caring folk,' chanted one of them.

'Yes, caring, sharing people,' said another.

The voices continued in turn.

'We wouldn't leave a very pretty female like this outside a men's toilet.'

'Left in some darkened corner to fend for herself.'

'Quite a relief was it? Getting rid of her that way?'

'Sticking her up, as it were!'

'Up against a wall. Outside a toilet!'

'What were you doing in there so long?'

'Such a long time.'

The voices droned on, sneering, menacing. They seemed to speed up in Reinhard's befuddled mind. He went to answer each accusation but they chanted on as if they had not heard. He tried to hurry his answers but the indictments came faster than his ability to form the answers and eventually he just stood there, open mouthed, barely able to breath.

'No compassion in you!'

'You abandoned her!'

'Heartless bugger.'

Reinhard managed: 'Just you -'

'Just nothing.'

'Hands off, old man.'

'Yes, hands off!'

'You'll contaminate her.'

'Filthy hands, just out of the toilet.'

'Hands off!'

'We're going to look after her. Gentle hands. Caring hands.

Sharing hands.'

'Cardboard needs special treatment.'

'Just toddle off, old man, and leave her to us.'

'Go!'

'Walk!'

'Run!'

'However you want to go.'

'Or stay!'

'You, dear girl, come with us.'

Adult cynicism suddenly turned to infantile sniggering when one of the tormentors lost his balance and stumbled out of the mocking cordon, throwing upwards the shoulder he was holding. Stephanie as a result stood upright for a few seconds facing sweetly and serenely towards the object of the ridicule. Taking advantage of the scene change, Reinhard again tried to get to his feet. But their intimidating attitude was quickly restored. Reforming as one, the group moved back towards Reinhard, then stopped. Each continued to hold his allotted part of Stephanie with one hand while, with outstretched, upturned fingertips of the other hand, moving in perfect unison, invited Reinhard to rise. When Reinhard was on his feet, Hans tucked Stephanie under his arm while the others smoothed hands over her legs. Then each of the yobs raised their right arms stiffly and diagonally towards the marquee's canvass top before returning to their task, about-turning as soldiers on a parade ground and striding towards the rain-soaked exit behind Hans and the horizontal cardboard figure.

In the distance, Reinhard saw them swing Stephanie into an upright position as they left the marquee and he emerged just in time to see them approach a car that had entered the site, off the Bavaria-Ring to his left. It had pulled into the side of a small fun-fair site, where Bröckwurst-stuffing couples were beginning to shelter from heavier rain. Reinhard slithered to a halt behind the group just as the car door opened. He snatched at Stephanie, tripped and almost fell, steadying himself by putting a hand down. In this position, he was shunted from behind and sent sprawling into the muddy roadway. The yobs burst into a laughter that contested the noise of the musical roundabouts and their screeching occupants. The four of them got into the car that spun in a tight figure-of-eight as a steamed-up window was opened and Stephanie was cast out to land a few feet away from Reinhard.

'She's in a pretty bad way. Really!' one of the occupants called out from the back seat. But before Reinhard could reach her, the car completed its turn and drove over her, its exhaust belching a bluish haze into the face of his girl as it came to rest. The occupants all looked towards him. Hans said, 'Yes, she could not come in person. Well, how could she? She was run over. ...' 'A bit like this, it could have been,' Ernst cut in, looking at the skid marks on the ground in front of him.' 'But we did not want to disappoint you,' Hans continued. 'For the moment at least,' he said, smiling sardonically at his friends.

Ernst, emerging from the car to stand right in front of Reinhard, said, 'The car hit her hard, we understand. She was unconscious when she was admitted to hospital, according to a friend. Touch and go or, more possibly appropriately, crash and going, going, gone. The wrong side of life's highway, so to speak. We are kind, however. You are going to join her.'

Reinhard bent down to pick up Stephanie but Hans and Heinrich stepped forward to stop him. Ernst and Siggie helped complete a circle around him.

'Reckon you're a doctor now, do you?' Hans sneered.

'Get in!' they said together.

Reinhard was forced into the back of the car and taken out through the main gates on to the Theresienhöhe. The car had travelled for only two or three minutes before it was slowed to stop behind a VW Westfahlia campervan.

'We'll all be a lot more comfortable in here,' Hans said. The other three murmured their agreement and each took a firm hold of him, walking him around to the sliding door.

'I don't know whether you know it or not, but this particular model was pretty well protected against rain and water generally. All the joints were given a special seal - here, let me show you,' he said enthusiastically.

Reinhard said he didn't at all care whether the vehicle had been completely covered in the stuff.

'Well not quite, but in all the important areas,' Hans countered evenly.

Reinhard tore himself free of his guards, 'Enough!'

Heinrich said calmly. 'Let's all go inside. Let's have a drink, OK?'

'I don't want a drink!'

'Oooooh, he doesn't want a drink!' they said together.

'Well, some sort of intake,' Ernst said.

'You've guessed it, eh Reinhard? The whole van is sealed, perfectly sealed - apart from this here,' he said, pointing to a hole just above the rear offside wheel arch. 'And into that goes this tight-fitting pipe,' he said, bending under the rear and bringing around a hose which he fitted in.

'Furthermore,' Hans said, 'Since you're so unsociable, you can share the memory of your flat-chested woman on your own. You can contemplate her refusal to accept what was good for Germany and your weakness in not seeing it through. Germany is going to get another chance through this imaginative party of ours but you will not see that day. You had your chance but you lost your nerve. The new Germany will tolerate no weaklings anywhere on German soil.'

Heinrich added, 'In you get!'

With help from his colleagues, Heinrich bundled Reinhard into the van and said, 'You will notice the division between you and the cab. It's strong enough to restrain a rabid Alsatian, so you'll not be able to get to the ignition. And the vehicle is sound-proofed. Goodbye!'

The sliding door was shut tight and locked with ceremony. Two of the men entered the cab from the nearside and the other two on the driver's side. As Ernst bent forward to turn the key, the other three leaned over, each placing a hand on the others, linking their responsibility. The engine burst into life and they vacated the vehicle, standing back, for a moment, on the wide, tree-lined pavement, before walking towards a blue Mercedes a little further along the road.

Reinhard tried to open the iron grilled black opaque windows but they refused to budge. He opened lockers, cupboards and drawers but they were empty of anything that could be used to smash the glass. He felt like a dog as he pawed at the cab division. His view of the pavement was partially blocked by the silvery trunk of a tree on the other side of which passed a few strolling couples. A noise made Reinhard look up. There was a plastic covered light in the roof of the vehicle and in it were several holes. He put his hand towards the shade. There was a warm disturbance of air with a smell that made him immediately put his hand over his mouth and nose, bending down towards the floor of the vehicle to draw in as much fresh air as he could. He counted the seconds. Twenty one, twenty-two, twenty three … he slowly stretched himself out face down on the floor, his head close to the inside edge of the sliding door. Thirty-five, thirty-six … it was the end. He raised a hand to smash against the door … forty … and gasped in the foul smelling air. Reinhard's chest hurt and he felt giddy. Another gulp, yet the pain eased and his head cleared a little. Another deep breath and … he slowly got to his feet. He reached up to the lamp. It was still coming in. He dared to lift his mouth towards the lamp, and breathed in, tentatively.

Nothing.

The smell was awful but it was not carbon monoxide or hydrogen cyanide.

It was an elaborate hoax.

Reinhard let go a long exhalation of immense joyfulness. He thought he might try to beat forty seconds but satisfied his relief by closing his eyes. He was not going to die. After a moment he suddenly leaned over and yanked at the sliding door handle and as he now thought, it readily opened. It was one almighty prank. Unless this was just the first stage of some double bluffing slow torture, he was again free.

Had anything really happened to Stephanie? Reinhard panicked. He stepped out and looked up and down the avenue but so far as he could see, the louts had gone. He pulled the door closed and walked away. The rain had stopped and back at the Theresienwiese parkland, at the Bavaria-Ring entrance, the bustle and music that had previously excited him, was now a noisy imposition. He scanned the ground in front of him. Then he saw her. The mud-covered tyre had run from her left thigh across her belted dress and up to just below her left shoulder, leaving what he saw as a Swastika-like pattern. Mud clogged the gaps beneath his fingernails as he picked away at the filthy covering. When it had mostly gone, he gave Stephanie an affectionate sweep of his open hand. He lifted her upright, and as he did so, he noticed her neck. The rain intensified to a thunderous downpour and he moved to partial cover by a fence at the rear of the funfair. They stood there, the pair of them, rain dripping down their faces. He held her by the shoulders and they looked at each other. The rain came in at them at a new angle and with fresh force and he tried to protect her head, no longer up to the occasion. For several minutes, Reinhard remained with her, upright, still, seeking some kind of comfort from this moment, in which he was numb and she was a piece of cardboard. The wind blew the fiercest in all his life. He bent to protect her further, lowering his eyes to Stephanie's face. Her head slowly bent forwards. Suddenly it flopped on to his chest. He could see the fracture at the back of her slim neck.

45

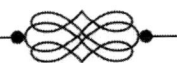

REINHARD wanted to be able to drive to the hospital. He would not mind being told to wait because things were critical if eventually, on say about the third day, if things had been that bad, to be allowed at her bedside, for just a short time, just to see her, all tubes and dials but breathing. He would understand that she might still be very ill but that with her not dead, not actually killed by any car as Heinrich had said, she could improve. There could be offered some hope that she would recover, however long that might take. Or, even if she were unable fully to recover, she would still be alive. Because while there was ... he would want to be able to say, 'What, you mean she might recover, be able to speak and everything, like always?' and he would accept any reply like, 'Well, maybe not everything, we'll see.'

Reinhard wanted to be able to get to the hospital, wherever it was, and squeeze her hand. She might of course not be in a position to squeeze back, then or ever, but if that were the case, he would be happy enough to resign himself to a different life than he had imagined so often but in these unknown but possible circumstances, be so grateful that she was still alive.

Stephanie's house was across the other side of the city and the taxi's progress - which regularly seemed to fall prey to every red traffic light, road works or traffic jam imaginable - switched Reinhard's mind between sinister to pleasant assessment of Stephanie's condition. As the taxi made gains, Stephanie was practically waving goodbye to the nurses and thanking everyone for looking after her so well during her stay. During hold-ups, she was on life-support and fading.

All the time he tried to counter Heinrich's words of mocking fatalism. He closed his eyes. Everything was a requirement of guilt, including the nightmarish dream in which Stephanie had died and he had suffered a courtroom accusation of deserting her. He had acted on the female judge's words. Images, she said, were not only in the mind. With a photograph of Stephanie, he could go the Oktoberfest with her. Yes, he could have the photograph greatly enlarged. Be bold. Some people might think it strange. There might be scores of them, even hundreds, a whole huge crowd, and maybe people would gather round and laugh. Perhaps when the crowd had stopped laughing, in quieter moments later on, when wide-mouthed convulsions had given way to hardly smiles, then just slightly parted, wondering lips, individually they might imagine much, perhaps more than they had thought possible.

In the nightmare, he had taken Stephanie as a full-length cardboard figure to the Oktoberfest to fulfil his Thirties' promise and he had blurted out the entire dream sequence to his old photographer friend. Some of it had happened, too - thanks to the spying Erich. Yes, another requirement of guilt. Lightly into cupped hands he sang the ditty as he remembered his dream.

A requirement of guilt!

A requirement of guilt!

Requirements of guilt, more like!

Requirements that guilt has forced me to face!

Requirements of guilt, oompah!

That first night, after being cleared by the newly opened war crimes office in Ludwigsburg, he had fallen asleep but there had been no sweet dreams.

He is arraigned before a Frankfurt court, found guilty of desertion and sentenced to a period of public retribution during which time the normal restrictions imposed by the law are suspended. He has to deliver in the centre of Jerusalem a compilation of the recorded words of prominent National Socialist speakers of the Thirties before finishing off with the main points of the Wannsee Conference - and he has to dress in his old SS uniform for the occasion. This is followed by his accompanied trip to the Oktoberfest when a woman comes out of the body of the marquee and puts her head back and blows upwards into a fringe of fine, auburn hair and a man joins her from the hall. The couple smile. The woman looks again at Reinhard and approaches him.

'Are you all right? I mean, it is so warm, actually quite hot in there.'

'Yes, I'm fine, thank you.'

She goes to turn away but faces him again, 'Only, I wondered whether you had a table.'

'No. You see, I just ... wanted ... to come.'

'Well, you can be on our table if you want. I'm sure we can squeeze you both in. I am Anna. This is my husband Gregor.'

'Reinhard.'

'An important date, eh, Reinhard?'

'Yes. This is Stephanie.' *He hesitates.* 'She -'

The woman smiles and brings up an open hand between their faces, slowly shaking her head. 'Let's all four of us go and enjoy ourselves.' *As they quaff their second steins, she tells him she is a psychiatrist and her husband a retired architect. They had always said they would go to the Oktoberfest but had only this year managed it. They had always had something else to do. Then earlier in the year, they nearly lost the chance when Gregor just survived a serious heart operation. She looks away momentarily before turning back to Reinhard.* 'I want not to ask any questions, only to imagine your feelings and to welcome you with us at our table.' *After a couple of hours, the Löwenbräu-Festhalle marquee revellers gradually begin standing on the wooden bench seats, singing and drinking from there. Reinhard opens his mouth, as wide as the frothing tops of litre steins and he clinks glasses with those at his table and every so often leans across the aisle to meet extended arms and touch glasses. He can pick out wonder on some faces but it never forms itself into a question. He smiles and they smile. One female reveller leans over and puts a hand on his shoulder and a thumb into the air level with a face that beams and blasts out the chorus of a song that soon engages the entire hall. His cardboard Stephanie starts as a requirement of guilt but now he feels himself almost unimpeachable. Glasses are recharged and as the trumpets and the euphoniums encourage a fresh response, he raises his glass to Anna and Gregor who stand either side of him and his girl wanting the feeling he has to last forever. An hour later he shakes Anna's hand and Gregor's and everyone else's on the table and unsteadily steps down from the rocking bench. He waves merrily to the table and its fuzzy occupants. He carries Stephanie between the rows of tables to the toilets before propping her up by a palm in a corner of the vast room of merriment and before propping himself up against the wall inside.*

Reinhard leant forward to engage the taxi driver, 'How much longer?'

The man half-turned. 'Sorry. It would have been quicker but for these road works. Just a while longer.'

Reinhard sank his head into his hands. How wonderful if she were there, mystified, even annoyed that he was late but all present and correct. When he looked out through the window again, he recognised the road and prepared the fare. He asked, 'Would you mind waiting a few minutes? Only I may need you again right away. If she's not in …'

'Five minutes!'

With a thumping heart, Reinhard walked briskly up to her front door and rang the bell. There was no answer. He rang again, willing her to turn the latch and pull the door open, to smile, to end his agony. Thomas opened the door. He hung his head and Reinhard felt the chill of bad news.

'Stephanie has had an accident …'

For what seemed the umpteenth time, Heinrich's words rang out in Reinhard's head, this time banging against the sides with such force that his temples twitched. His open hands pushed in at the sides until he could hear nothing. Her life was in danger and he had been drinking in celebration of Germany's annual piss-up.

'No!' he practically shouted.

Thomas put an arm around him and guided him into the hall.

'Let's go in here,' he said, passing double glass-panelled doors into a room with little furniture but floor-to-ceiling shelves full of books that took up the whole of one end. It's where he would have come, he thought, and he wondered which seat she would have offered to him before inviting him to take tea and cakes. He imagined Thomas was not there and she had excused herself and would be back soon. He stared at the kitchen door.

'I have just come from the hospital,' Thomas said, reappearing from the hall. 'She is in theatre. It was bad but she has a fair chance, Reinhard. I have just come home for some things I know she would want. Please, sit down.'

Reinhard chose the winged armchair. 'When, where did this happen? Can I see her?'

'We shall both be able to see her. I am just about ready to leave for the hospital now. Shall you accompany me?'

Reinhard remembered the taxi but when he looked out it had gone.

They sat in the car, fumbling their way to conversation. Thomas's steering was exaggerated and, leaning forward, Reinhard tightened to the point where he seemed to be examining every item of street furniture. He cleared his throat and asked softly 'What happened, Thomas?'

'There is something you must hear, Reinhard,' Thomas began, accelerating onto the ring road he had said would take them to the hospital in twenty minutes or so.

'Stephanie spoke to me right after you telephoned her. She asked me to pick up two tickets in anticipation because she was sure that when you arrived, you would want to keep the date just because the intervening time had been so long, because here there was another chance, two tickets, two people, talking eagerly despite so much silence.'

Reinhard looked at Thomas.

'Yes. She even said it was perhaps the start of a new life, at least something to finish off with. So I know how she felt. Her mood was ... well to be honest, Reinhard, her voice was dancing, the words coming over like extravagant arms punching the air, though sometimes caressing arms.'

Reinhard tried to picture the scene.

Thomas continued, 'She went on about what she should wear for your visit and even went into the question of the food she should have in for you. I made enquiries near the Kaufhof area and the owner of an expensive shop nearby remembered this woman staring into her store, then pressing down the door handle so fiercely that she almost stumbled in. Reinhard, she was talking to me about shopping almost all the time, what she would wear, how she would wear it. She asked my advice but went on non-stop about styles, colours, materials, the whole fashion scene. She was bubbling. I found myself smiling most of the time, laughing I was, yes, excited by her excitement. God, I see her so happy.'

Thomas fell silent. Then he sighed loudly.

'What happened, Thomas?' Reinhard said urgently.

Thomas at first seemed not to hear. Then he said, 'I hope it all doesn't sound heartless in the circumstance but I feel it has to be said so you will know and appreciate that even after so many years, her love is deep, and there was I toying with the notion that I had some local rival who with a bit more time could easily be seen off.'

Reinhard's body filled with an unknown energy, but he persisted, 'Thomas, please tell me, what happened?' When eventually he got Thomas's full attention, Reinhard added, 'How was she injured? I mean, how bad are her injuries?'

'As I said, she had just come out of this quite exclusive fashion shop almost next to the departmental store Kaufhof, in the Rinterstrasse. According to the owner of that small but very smart shop she bought this suit and left the shop with a kind of joy that made the woman feel that doing something for the soul was so much more important than selling clothes. By the owner's account, Stephanie had fairly clutched her package - well almost strangled it so fiercely did she hug it. She was so fascinated by Stephanie's manner that she went up to the shop door and watched her walk away, well practically skipping at times. She went straight out into the road and was hit by this car. It had no chance of avoiding her. She had no chance of avoiding it.'

Thomas was clearly upset and, for a moment, Reinhard felt the odd man out. When they reached the hospital, however, Reinhard knew this was no time to step aside. He felt the need to assert himself. The impulse to physically shoulder-charge Thomas out of the way and rush into the hospital ahead of him was, however, suppressed and the remaining aggression was satisfied by giving Thomas a jerky look as he thought of him as an impostor, a sort of Johnny-come-lately. Why, he was little more than a carrier bag for an acquaintance. Reinhard's Stephanie experience went back more than thirty years. She had been on his mind much longer than she had ever been on Thomas's. She had hardly ever been out of Reinhard's mind. At times she had practically driven him *out* of his mind. They had practically been as man and wife, for goodness sake. It seemed impossible, now more than ever, that he had allowed himself to be content with fairy-tale love. It had fortified his lonely days, for certain, provided a background for practically everything he did, but he realised with gathering exasperation, filling his head with embellishments on a theme had been inadequate in the extreme. He did not want to say it had all left him with a pitifully hollow and self-deceiving joy; that would be to denigrate a huge chunk of a life that she had anchored and negate a comfort he could hardly explain. That the thought had crossed his mind at all was really only an expression of his amassed frustration. Yet he could not deny that in all practical means, his half-heartedness - no, downright apathy - had left him empty-handed from a sublime experience not given to everyone. It had taken this forced trip to his old Fatherland to break inertia's ungracious and cowardly grip. No, Thomas had nothing to reproach himself about, and Reinhard told him quietly, 'We should go separately, yes?'

'Well, if you like, Reinhard. You first, eh?' But Reinhard gestured Thomas forward. 'I'll wait here for you. Please don't tell her I'm here. OK?'

'I understand.'

Reinhard watched him go through one line of cars, then a saw tooth passage diagonally through other ranks until he reached the paved entrance of the hospital where he hesitated, swapped the bag of Stephanie's things from one hand to the other and disappeared through the double doors.

The end of the past, Reinhard thought. It was over and he would never again take breath from imagination. The air he would take down from now on would be future fresh. He looked at his watch. He brought it to his ear. He sat back, still staring at the hospital entrance. Reinhard's eyes closed and he forced them open with a wide-eyed stare that took him to her bedside where Stephanie was smiling up at Thomas. Thomas had been kind. He was a friend. Of course they smiled; yes, Thomas was smiling too. They were close but apart. Reinhard looked at his watch again. They had been together for more than twenty minutes. He got out of the car and walked up to the hospital entrance. He touched the glass-plated door but did not push it. He retreated, resting on a low wall where he could see both entrance and Thomas's car. What would he say, those first awkward words, as he neared her bed, within hearing distance? Would she be able to hear him? Was Thomas not yet out because he had been taken aside by one of the sisters, or the doctor? Maybe Thomas was also waiting. Reinhard thought he would try to find out and pushed on the glass just as Thomas appeared from a side corridor. A young woman looked up from the enquiry desk but resumed what she had been doing as the two men started talking.

'She's out of danger, Reinhard.'

'Gott sei Dank!'

'But there is a problem, I'm afraid. Apparently, she had a nasty bang to the head in addition to other injuries caused in the collision. The doctor said these other injuries had been taken care off, near enough. There has, however, been damage to that part of her brain controlling memory, which is quite common with violent impacts. And again, in such cases, an accurate prognosis cannot dependably be given just yet.'

'Christ, but she recognised you all right?'

Thomas hesitated. 'Not so as I could be certain. I detected ... bewilderment ... I don't know. Odd. She sort of said Hello and Goodbye but the rest . . . see what you think. Take what time you need. I'll be outside.'

Thomas had earlier invited Reinhard to spend more time at his place so he said he would make his own way back after seeing Stephanie. Reinhard said he needed some time alone. And after everything, he needed some new clothes. After checking in at reception, Reinhard strode into an open corridor where, twenty metres in, a man dressed in a green uniform stepped forward from a doorway. 'Good evening, Sir - security. We have reason to be extra careful at this time about visitors to this hospital, extra vigilance you know, at least for the time being. May I have your name and the person you are visiting?' he said, unfolding a clipboard.

'I see. What's happened, then?'

'I am not at liberty to divulge that, Sir. Suffice to say there is currently a need to check people in and out. If you could give me your name I will sign you in against the person you are visiting. It's just a precaution.'

The bespectacled man, with the close-cropped hair and sharp features of what Reinhard recalled of servicemen, turned a couple of pages before laying an open-hand over what looked like a two-column list of names.

'Who are you visiting please?'

Reinhard told him. The man ran a finger up and down the list and confirmed Dorman Ward. Reinhard identified himself.

'Thank you, sir. One more thing. An address, please.'

Slightly irritated, Reinhard obliged, pushing the pen back into the man's hand before quickly making off along the corridor. His anxious feet picked up the mortal messages, hanging stiffly from the ceiling. He sought a simple word but to his right was nuclear medicine, then suffocating words like pulmonary straight ahead in Area B. Cardiology pointed left. Only parts of haemophilias, ophthalmology, neuro-rehabilitation, neurology and oncology could be processed as they swooped overhead. Clearer but cuttingly came the renal unit, an arrow mercifully pointing up a flight of stairs. Out of immediate reach, too, via stairs down to Level One, was Acute Stroke. Reinhard felt a pain in his left arm, then a twinge in his left thigh. They passed quickly, like the never-ending, express signs overhead that pointed to where fear and hope were being trollied about and where starched dedication came with the unpleasant whiff of spotlessness. Then it came, pushing the rest out of the way, huge and important: Dormann Ward, different from everything else, wholesome rather than sterile. Reinhard shouldered open the double doors and stopped almost immediately by the first of a number of watercolour paintings that stretched down one wall to the ward reception desk. He took a deep breath. The future. That was the thing. He'd have a big smile, a cheerful greeting, words that meant it was just a matter of time before she'd be able to leave. Oh, how he'd love to go this far, during this first visit, to suggest a life together, forever, in West Germany, in London, anywhere. He wanted to freshen their stale brain boxes. She would understand. At the ward desk, he was told a doctor would see him after what should be only a short visit. Reinhard nodded.

46

REINHARD wanted to cry when he saw Stephanie. Facial injuries resembled a blooded string vest stretched from ear to ear. She had her eyes closed and he was grateful for that as he struggled to match something of the face that had been so clearly etched on his mind for such a long time. That was his Stephanie. This *is* his Stephanie, he corrected as she suddenly opened her eyes.

Reinhard smiled, 'Hello.'

She moved her head slowly in his direction but her eyes were only partially open and she did not look at him directly. Her lips parted but she gave no indication that she recognised him or that anyone was standing over her. What Reinhard could see of her eyes - nothing more than slits of moist dark brown between heavy lids - seemed to move agitatedly from side to side. After a few moments, the flickering stopped and she seemed to sink into a deep slumber. He closed his own eyes, pressing two fingers firmly over his forehead, backwards and forwards several times. When he looked at her again, he strained to hear her breathing for there seemed to be nothing. He studied her face with increasing alarm but when he moved closer he noticed the slight yet silent sign of life in a slow rise and fall of the bed sheet that stretched across her. He felt helpless and troubled in the same way he had as a boy when his normally unflagging mother announced that she did not feel well and how her small voice had so unsettled him, prompting him readily to busy himself with all the jobs he knew she would have liked him to do for her before he went to school and which he knew would keep him occupied and responsible. It had been a Tuesday and for years he hated it when Tuesdays came round. Reinhard wished the doctor would come. He looked around, then heard another small voice.

'Who - are - you?' Stephanie managed.

His strength returned. He wanted to hug her.

'It's Reinhard,' he said nervously, fumbling for the right words. 'I phoned you a few days ago, Stephanie, and we arranged to meet at your home. It was for a special date you spoke of, you remember.'

But Stephanie did not seem to remember or she had fallen asleep again. Reinhard moved gingerly to the other side of her bed and put out a hand. 'It's Reinhard. You know.' But he knew instinctively that she did not know. He again looked around, hoping for a nurse if not the doctor.

Stephanie stirred again.

'Stephanie?' she said, suddenly opening both eyes widely, the creases of surprise gradually taking on the lines of a frown. But it was some time before her eyes seemed to focus and even then, not directly on him. She appeared to be looking but not seeing anything and briefly the rapid lateral eye movement returned. He tried to comfort her.

'Stephanie it most certainly is,' he said, forcing composure. 'Time, and ...' he swallowed, '... a car accident, they have managed to create only a very thin disguise.'

There was no reaction. Her eyes again closed. Reinhard waited breathlessly but she remained still. He shifted uneasily. He turned away, suddenly angry at his convoluted and exaggerated attempt to please her. Sub-consciously she had probably recoiled at such embellishment of a straightforward reaction. *'Liebling!'* might have risked presumption but little else.

'Liebling!' he dared, leaning forward.

For a moment, she seemed to breath more deeply but otherwise remained motionless. He said it again. He did not know what else to say now. He looked for a sign but could not say he found one. He repeated the word, again and again, then rapidly, crazily in his mind as if to substantiate all the *lieblings* he had mentioned over all the years.

REQUIREMENTS OF GUILT

'Liebling!' he said once more, aloud, confidently, earnestly, lovingly. There was need for nothing else. It was that simple. Nothing clever. No embroidery of any kind. Why had he ever made so much of everything during his life? Why had he not seen things in simple black or white? Shades of grey were for artists and decorators, not means of delay and pathways to doubt. He had been wrong; that was the end of it. In this moment, beside her bed, at this latish stage in his life and with the partially open window behind Stephanie's bed hopefully sucking out his wordiness, he challenged everything about himself, what it was that had made him who he was. He had for far too long considered unworthy anything that smacked of the ordinary or the imperfect, whereas shortcomings and flaws - and certainly humility - was what made humanity the stronger. And he would give his past a mental exorcism: he tossed the contents of his Berlin filing cabinets in every direction and cursed authority worldwide, slashed directives with a five-foot pen, raged at superiority in all its guises, hit out at desks, condemned paperwork, defaced walls, applauded graffiti, sloshed the contents of pan-size inkwells over practically every inch of floor space, and for good measure, spat at the very idea of any kind of preconceived order. And, while he was about it, he mentally entered his Hammersmith flat to tip up his draw of referenced papers, scattered his folded pullovers, saw himself remaining at rest while the telephone rang, scorned those occasions when servility had left him breathless, listened to the radio instead of judging it, decided that wearing scruffy clothes was a flimsy cover up, left the dirty dishes to do as they pleased in the kitchen until he was ready for them, refused to make the bed and abandoned totally any discretion with caffeine. And he felt lighter.

Reinhard looked intently into Stephanie's face. She was next to him. Injured - perhaps badly - but she was next to him. Thinking about someone could be powerful but being with that person was all but overwhelming. He had been given a chance he hardly deserved. Perhaps already he was kidding himself. Hark at him! A chance! She had entered his soul at their first meeting. She became part of him. Gentle thoughts about her sometimes came as often and as natural as returning the carriage of his typewriter, a really deep feeling as often and intense as hunger. There never had been rhythm to his thoughts about her but there was one constant: now and again, and often ill-timed, his breath would be caught and there would be that horrible pain, regret. Now it was going to be different. No backward thinking. Forward, ever forward. He was here in front of her once again. And if ever he should be the person he believed he was deep down, certainly the one he thought himself capable of being, then it had to be now. A life likened to thin coffee was at an end. Now he would dare to make it rich and full. He would fight for Stephanie as if he had been restrained by chains from doing so until this moment. He flexed his arms for the task. Shoulders back, chest out, head up.

Stephanie had not moved. She breathed lightly though regularly. He looked away through the doorway and got up to walk to the ward reception area, occupied by three female clerks, two of whom were on the phone and the third speaking to a visitor. He trailed a hand over Stephanie's shoulder as he made for the desk. Off to one side were two white-coated males deep in conversation, both holding clipboards. Reinhard wanted Stephanie's doctor but he was off duty. Her case notes were with an assistant. The starched-face nurse in her white uniform who marched towards him almost made Reinhard laugh out loud. The consultant would see him now, she told Reinhard. She led him along a corridor before tapping on a frosted glass door.

'Thank you Angela,' the neurologist said. And turning to Reinhard: 'Please take a seat. Just give me a minute', at the same time lifting a hand in the direction of a tubular but well-padded chair. Reinhard sank into it gratefully and suddenly thought of Stephanie's father and his probably high position in the grind of Germany's heavy industry. It yielded much for humankind thanks to the practicalities of moulded metal. He smoothed the arms.

'Mr Hänsel ...' the consultant said, slowly looking up. 'Stephanie has suffered a head injury. Exactly how bad that injury is we will not know immediately, not perhaps for days, even weeks. You see, apart from visible injury caused during the kind of impact Stephanie suffered, brain trauma can be the bigger problem. Alterations in cerebral blood flow and pressure within the skull may quite severely add to what happens at the time of the crash. The one thing we can be sure about is that beside the care that she will need here, you or someone she trusts, will have to minister to the psychological needs that will almost certainly manifest themselves on discharge and perhaps for some time as she attempts to recognise her place in a world that will on occasions seem mildly strange, bewildering or downright alien. She might well need the entire thesaurus of the words we all freely use. How complete that love is could determine the length of time it takes for her to recover.'

The consultant continued, 'Traumatic brain injury can have a number of cognitive, behavioural, physical and emotional effects and in certain states can cause permanent disability or, rarely, death. Happily, I hasten to add, we are sure we are not in this area. Based on my observations and tests carried out, and those of my colleagues, we think Stephanie may be suffering from a quite severe case of loss of memory. It is entirely possible that messages between certain areas of the brain are not getting through. The encoding process has been interrupted. There may be a certain amount of re-wiring that may be necessary mentally. So that if memories are fogged at present, that fog can be cleared.'

Another consultant accompanied Reinhard back to the ward, talking non-stop as if lecturing university students. Reinhard hated his constant use of what he saw as 'double dagger' phases, conspiratorial twins: he spoke of retrograde amnesia, temporal lobe, cerebral cortex, contextual knowledge, episodic memory. And what was that? Hippocampus? If he had been asked to sum up what he had now been told, Reinhard would have to say that Stephanie's chances of recovery were based on possibilities, maybes and probabilities depending on this, that or the other.

'Oh, I'm sorry,' Reinhard said, interrupting, and stopping suddenly to turn his head briefly and apologetically towards the dapper assistant in his stiffly starched whites.

'What for?'

'Inner thoughts, doctor. Inner thoughts. Just make her better, please,' Reinhard pleaded.

'We'll do our very best from a medical point of view. But in the long run much is probably going to have to depend on you. I understand you may well be best placed in this regard. You must do your best to help her re-index the past, Herr Hänsel. I probably don't need to tell you this but you may have to be prepared to tolerate a lack of comprehension, strangeness if you will, especially in the early weeks. Surgery may not become necessary, especially if the instruments of incisions and manipulation are the kind encouragements of a close friend, supported where appropriate by specific images that are currently locked in there. Sometimes it is as simple as finding the key. We would always prefer that. Good luck, Herr Hänsel.'

'May I see ...'

'Of course, but stay only a short while longer. Rest in the early days is essential.'

Reinhard hurried to her bedside, said, 'I love you, *liebling* Stephanie,' and left the occupant for the time being in her locked-in state.

Outside the hospital, Reinhard compared the way she looked with how she would have planned to appear in front of him. She had obviously wanted to look good for him and he would look good for her. He had nevertheless seen her. She was alive. She had a chance. He had a chance. They, he dared, had a chance.

47

YES, a yellow shirt and a tie of predominantly pale lemon with some blue. And a beige suit. Also a pair of soft brown, lace-up suede shoes. Oh, and a deep brown felt hat, with a light tan band if you have it, fedora-style. No, nothing else, thank you. The assistant packaged up the items and smiling, projected the carrier bags towards Reinhard who looked across the department store, out of the men's section, to the far side. He walked over the pampering mauve carpet towards the cocked heads, tilted hats, smoothing hands, slender, searching fingers, all the female animations of fresh purchase. He stood there for a while, eyes closed, and then made for the door, standing in the entrance, where he looked out over the busy shopping scene before walking up to the window of the shop next door. He guided his eyes over everything on the shelves around the walls and on to the more presumptuous items lining themselves up in the centre of the store. Reinhard kept his hand on the door handle for some time before pushing forward. He walked towards the counter, looked at where his shoes trod, made them pointed and turned first one way, then the other, undecided, before he made for the first rack and smoothed an early sleeve. He looked up at the advancing assistant. She asked him if she could help but he could not think of how he could tell her how she could help. He said he was just looking. When she turned back to the counter, he left the shop, trailing a hand over the side of a modelled suit.

Reinhard told himself how extraordinarily fortunate he had been to find Stephanie and to have had his telephone call received with such grace, with even a touch of playful delight. Now their date had been cruelly interrupted. He remained in the shop doorway until he regained his composure and his resolve to think positively. In the street, at the kerbside, it came out, 'There, Stephanie, I am ready.' He mouthed the assurance into a sharp wind that suddenly raced down the street in front of him, chilling his right side.

48

THERE were days when a flicker of recognition seemed to cross Stephanie's improving face during Reinhard's visits to the hospital. Such occasions were blissful and he had a hard time keeping his reaction in check. Then, on other days, there was nothing. Not a trace of anything and such visits left him flat. The hoped-for Oktoberfest date had come and gone, as had the entire fortnight's jollifications. Yet another year gone, he thought, but who cared!

He was by then, though, having no difficulty in recognising her; it was his Stephanie right enough – like himself, just a little older. When she finally came out of hospital, looking really good, she continued to drift in and out of uncertain present and hopeful future. Reinhard had thought that she might well return to live with Thomas until she felt stronger all round when her recovery could be concentrated in a place she knew well and with someone she had grown to trust. Thomas had told Reinhard that he would certainly have gone along with that suggestion if Stephanie had wanted it but she was quite insistent that she would feel better in her own place, new though it was. And, again she was very insistent: she wanted Reinhard to continue to look after her, if Thomas didn't mind.

Thomas told Reinhard, 'Even though Stephanie's decision is more than likely the result of some repressed impulse, knowing what we both know, the arrangement is befitting.'

Reinhard was happy to go along with that and he wanted to believe that he noticed during the next few days some very small signs that he was really welcome in her place. She had had a bed made up for him in a spare room and he couldn't help recalling Thomas telling him that he would put up with anything so long as he knew Stephanie was under the same roof as he was. Visits to the hospital for Stephanie to have check-ups were interspersed on other days with just walking. It was a fairly regular routine but one that for a long while looked to be getting nowhere or nearly so. On returning home by bus from one of their walks around a large park on the outskirts of München, there were several letters waiting for Stephanie on the mat, one of which Reinhard learned later that day was from Stephanie's daughter, Christine. Christine was studying law in England, at King's College London, and would be flying back to Germany in a couple of days's time.

'She's a good girl. She's certainly looking forward to seeing you. Read for yourself,' Stephanie said, leaning across to pass the letter to him. 'But there's no need for her to break her studies in England on account of me. I'm fine,' she added.

Reinhard learned from the letter that Christine was nearing completion of her studies at the School's Centres of European Law and Crime and Justice Studies.

'A lawyer, eh?'

Stephanie smiled.

The letter was a long and mostly cheerful daughter's dialogue. But Reinhard was a little startled by two things. Christine mentioned that her new job was with the war crimes unit at Ludwigsburg and that she 'couldn't wait' to meet him. Well, it was not so much the 'couldn't wait' bit, because that's the sort of thing people were given to saying even though it so often turned out to be quite an ordinary handshake or feather embrace and little else. No, she had added that after all the nice things Stephanie had said about him over the years, she would find it difficult to keep her hands off him! Of course, it was a gross over-statement and no real intent meant.

Reinhard never felt like a stranger in Stephanie's home but he did think it a little strange that Stephanie seemed reluctant fully to engage in the present special situation of his now being part of that home.

'Do you have a photograph of Christine?' he asked casually.

'Somewhere, I am sure. I will try to look one out. Actually, I had one at Thomas's place and I think it may be among the stuff I still have to collect from him.'

Reinhard did not want to tax her memory, or anything else, to the point of irritation so he suggested he make some tea. She smiled and said that would be nice. It was safe ground and again Reinhard got an inkling of how Thomas must sometimes have felt.

The following day it was raining but she put on some rather luminous all-weather gear and in the coal shed at the back of her home she found an old overcoat and hat for Reinhard that Thomas had given her for gardening. Thus attired, they set off for a walk. Reinhard thought of their first ever meeting in the Berlin club and, with a nervousness that crazily felt just as extreme as it did those thirty years before, he suddenly came out with, 'Would you like Coca-Cola or something?' without a shop in sight.

Stephanie didn't just nod acceptance but stopped, turned to him, touched his arm, and said, 'That would be very nice.'

Reinhard could swear she had used those very words in the club that night, before their game of table tennis, when he had placed a bottle of the stuff on an edge of the table and invited her to beat him for it. They eventually located a general store and sat at a table outside and had their drink. It was nice but nothing important came of it.

One day (there were others and they were always obvious by the frown that greeted his arrival) she seemed to recognise nothing about their relationship or about anything. It was as if they were complete strangers. Even on one fairly good day she could still not recall the telephone conversation that had brought them together again after three decades. The starting point for their renewed friendship had apparently, for the time being at least, been lost to her memory. He sometimes thought of holding her hand, but he held back because of what the consultant had said. Certainly, he did not wish to push her away with some random and premature advance. It had to be done gently and very patiently. During the difficult days when the mood between them was flat - even, he might say, strained - they walked stiffly and mainly in silence, as if they were walking through gravestones to a funeral. Reinhard knew that somehow he had to change this. He just had to keep plugging away at anything he could remember that had happened between them, mention them if and when they seemed appropriate and hope something would click. Big things, little things, anything, things like the Coca-Cola bottle, specifics of their past.

Reinhard had been told that Stephanie's explicit, episodic memory was what was probably blocked. Stephanie would likely retain both personality and identity, along with her procedural memory because her motor skills and instinctive physical memories were stored separately and away from the injury zone. What Reinhard had not been told but feared was that the longer memories were unable to be accessed the more likely it was that they ever could again be extracted. He felt himself to be in a hurry.

The previous evening, just over three weeks into her recuperation, Reinhard thought of something special and decided that during their next walk, choosing a moment when she seemed at her most receptive, he would ask her if she would be prepared to be a bit more adventurous. When he did this, Stephanie stopped in her tracks and looked sternly at him.

Reinhard began, 'I didn't mean …' But she interrupted, her face breaking into a smile. 'These walks are not really working, are they? What did you have in mind?'

Reinhard drew breath and said, 'Oh, well, it was just that I thought . . . would you come with me to Berlin? I have been thinking about it for some time, something that might just work. Would you?'

'Just so long as it's not another long walk!' she said impishly.

Reinhard was delighted with her reaction and said, 'Actually, there is just a short walk involved but it leads to something else, I promise.' The stern look now completely absent, she rested a hand on his arm.

'Berlin, though?' she said playfully, keeping his spirits up. Reinhard nodded several times, inside bursting with excitement at the thought of the forest tavern and the artless collaboration of merrily intoxicated sweethearts, feeling again as young as tent life. He wanted to turn to her, put his arms upon her shoulders and put his so mature eyes upon her lovely face and ask her right here and now. But he knew that he had to wait.

*

Layers of pine debris beneath their feet softened the steps they took along the track in the forest towards the Tavern in the Trees.

REQUIREMENTS OF GUILT

Reinhard had checked the place out and had hurried round to open the car door for Stephanie. Immediately he pointed her onto the track, he felt the surge of joy that probably he did that special night so long ago. After just a few silent steps, it was as if he was walking with her that last time, around the bends of their track, their clumps of trees, those that leant in on them from both sides, their time. The echo of hand in excited hand conversation that had surrounded them then, drifted into his mind. Continuing to look straight ahead, he felt for her hand and curled his around it. She let it be and Reinhard could hear his own heart beat. He wanted to tell her straight away. Surely she would remember. It had meant so much to them both. There was so much of the past within him, and Stephanie, too, he was sure if only her wires would sort themselves out. He felt sorry for Stephanie. This little outing had probably made her aware of something but almost certainly it made little or no sense. On the other hand, he knew the story, yet as things were between them, it felt very intrusive. He kept quiet, just happy having her hand. He would hope on the walk back that they would truly be retracing their Thirties' promenade.

Reinhard asked if she was all right, because he noticed she looked to be limping slightly. She glanced at him and nodded. 'My hip is still troubling me a bit. I must tell them at the hospital.' Then, encouragingly, she added that she felt looked after. He still hoped that at any time she might sling her arms around his neck and say she knew where they were going but her generally detached bearing held out little hope of that. Despite the fact that Reinhard was still holding her hand, yards from the tavern, he still did not feel over confident that his plan would work yet at the same time he knew it was an occasion that had meant a great deal to both of them at the time and positivity reasserted itself. Before mounting the wooden steps to the tavern, he looked back at the forest and breathed deeply on its bouquet of glorious young days hoping Stephanie might recognise the scent. As he pushed open the tavern door a wonderful future flashed before him but knew that this was much more about Stephanie remembering the past. Stephanie hesitated as if she was trying to remember but she walked on. He looked across to the bar area and acknowledged the greeting of Torsten, a stout man with an orange beard, who he had earlier told something of why they would be present. The man was pulling a drink and inclined his head towards a vacant table almost central in the wood-panelled room that was already more than half full. Reinhard kept hold of Stephanie's hand and led her to the table. He felt comforted by being in the company of relaxed drinkers, the soft buzz from whom came in pleasant waves that placed him back in that long-ago evening scene. Stephanie, had she been asked, may have wanted something quieter, though had she remembered the last time they had been there, Reinhard and she had been part of quite a high-spirited, perhaps a little rowdy occasion.

Although it was not difficult to notice the dubiety in her voice, Reinhard detected at the same time an eagerness for this night to succeed and she was obviously not displeased to be present. They settled around the small table and Reinhard looked up at the approaching *Kellner*.

'*Zwei Bier bitte*,' he ordered. It had started like that. Two small beers. They picked them up, touched glasses and settled back. They sipped in silence.

She leans forward, her eyes sparkling as she looks at Reinhard with a sudden intensity he instantly recognises. Reinhard cups her face in his hands. Their eyes, expressing now more than the power of speech was capable of, are still fixed on each other when the two beers arrive at the table. Slowly, almost reverently, der Kellner sets the glasses down and strikes two Biro marks on Reinhard's beer mat.

'*Danke Schön.*'

'*Bitte Schön.*'

Reinhard snatches at his beer. She follows, but slowly. They link arms, the glasses making way for their lips. Reinhard says, 'Prost. Here's to us.' They drain the glasses and two more are soon seen off. Replacements mean there are now six ticks around the beer mat. Each drink that arrives at the table seems to make them ever more thirsty. Two more marks, and another two. Their hands fidget, touching each other lightly at first. The tavern is full but they are by themselves. They speak sparingly but they are out of breath with thought. She puts a hand to his face and his heart leaps. He looks at his beer mat. The marks seem to move, occasionally spinning, like a bike's spinning spoked wheel, reversing to a stop, then speeding forward. He concentrates extra hard and sees that the marks have almost linked up around the circumference of the beer mat, nearly a circle. Reinhard thinks it looks like a chain. No. Not a chain. He starts to count the links, but looks up.

REQUIREMENTS OF GUILT

'Liebling, we shall complete this circle, eh? Let's drink on until the marks on the beer mat join up. And ...'

Stephanie suddenly stiffened. She bent forward, for a few seconds resting her forehead on the backs of her hands flat out in front of her. In that time, Reinhard's room fell silent while Stephanie's obviously roared. 'Reinhard!' she almost yelled out. Animated for the first time since entering the tavern, she shouted 'Yes!', turning to take in every part of the room. Slowly, affectionately, a faint smile on her face imaging a panorama of the old happiness he had drawn on during all the lonely years, she went on, her face now inches from his and looking intently into his eyes, 'Reinhard!' And then, softer, 'Reinhard! Reinhard!' And softer still, 'Reinhard ... You are wonderful.'

This moment of intimacy was followed by a sudden explosive gesture in which she brought her open hands up from the table, then heavily down onto its surface, at the same time as she sank back into her chair. She did not try to hide the tears that now poured down her cheeks. She shook, in small, breathless jerks, her heaving body setting her mouth in an enchanted expression. She could not speak for emotion but he knew what had to be happening. It had worked. In front of him was the result of recall and release.

She apologised but by now Reinhard was in the same state and gestured sympathetically. Words seemed totally inadequate for what they were experiencing. For a moment more, she said nothing, and he waited patiently, alarmed and excited in equal measure. Composing herself, Stephanie asked, 'Shall we have some more beers, perhaps finish off that ring of marks?'

Reinhard wanted to marry her straight away and nearly said so. But he held back. He wondered now whether in her condition she should be drinking so much, whether she should be drinking at all, and that his plan had unfortunately involved the one thing that might be no good for her despite what he was sure was actually happening. He was helped out when, without any bidding, another couple of drinks appeared at the table and *der Kellner* made two more marks.

'Just drink,' she said, seemingly anticipating Reinhard's thoughts. 'For now, nothing else. Like it was, eh?'

Reinhard's insides were afire. Also, he had some difficulty in keeping up with Stephanie. She downed her first in just three gulps, rested the glass heavily and wiped her mouth with a huge sweep of the back of her hand. She again put up her hands as he drew breath.

'It will form a ring!' she gushed, her face again awash with tearful happiness.

Reinhard stood up, threw his hands around her across the table and whispered hoarsely into her neck. 'And we said we should marry!'

'Yes, Yes! I remember. I recall it, everything,' she said loudspeaker like. Then, intimately, she said, 'Thank you Reinhard. Thank you. Thank you.' She kept repeating it, 'Thank you. I am back. I would not have missed this for the world!'

She got up from the table, walked round to him, slipped her arms around his neck and kissed him long and lovingly (to relieved Tavern approval, he could now hear) but they sat back in silence, ignoring the attention, staring past each other, hardly daring to think what next was due. For sure and with the certainty of young love they were back in their past and for now each wanted to remain there, drinking in the beauty of that Thirties' evening. The feelings Reinhard had were not those of a middle-aged man remembering but of a teenager experiencing. He wanted to stay in that past where the tavern had offered them the world. Here was another chance. Stephanie appeared to feel it, too. A miracle seemed to be happening.

'That's what we agreed, wasn't it? Back then?'

Reinhard rushed his agreement, eager to take the matter further. 'Yes, it was. That we should marry because when the beer mat marks joined up it would form a kind of chain. A ring.'

'Yes, a wedding ring. That's what you said out of the blue that night,' Stephanie recalled, her nose almost touching his as she stretched across the table. 'And I loved it. Then, since and … and I …'

Their dialogue, already the subject of interest among those people on the nearest tables, now seemed to have the attention of the entire tavern. Drinkers chinked their glasses towards them and they both responded with abandon. The interlude seemed to go on forever. The reappearance of *der Kellner* broke the spell. 'I always knew my beer had magical qualities. Now everyone knows! Do I understand correctly? Is it congratulations?' Other far-off drinkers started to applaud and soon the whole room was turned their way, clapping, smiling and cheering.

'Yes, your beer certainly has magical qualities,' Reinhard responded. 'Your tavern, too. We are sorry if we have also told the world,' he cried, turning to Stephanie. 'You particularly are magical, Stephanie,' he said, folding his arms around her.

They sat back and *der Kellner* brought in four more beers, completed the marks around the beer mat, and said quietly to Reinhard, 'Take the beer mat when you have finished. You owe me nothing!' He put a hand on *der Kellner's* arm. Now he did feel drunk.

'We are drunk,' they confessed to each other. 'But not too drunk to know what I am saying,' Reinhard confessed. Holding up the beer mat, he said, 'So, Stephanie, as we have rediscovered our ring, will you marry me?' His voiced trailed away to nothing.

'Stephanie,' he repeated huskily, *'Willst du mich Heiraten?'*

She whispered something into his ear that was drowned out by the tavern revellers. He was puzzled at first but as she left for the toilet, she looked back into his face and he knew what she must have said.

49

OFF you go then adolf. You know what to do. Where he goes, nothing else. I'll wait here, inside or out.

Tschüss!

A fine name, Adolf.

A fine brandy, too.

The name's known everywhere. A forever name. Picked him for his name, really. It motivates me, just saying it.

'course, he's not a proper Adolf, a proper upper case version.

adolf, Kommen sie!

Gehen Sie hinaus, adolf!

He's a fool in fact. But he'll do this; a simple enough job. It'll be his last for me, though.

Best to work alone, anyway. I'm like Him. Not him. Upper case Him.

I'm single-minded. Blessed with commanding oratory. Threatening and beseeching in turn. Luring them in. Very effective. As then, so now. Folk will follow. They'll see reason. Or be removed.

Noch einer, Herr Ober.

Danke …

Aahhhh! Sehr gut.

REQUIREMENTS OF GUILT

They conjure world domination with a bleary stare into the bottom of a crystal glass stein, those Fest freaks Hans and Ernst and what's it, *ja* Siggi, and probably Heinrich and, um, ja Gandolf. My sights are more focussed, set on one individual, perhaps two, the recently departed, and soon to be just that.

adolf's out there, right now, strolling but not aimlessly, behind the couple, suitably distant to their rear, like I told him.

It's not a lonely life, being alone. Thoughts make constant company. You can call on individuals by lifting a hand or the masses by standing on a platform. In private, by myself, I can think properly, read a lot. Schopenhauer, Kleist, Nietzsche, His old but still fresh words. Worthy minds, all of them. Only he who lives dangerously lives fully, one of them said. I agree.

My, this brandy's good.

Bet the Fest freaks haven't heard of, let alone read, *Die Hermannsschlacht*. That's a great bit - Act IV, scene 7, if I remember rightly. Faced with Thusnelda's entreaty for compassion, Hermann retorts *Hate is my office and my virtue vengeance*.

That's the trouble with Hänsel. He is all love and no hate. It can't be so.

I wonder if adolf has found out yet.

Our kind must be ruthless. Compassion equals compromise. Arbitration and its dithering cousins represent weakness. I can separate emotion from intellect. My audiences will see that.

Hänsel would only recognise me as hospital security. The name would have meant little unless one of that Fest gang of drunks piped up. They're bound to have tried to degrade me. They fear me. I have no equal; many aspirants, but no claimants. They can say what they like, anyway. Everyone can say and do what they like. It will make no difference. I am set on my course. It *will* happen. The Will has always been the important thing.

adolf shouldn't have mentioned my name at all, though. Leader, I told him. Call me My Leader. *Mein Fuhrer!*

Maybe I'll change my name to Adolf. Yes. Why not? They'll recall Him and those glory days. Maybe I'll make my mark even before thirty.

I had to allow Hänsel to indulge his moment. But that's all he gets. He's attracted to this unworthy woman. She to him, too, by the looks of it. Magnets. But like poles repel! They certainly do me!

This brandy's *very* good.

Yes. Adolf. I like it. I will not miss the name Konrad. No emotional resonance. None whatsoever.

Nochmal Weinbrand, bitte!

I will show them all!

Ah, there you are. Where will I find them, then adolf?

Danke.

Tschüss!

50

IT WAS Stephanie's idea that they ride the trams that night. Reinhard readily agreed, realising it would act as a natural restraint on the night ahead because recounting the amazing breakthrough at the Tavern in the Trees would generate only so much excitement that words could satisfy. It would give decency due priority and provide time to begin the task of filling each other in on their pasts. Besides, they were both aware that they had to be up early in the morning to meet Christine at the airport, so it was as well to get as much sleep as possible on this first night. They did go over the evening at the Tavern, alternately extracting huge delight in describing the expressions that crossed each other's faces at the various stages. They relived the moments with such intensity and euphoria that other people started joining in just like back in the tavern. It got a little ridiculous and when Reinhard started losing his ability to say anything coherent, this sent Stephanie over the top and they had to help each off at the next stop, neither of them even able to say good-bye to the other passengers. They weren't much better while looking for another tram number. A crowded number 8 arrived but they boarded it, hanging on tightly to a central pole. 'It's been a bit of a bumpy ride, you know!' Reinhard said, suddenly serious.

'Smoother road ahead, eh?' she shot back with the grin that so often marked her zest for life. Then, suddenly she was serious, 'There's always been thoughts about you, Reinhard. I'm sorry about that time just after the war but I did understand about your wife and actually loved you even more for that decision. And in view of what has happened now, I realise how thwarted you also must have felt.'

Reinhard was on the verge of being overwhelmed to hear her say these things. His eyes gave him away but he breathed out her name, squeezed her hand and kissed her on the forehead.

'What about you?' she asked brightly, fully restoring the naturally radiant look to her face and guiding Reinhard into a seat that had just been vacated. He said, 'We have lived as man and wife, you and I Stephanie, in absentia. But I wish everything was as clear-cut and as wholesome as …' Stephanie leant forward to grab Reinhard's arm as the tram stopped opposite a café quarter. 'Let's get off here for a while.'

When they alighted, she said: 'I think I know what you were going to say just then, Reinhard. Christine has told me. I know about your brush with the Central Crimes Unit. Look, let's sit over there for a while,' she said, pointing to a street bench. They relaxed into it and she put an arm around him. 'Christine dealt with the interview papers when she returned for a spell from her studies at King's. She thought I ought to know how rough a time you had actually had.' Reinhard went to speak but she put her hand gently over his mouth. 'Because you told the officers everything, I also know about your time with the camps inspectorate and what happened at that awful place, and later. I know most of all that. And there's very little I cannot imagine.' He drew breath to speak but she repeated her action and went on, 'And frankly I am not surprised Ludwigsburg came to the decision they did over you. You once told me you were proud of me. Well, I want you to know for sure that we both know how that feels. I shall look forward to hearing about the rest of your life in greater detail but not now. Pulling at his hand she said, '*Ich liebe dich immer noch.*'

Reinhard liked being led by her as she closed in on another tram. They got off again soon after, this time at his behest, when he spotted a band or a small orchestra playing to the side of a crowded square. It was an orchestra and he recognised the music. After just a few bars, the musicians seemed to become entranced as they produced a brilliant rendering of Dvorak's *Song to the Moon*. Or was it his interest in the music that made it appears so? Because he had shown such rapt attention to the piece, Stephanie let it be heard through to the end without speaking. Reinhard then told Stephanie the story of the Jewish woman he had met while camping with his London neighbour. She slung her arms about his neck, then hugged him tightly.

'Do you remember this?' she said as she began humming the first few lines of another classical piece. Reinhard remembered the occasion immediately and vividly and as his mind went back he stared away from the orchestra, away from Stephanie, to that time when, hand in hand, they had walked jauntily into some wood humming the opening bars of the overture to Otto Nicolai's *The Merry Wives of Windsor*. He could see them both as if were yesterday. She had been totally beguiling that evening, his Stephanie. It was so real to him, just then, that he must have reached out or something to hold her young hand and started on the tune because when he felt a tug on his sleeve and turned around, for just an instance, he felt distressed that she had vanished. He feared he must have conveyed a measure of disappointment because Stephanie said, 'You don't remember? Or you didn't like what you remembered?'

'Oh no, Stephanie darling,' he said. 'I liked immensely what I remembered! Of course, it was *The Merry Wives of Windsor*.' And to hide his embarrassment, he tried to hum it, too, but he was crying inside. Stephanie gave him a sideways glance before getting hold of his hand and swinging it into the air that made him feel much better.

The next tram trip took them back into the city centre. They were getting tired because for the first time since they had set out, their conversation had slowed and he suggested they make their way home. She agreed and they snuggled up to one another as the tram slowed to its stop. As they waited to alight, Reinhard saw a man looking their way that he was sure he had seen on the previous tram. His face was vaguely familiar, perhaps from a time before their time in riding the city, but Stephanie snuggled up even closer and he whispered, 'Stephanie!'

'Yes, Reinhard?'

'I just like saying your name,' he said quietly.

She laughed.

'Reinhard?'

'Yes ... Stephanie?'

'I just like saying your name!'

They hugged.

They walked on for a while, almost in silence, with just a contented, occasional squeeze of the hand. Reinhard wanted to hear something about her life but they were only a couple of streets from home and it was getting dark. She must have read his mind, however, because she said she had married a doctor, Theodore, but he had died just months later, only weeks before the end of the war, following an air-raid on Nürnberg.

'He never saw Christine,' she said, adding, 'You will like Christine. She's so pleasant. I think she has a bright future.'

'Like us,' Reinhard said.

Stephanie broke free, pressed her hands together and arched her body to bring an excited face close to his. 'I can't believe it!' she said. 'You . . . and me!' And she flung her arms into the air, head back and letting go a long and loving 'Ahhhhhh' before dancing over the grass and around a couple of trees and returning to raise Reinhard's right hand aloft, rest her other hand on his shoulder, and give him a gentle nudge backwards and one of her special expectant dance floor looks.

Reinhard felt a thrill as they passed through the door of her apartment. They were together again.

51

THEY kept to their separate rooms routine and Reinhard slept soundly enough once he had got over a restless couple of hours. In fact, they were late getting up but their early blur and disjointed attempts to dress, which at one point had them hopping into one another in the hallway, kept them in good spirits. They had a hurried breakfast of strong coffee and rather overdone toast with marmalade.

Reinhard locked up and she got the car out - a light green Opel Rekord - and they set off like a practised married couple, Reinhard checking with her that she had turned off the gas cooker while she asked him if he had been sure to double lock the front door. She put the car into top gear on reaching the autobahn and raced ahead to try to catch up a little on time. They travelled in silence to start with. Then, after about a dozen kilometres, she said, 'You look better than your picture.'

'What picture?'

'Ah, I had one given to me just just recently. It was extraordinary, really. Christine visited me one afternoon, quite out of the blue, and over tea she suddenly opened her handbag and brought out this very recent photograph of you! I couldn't believe it. You had telephoned me only a couple of days before her visit and I had idly wondered what you looked like now, and here you were. By the way, I now do remember that call most clearly. Everything's come back. You sounded anxious. I suppose you might have been.'

'Well, I was, just a little. But what picture are you talking about, Stephanie?'

'No mystery really; the one they took of you at the time of your arrest.'

'Oh, that picture! Wouldn't take much to improve a police profile!'

'Ah, but Christine saw you at the unit headquarters. Only briefly, but she saw you and she said for me not to walk out on you again. She was able to fill in the photograph quite a bit, so to speak.'

Reinhard said, 'Stephanie, it was *I* who made it impossible for you. I was sure I was right but in the end I was sure I had made a big mistake. Now we're together. And together let's return to that time when we thought everything was ours by right. I love you. You need to hear me say what only our stars have heard of late!' She pressed a hand on his thigh. 'Ditto.'

Reinhard had already seen the signs for München-Riem Airport and within minutes they arrived at the main terminal. They had caught up on time with the result that when they approached the arrivals lounge, the passengers had not yet begun to filter through. Stephanie said, 'I'm sure Christine would recognise you even if I were not here. Tell you what, you remain right here and I'll go and stand behind that billboard over there. Just see if I am right.'

Reinhard protested, 'She will be looking for you,' but the words did not reach her or were being ignored as she took up her position and the passengers from flight FH357 began filing into the lounge. He leant against a pillar and tried to look as ordinary as possible but found himself responding to the dare, straightening himself off the pillar, plunging his hands into his pockets and walking a little way towards the passengers. He wondered what she would look like. Then the passengers started in his direction: two elderly women, a young man and his wife or girlfriend, three young females, probably students, a man struggling on sticks, what looked like two middle-aged lesbians, two kids causing their parents to argue, a man in a panama hat trying to read something in one hand while wheeling a suitcase with the other …

Reinhard walked back to the pillar. She had probably missed her connection. He looked for Stephanie and saw she was giggling, shooing Reinhard back, urging him to face up again. He laughed but complied. And there was Stephanie! Young Stephanie! His Thirties' Stephanie! The same Stephanie he had seen while the city orchestra had played the Dvorák piece. His mind's forever Stephanie. Without hesitation, she walked quickly up to him and said, 'I knew I would recognise you straight away.' But Reinhard was rendered practically speechless and when she put both arms around his neck and kissed him on the cheek, he experienced a rush of emotions that left him gasping for air as she dashed on round to Stephanie who had reappeared from behind the pillar.

That much of the airport meeting, Reinhard remembered very clearly. The rest was fuzzy. He tried to compose himself but his mind was in turmoil. For some time, he was virtually unable to join any thoughts together, either to speak or understand anything that was said to him. He tried not to look at Christine and concentrating on Stephanie did not help much at this time. He closed his eyes as Stephanie turned to ask him whether he was OK. He told her he was actually feeling a little unwell. Perhaps it was the heat, he suggested. So that when they arrived home he was able to excuse himself for a while and he laid down on his single bed in the spare room. Christine had bowled him over, good and proper. She was the stunning version of Stephanie he had fallen in love with and had lived with in fantasyland for the past three decades. He was so shocked when he unscrambled the thinking in his head that he felt he would not be able to act normally when he was in their presence together. And that would be shortly. He knew he had to pull himself together and face the situation head on.

On the way home, Stephanie had filled Christine in on everything. Christine had said she was happy for her and that she would like to work on the wedding outfits. She would use the two mannequins she had acquired and make a proper job of it. Christine was keen on dress designing but had said she also had a male mannequin and would gladly create an outfit for Reinhard. Fashion designing was only a hobby but she was getting quite good at it and enjoying it.

After a little while, Christine knocked at Reinhard's door to see how he was. He had only just got up after stretching out on the settee and she went over to sit next to him. He did not feel the angst he might have felt at having her so close to him and said, 'So you're into a career with the war crimes unit. I imagine that can be quite a satisfying job at times.'

'Very,' she said, 'especially with unusual cases like yours. 'Do you want me to bring you anything to eat or drink?'

'No, that's all right. I'm feeling much better now, thank you. I'll come out and join you in a while. Thanks anyway.'

She nodded and levered herself up with a hand laid firmly on Reinhard's thigh. She turned to him, 'I just wanted to say I think what you did back along was courageous. It was so very sad about Dieter but it is wonderful that the darkness of that time did not in the end swamp you and that mum and I can know and be with such a person. I hope we can be good friends, because - and I hope you don't mind my saying this - we can all make mistakes in our lives but it takes courage to admit them, and even more courage to try to face up to any wrong and try to somehow put things right. And when you are not just talking of some trifling off-the-cuff remark or a wrong conclusion of paltry significance, well I admire folk like that. It also gives me solid, extra faith in my nation that recent history practically destroyed.'

'I'll be out in a tick,' he said, adding, 'and thank you.'

She leaned back in at the door and enquired about the wedding suit. He agreed. Reinhard was sure she would make a good job of it. 'Something like charcoal with a feint stripe, single vent, two-button jacket, OK?'

Reinhard entered the lounge and settled into the remaining outside space on the luxurious three-seater settee, next to Christine. Straight away he said: 'It's all been a bit hectic, eh? But here we are together. This particular point in our lives seems to be all round wonderful. For Christine, because of her successful studies in England and new job with the war crimes unit to say nothing of her fame-to-be as a fashion designer! and for Stephanie and me because after far too long we have found each other again.'

Conversation was helped along with several glasses of Riojo. Christine reminded her mother that she had to be back at King's in three days' time but that she would soon be leaving permanently to join the unit in Ludwigsburg. The present few days at home were the result of some earned time but she understood she would be undertaking a fortnight-long intensive course, fortunately in München, to prepare her for what they said would be a demanding career.

Stephanie and Reinhard smiled at one another and stretched out an arm to touch hands behind Christine's chair. Reinhard happened to lightly brush the back of Christine's hair as he took his hand away. All in all, it was a very pleasant evening, oiled with a further bottle and a half of Shiraz. Christine left Reinhard and Stephanie alone an hour before midnight. Stephanie sank into her armchair and after they had listened to an absorbing mixture of classical and folk music, she wondered whether Reinhard would mind very much if they made the marriage special 'in every way'. Reinhard took a little while to absorb what he imagined she meant and when he did so he thought the best reply would be to kiss her lightly and say it was time they retired to their rooms.

In the morning Christine said that before she left for England, she had to try to get hold of a particular law book. She went on, 'There is a quite remarkable bookshop I've discovered in München, housed on three floors, with a fabulous second-hand section and I wondered whether you would like to join me today to take a look at the place because mum has told me about your interest in first edition modern fiction. You won't be disappointed, I guarantee it. As you know, mum has an appointment at the hospital this morning and is being taken by Thomas because he has to see a practice nurse there around the same time.'

Reinhard looked briefly at Christine and wondered whether it was such a good idea.

Stephanie seemed more interested in addressing the dishes than the arrangement and Reinhard wondered whether this had been the cause of a little contretemps between the two of them that he had overheard. He called out to Stephanie, 'We'll go to Molly Malone's tonight, Stephanie, if you like. I've already booked a table for two,' whereupon she noticeably cheered up.

'OK, you two enjoy yourselves,' she said looking between them.

*

The first thing Reinhard and Christine did at the bookshop, just off the city's central area, was to have a coffee and cake in the quite exquisite café on the top floor. Christine made for a cozy-looking settee in the corner and Reinhard immediately felt uneasy when she leaned across to pick up a discarded newspaper. He stretched back a little to make it easier for her to pick it up but she almost slumped into his lap, easing herself off with both hands. She laughed a little, saying she was sorry.

'Not at all,' Reinhard said tensely.

After scanning the front page, she cast the newspaper aside and said, 'I couldn't help noticing your reaction at the airport. Mum has shown me photos of herself about the time you knew her and it is amazing just how alike I know I am now to the way she looked then. Since you have grown up only with the one vision you could ever recall, well I sensed your ... warmth. It was natural. I can understand. Normally, this would not concern me but for the fact, as I've said, I have come to admire you greatly through the many things mum's told me of your time together and shortly afterwards, what I learned about you after the unit interview and seeing you briefly in person at the unit - when I saw something I cannot properly explain - and then again at München-Riem. Perhaps I have convinced myself that that was what I would see, I don't know. Sorry Reinhard but I have to be honest as to how I feel. You've been comforted by the memory of Stephanie all this time but for quite a few years now I have sort of lived with you ...'

She stopped with lips parted, slightly breathless, slowly shaking her head. 'This is no schoolgirl crush. Reinhard,' she continued. Then louder, 'I'm twenty-two for God's sake!' Then she leaned back and smiled through a long sigh. 'I hope you don't mind my telling you that. Anyway, I feel unburdened. It's a bit of a relief,' she said coyly.

It was too much for Reinhard to take in. He thought he sounded dismissive the way he said, 'I think you should try to get your book and I'll rummage through modern fiction, OK?' If it had sounded dismissive, he was glad. Because it would have to be dismissed. Yet he could not deny that he actually felt simultaneously adventurous even if twice as guilty. But again, he dismissed the thought and said as casually as he could, 'Böll's a favourite of mine.' Then, as if to organise her immediate itinerary, he said, 'Perhaps we'll have another drink before you fly off. Good luck with your book search.'

As she disappeared downstairs, Reinhard slumped into a seat by the window and looked out over rooftops. He felt miserably disloyal. He had suffered this long, frustrating and tragic journey and just as

REQUIREMENTS OF GUILT

he was to be miraculously rewarded with the grand prize of reuniting with Stephanie, something else was glittering off stage. Christine was just how Reinhard had always remembered Stephanie. How could life be so cruel? He shifted, felt very hot and was decidedly bothered. He announced to himself that he did not want a Böll or any other author. Books were crap! All of them! He hated books! There was so much more to life than books . After a while, however, and just to deflect his mind, he decided to give the shelves a cursory glance just a jubilant Christine came in holding a book aloft.

'I found it almost straight away!' she cried. 'What an enriching shop this is!'

'*War and the Law,*' Reinhard read out slowly, smoothing a hand over the cover before flicking through some pages. 'It certainly looks comprehensive,' he said, returning the book to her. 'Let's have this drink then, eh?' he said warily. In her other hand she had what looked like a book wrapped up and said, 'It's for you, Reinhard. Just a small gift. Open it later.'

Over hot chocolate, Christine said, 'I'm sorry, Reinhard. I should not have been so forward over there. It's just that, through mum, I have grown up with your name and the kind of person you are. Then I read about you and actually saw you, and now again, in more relaxed circumstances. Still, I'm sorry; I don't know what has come over me unless it has something to do with what came over you at the airport. Please forgive me. If we can remain good friends I will be very happy. What do you say?'

Her frankness was disarming. 'You know, Christine, if at the unit you read my story as I related it to the war crimes officials, then I do not deny that I am that person. But I made one huge mistake with Stephanie and I do not intend making another by abandoning her now. Good friends I hope we will continue to be, always, but Stephanie is hopefully, a final requirement of my guilt. Miraculously, Stephanie remembers again. Everything. And I heard through Thomas that it was because she was so dancing with joy after I telephoned her, that she had her accident.'

Christine said, 'I know and it is wonderful there was such a great reaction to your call. As I said, I am sorry.'

52

CHRISTINE's writing was as powerful as her spoken word. Her visiting card, slipped into a copy of *A Time to Love and a Time to Die* by Erich Maria Remarque, read '*Alles ... jederzeit*'.

Reinhard immediately tried to forget the message but 'anything ... any time' was hard to dismiss. He stood staring at the card, seeking innocence, some well-meaning but everyday courtesy from the words. He certainly did not want mere infatuation to gain any kind of strength. He certainly did not want the words to germinate in his mind and present him with totally destructive consequences. What was happening? Stop!

Stephanie and Reinhard went out for the evening as planned to Molly Malone's. Reinhard was totally at ease with Stephanie though he could not totally ignore Christine's card and he began to think that the problem could be solved if Christine simply slipped away. Perhaps he could tell her that he actually thought it was very unkind of her to push herself forward like she had. Damn her! And thereby force her to change her mind about how nice a guy he was supposed to be. Even tell Stephanie. Yes, tell her and have it all out in the open, as soon as possible. Just because he was so pleasantly shocked to see how much she looked like his Stephanie of old, did not mean ...

No, it did not mean that. He was with Stephanie and after a couple of glasses of wine he started ticking them off on a coaster. Stephanie looked at him lovingly and said, 'Yes, let's fix a date; I've been thinking about it a lot. What do you think about September?'

REQUIREMENTS OF GUILT

Reinhard said that was fine. September, particularly the weather that could be expected then, would be wonderful. But when he recalled Stephanie's casually delivered entreaty to have 'a proper marriage in all respects', he was initially disconsolate but determined to bring her round. This is a time to love and here he was dying! Yet he knew the problem would not be resolved by words alone, perhaps no words at all. He simply nodded, leant over their table and lightly patted her cheek.

'No, I am serious, Reinhard.'

'Oh, that's all right then because so am I!' he said, winking at her but wondering how much charm he actually had. To change the subject, he added, 'Tell me a little more of what you did after our last meeting.'

She sat back and said, 'I have made loads of notes about us over the years, memories mainly but also little hopes, even expectations. They're in a special box I have. I was thinking of getting a bigger box but now there's no need. Music has always helped me out when I am a bit low. It's like a fix. It makes me cry but makes me happy at the same time.'

Reinhard exclaimed, 'Well, that is amazing. I have done even more, Stephanie. Honest I have. I have written a novel. We can work together on a revision, eh? Find a publisher! This might be a first in publishing history,' he said. 'We could be very busy. Think of the deadlines we may have to face, the book signings. Then perhaps a sequel!'

Whimsically, they thought of all the money they would earn on publication, the dozens of editions that could follow, the film rights, royalties, the sheer delight of wallowing in the luxury of being very rich, with expensive cars and homes in half a dozen of the best places in the world in each of which they could settle down to a couple of months of bliss at a time, seeing so much, loving so much, learning so much, catching up on so much lost time. They drank to that, linking arms and generally behaving like a couple of fanciful teenagers.

It turned out to be a lovely evening and Reinhard wondered how he had managed for so long on the friendship of neighbours, good though George and Irma had always been. On the way back home, Stephanie mentioned work for the first time and he learned that she was a crossword compiler besides being a part-time secretary at a doctors' surgery.

'I shall be returning to the medical partnership the day after tomorrow,' she announced as she made coffee. 'I'm trying out this new coffee machine; how do you like yours?'

'Quite strong,' he said, thinking of staying awake a while longer but hearing her say that coffee acted as the perfect nightcap for her. He sat in her beautiful matte-finish brown leather settee and she joined him, drawing up a small table for the coffees. They talked a little about how good Molly Malone's was and when they finished their drink, Reinhard put an arm around her and leaned forward to kiss her. He could feel her reaction was somehow different from the way she had responded in the tavern, on the park bench or in the tram, for instance, and when she straightened his arm, he knew she saw a danger in privacy and was in effect repeating her special request. All right, he said to himself, perhaps lunch time can be night time! But it wasn't and then she was back to work. After breakfast, she liked to get straight on with her crossword compiling work so Reinhard was left with virtually only one other slot: tea time. One day, therefore, he waited until she had left for an afternoon shift at the surgery and straight away started prepping a special meal and set the scene for a relaxing time. He had kept a magazine article about a Black Forest food delight of lentil stew with Spätzle noodles and decided to give it a go. He really wanted to please her so he set up square red pillar candles in the centre of a finely dressed table which included a couple of miniature vases filled with varieties of wild flowers from her cottage garden. And for further soft illumination he prepared floater candles at points around the room. When all was ready, he decided he had enough time to do two other things and immediately set out for the city centre. Reinhard was after a smart casual shirt and slacks and, why not he thought, Dior's Eau Sauvage. The thought he put into this on his return had him adjusting every fine detail of the lounge-diner scene, including putting flame to the floater candles. He adjusted this and that for a full thirty minutes before Stephanie again stepped through the door.

It didn't work. She noticed everything, liked the illumination a lot and the meal went down exceptionally well but afterwards there was nothing to suggest that, together with the attention he had given to himself, anything had changed. And this routine continued. It was obvious she still very much wanted to marry him besides the number of times she told him. Apart from the slight limp he observed near the tavern that night, Reinhard had never become aware that her hip restricted movements in any material way and was vexed at the constraint she imposed on their relationship, because she extended it to virtually any kind of physical contact when they were alone. One way or another she spent a fair amount of time outside the house but at the same time was keen on her return to tell him how much he had been missed. Reinhard loved that part but she did not seem either to recognise or understand the other matter. She simply avoided it. It was, however, not a subject he cared to discuss. If nothing were forthcoming, he would seek nothing, even though he was hurting inside.

Stephanie spent any spare time on looking through her box of notes and although she was always blowing kisses at him, on the rare occasions they relaxed together, they were somehow always of short-lived duration. Reinhard tried to say that they could work on the manuscript together, adjusting here and there, until they had it just right. It seemed a fair suggestion but she said she was not quite ready for this. He felt it was almost like she was being evasive and Reinhard told her as much. He concluded a rather testy analysis of how he saw things with, 'It's a worthy project that need not be a total distraction, Stephanie.' But she shot back with 'Surely not that again!'

Cheapening, almost devaluing what she correctly guessed took little to be switched on in Reinhard's head sucked the life out of him and triggered the lure of those simple words, *'Alles ... jederzeit'*. Stephanie and Reinhard did not even say good-night to each other and they were not on the best of terms in the morning. She was going to be out all day on crossword business, she announced plainly. Reinhard hoped to lighten the atmosphere between them by saying they already had cross words and did she really have to go out? But the remark softened nothing. He let her leave the house without another word and when she had driven off, Reinhard sat for a while, very unhappy and very worried. Twice he got up and then sat back. Eventually, however, he picked up the phone.

53

CHRISTINE'S place was some miles outside the city boundary with views over a small but attractive lake. It was a beautiful home close to the water's edge. She had obviously not long been up and was wrapping a white waffle loungewear about herself as she ushered him into a luxuriously appointed room with a picture window that took in a large aspect of the lake on which shafts of light shimmered under a patchy but bright sky. Then she brought in coffee, still in her loungewear.

Christine said, 'We can have a little chat now and then go into town if you like. I have a very special café to let you experience. They have the most delightful cakes and pastries for miles around, Reinhard.' She offered him a cigarette, a Gauloises, and he accepted it. Christine leaned forward with a lighter and Reinhard drew heavily on the crackling cigarette but it was her perfume that had the greater effect. She said, 'This place is so refreshing. The people all seem so nice here, special if you know what I mean. I have lived here a couple of years now. This property is a bit big for just me but I do not suppose I will remain alone here for ever.' Reinhard fidgeted a bit because he felt himself to be going under her spell and when she said, 'You look a little flushed, Reinhard,' he wanted to tell her that actually he felt *very* flushed. She said, 'Is your interest in my little home the only reason for your being here? Only mum seemed a bit down when I spoke to her yesterday. Is everything all right? I mean, you know . . .' Reinhard shook his head defiantly. There was nothing he wanted to put into words.

She remained quite still for a while, then rose and moved round to the back of his chair and put her arms on his shoulders. Her hands remained there unmoving but the length of time they were in this position and the fragrance that was finding its way around him, forced Reinhard to put out the cigarette and say rather curtly, 'Shall we go into town?'

'I understand, Reinhard,' she said gently, sliding her hands from his shoulders only slowly. 'I can imagine how you feel.'

Ignoring the prompt, he said, now gruffly, 'Shall we go then!'

'Very well,' she said.

They travelled in silence as she drove her green open top BMW roadster at quite a pace into town and still had her foot down quite a bit along the tree-lined approach road to the shops. It seemed that her manner relaxed with the revs of the car so that by the time she had parked in the main street she was her usual sweet self again.

'The café's right over there,' she pointed excitedly. 'Hope you are hungry!'

He wasn't really but he didn't reply, silently cursing the situation as they were ushered to a window seat she had obviously pre-booked. She immediately ordered her favourite, apricot cake with almond filling and a lavish chocolate drink and said she knew what he would like - a *schillerloche*. She pointed out the luxury cream horns and they did look nice but he wanted to stay in control and said, 'I prefer raspberries, so may I have a double helping of *obsttorte*? And a strong coffee with pouring cream.'

'*Natürlich,*' she said, adding, 'my, you are a hungry boy!'

He let that one go, too, and settled back to try to enjoy the occasion. Afterwards, they had a quick walk around the town and then made their way back home. She said she was hot and needed to change and Reinhard was surprised when she again reappeared in her white loungewear. She walked around the back of his seat and then completed the circle to face him. She put out a hand, her loungewear now much looser about her body, her face with all the wondrous allure from his past. To begin with, he let himself be led away from the lounge, wanting momentarily to feel the wonder of such an experience but feeling strong enough to resist anything, even when confronted by the sight of drapes of cool silks hanging around the four-poster bed, threatening to replace clothes. She slipped off her loungewear, whispering that it must be hard for him. He expected this and asked what she meant and she said, 'I'll tell you … later.'

Reinhard's strength was now total and he said 'later is now'. He wanted to know straight away. She tightened her lips and sighed. At length, she said, 'Well, you remember when you overheard mum and I arguing a bit that day, it was to do with something that happened to her a few years after the war. Mum asked me not to tell you and that she would sort it out but I said I thought you had a right to know. And I do. While walking home from the cinema one evening in Nürnberg – a couple years after dad had been killed in that air-raid - she was followed by three young men who suddenly surrounded her by a derelict area and forced her down a narrow passageway and into a bomb-damaged building. We still don't know exactly what happened but these men apparently delivered her to about a dozen boys – I mean real youngsters, boys of no more than ten or eleven. Apparently they called themselves the Wolf Pack and as far as we can gather, though mum was never too clear about exactly how, threatened her in some awful way. She was terrified. Fortunately during some ceremonial build-up during which the boys circled her chanting softly but menacingly, the three men beat heavy oar-like sticks against a wall and this action suddenly unsettled the brickwork and part of the wall started moving and a fair part of one side of the room collapsed, making the hooligans run for their lives. Mum was found by a patrolling policeman still sobbing from the ordeal. For years she would hardly look at another man, apart from you, of course, in picture form. And she was always afraid that, if by some miracle you were ever to come on the scene again and the two of you met up, whether her responses would be, well normal. The doctors said they could not be sure.

'You love her, I know, but perhaps you also need me as I need a man like you.' She looked unflinchingly into his eyes. 'The arrangement could be ideal, eh?' she said in a tone that bordered on pleading. Then, relaxing, she laughed, stretching across to him. Reinhard recoiled and stood impassively, facing the bedroom door. He turned and looked down at her, still outstretched, but now she was just a pretty girl, nothing like his darling Stephanie. He moved slowly towards the door as she said, 'Another time then, Reinhard.' But he had already begun making his way back to the lounge where he stood looking out on to the lake, fear pushing anger aside.

'Another coffee, if I may' he said as calmly and correctly as he could as she walked up to him.

Christine poured more coffee, her attire now modestly tight around her body. Reinhard decided to do some leading of his own since he felt haunted by events. 'Christine,' he said somewhat loudly and pointing back towards the bedroom, 'That in there was never going to be. And in the circumstances you've mentioned, that was very wrong.' Then, lowering his voice only slightly, he added stiffly, 'However, I am glad you told me. Please listen. I am going to give faith a good long run. I want to hope, like probably Stephanie so desperately wants to hope. Thanks to ... ' Reinhard's voice became almost a whisper as he turned to face Christine squarely. Looking straight into her eyes, he continued, 'I will not have another requirement for a new guilt. Never. Ever. Stephanie and I will be just fine, no matter how long it takes, no matter if we are just extremely good friends, no matter what, we will be fine.'

Christine lowered her head and announced sadly, 'I really wish I had listened to mum.'

At the door she added mechanically and with a distinct note of resignation, 'Anyway, you have my card.'

After he got back in the car, he took out the card and tore it into small pieces, letting the bits fly out at intervals on the journey back to Stephanie.

*

When Reinhard arrived back at Stephanie's apartment, she was already home. Straight away she asked him if he had liked Christine's place and it threw him a bit.

'Why, yes. A nice town, too,' he added as casually as possible.

Stephanie said, 'I haven't long put the phone down from Christine. She told me you went to see her. I knew you would want to see her. She went through your whole visit. She said everything went well and how excited you were with the scenery but that she could not tempt you with a *piece de resistance*!

Reinhard felt terrible. But he tried to stay strong and quipped hopefully, 'Well, I'm older now. I still fancy my real favourite; remember what it is?'

Stephanie instantly spun around, away from him, without a word. He was sure she knew.

She went into the kitchen and when she returned, Stephanie said, 'Christine told you about my problem, then.'

The words struck out at Reinhard. They actually hurt and his head was whirling, like he was about to lose everything.

She looked down, both hands behind her back.

Reinhard shifted, emptied of all he had hoped for, the way things were turning out. He felt angry at himself but helpless, destroyed.

She added, 'I'm just surprised that Christine did not know your speciality. I've mentioned it often enough over the years. A *schillerloche* indeed! Some temptation!'

Although Reinhard relaxed a little, he wondered about the symbolism.

She said 'I told Christine not to tell you about my problem but actually, the way I now feel, I am glad she did. It's in the open. And do you know, the impact of that time years ago has now, even during this short time since putting the phone down, suddenly to have been dispelled and I feel strongly that it has lost its hold over me. Besides, keeping the secret in, hoping you would understand because you are Reinhard, was selfish of me and the whole thing became an unnecessary burden. I am so sorry Reinhard. Mum doesn't always know best, does she?'

As his body replenished itself, she stood back smiling, taking on much more of the look of the Stephanie he remembered. She produced from behind her back a small lunchbox and placed it onto the table.

'That would be more like it, right?'

Inside was a freshly made bread and butter jam sandwich.

'Right. So right!' he said, his head making sense again.

She said it had been one of the items she had considered having ready for him when he arrived at the apartment for the date that was interrupted by the car accident. Her face beamed as she said softly, 'Eat up.'

Reinhard loved to see her so happy and teasing, like Berlin, like before. Almost toe-to-toe, they watched each other as he took great hungry chunks out of the sandwich, wanting to put her in the mix.

She spun around again, but this time lost her balance a little and put out first one arm to steady herself, then the other, adjusting her feet. Reinhard's whole body became rigid as he stared at the disarranged but immensely attractive figure in front of him.

'That was it! You! When I first saw you, playing table tennis,' he shrieked, smiling widely.

It was *her* hands. *Her* feet. *Her* wonderful look. Christine's hands and feet had been those of a stranger.

He was back in the city's sports club. And right there and then, though only the kitchen island, he wanted to put a bat in her hand, place a bottle of Cola on the surface and stand ready to receive her service.

'You were there, playing table tennis,' he said gently, his eyes moistening. 'Like it looked for a second, just then!' And now he could not stop the tears as he said, 'I saw you, so attractively tomboyish, alert, jumping to the backhand and reaching wide to the forehand. I saw neither tactic nor strategy, just bouncing hair, a jovial and so pleasant face and slim hands emerging on the stretch from a baggy jumper.'

Stephanie slung her arms around him and as if experiencing the same moments of that now distant past said excitedly, 'Yes, I noticed you several times. I knew I was being gripped by something new and could not help once or twice returning your smile.'

Matching her mood completely, Reinhard said, 'When, eventually, I asked you for a game, in going for a simple put-away (it must have been the impish look you wrapped around the ball) I somehow mixed *my* feet up, remember, like you did just then, and the ball flew off the edge of my bat and hit the ceiling.'

Stephanie bent practically double as the words mixed with laughter, 'You mocked your clumsiness by lightly head-butting the top of the table …'

Reinhard joined in the mirth of this momentous recall. Then suddenly serious, he said, 'I was so proud of you, Stephanie, daring to hope that you could be my girl.'

Stephanie's eyes also filled with tears as she put the crust into the waste bin and took Reinhard by the hand.

'Shall we perhaps have a game now?' she enquired. 'I've kept my hand in, you know?' turning to simulate a classy backhand loop drive only just missing the kitchen plate rack, then, stepping back, went through the action of a heavy forehand chop an inch above the floor tiles.

'What do you say, then?'

Reinhard visualised Thomas's dining room table. A blurred picture of Christine flashed in front of him and, inexplicably, the name Konrad entered his head.

But they were soon driven out during an extremely close and satisfying game.

Ends.

Printed in Poland
by Amazon Fulfillment
Poland Sp. z o.o., Wrocław